AFTER LUCY

Perennial

An Imprint of HarperCollins*Publishers*

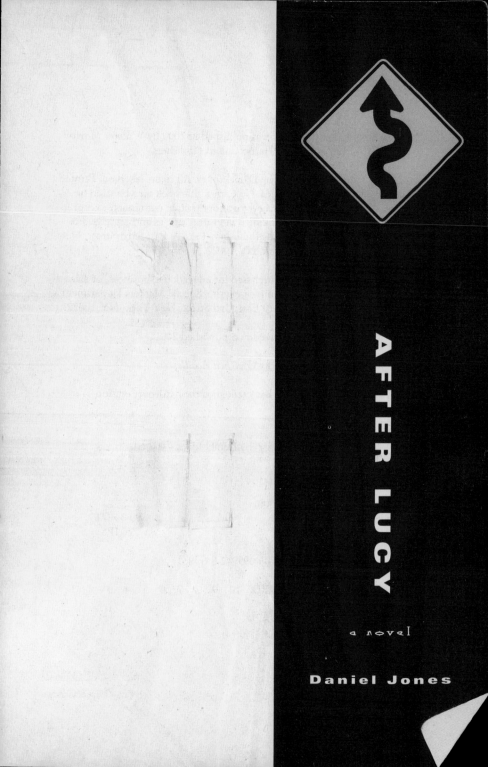

AFTER LUCY

a novel

Daniel Jones

HarperCollins books may be purchased for educational, business, or sales promotional use. For information please write: Special Markets Department, HarperCollins Publishers Inc., 10 East 53rd Street, New York, NY 10022.

First Perennial edition published 2001.

Designed by Gretchen Achilles

The Library of Congress has catalogued the hardcover edition as follows:

Jones, Daniel.
    After Lucy : a novel / by Daniel Jones.—1st ed.
      p. cm.
    ISBN 0-688-17456-6
    I. Title.
    PS3560.04747A69   2000
    813'.54—dc21   99-35871
                                 CIP

ISBN 0-06-095942-8 (pbk.)

01 02 03 04 05 WB/RRD 10 9 8 7 6 5 4 3 2 1

FOR CATHI, PHOEBE, AND NATHANIEL

AFTER LUCY

CHAPTER ONE

PITTSBURGH in mid-June, dry and bright with a high sun, and Porter Ellis was in that kind of fragile mood where something as dumb as the weather could make him feel good. As he cruised along Washington Boulevard and rumbled out onto the potholed span of the Highland Park Bridge, Porter couldn't believe this was the same gloomy city where he'd spent his entire adult life. The Allegheny River—that smelly trough of green goo—looked like one big vacation. Sleek boats shot up and down its shimmering surface. Clusters of fishermen dotted the industrial shoreline, casting their lines merrily into the swill.

It had been three weeks since Porter's wife had died. And today— after all the well-wishers had come and gone, after the phone calls had slowed to a trickle, after Porter's boss had delicately hinted that maybe he should return to work soon—Porter traded in his wife's old Mazda on a used truck with a camper on the back and decided that, starting now, he was going to try to be happy. He was going to appreciate his life, damn it. And he wasn't going to allow himself to be dragged down any further by grief or by his in-laws' opinions of how he ought to conduct his life and the lives of his two children, who now, as he did not need to be reminded, had no mother.

Porter descended the off-ramp into Sharpsburg, drifted past its bars—IRON CITY BEER!—and pizza pubs and auto-body shops, then turned onto Kittanning Pike and began the steep climb to Fox Chapel.

How many times had he made this drive in the past twelve years? A thousand? Three thousand? But always in Lucy's Mazda. He'd spent so many hours behind the wheel of that car, the stick shift felt like an extension of his hand. Downshifting his way up Kittanning Pike was a rhythm as familiar as breathing—fourth to third at Oakhurst, third to second at the Greenwood Cemetery, and then the slow, grinding push over the top into Fox Chapel, where the road left behind all the lower-class drudgery and pollution of the valley and began its happy journey through forested enclaves of million-dollar homes and sprawling golf courses.

As he climbed the hill today, Porter kept waiting for the drag of gravity to pull at him, for that plaintive sigh of the engine to tell him to downshift, but this truck, despite its age and the added burden of carrying the camper, powered on up like a mighty plowhorse. The camper itself was a faded Magic Bus—a purple-and-green tin shack complete with shag carpeting, velvet curtains, and a spare gas can that had been affixed to the rear bumper with silver duct tape. But the truck's engine thrummed. Porter sailed over the top with an exhilarating lift and *whoosh* that he had experienced only inside the plush, suede comfort of his father-in-law's Mercedes E320. Porter kept it floored down the backside and carried too much speed into the first sharp corner, and as the camper rocked on its haunches, Porter had to grip the wheel and tap the brakes to bring it under control. Feeling chastened, he negotiated the three roller-coaster hills of Old Mill Road and swung into the entrance to his in-laws' house, which was marked on either side by decorative split-rail fencing.

The Winters' driveway was a hushed, leafy tunnel that served as a drumroll for the sight of the Winters' house, which burst into view at tunnel's end to the accompaniment—in Porter's mind, anyway—of trilling woodwinds and an angels' chorus. Sloping up toward the house, as if in homage, was an exquisite carpet of dandelion-free Kentucky bluegrass (which had arrived by flatbed truck, in stacked layers of sod, several summers before). The driveway ascended the lawn in two short switchbacks, graced along the way by terraced pockets of tulips and rosebushes, towering maples and Douglas firs. Porter had never seen nature so whipped into shape as it was here, always trimmed to perfection and dolled up in its Sunday best.

The house—sitting atop the yard like a statue on a podium—was an English Tudor jumble of eaves, peaked windows, and white stucco that William had built to match his childhood house in Oxford, England. Tucked neatly into the backyard, as if out of embarrassment, was a full recreation facility: a red-clay tennis court; a sand play area with slides, swings, a jungle gym, and an in-ground trampoline; and a teardrop-shaped pool surrounded on its fat end by an apron of pale-blue ceramic tile, at the edge of which sat a white cabana, with its minibar, bathroom, and TV den.

For years Porter and Lucy had managed to decline the Winters' offers of financial support, determined to forge their own way in life. But the Winters' backyard paradise was their one guilty indulgence. It had started that first summer, when Kaylie was eight months old. It was an evening in late May, a real scorcher of a day for so early in the summer, and, unfathomably, Porter had chosen to grill kielbasa on their cramped porch. Kaylie was a red-faced piglet in Lucy's arms, and Porter was circling their little hibachi with fork and hot pad in hand, cursing, trying to avoid the smoke. And Lucy said, "You know, we should call my parents and see what they're up to. I'll bet they'd love to have us come over and take a swim."

Normally Porter would have laughed at the thought. He had struggled to like Lucy's parents, or even just to be pleasant with them. But that evening, standing teary-eyed in the funnel of kielbasa smoke that kept pursuing him around the porch, he'd imagined that pristine pool and air-conditioned cabana and thought, *Why the hell not?* "Okay," he said. "Since it's so hot. But let's try not to make a habit of it. You know, plenty of people are able to make it through life without their own personal tennis court and pool."

But once Benny entered the picture three years later, forget it. At least they'd been semi-independent with just one child. Porter's self-reliant martyrdom had been fine when it was just the three of them. But when you had *two* kids—living, breathing creatures who were bored silly twelve minutes after lifting their pale skulls from their pillows every morning—principles fell by the wayside mighty fast. During the school year their schedules were tighter. But summers were a joke . . . all day, every day, those kids wanted to go up to their grandparents' house. In the pool. Hitting tennis balls. On the swings and the trampoline. Summer after summer, those kids bounced up and down, up and down, for days on end.

And what were Porter and Lucy supposed to do? Deprive them? They couldn't afford much of a vacation on their own, much less a membership in a pool club. Friends of theirs from college sent their kids to camp, but financially that, too, was out of the question. Plus, this was free! And the kids *loved* their grandparents. So Porter learned to tolerate them.

Actually, he felt pretty invisible most of the time. When he and Lucy had first married, Porter used to get a rise out of Claire by wearing ratty clothes: ripped jeans shorts and black Chuck Taylors with no socks, a tie-dyed T-shirt from his college days. But now it wasn't even worth it—no one paid any attention to him. He was no longer the bad boy, just a father like every other father, fading into the background as his kids took center stage. Claire would come out to the car to greet them, kiss and hug Kaylie and Ben, then walk off. Sometimes she'd turn around and at least acknowledge Porter—"Hi there!"—before swooping the kids under her wings, asking what they wanted to do, and did they want ice cream?

Porter was glad to have passed the torch of attention to his kids; it was easier on everybody. But every so often this arrangement nagged at him—all this money, and sponging off people he didn't even much like.

"Doesn't it make you feel guilty?" his brother, Alex, had once asked him. "To hang out up there all the time and eat their food and use their stuff?"

"Yeah, kind of," Porter had said. But after thinking about it, he realized that guilt was not what he felt. It was an equal exchange: The Winters got to see their grandchildren, the kids got to have a blast, Porter got to stuff his face with Brie and shrimp and smoked oysters and wash it all down with a never-ending supply of Guinness and Amstel Light. No one owed anyone anything over that arrangement. What he did feel, though, was a kind of laziness, a spiritual malaise.

On the drive home one night, the kids zonked out in the backseat, Porter tried to articulate his feelings to Lucy. "It just seems like our family time should be about something other than *leisure*," he said. "Especially when it's leisure we wouldn't be able to afford on our own."

"Everyone visits their parents," Lucy said. "If you ask me, we're just lucky that my parents both live close *and* have all that stuff."

"Well, it's a mixed blessing," Porter said.

And round and round they'd go. But this kind of talk had taken place before Lucy got sick. Afterward, Porter's very musings about "leisure" and "spiritual malaise" felt to him like some luxury of a previous life.

When Lucy was first diagnosed and went through her initial bout of chemotherapy, the Winters often would pick up the kids at school, hang out with them all afternoon, feed them dinner, and put them to bed in their spare bedrooms. Porter would stop by whenever he could

get away to check on them or, if it was late, just to see them asleep.
In the morning Claire would feed the kids breakfast and drive them
to school. For a good two months, it was fair to say that those kids
were living with their grandparents. And Claire was not likely to let
Porter forget it. Especially now that he wanted to put his kids in this
camper and drive them all the hell out of there.

PORTER PULLED THE camper to a stop right in front of the entryway
(might as well be bold about it) and stepped out. He walked up to
the front door and cupped his hands to the glass. Dark. He rang the
doorbell. No response. Where could they be? He started to reach for
his key, but the SafHom security system intimidated him. He knew
the code to disable it, had the six-digit number on a card in his wallet.
But the last time he'd been in this situation, last fall, he'd punched the
numbers in wrong. And then, instead of removing his key, reinserting
it, and trying the code again as you were supposed to, he'd panicked
and opened the door.

Once the siren started blaring, Porter knew he'd fucked up, and
he just sat on the stoop and waited for his punishment, which, he
figured, would be the humiliation of having to explain himself to the
SafHom Armed Response Team (who he imagined would be two
pimply-faced teenagers from Aspinwall wearing shorts and holsters).
According to the contract, their armed presence was guaranteed to
come screeching up the driveway in no more than ten minutes.

But there had been no armed response from SafHom. Ironically,
Porter wished there had been. SafHom's not showing up was worse,
because finally, after twenty minutes of ear-splitting alarm while Porter
sat on the front stoop waving off suspicious neighbors, Claire returned
from the grocery store, disabled the alarm, and then had to be told by
Porter that the Armed Response Team never showed up. More troubling still, SafHom then billed the Winters for an armed response
anyway (some $280). And this led to months of heated exchanges
between Claire and SafHom, first over the phone, then by fax, with

each party holding its ground as to whether a team had been sent or not. SafHom even faxed Claire a copy of the logbook entry that identified her correct address, with the correct date and time scrawled in the appropriate boxes, and the note "All Secure on Premises" signed by someone named Richy.

Claire had interrogated Porter about this issue on three separate occasions ("Are you sure you didn't see anyone? No one came? You're sure? You were paying attention?" Yes, he was sure. What else would he have been doing but paying attention while the alarm blared away?). She'd also threatened, during her exchanges with SafHom, to change security services. Yet the reality was that it would cost a fortune to have a new system installed, and then how could you be sure the new company would be reliable? "You'd just be starting all over again," she'd moan. "That's how they get you. They make you install all this damn equipment and then the first time you need a Response Team they leave you in the lurch!"

"But, Claire, you didn't need a Response Team," Porter said, trying, for the eightieth time, to mollify her. "It was just me."

"But they didn't know that! For all they knew, it was a real Four-one-one."

"Four-one-one" was the SafHom code number for "Instantaneous Response Required." The fact that this term had worked its way into the vocabulary of a white-haired, yellow-sweatered Wasp like Claire Winter (as a result of her thrice-weekly phone conversations with SafHom's nerve center) was a source of mounting agitation for Porter. But he knew better than to make any comment about it. She was likely to wallop him over the head with a polo mallet.

At any rate, on this particular afternoon Porter was not going to test the alarm system. He stared at the SafHom panel, its little green light blinking at two-second intervals as if daring him to attempt his code. But Porter just sighed and stepped away, back down to the walk. They wouldn't be long, he figured—probably just went down to Fox Chapel Plaza for some takeout.

He strolled around to the side of the house, across the flagstone patio, and into the backyard. The funeral reception for Lucy had been held out there only two weeks earlier. The place had been decked out with green tents and tables with white tablecloths. Smiling, aproned caterers—dressed in the same green and white as the tents and table-cloths—stood behind the tables like cadets at attention. "Stuffed mushrooms?" they'd snap if you strayed too close. "Pigs-in-blankets?"

Porter had geared himself up for a somber, depressing event where people hugged each other and wept, but the day turned out to be almost exactly like all of the other catered affairs the Winters had held in that backyard over the years: William's retirement picnic, William and Claire's thirty-fifth-anniversary picnic, even Porter and Lucy's wedding reception. The events were nearly indistinguishable—all held in the same yard with the same crowd, the same caterers, the same food. During Lucy's funeral reception Porter guessed that some of the tottering stiffs in attendance weren't even aware of the occasion. To them it was just another Winter soirée with steak tartare, crab cakes, and free-flowing bourbon. After all, most of the conversations Porter overheard had nothing to do with Lucy. There was even laughter, a lot of it, and people drinking and scavenging for hors d'oeuvres and kids chasing each other around the house as if it were just another party.

The only physical reminder of the reception's true purpose was a shrine for Lucy that Porter and Claire had assembled on a card table opposite the food tents. Porter's boss, Pete, had done the same thing for his father's funeral six months before, and Lucy had really admired it. This was during a particularly bleak period when those shadows were suddenly all over the place on Lucy's X rays, and she was having trouble even drawing a full breath. That being the case, Pete's father's funeral hardly seemed like the event to lift her spirits. They'd intended just to make a brief appearance and then sneak away. But they ended up spending nearly an hour at that shrine, studying the old photos of Pete's dad as a young boy, a family man, and finally, a grandfather.

They felt the heft of all those World War II medals and perused the assortment of cherished books and U.S. Marine Marching Band LPs.

It was a life. You could see the arc of it, and there was something comforting in that.

Lucy's favorite item was a framed letter from the thirteen-year-old granddaughter of the deceased explaining how "totally harsh" it was that her grandpa had died. Yes, she understood the fact that all living creatures, "including even people," have to die, but she was glad at least that her grandpa had lived a long life and been "totally happy" and that one day in the far distant future she was going to be reunited with him in heaven, which made her "totally not fear death."

Later, as Porter and Lucy were driving home, Lucy turned to him with a wry smile and said in her pained wheeze, "You know what? I *totally* want a shrine like that at my funeral. Okay? Like, *totally*."

So there it was. A "no-brainer," as Pete would say.

Of course, Claire was a little skittish of the idea at the start, but once she steeled herself for the effort and started rummaging around in Lucy's childhood things, it only became a matter of what to include. In the end, they decided on a range of items from elementary school on up: a blue ceramic moose Lucy had sculpted in fifth grade, her tennis trophy from the state semifinals, her equestrian boots and helmet, a plastic bead necklace that Kaylie made for her (which Lucy liked to wear to fancy occasions), a plaque from the Fox Chapel PTA honoring her "Leadership and Commitment," three large photo collages, and a framed poem Benny had written in school just three months earlier, entitled "My Mommy Has No Hair." It read:

> My mommy has no hair
> But she has a wig to wear
> And she still looks really pretty.
> She's the best mom in the city.
> —BENJAMIN ELLIS, GRADE 2

Porter felt good about the shrine, and especially about his kids' contributions. But most of the crowd pretty much steered clear of it. A few dozen people did stroll over at one time or another, and some even left little notes or contributed a flower. But the most awkward scenes involved the people who'd wandered over by mistake, thinking the shrine was some sort of satellite wine-and-cheese station, and after realizing their error, had felt as if they had to paw through Lucy's stuff for a requisite minute or two before they could make a break for the food tents.

Porter wasn't so bothered that the funeral reception had turned out that way. As the event wore on, he even began smiling and talking about things completely off the subject of his wife's death. He got choked up only once, when a friend of Lucy's mother—an overbearing linebacker of a woman Porter had always disliked—had said, almost as a way of ending their awkward conversation, "Well, I'm sure Lucy's happy, wherever she is."

And it was that image of Lucy being someplace else, away from them, that had so disturbed him. It wasn't as bad when he thought of Lucy as just not existing anymore, or else when he simply remembered her being alive and part of their family. What he found unsettling was the idea of her being in some other place without them, knowing she would never see them again.

Still, all told, the occasion was less fraught with tension and bad feelings than their wedding reception had been. If anything, this reception, for her death, had seemed *more* celebratory, with people speaking so glowingly about her, as opposed to their wedding, which had been cloaked in despair. After all, this promising girl they all had watched grow up was now scandalously pregnant and about to marry an unemployed wannabe artist from Minnesota who didn't even own a car. Even if the marriage broke up, which everyone was certain it would, Lucy would still be saddled with raising this child as a single mother.

The day of the ceremony Lucy had been six months pregnant with

Kaylie and felt bloated and ugly in her white tent of a wedding dress. She was sweating and miserable. And her mother's discomfort with the marriage had infected the crowd like a flu—they were Claire and William's friends, after all. They had all been turned against Porter, the poor slob who had ruined Lucy's life. The day was humid, oppressive; disapproval hung in the air like a mist. William's lifelong pals gripped Porter's shoulder more in reprimand than in congratulation and said, with the air of a threat, "You take care of her, all right?"

It had all seemed so hopeless at the time: a dead end, a trap. A clichéd trap at that! "Needless to say, this is *not* how I pictured my wedding day," Lucy had said to one grinning couple after another, just trying to say something, *anything,* to ease the tension, with Porter standing next to her, teeth dry, his face frozen in a terrified smile.

And what about Porter? It was hardly what he'd wanted for himself either. What had happened to bumming around the country for a couple of years after college? Living in San Francisco and painting? Hanging out in some seaside Mexican village for a winter on three dollars a day? Working on a fishing boat in Alaska? All the things his college roommates were off doing? This wedding wasn't exactly his vision of utopia.

Looking back on it now, and thinking about his daughter, Kaylie, Porter considered how wrong those hopeless feelings had been, how young he must have been to have felt that way. If only he'd known then what joy it was to have a daughter. . . .

It hadn't been easy, of course. There were times he felt burdened, yes. His choices limited, sure. But a trap? A dead end? Hardly. More like a rocket launch. And then to have a son, too. He didn't know what he would have done without them. He wouldn't have made it through the events of this past year, that's for sure. They were everything to him. Everything. Occasionally, more often than he ever would have predicted, Porter would look at them, or daydream about them at work, and think, *They are my whole life.*

Porter was caught up in the reverie of this thought when he heard his name being called. Then he heard it again—"Porter?"

He wheeled around, and it was Claire, by herself, standing at the back door. She held shopping bags in each hand. Her expression was puzzled but friendly. She wore white sneakers and khakis with a billowy azure blouse and, of all things, a straw hat. Porter had never seen her in a straw hat before, or in any hat that he could recall, although this one looked perfectly fine. The rest was Claire's standard uniform: no-nonsense cotton clothes with splashes of bright color here and there. Stylish in a sturdy way, Claire's wardrobe was not expensive— she rarely dressed up, and she never wore much makeup or jewelry— but she looked unmistakably wealthy at all times. Porter thought it had something to do with her skin tone, or maybe her hair, which had grayed intelligently at the temples and which she kept swooped up in a Katharine Hepburn bun.

Claire put her shopping bags down on the patio and placed one hand on her hip. With the other hand she was pointing back at the driveway, but she hadn't yet formed the words she wanted to speak. "Is that . . ." she began. "That camper around front . . . That isn't yours, is it?"

Porter smiled. He'd forgotten already. "Actually, it is. I just got it today. I can't say I was planning to. It just sort of happened."

Claire sighed and shook her head, her expression one of familiar exasperation. "You *bought* it? I thought you were going in to work today. To try to catch up so you could go back on Monday. Wasn't that the plan? I thought that was the whole reason you dropped off Kaylie and Ben."

"That *was* the plan," Porter said. "But I decided I just can't go back yet."

"And Pete is okay with that?"

Porter shrugged. "He'll understand." Really, what could Pete do? Fire him because his grieving process was rolling over into a fourth week? Besides, his job was going nowhere anyway. Porter worked as a graphic designer for a second-rate advertising firm that specialized in nonprofits—museums, performing-arts organizations. He'd spent almost a decade churning out posters and pamphlets for festivals and exhibits from Wheeling to Moon Township—a veritable blur of mediocre cultural activities requiring packaging and promotion. Yet he still barely made enough for them to live on.

On the good side, Porter liked the people he worked with. But during the drive in today, he'd begun to feel that he couldn't yet deal with them—their hushed words of consolation and their well-meaning but claustrophobic hugs. True, it was a Saturday, and only a handful of people would be in. Or might that make it worse, allowing for an intimacy that a normal workday would discourage? Apprehension had surged up his spine, crowding out his thoughts. He'd driven on for a while, trying to fight it back, but then had decided to turn around and head home. It was within three blocks of making that decision that Porter stopped at a red light, gazed into the used-car lot, and saw the camper.

"So where's Lucy's Mazda?" Claire asked him.

"I traded it in!" Porter boomed. "A straight trade, if you can believe it. I just figured this was more practical, you know, for vacationing and whatnot. I mean, from now on, wherever I go, the kids've got to go too. So I just thought this was a good idea."

Claire regarded him. "A good idea for whom?"

"For all of us."

Claire looked down exhaustedly, already drained by the conversation. "You know, Porter, the children don't *have* to go wherever you go. They're welcome to stay with us if you feel you need some time. I've told you that. Where are you planning to go, anyway? On a vacation?"

"Yeah, actually, I thought we would. Not a vacation, really, but just a little getaway. You know, I haven't been able to give the kids the attention they've needed, and it's really been terrific that you and William have been around to fill in. But I feel like the kids and I should spend some time together, you know? And we can see a little bit of America while we're at it." He sensed that saying that last part had been a mistake. Why hadn't he planned better what to say to her?

Claire's eyes searched him frantically. "See *America*? For how long?"

"A couple of weeks. I don't know. We'll see how it works out. To be honest, I haven't figured that part out yet. Maybe we'll only go for a few days." He wasn't lying. He didn't know what to expect. They'd figure it out as they went. And what did it matter? It was the beginning of the summer. They could go off for three months if they wanted to. The kids would probably love it. When he and Alex were growing up in the stultifying boredom of St. Cloud, Minnesota, hoping for a tornado to rip through town just to rearrange the scenery, they used to look forward to trips like this for months, setting off with their parents for a few weeks of camping. "Where are they, anyway?" Porter said brightly, trying to change the subject. "William and the kids?"

"They're coming back from the mall. I had to pick up some things at the grocery store, so I took the Acura. They'll be here soon. I thought they'd beat me here, actually." She paused, once again looking at him with great concern, or more likely, contempt. "Porter, is that thing safe for highway travel? It looks kind of, I don't know, junky."

"Sure it's safe. It's got a lot of miles on it, but it's not that old. And it's been well taken care of. You should've seen it power up Kittanning Pike. It's an ox."

"But you're just going off in it? Just off somewhere? To live in it?"

"Claire," Porter said, his patience fraying at the edges, "we're not going off to *live* in it. We're taking a trip. That's all. You act like I'm kidnapping my own kids."

"Well, this just seems like a rash decision to me. It's all out of the blue. I mean, how long have you been planning this? You can't have been planning this for very long."

"No," Porter said. "I haven't been planning anything lately." Then he started to get angry. "When would I have planned it? All I've been doing is trying to hold things together. That's all I've been doing for two years! But I want to do more than that now. Okay? I want us to enjoy ourselves. Is that so awful?"

Claire sat down on the steps and gazed into the yard beyond him. "I'm sorry. I don't mean to get you so exercised. I'm just trying to figure this out. I thought we'd get a breather finally. That we'd spend this summer trying to just settle down and get used to things. And now for you to take the children and run off in that rattletrap camper just throws me for a loop." She turned to him with a resolute expression, her cheeks slightly flushed. "I just don't want you to do it. It's as simple as that. I want you and the children to stay here this summer. I thought that's what we'd agreed to. And if you must take a vacation to get some rest, then I think you should go and leave the children with us, so at least they can have some stability."

"It's really no big deal, Claire. I think *you* should try not to get so 'exercised' about it. We'll leave, we'll come back, and that's it. To tell you the truth, I think it bothers the kids to be in the apartment with all of Lucy's stuff and not have her there anymore. It's like the place is haunted or something. And I think it would do them some good to take a break from it."

Claire stood up again, brushing off the back of her pants. "If you need to get out of the apartment for a while, you can stay here. You can move into the apartment over the garages."

Porter broke into an open smile at the ridiculousness of her offer. "How about this, Claire? I'll ask the kids. I'll ask them what they want to do. And then I'll take that into consideration."

"But you'll influence them. You can't help but influence them to do what you want. They'll want to please you."

"I'll try not to," Porter said.

"Before you decide anything for certain, promise me that we'll talk this over with William," Claire said. "I know it sounds selfish, but I really want the kids around these days. And you too. It makes me feel so much better to have you all here. And I know William feels the same way."

"I appreciate that," Porter said. "I do."

Claire's face brightened. "We could all go down to Disney World like last year. That was kind of fun. You liked that."

Go to Disney World? Was she kidding? You win the Super Bowl, you go to Disney World. Your wife dies, you don't go to Disney World. Besides, Claire and William *hated* Disney World. They ridiculed it every time Kaylie and Ben were out of earshot. If Porter liked it, or acted as if he did, it was only because they hated it so much. "I want to go *camping* with the kids. They should spend some time in the woods. That's what I did as a kid."

Claire let out her breath. "But you promise me that thing is safe? You and the children aren't going to wind up stuck on the side of the road somewhere?"

"We won't."

Claire said suddenly, "You'll take one of the cell phones!"

"No, no." Porter waved her off. "No cell phones."

"I insist," Claire said. "Then you can call us anytime. Tell us where you are."

So you *can call* us, Porter thought, but he nodded. "Okay."

"But I still want to talk this over with William. All right?"

"You know," Porter said, "you guys have been doing double-time—triple-time—taking care of us all. You may think you want us around forever, but I'll bet once we're gone you'll be happy for the rest. I bet you don't even realize how worn out you are."

"I *am* worn out," Claire said. "Absolutely I am. But not from the children. From everything else. I'm afraid I'll start to feel even more worn out if you go off with them. That's when I fear everything's going to come crashing down."

Porter was actually happy to hear Claire talking this way. Maybe it explained her relative calm, her impeccable dress and appearance throughout Lucy's final days and the funeral, and through until now. Maybe it all *would* come crashing down at some point. And Porter couldn't help but think it would be a good thing when it finally did. Being with Claire lately was like watching a balloon filling, waiting for it to pop. You wanted it to happen already. "We'll be back before you know it," Porter said cheerfully. "The kids'll probably get homesick the second we hit the Ohio border. But if that happens, then fine. At least they'll want to be back here. Right now that apartment just has them spooked."

"Have they said that?"

"Not in so many words, no. But I can tell they're bothered by it. And they wouldn't say anything anyway. They'd think they were saying something bad about their mother to admit it."

Claire grimaced. "You might be right about that."

Just then the back door opened, and out stepped Kaylie, followed by William.

William Winter was nearly seventy, eight years older than Claire, and just in the past year he had begun to display the vaguely disoriented manner of an elderly person. Even six months earlier he'd seemed much more vigorous, whacking a tennis ball with Kaylie or diving off the board into their pool with a resounding *thwump* and splash. But now everything seemed a struggle. He was always fiddling with his hearing aid, and he startled easily when spoken to. He'd taken to reaching out for railings and walls and other people's shoulders, no longer trusting of his own balance. Increasingly, he winced and sighed and squinted his way through life.

Still, William's face remained young and flush as a boy's, and he had a headful of thick gray hair that he wore like a helmet, with bangs, in a style that made Porter think of English knights. William's family had moved to the United States when he was a teenager, but he maintained a trace of his British accent and still used words like "lorry," "lift," and "fortnight." People found him charming. Porter could still be charmed by him, but he'd also seen the dark underbelly, the old wounds of a long marriage, the raw nerves exposed by fathering a dying daughter.

William stood at the top of the steps gripping the railing, one hand cupped above his eyes, while Kaylie bounded down to the cement patio. A skinny twelve-year-old, she was wearing orange stirrup pants and a dark-green sweatshirt that hung on her like a trash bag. Her sandy hair dropped in a braid down the middle of her back. She rushed over toward Porter but jumped to a stop a couple of yards away. She smirked at him. "Don't tell me you really bought that, Dad. That Peacemobile out front?"

Porter smiled. "I did." Kaylie's dry remarks had been returning in recent days—a sign of her good emotional health coming back? "You like it?"

"Sort of embarrassing, don't you think?"

William descended the steps to the patio, combing his hair with his fingers and looking at Porter in a bewildered way. "You *bought* it?"

Claire glanced at him conspiratorially. "He traded in Lucy's coupe."

"It was a great deal, actually," Porter said, "for such an old car." He looked beyond them. "So where's Ben? Is he with you guys?"

"He's snoring away in the backseat," Kaylie said. "Major sugar coma. On the way out Grampa bought him a hot fudge sundae at Friendly's. Big mistake."

"But what do you need a camper for?" William said. "What was wrong with Lucy's car?"

Kaylie set off across the grass toward the pool cabana, swinging her arms in big circles as she went. "I'm getting a Pepsi," she yelled over her shoulder, then raised her eyebrows at Porter as if to say, *You're on your own with this one.*

Porter looked at William and Claire. "There was nothing wrong with Lucy's car. But there was no reason to hang on to it either. I just wanted to be able to take some camping trips with the kids. I've already explained this to Claire."

"But you've never gone camping before," William said. "Have you?"

"Not lately, no." Even before she was sick, Lucy wasn't much for roughing it. Their vacations were either three-day getaways at tacky resorts in the hills east of Pittsburgh (leaving the kids with Claire and William) or else fully paid, luxury weeks with the Winters in Bongo Bongo or Tiki Niki or wherever the hell Club Med had managed to secure the best swimming lagoons from the local populace. "But I used to go camping all the time when I was growing up. It was the only way we vacationed. In a camper not too unlike the one I bought, in fact. Alex and I would ride up top. We loved it."

"I never knew that," Claire said, sounding genuinely impressed.

"Sure," Porter said. "My dad loved to drive. We'd go from Minnesota to San Diego every Christmas to visit my aunt and uncle. Took us two weeks of solid driving. We'd camp along the roadside, up in the mountains in snow, wherever we happened to be when my dad got tired."

William said, "But Kaylie and Ben—they're not used to that."

"We'll avoid the snow, I promise. And no stopping at the roadside. Only certified campgrounds."

William felt around behind him for the deck chair and then lowered himself into it.

In truth, Porter thought, William probably wasn't so against the idea. Sure he wanted to be around his grandkids, especially now. But he would understand Porter's wanting to go camping. He would. All this huffing and puffing was really for Claire. He sensed she was upset, and he was trying to do the manly thing for her. For a moment it seemed he was going to pursue it further, but then he said, "Well, perhaps that would be all right. What do you think about all of this, Claire?"

"We'll have to talk about it," she said. "Porter even agreed that you and I could discuss it first, before any plans were set in stone." She nodded at Porter as if in confirmation.

He'd agreed to that? Whatever. He was going camping one way or another, and he was taking his kids with him. He hardly needed their permission for that.

"We just need to be able to feel good about this too," Claire said.

"All right," Porter said. "Fine."

Claire motioned for William to stand, which he did, stiffly. And with that, Claire took him by the arm and they ascended the steps of the house.

Porter watched with relief as the door closed behind them, then looked over at the cabana for Kaylie. The door was open, but she wasn't in sight. As he began to walk over, he spied her next to the pool, halfway reclined in a deck chair, sipping her Pepsi. He strode down the carpet of lawn toward the pool. It never ceased to amaze him that this lawn was actually a part of nature, a living thing, so perfect and springy was it under his feet.

"They're really pissed," Kaylie said as Porter approached, giving him a quick glance out of the corner of her eye. "You should've seen Grampa's face when he saw that thing. He freaked." She took another swig of Pepsi and swallowed. "I knew right away it was yours. I knew you were going to do something like that today. It was like déjà vu or something. I saw it parked there, and I wasn't even surprised."

"You weren't?" Porter said.

"Well, I mean, I didn't know you were going to do something that retarded."

"What's Ben going to think?"

"Are you kidding? He's going to love it."

Porter smiled. He sat down on the chair next to her and extended his legs, cupping his hands behind his head. "And how about you? You feel like going on a little road trip? Doing some camping?"

"Where?"

"I don't know . . . maybe head west. The problem is, it takes a

long time before you reach any country that's interesting. You've got
to get all the way to Colorado before there's mountains. That's almost
a week of driving just to get there. Your grandparents don't even want
us to be gone a week for the whole trip."

"That's the understatement of the century," Kaylie said. "On the
way home today Grampa asked if me and Benny wanted to live with
them for the rest of the summer. If it was all right with you, he said.
He said it would give you a break so you could take care of things.
And he said it might be better for everyone for a while, until we all
get used to Mom being gone. I said I already *was* used to Mom being
gone, which I didn't mean the way it sounded—it just came out that
way. I tried to tell him I didn't mean it that way, but I think he was
crying a little and couldn't really talk. He was all blinking and wiping
at his nose and stuff." She looked at Porter. "I didn't mean it that
way, Dad. I didn't."

Porter put his hand on her knobby knee and gave it a fatherly
squeeze. "So how did you mean it?"

She looked at the pool. "I don't know. Just that . . . I mean, I don't
want him to think I'm like Benny."

"Like Benny, how?"

"You know . . . how he thinks Mom's going to come back as an
angel or something and take care of us."

Porter sighed. "He's only eight, Kaylie. If it helps him to believe
that for a while, then . . ."

Kaylie wheeled to face him, her cheeks flushed. "But I *hate* it when
he says stuff like that. I *hate* it. It's so *stupid*." She blinked, sending a
rare tear down the side of her nose. She wiped at it quickly and then
turned away.

Porter scooted forward in his deck chair, laid his arm around his
daughter's shoulders, and tried to draw her in, but she stiffened in his
embrace. He kept his arm around her anyway, waiting for her to relax
and slump against him. "Hey," he said, jostling her. But apparently
she didn't want this now, not right now. So finally Porter released her

and settled back in his chair. After a while he said, "I wonder what they're talking about inside."

"You can hear them if you want," Kaylie said, not looking at him. "There's an intercom in the cabana. All you do is push 'Listen.' If they're talking near one of the inside intercoms, you'll hear them. Benny figured that one out. I've got to give him credit for that."

"Is that right?" Porter said.

Kaylie nodded.

"I don't want to spy on them," Porter said. "I'm just curious about what they're saying. I don't always agree with them, but I feel like we should be honest with each other."

"I guess." Kaylie yawned.

Porter looked out at the pool, which was clear and smooth except for a huge black spider standing improbably on the surface. He had an urge to toss a pebble into the water to see if that spider would sink or skitter away. But then, he realized, he'd be responsible for that pebble at the bottom of the pool. No doubt the pebble would get sucked into the pool vacuum and fuck that up, setting off a chain of events so costly it would boggle the mind.

"So with this camping trip," Kaylie said. "How are we going to eat?"

"What do you mean, 'how'?"

"Do we have to cook everything on a fire? And catch fish? Stuff like that?"

Porter sat up and turned to Kaylie. "We could cook on a fire if we want. But that camper has a little kitchen and a refrigerator. It even has electricity. So we'll probably cook the same as we've been doing at home. It'll just be a little more cozy."

"That sounds okay," Kaylie said. "Maybe it'll be fun." She furrowed her eyebrows at him. "But can we paint that thing first? That purple and green is really, really gross."

Porter laughed. "How about after we get back? There won't be time before we leave. I want to be out of here in a couple of days. Monday or Tuesday at the latest."

"But aren't people going to see us in it?"

"No one you know. Not unless they catch us on our way out of town." Porter looked back at the house. "You think Ben's up yet? You think he's wondering where we are?"

"Nah. He'll sleep until tomorrow unless we wake him."

She was probably right. Kaylie's response to her mother's illness had been mostly icy glares and flip remarks and sullen denial, but Benny's way of coping had been either to bawl his eyes out or retreat into a cocoon of impenetrable slumber or both. It was not unheard of for him to sleep for fifteen hours straight.

Kaylie took the last sip of her Pepsi and then sat bolt upright, zinging with sudden energy. "Wanna hit some tennis balls?"

Porter groaned. "Okay."

"You don't have to. I can just hit against the backboard."

But Porter pushed himself wearily to a stand. Kaylie dashed to the cabana and a moment later emerged with two tennis rackets and a ball caddy. "Take these," she said, giving Porter a racket and the ball caddy. She then went skipping across the sloping lawn toward the court. Porter looked down at his ratty orange T-shirt, cutoff jeans, and black Chuck Taylor sneakers, no socks. He wasn't supposed to play tennis in such attire. This was pretty much the exact outfit he'd worn back when he and Lucy were just mindless twenty-year-olds, getting stoned in the cabana and then stumbling around the tennis court in hysterics, smashing balls sixty yards into the glen beyond the far end of the court.

One evening Claire had caught them doing this. Porter had just smacked a ball overhead, and it was in midflight over the fence when out of nowhere she'd stomped onto the court in a tightfisted, red-faced rage. Porter thought they were completely busted. The cabana must have reeked of pot. But Claire looked only at Porter's feet and boomed, "I've told Lucy a hundred times that you must have proper tennis shoes if you want to play on this court." She gazed with a distraught expression at the scuffs he'd made, then turned to Lucy. "I'm happy to buy him tennis shoes, if that's what I have to do. But I will not have this court ruined."

"Sorry," Lucy said, battling to withhold her laughter.

"Sorry is for children," Claire said. "Are you still children?"

"No," Lucy said.

Porter wanted to say, *Yes!*

Claire eyed them suspiciously, then gestured back up the slope. "And what is that burned smell in the cabana? Did you burn something in there?"

Porter couldn't stand it. He was about to piss his pants.

"Um, I'm not sure," Lucy said, glancing at Porter for help. "Maybe toast?"

For years afterward that story would absolutely double them over with laughter. One of them just had to say "Maybe toast?" and they'd be out of commission, rolling on the floor for fifteen minutes.

But now, as Porter watched Kaylie run off before him down to that same tennis court, he felt a sudden wave of sorrow for Claire. He thought about her walking off that day, stiffly ascending the lawn, passing the pool and the cabana, not looking back once, not even turning around after their giggling began and quickly erupted into full-blown, cackling laughter. For a while he and Lucy had to hang on to the tennis net for support, but finally they let go and lay on their backs on the red clay, tears streaming down their cheeks, where they laughed until they'd laughed themselves out.

Claire had been so twisted up in knots over . . . *what*? Not his improper shoes. But *what*? That her own daughter didn't care about what she thought was important? That her only child already was beginning to regard her as a silly, uptight old fool? Suddenly it tore Porter up to think about it. It tore him up to think that someday Kaylie was going to treat him that way—getting high with some arrogant slob and then laughing Porter out of his own yard. And what else? Would she then get pregnant and have to marry the slob, before her own life had even started?

Porter tried not to allow himself to think it out to the next step, but he couldn't help it. "So am I going to catch it too?" Kaylie had asked him once, early on, when their family discussions of Lucy's cancer had used only words like "sick" and "under the weather." But what if Kaylie did "catch it" someday, as she very well might, given her inauspicious genetic history? What then?

Porter shook his head to try to clear it of such thoughts and gazed at Kaylie waiting for him on the court.

"C'mon!" Kaylie shouted. "What are you *doing*?"

As he started down, she began to play leapfrog with her racket.

Poor Claire. Difficult as she was, she really didn't deserve to be abandoned right now. She didn't deserve to be without her beloved grandchildren in the midst of her loss. Not for two weeks. Not at all.

The only problem was, Porter didn't deserve to have to stay either.

CHAPTER TWO

AFTER only ten minutes of chasing down Kaylie's wild overhead slams and dribbling drop shots, Porter was gasping for breath and feeling light-headed, so he convinced Kaylie that they should call it a game and head back up to the house. They dumped the balls and rackets in the cabana, then ascended the lawn.

Kaylie stopped on the patio. "Should we go in?"

Porter was bent over with his hands on his knees. "We'd better wait."

So they plopped themselves on the deck chairs and lay back in the late-afternoon sun.

As they waited, Porter began to wonder what Claire and William were doing inside for so long. He knew Claire would be browbeating William for somehow allowing this situation to arise (as if he'd had any hand in it at all), but he couldn't imagine William taking her abuse for more than five minutes. Sure, he'd play rope-a-dope, allow Claire

to spend her frustration, but if she persisted beyond a reasonable period, he'd say something like "That's quite enough on that subject, my
dear." And then, if necessary, "That's *quite enough*!"

Porter thought it was sad and ridiculous that after all they'd been
through together these past two years, Claire and William still had to
erect their walls and talk in secret. Actually, he did at least feel closer
to them in the sense that he understood the rhythms of their marriage,
their little quirks and strategies for coping. But he did not feel
"bonded" with them. Physical contact at greetings and good-byes was
as awkward as ever. Conversations were the same tense struggles
they'd always been.

Porter wasn't religious, but up until Lucy died he'd always felt
that there was a greater force at work in life, balancing things out, and
that every cloud had a silver lining, and all that crap. If you suffered
a loss, you got something else in return, and that thing you got in
return might prove to be even more valuable than what you lost.

For a while he preached this stuff to Lucy. He just wanted to look
on the bright side, and was that such a crime? But Lucy's threshold
for putting up with his plucky sentiments was pretty low. It took
enough energy for her to be cheery in front of the kids. Did she have
to spend it on him too?

"But if you look at it right," he'd tried, "it should give you
energy."

She'd squinted at him. "If I *look* at it right?"

Last year, when Lucy was deep into her treatments and feeling
especially awful, she and Porter had rented a documentary by a filmmaker with cancer who had decided to capture his battle on film.
Touching on Porter's point, the filmmaker had said, with great pleasure and conviction, that having cancer had given him an edge on life.
Cancer had made life matter to him, had heightened his senses and
appreciation. Cancer, he said, had made him more loving and in love
with the world. Moreover, it had done the same thing for the people
close to him.

That's it, Porter thought. *That's exactly what I've been talking about!* And he said so to Lucy.

"Wouldn't that be nice," she said, "if it were true."

"It was true for him!"

"Oh, I don't know," Lucy said wearily. "Maybe that'll happen with us. I'm not saying it won't."

If it had happened with them, though, Porter wasn't aware of it. Had cancer given them an edge on life? Not that he could tell. More love? Nope. Enlightenment? Sorry. In the end, it was just a lot of work and sadness, arguments with doctors and relatives, endless excuses to his boss, a parade of promising and then failed treatments, the care and feeding of two grief-stricken and angry children, and the final void—Lucy lying there on her air-flow hospital bed, eyes closed, muttering something about celery and rice cakes, and then, suddenly, stillness and silence.

Porter thought, *That's all?*

Later it occurred to Porter that maybe the enlightenment he'd been searching for—the "edge" the filmmaker had described—was an understanding, and acceptance, of the meaninglessness of life. Was it possible that this knowledge gave you an edge? And had he and Lucy gained this edge at some point and just not realized it? Had they just not been focused enough to think of it in quite the same way as the filmmaker, who, after all, was more tuned in to such things because he was making a goddamn documentary about it?

But just as it had entered his mind, this whole line of reasoning struck Porter as the biggest crock of rationalized bullshit he'd ever dreamed up.

PORTER WAS WATCHING the red shapes on the insides of his eyelids expand and contract when he heard the back door open. He sat up, squinting, to see Claire emerge sunnily from the back door with William trailing her like an afterthought. "Look at you two!" she gushed. "You look like you've run a marathon!"

"Tennis is not without casualties," Porter said ridiculously.

"Anyway," Claire said, ignoring him. She came down the three steps to the patio and stood there a moment, heels together, gathering herself to make an announcement. "Porter," she began, "I feel like I should apologize about all this vacation nonsense. Of course you and the children should take a trip. We'll miss you. But that's not so bad. It's nice to have someone to miss."

Porter breathed with relief. Who would have thought she'd come around so easily? He leaned back in the patio chair, stretching his hands over his head.

"I just have *one simple request*," Claire continued. "William and I arranged for Jim Nathan to look over that camper first, just to make sure it's in good shape. Otherwise I'll have nightmares about you three stuck out on the highway somewhere. I explained the situation to him, and he was willing to stop by your apartment first thing Monday morning and give it a thorough look-see. Said he'd be happy to do it. And if anything needs to be fixed, he'll take it into his shop in Sharpsburg and then bring it right back."

Porter blinked with surprise. "You already set this up?"

She smiled. "For Monday morning. At nine." Then the smile left her face, and she squinted at him. "You needn't worry. It's on us. I know you don't like to accept most of our acts of generosity, but in this case I insist."

"But what if something needs to be fixed?"

"William and I agreed that we'd pay for that too. Though I wouldn't be surprised if Jim did the whole thing pro bono anyway, for the amount of business we give him. So don't worry about it. And if it does need repairs, you can use the Audi in the interim."

Porter smiled uneasily. The Audi had been Claire's car for a few years before she got the Acura. At the time, Porter had hoped Claire and William would give them the Audi so that he could finally junk Lucy's Mazda. Now *that* was an act of generosity he would have embraced. But instead William announced their intention to hold on to the Audi as their "runabout" car. As he had joked crassly to Porter at the time, "If you have a three-car garage, why not keep it filled to capacity?"

Porter had used the Audi once before, when Jim Nathan had installed a new clutch in the Mazda. But he'd made sure to have it back in its stall within twenty-four hours. The question was: Why had Claire and William already thought through lending him the Audi this time?

Suddenly Porter could see where all of this was headed. He looked at William, but William wouldn't meet his eyes. "I don't expect any problems like that," he said, standing up. "The camper drove fine all the way here from the dealer. But thanks anyway."

"Oh, I'm sure there won't be anything wrong," Claire said. "It's only to be safe."

"Right," Porter said. "Well, should we go rouse Benny? We should probably be getting home."

And with that they all started to troop around to the front, Claire taking Kaylie by the arm and walking ahead in a whispering twosome, leaving Porter to fend for himself with William. The problem with William was that you couldn't small-talk him. He wasn't interested in American sports—only rugby!—and he was too impatient to blather about the weather for more than a few seconds. Sometimes, by asking the right questions, Porter could get him to talk about his childhood in Oxford, which Porter found endlessly entertaining. When William really got going, it was like watching *Masterpiece Theatre* as a live monologue. But during the past two years of being trapped with William in various hospital waiting rooms, Porter had mined that vein for all it was worth. So that left jokes, William's jokes, which he made up himself as a sort of hobby. They were shamefully unfunny, all haughty jabs at immigrants and the poor—". . . and so the homeless fellow says, he says, 'I may live in a cardboard box, but you shouldn't assume that reflects my taste in architecture!' " *Har, har, har.*

Today, however, William was apparently not in the mood even

for jokes. He walked gingerly around the west wing of his house in scowling silence, with Porter next to him.

Ben was still sound asleep where they'd left him in William's Mercedes. He was laid out across the backseat, his face wedged into the corner. Porter thought his son looked so tall that way, splayed as he was. He stretched clear from one side to the other. Ben was not tall; in fact, he was shorter than almost every boy in the second grade.

Porter rapped his knuckles on the window, and Ben stirred, then looked up groggily, squinting in the soft evening light.

"Get up," Porter mouthed through the glass. "I've got something to show you."

Ben gazed out at him, unresponsive. The Mercedes was like an encased tomb. Porter liked traveling in it, although he found the ride to be disconcertingly quiet, as if the world outside were one big pantomime.

Porter tried to open the door, but it was locked. A quick survey of the car's interior revealed that all the doors were locked. "Unlock it," Porter mouthed, motioning to the lock.

"Oh, I'm sorry," William said. "I locked him in. I thought it might be dangerous for him to just be sleeping out here all by himself. You never know who might be lurking around these days." He produced the keys from his pocket, but by then Ben had unlocked it from the inside. He unfolded his legs out the door and stood up. "What?" Ben said. He yawned hugely and rubbed at his eyes. A trail of white dust, drool residue, led down from the corner of his mouth under his chin.

"Look over there," Kaylie said, all smiles.

Ben turned and saw the camper. His eyes widened. "Whose is that?"

Kaylie grinned. "Dad wigged out today and bought it."

Ben stared at it, dumbstruck. "You're kidding."

"Nope," Porter said.

"We're going camping," Kaylie added.

"No way," Ben said. "Really?"

Claire said, "We've just got to make sure it's safe first. . . ."

But Ben was already off and running, his stick legs and huge white sneakers in full awkward dash to the back bumper. He laid his hands against the little door and looked back at them. "Can I go inside?"

"Of course!" Porter said. "Explore all you want."

Ben opened the door, clambered up, and quickly disappeared inside.

DURING THE DESCENT into Aspinwall, as Kaylie and Ben romped around in the back of the camper, Porter kept playing back Claire's "one simple request" in his head, attempting to unravel its intricacies, because with Claire there were always intricacies, little sleights of hand, hidden bombs with ticking timers. He should have known what the woman was up to. He should have realized that the whole time he and Kaylie were outside, Claire and William had been plotting. They'd been strategizing and making phone calls, searching for some way to head off Porter's trip. What else would have kept them in there for so long?

Porter turned off Guyasuta Road into Aspinwall. The gloom of the evening had already descended on the cramped river town: the streetlights flickered on, the surrounding hills rose like gray shadows. They crossed beneath the dark, wet underside of Route 28—under the nonstop rush of cars—and emerged into the grid layout of cobbled streets and row houses, redbrick porches with grimy aluminum siding. The fishy waft of the Allegheny River swept in through the windows.

Porter could kick himself. He felt completely blindsided by Claire's plan. How could he have agreed to such a stupid thing as having Jim Nathan come over on Monday morning to check out the camper?

Here's what would happen: Jim Nathan would take one look under the hood, sigh with grief, and haul the truck into his shop. And there it would stay, in dry dock, mothballed for eternity. That was the deal struck during Claire's phone call—Porter knew it. He only wondered how much it had cost her.

Could he simply call Jim and cancel the appointment? Two problems with that. First would be the agonizing phone call. He could already see Jim's doughy face flushed with disappointment. "Porter," he would say, "you gotta have the thing checked out. *[Sigh.]* You can't just haul off across the country without having it checked out. You know that, right? You'd be puttin' your kids at risk out on the highway. In danger out there. And without the proper belts and tools to undertake a repair. *[Sigh.]* Besides, Mrs. Winter said she'd pay for it, hey? A very generous lady, that Mrs. Winter. So what have you got to lose, hey?"

And what could he say to that? Even if he were able to convince Jim that the appointment was unnecessary (impossible), he knew that Jim would still have to report back to Claire. And then he'd be back on the phone with Claire about it, with no way out.

The more Porter thought about it, the more trapped he felt, and the more trapped he felt, the angrier he grew. When he finally arrived at their parking lot, he swung into his space too quickly—he'd forgotten yet again that he wasn't in Lucy's little Mazda—and found himself overly angled in the spot. He slammed the stick shift into reverse, backed out, and eased forward again, this time sliding it into berth like a docking cruise liner. He looked back into the camper through the little padded passageway. His own parents, he suddenly remembered, had called that passageway the "boot." Was it really called that, or had they just made it up?

"Home," Porter yelled over his shoulder.

Ben's head appeared in the boot. "Already?"

"Afraid so."

"Can't we stay out here tonight?"

"Oh, get real," came Kaylie's voice from the back. "What is it with boys that they always want to sleep outside?"

Porter laughed. "No, we'll sleep inside. You'll have plenty of nights in here on our trip. You'll probably get sick of it."

"No way."

Porter wasn't used to seeing Ben so excited. He'd forgotten the boy's capacity for it.

Kaylie was in the back twisting the little door's knob back and forth, without result. "How do you open this stupid thing?"

"Hang on," Porter said. "I'll come around." He opened his own door and stepped out. The camper still surprised him—had he really bought it? It was so . . . Grateful Dead. There was even a Dancing Bear bumper sticker on the back. And this swirling purple-and-green paint job—what the hell was that all about? The curtains too were a riot: faded purple velvet with gold tassels. What a deal, though. A straight trade for the Mazda? He'd thought the guy was joking. But the salesman—a bald, flat-butted Steelers fanatic named Joe Hinch-cliff—had just seemed to want to get rid of it. "Didn't much want to take it on in the first place," he'd roared at Porter. "Wasn't worth much. But I just couldn't turn those kids down when they brung it in. They were flat broke, those kids. And they looked it, you know? They were hippies. Wearing bell-bottoms . . . the whole friggin' deal, you know? But nice kids. That girl, she kissed me when I agreed to take it. A big smooch right on the cheek. Called me a 'lovely man.' " He smiled a big, gap-toothed smile. "First time for that."

Porter grinned, thinking about Joe Hinchcliff, then walked around to the back of the camper, where his kids were already clambering out. "*I* opened it," Ben announced.

Kaylie made a face. "Conehead wants a medal for figuring out how to unlock the door when he's the one who locked it in the first place."

"Kaylie," Porter said. "I thought we agreed you wouldn't call Ben that."

Ben's hair was an exploding Brillo pad of tight curls, which a girl at school had recently referred to as a "nice Afro." As a result, he'd begun sleeping with a segment of green plastic fruit netting over his hair to mash it down. The resulting shape was, Porter had to admit, coneheaded—almost a bouffant.

"Sorry," Kaylie said.

"No you're not." Ben ambled off toward their building in his slouching walk, his head down and his shoulders sloping to the right.

"Okay, I'm *not*," she yelled after him.

Porter waited until Ben was out of earshot, then said to Kaylie, "Just be nice."

"I'm only trying to save him some embarrassment," Kaylie said. "He's going to be in serious trouble if anyone finds out he wears that net to bed."

"And how's anyone going to find that out?"

"I don't know. Maybe they'll guess it."

Porter sighed. "You've got to be easy on him, Kaylie. He's not like you. Stuff doesn't roll off him like it does with you." In truth, he didn't believe anything rolled off her. She kept everything bottled up inside much more than Ben did. But Porter wanted to compliment her on something. He wanted to tell her she was coping well even if he believed that somewhere down the line she was really going to lose it. Or was she? What did he know? For all he knew, both his kids were fine and *he* was the one who was going to lose it.

Kaylie walked off across the parking lot, and Porter closed the camper door, locked it, and followed her. He looked up at their building—a four-story, blue-brick monstrosity that the realtor had described as "functional" when she'd first told them about it. As they'd ridden up the desolate elevator, the realtor's only words about the apartment they were about to see—the same one they now lived in— were "It's a nice unit."

To Porter, the most depressing thing about the building was the fact that the architect had seen fit to equip the third- and fourth-floor units with little four-by-eight-foot porches. At that size, they were too narrow for chairs, and besides, they all looked out upon either the parking lot in the front or, like Porter's, the elevated highway in the back (which they were actually *beneath*). So rather than providing you with a private piece of the outdoors, these porches only made you feel exposed and trapped. In seven years, Porter had never, ever, seen any of his neighbors relaxing or enjoying themselves on their porch. Some used the space for storage: rusting bicycles, car parts, soiled couches standing on end. Others crammed it with potted plants, which then leaked yellow swaths of mineral stains onto the walls below.

Over the years, Porter and Lucy had done what they could with their apartment. Lucy had retiled the kitchen and the bathrooms. Porter had built bookshelves in the living room and furniture for the kids (little desks and bookcases in primary colors), spending his evenings and weekends painting like a madman. But now, as he stepped inside behind his children, he couldn't help but think the place was a tacky dump, a big wasted effort. All the time they'd spent trying to fix it up had been like pushing sand up a hill. No matter how much they'd fussed with warm lighting or mellow Southwestern furniture themes, the place still looked like a sickly, fluorescent box. The heavily stuccoed ceiling—created, Porter imagined, by trowel-wielding apes on stilts—was so deeply textured that thick eddies of dust had gathered in the tortured sea of swoops and swirls.

Surprisingly, the only time their apartment had felt more welcoming was while Lucy was sick. It became the place they returned to, the warm home that took them in amid all the stress and bullshit and bad news. It didn't look any different; if anything, it looked worse from the neglect. But it felt like shelter. On the way home after a long stint in the hospital, Lucy would say, "I just can't wait to be home. I've been so anxious to come home." And Porter had felt almost tingly with warmth about their "unit" then.

When Lucy died, however, the apartment lost all those associations pretty much instantly. Porter was surprised at how indifferent the apartment seemed to her death. As if he expected it to change somehow, to accommodate her loss, or to understand! Now all he wanted was to get out. *Fast.*

AFTER A WHIPPED-TOGETHER dinner of canned ravioli, cucumber salad, and Hawaiian Punch, Porter allowed Kaylie and Ben to watch a rerun of *Beverly Hills 90210* while he sat at the kitchen table studying the road atlas. He loved road atlases, could pore over them for hours plotting routes and searching for obscure landmarks. As a boy he'd navigated for his father on their many trips, and looking back, that seemed like the high point of his childhood. He hadn't realized how much he'd missed taking road trips until now. His heart felt light with anticipation as he flipped from state to state: Ohio, Indiana, Illinois, Missouri, then either Kansas or Nebraska as a route into northern Colorado and Rocky Mountain National Park. And maybe from there over to Jackson Hole. Incredible. And to think that earlier today he had been less than a mile from walking back into an office for the rest of his life.

Counting miles, Porter figured they could make it to the far side of Indiana in their first day, depending on when they were able to leave. They'd have to be all packed and ready to go the night before in order to be on the road before nine. Jim Nathan would come cruising up in his gleaming white tow truck promptly at nine o'clock, and Porter already had decided that they weren't going to be around when he did. He didn't care about whatever explaining he'd have to do later. Claire and William would be upset, sure, but that's what they got for scheduling the appointment without consulting him first.

After half an hour, Porter looked up from the atlas to see Kaylie and Ben sprawled atop each other on the couch, sound asleep. Kaylie would be mortified to be sleeping so close to her brother; Porter almost wanted to take a picture to show her later. Instead, he carried them to bed. Then he turned off the TV, undressed, and crawled into bed himself.

But he couldn't sleep. The night had grown hot and muggy; plus, he was wired. He tossed and rolled under the sheets, vaguely aware that it had begun to rain. Then there was a thunderclap, and raindrops began to batter the air-conditioner. Porter lay there, semiconscious, wondering how the camper was doing in the rain. He drifted into a nightmare involving the camper's purple-and-green paint washing off into the parking lot to create a mess that he would later be fined and jailed for. A dull panic pierced his brain, and he felt he should take action to prevent the mess, but he couldn't move. Then he heard something, someone talking, and Porter opened his eyes and was awake. It was Ben, saying something in his plaintive whine. He heard Kaylie's voice in response, brash and dismissive, followed again by Ben, more plaintively this time, and then Benny started to bawl.

Porter heard the padding of feet, then the knock on his door. "Dad!" It was Kaylie.

"What is it?" Porter said, sitting up.

She came in. "He needs you," she said sleepily. "He's all scared."

"Of the thunder?"

Kaylie brushed the hair from her face. "Don't ask me. I can't understand what he's saying. I told him to go back to sleep, but he just started to cry. I think he had a nightmare."

Porter got up and put on his bathrobe, but by the time he reached the hallway, Ben was standing in his own doorway, sniffing and rubbing his eyes. "I wanna sleep in your bed," he whined.

"Okay," Porter said. "You can." He stooped down, and Ben walked into his arms. "You have a nightmare?"

"Uh-huh."

"About what?"

"Nothing," Ben said woefully. "There was clouds and stuff. And then a plane or something went by, but it wasn't really a plane."

"What was it?"

Ben sniffed. "Maybe a boat." He tucked his head in against Porter's neck.

Porter glanced at Kaylie, who rolled her eyes. He shook his head at her, meaning, *Don't, please.*

"I'm trying to forget about Mommy," Ben said.

Porter winced. "You don't have to do that, Benny. You don't have to do that at all."

"That's what *I* told him to do," Kaylie admitted. "That was *my* idea."

Talk like this made Porter's stomach hurt. "You shouldn't forget about her. Either of you. Not even if you want to." He turned to Kaylie. "Does that really make it easier for you? To forget about her?"

"Yeah, I mean, just to not think about it. And to keep busy. That's what Gramma says."

"Says what?"

"That you should stay busy."

"But that's not the same as forgetting about her."

Kaylie rolled her eyes. This gesture was becoming almost a facial tick with her. "What-*ever.*"

Porter hated it when Kaylie acted this way, but what was he supposed to do? Punish her? Is that what she wanted? Or should he give her "space" to try to work through this crap on her own? He had no idea what his role was supposed to be at times like this, so he'd end up being schizophrenic about it, scolding her in one instance and ignoring the exact same response in another, wholly dependent on his own mood.

Over the winter, when this behavior of Kaylie's had first begun to manifest itself, Porter had mentioned it to his therapist, Carole Levine. Actually, she was Lucy's therapist, and Porter had begun to see her only at Lucy's request.

Porter had to admit that he didn't have much faith in the woman. All she seemed to do was hide behind her huge glasses and underneath her tightly wrapped bun of hair and say things like, "What do you think?" or "What is your fantasy about that?"

Part of the problem was that Porter's expectations of therapy

had been formed by movies like *Ordinary People*, and he'd imagined that your therapist was someone like Judd Hirsch looking out
for you like a best friend, or else really rattling your cage if need
be, but in any event putting some heart and soul into it. All Carole
Levine would do was sit there like a stone, unless Porter, to please
her, attempted to answer her questions about "fantasies," at which
point she started scrawling on her little pad like a woman possessed.

Carole's advice about dealing with Kaylie, however, actually
struck Porter as well reasoned and insightful. "I suggest you try to be
consistent," she said. "Mostly what Kaylie needs right now is something to count on, even if that means knowing she'll get punished for
saying certain things."

This made perfect sense, in theory. But in practice, Porter found
it very difficult to punish a girl whose mother was dying. Plus, he
simply didn't have the energy to punish her. Ben was easier. No matter
how upset he became or how much he cried, it was a cinch. You
hugged him. You took him into your bed. But with Kaylie, if what she
needed to get through this trauma was for Porter to punish her, he
didn't think he was the right man for the job.

"Kaylie," he said now, "you want to sleep with us too?"

"No, thanks," she said. "I'm looking for some cherished peace
and quiet." And with that she headed down the hallway.

Cherished peace and quiet? It was lines like this that made Porter
feel she was going to be okay after all. He gathered Ben into his arms
and carried him into bed. Within thirty seconds the boy was out cold.
The rain continued to batter the air-conditioner, louder than ever.
Porter rolled over and stared out the window. Water slid down it in
sheets, blurring the scene into a dark, undersea world.

IN THE MORNING, Porter awoke with Benny's hair in his face. His
arms were wrapped around his boy like a lover's, his knees tucked in
behind Ben's. This was how he'd liked to sleep with Lucy, in this

position. Now, with Ben, it felt comfortable, like a memory. The only surprise was the hair. He'd grown used to Lucy's bald head—smooth, blue-veined, pulsing at the vortex of her neck. By contrast, Ben's mat of hair felt like an animal between them.

Porter closed his eyes and nuzzled his face into the oily musk of his boy's scalp. At moments like this, Porter was convinced that love was an aroma, something you could breathe in and consume. He hugged Benny tightly, wrapping himself around his sleeping boy, and doing so filled him with a feeling of such pure joy that he was astonished to find himself suddenly weeping. He cried quietly for a few minutes, sniffing and breathing shallowly against Benny's neck, as his mind began to feast on dark memories of Lucy's final night. Her last comprehensible words to him, whispered with eyes closed and lips barely moving, had been "Just don't let go of me, okay? I don't want to do this all alone, okay? Please?"

"I won't let go," he'd promised, squeezing her hand. "I won't."

And for a long time he didn't let go. For at least forty-five minutes Porter held on to her hand and stroked her forehead and told her stories about what the kids had been doing. But eventually he had to stand up and move around. He had to use the bathroom and get a drink of water. Plus he had to phone Claire and William to tell them that this might be it, tonight might really be it, and that they'd better call the sitter and come on down to the hospital.

But even when Porter returned to Lucy's bedside, he didn't hold on to her the entire time. There were other seemingly important tasks to be performed that required the use of both hands—sheets to be straightened, curtains fiddled with, pillows adjusted. But he could tend to these things because Lucy wasn't going to die while he wasn't holding on, right? She wasn't going to exit this world at the precise moment when Porter was, in fact, rummaging thoughtlessly through his pockets in search of his misplaced parking token, was she? But that's what she did. That's exactly what she did.

Porter took a deep breath to try to clear his mind of these

thoughts, then wiped his eyes on Benny's flannel collar. Finally, being careful not to wake Ben, he sat up and got out of bed.

In the kitchen, Kaylie was already at the table with a plate of toast and a glass of orange Gatorade.

"Sunday-morning sleep-in?" she said, licking crumbs off her fingers. "I've been up since seven."

"What time is it?"

"Nine-thirty."

Porter made a big showy yawn and stretched his arms behind his back. "Yesterday wore me out."

"All that tension," Kaylie said.

Porter laughed, letting his arms fall forward. "Well," he began, but he was interrupted by the ringing phone. Porter froze with dread. *Claire.* She was already calling to confirm plans for Jim Nathan's inspection and the subsequent removal of the camper from their lives. It rang again. Should he pick up? Claire had to know they'd be around, first thing Sunday morning.

Kaylie stopped mid-chew. "You gonna get that?"

Porter nodded reluctantly and reached for the phone on the counter. But just as his hand touched the receiver, the answering machine clicked, and he thought, *Why not wait and see who it is?*

"Hi, Porter, it's me. Just calling to check in. . . ."

His brother. Porter picked it up. "Hey, Alex."

"Hey, you're there. I didn't wake you up, did I?"

"No, of course not. Kaylie and I have been up. Benny's still asleep."

"That kid really gets a lot of sleep."

Porter could already sense the restrained judgment in his brother's voice. "I guess he must need it."

"I guess," Alex said.

And they were silent. Porter tried to think of something to say. These phone calls with his brother could be excruciating. They had little to say to each other and over the years had spoken only on holidays—a perfunctory greeting. They'd always been like this, short on conversation yet supportive in ways that were expected. But ever since Lucy had been sick, Alex had been making an effort to check in every so often. Lately, over the past month or so, he'd been calling every two or three days. "So what's new?" Porter said.

"Not much," Alex said. "What's up with you and the kids? How is everybody?"

"We're all right. Hey, I bought a camper yesterday. Traded in Lucy's Mazda."

"Really?" Alex seemed truly startled. "I didn't know you were thinking about that."

"I wasn't," Porter said. "Sheer impulse."

"Well, that's great. Are you going somewhere?"

"Yeah, we're going camping for a week or so, just heading out West. I need to shake things up a little. You know. It's hard, staying here."

"I can imagine."

But could he? Porter wondered how much Alex could really understand. He was two years younger than Porter, unmarried, and living with a woman named Chloe in a third-floor walk-up in Park Slope, Brooklyn. He worked all of four evenings a week as a waiter in a fancy Manhattan restaurant called Room, where supposedly he earned as much as several hundred dollars a night. As far as Porter could tell, Alex spent the rest of his time writing and socializing—an existence that was recently rewarded when he sold his first novel, *Lifetime Moon*, for an amount, as he coyly told Porter, "in the high double figures."

To Porter, Alex's life seemed absolutely untouched by complication, unscathed by loss or even much suffering, though Porter knew it was unfair to think that way. Sure, everybody had problems. And you couldn't know that until you walked in the person's shoes, etc. But the stuff Alex wrote! Story after story of emotional mayhem, of characters so royally screwed up that just the weight of their suffering seemed enough to snuff out their lives. Porter couldn't deny that the stories were well written and that the suffering *seemed* authentic. But when he pictured his brother writing them—when he'd imagine Alex hunched over his desk sipping his mocha cappuccino latte, typing away on his four-thousand-dollar laptop, leering every so often at Chloe (who was no doubt lying naked in bed, waiting for him to finish so they could have sex all night)—the stories would collapse like a house of cards.

Alex hadn't shown him any of *Lifetime Moon*, but Porter had a pretty good idea that at least part of the story involved a man with two kids whose wife gets cancer. This occurred to him during one particular phone call when Alex seemed a little too interested in the details of Lucy's treatments. The telltale question had been "Is it red, that medicine?" And Porter, suddenly wary, had said, "Why do you want to know that?"

"Oh, it's just that this friend I know, she has breast cancer, and I was just wondering, you know . . ." but Alex couldn't even finish off the sentence.

That had happened a year ago. Ever since, Porter had been more circumspect on the phone with Alex, which only added to the awkwardness of their conversations. But Porter's real problem with his brother was that he believed Alex viewed their divergent lives as follows: Alex led a happy life because he had stayed true to his art, while Porter led a miserable life because he had traded in his art for a wife, family, and career.

Alex had never said anything like that. But there was always an undercurrent of self-satisfaction whenever Alex got onto the subject of his own apparent success: "I'm just glad I stuck it out," he said during the conversation in which he'd broken the news about the novel sale. "I could have given up at about a hundred points along the way."

Of course, Porter took this as a direct jab at the fact that he *had* given up on his painting. Or was it just Porter's own insecurity and regret that made him feel that way? In any event, there were times when he'd wished for Alex to say something judgmental along those lines—about choosing family over art—just so he could tell him off.

First of all, you little fucker, he'd planned to say, *having kids is way more important—and much less selfish, I might add—than staying true to your art. And second of all, fucker, I am still using my art, but I happen to be using it to help other people get the word out about their fucking art so that people in rural places, outside of goddamn New York City, can also look at paintings or see someone play the flute for once in their fucking lives.*

Now, though, Porter was glad he'd never exploded at Alex that way. For one, Alex would have seen it for the defensive and transparently false argument that it was, which only would have increased his sense of superiority. But on a more basic level, Porter felt that he needed Alex in his life these days; he had come to depend on these phone calls, however awkward.

"The kids are actually excited about this trip," Porter went on. "Even Kaylie." He winked at her. "And it's the first time I've seen Benny excited about anything in months."

"That's great." Alex paused. "So what about work? Are they being understanding about all this?"

"I can't tell what they want out of me. It's too awkward for them to say if they really need me or not."

"Then you should go for it," Alex said. "You should just get in that camper and go for it."

Somehow hearing Alex talk that way raised Porter's hackles, made him want to defend people who had to work at jobs they didn't like in order to be responsible. Not everyone could just bolt on a moment's notice—fly to Peru or Tunisia, as Alex and Chloe had done within the past year. "Well, it's not that simple," Porter said. But hadn't he just made it that simple by deciding to blow off work and go? "They're way behind because of me. In fact, they're having to pass on jobs."

"I'm sure they are," Alex said. "But you should still do it. I mean, when was the last time you didn't have a full-time job? Back when you were trying to paint? That was twelve years ago."

Porter almost laughed at the memory. He'd just graduated from Carnegie Mellon, having racked up twenty thousand dollars in student loans in the process, and was living with Lucy in a sprawling apartment in Squirrel Hill that her parents were paying for. For some reason, it was okay to have them footing the bill then. It was even socially honorable in a Robin Hood kind of way—using dirty capitalist wealth to subsidize the creation of art.

By day, Porter wandered the city simply looking at things to get inspired: images, angles, human moments. The evenings were for painting. First he downed some coffee and let the caffeine work its magic. Later he turned to Grand Marnier, with ice, in a highball glass. He cranked up the music—Grand Funk Railroad, Van Morrison, Springsteen—and painted until about midnight, then fell into bed with Lucy. Each morning he and Lucy carried their bowls of cereal into the living room and surveyed the horror of what he'd done the night before.

Gradually Porter painted less and less. After four months he found himself painting only one or two nights a week and spending the remaining nights watching TV. He became a rabid fan of college basketball. It didn't matter who was on (Lamar vs. Mc-Neese State?); within minutes he was pulling for one team or another, scooting nervously around the couch, shouting at Lucy to come in and see plays that she wouldn't believe. His daylong jaunts around the city were no longer so much about finding inspiration as they were about whiling away the hours until the primetime lineup commenced.

But it gnawed at him, this existence. He knew his life was adding up to a big fat goose egg and that he'd better do something about it. Sooner or later he was going to have to buckle down and make some decisions about what mattered to him. But just when he was beginning to think that what he really needed to refire his creative pilot light was a change in medium—say, from oils to watercolor—Lucy got pregnant, and that was the beginning of this new life.

"You know," Porter said now, "the other thing is that this trip is not only about leaving work. Claire and William aren't exactly ecstatic over the prospect of us leaving either." He wanted to tell Alex about the arrangement Claire had made with Jim Nathan, but he didn't want to do so in front of Kaylie. Plus, he realized, that was exactly the sort of juicy tidbit Alex was likely to seize upon and then include in the sequel to *Lifetime Moon.*

"What did they say about it?" Alex asked.

"Oh, just that they want us around for the summer. You know what? Claire actually insisted that I take one of their cell phones, but luckily she forgot to give it to me."

Kaylie looked up from her toast. "She gave it to *me.*"

"What?" Porter asked her. Then to Alex: "Hold on." He cupped his hand over the phone. "She did what?"

"Gramma gave *me* the cell phone. When we were walking around to get Benny."

"You're kidding." Porter grinned, shaking his head in disbelief. "What did you do with it?"

"It's in my backpack."

He spoke into the phone. "She slipped the cell phone to Kaylie. I swear. What a master plotter that woman is."

Alex laughed. "You know, it'll probably be good to have on the road. Cell phones are the best."

Porter took this to mean that Alex now had a cell phone and was ready to be asked about it, but he didn't take the bait.

"You should give me the number," Alex said. "I'll track you across the country. Plus, if Mom and Dad ask about you, I can tell them where you are."

"They won't ask about me," Porter said. "I've talked to them a bunch of times in the past three weeks, besides seeing them at the reception. That ought to cover us for a good six months."

Porter thought it was funny that Alex was now the one his parents kept in touch with. After more than forty years as a welder (that thought alone was enough to make Porter's brain go numb), his father had retired and sold the house in St. Cloud, and they'd moved all the way to Thatcher, Arizona, where they now lived a life of almost total seclusion in a bustling retirement community filled with people they claimed to "hate." Porter had been the one they called back then—The Favored Son. And soon after they'd moved, he was the lucky recipient of their rambling explanations for this hate in a series of costly and migraine-inducing phone calls—"It's fucking *politics*," his father kept shouting incomprehensibly.

After this episode, Porter decided to screen his parents' calls and return them only when absolutely necessary. In response, they turned to Alex.

Porter was surprised that Alex was willing to take them on again in this way. Alex's prior reign as The Favored Son had come to an end years before, after he'd sent them his first published story, "The Beating," in which a father (who was exactly like their father in dress, looks, and manner of speech) savagely beats his two sons (who precisely resembled Porter and Alex) with the flat back of a shovel, sending them both to the hospital in Minneapolis. At the end of the story, the narrator, a grown man named Alan living—guess where?—in Park Slope, Brooklyn, forgives his father for this traumatizing beating in an eloquent and devastatingly convincing final moment involving his older brother, "Palmer," who happens to work as a graphic designer in Pittsburgh.

After his parents read "The Beating" and dismissed Alex from their lives, Porter began his first and only reign as The Favored Son, and, as such, he had to hear his father's shocked and pained denials: "Who put this idea in that boy's head, anyway? I never laid a hand on either of you, much less a shovel. Your mother confirms this. She feels as betrayed as I do."

At the time, Porter made a minor attempt to explain to his father about fiction, but to no avail. The fact was, Alex also had portrayed "Palmer" as something of an underaccomplishing sellout, so he was in no mood to defend his brother or his work.

"Well," Alex said now, "give me that cell-phone number anyway. I hate to say it, but I sort of know where Claire's coming from. This just isn't a time when . . . I don't know . . . when I feel like I can go without talking to you for a few weeks."

Porter felt a swelling in his chest followed by a moistening of his eyes. God, what a softie he'd become! Anything could nudge him over the brink to tears these days. He swallowed, trying to gain his composure, and said, "Yeah, okay. Yeah, I want to keep in touch with you too. Hang on a sec." He lowered the phone. "Kaylie, can you get the cell phone and read me the number?"

Kaylie stomped off into her room and then yelled the phone number from there at peak volume.

"You hear that?" Porter asked Alex.

Alex laughed. "Got it. Okay, well, good luck with it all. I hope you guys have fun!"

"Thanks," Porter said. "I'll be talking to you."

And with that they hung up.

Porter thought Kaylie's shouting of the phone number would wake Ben, but it didn't. He continued to sleep for another three hours as Porter and Kaylie went through kitchen stuff, deciding what they might need and packing it into plastic milk crates that Porter had been using for storage. From there, they moved on to Kaylie's room, where negotiations commenced over what she should bring. When Ben finally woke up an hour later, he walked out looking groggy and morose, but when he saw them packing, a lightbulb went off in his head. "Oh, yeah," he said, smiling hugely, and then they started to tackle his stuff and Porter's.

The afternoon was spent cleaning the camper: scrubbing down the interior and exterior, washing the windows, vacuuming the nooks and crannies (this last chore conducted by Porter with a horrified grin as the nozzle exposed and sucked up one pile of spilled marijuana seeds after another). The outside of the camper had been filthy, coated with a layer of oily grime, and now—wet and gleaming in the evening sun—the purple-and-green swirls looked absolutely electric. The paint job, he realized, had been done by hand, with high-quality enamels. The sides of this camper had been somebody's canvas, the finished product a work of art. Also, the layer of grime had hidden the fact that the green paint was not just random swirls as Porter had thought but was instead an elaborate picture of a wooded area surrounding a grouping of Indian tepees. The image was just abstract enough that you wouldn't notice it with merely a glance. But upon inspection, it was a competent, complicated work—all the more impressive in that it was done in only two colors on a ribbed, metallic surface.

The only part Porter and his kids hadn't gotten to was the cab, but he was willing to pass on that. It wasn't where they'd have to sleep or eat. Besides, Kaylie and Ben were already sprawled half asleep on the lawn, wet rags still in their hands. He needed to get them upstairs and shovel some food into them.

Over dinner, Porter told Kaylie and Ben that he'd canceled Jim Nathan's inspection of the camper and that they were going to leave first thing in the morning. "They already inspected it at the dealer," he said, which probably wasn't a lie. "So I don't want to waste his time." And they seemed to accept this without suspicion.

Much to Porter's relief, the whole day passed without a single call from Claire. They got the camper completely packed and ready, and Porter plotted out a route for the first three days, which, at an aggressive pace, would take them almost all the way to Rocky Mountain National Park. He'd see how the kids held up. He wouldn't mind taking longer if they wanted to stop and see things along the way, but he wanted to avoid getting bogged down anywhere in the Midwest. He was anxious to do some real camping in real mountains.

At nine he put the kids to bed, then cleaned up the kitchen and the living room. At ten he called his boss's voice mail, waited through that idiotic greeting for the two-millionth time—"Hi! I may sound like Pete, but actually I'm his voice mail! Pete is either . . ."—and left the message that he and the kids needed just a little more time together and that he was sorry and would be in touch. *Perfect*. He looked at the clock. One more hour and he could stop worrying about Claire. He was shocked she hadn't called. If it held up, it would be the first day in weeks that she'd left them alone. Perhaps she was feeling so smug about her brilliant plan that it hadn't even occurred to her to check in on them. Or maybe that was unfair.

At any rate, when the clock struck eleven, Porter popped open a beer in celebration and sat down on the couch to drink it. He lay back, put his feet up on the coffee table, gazed at the stuccoed ceiling he hated so much, and decided to let the enormous weight he'd been hauling around on his shoulders these past few weeks slide off onto the couch cushions. His mind tingled with the first gulps of beer, his muscles loosened, his chest warmed, and he allowed himself to feel, for the first time since Lucy had gotten sick, something he thought might be the beginning of happiness.

CHAPTER THREE

PORTER awoke to the drone of the radio—KDKA morning news, weather, and traffic—and he was hearing about the overturned car on the Highland Park Bridge, but hadn't that been in his dream, that overturned car, and the traffic jam too? And the twelve-year-old boy who'd been shot in Homewood? Then his eyes focused on the red numbers of the clock: *8:30!* The radio must have been droning away for almost an hour.

Porter sat up, his heart bouncing around his rib cage. Jim Nathan would arrive in thirty minutes, possibly sooner. He pulled himself out of bed, got into the clothes he'd laid out the night before, then walked stiffly down the hall to wake Kaylie and Ben. "Get up, you two!" he shouted as he approached. "Up, up, up! We've got to get on the road. I slept through my alarm."

He stuck his head into Kaylie's room. She was lying on her back, hands clasped over her stomach, like a corpse in a casket. It was the way she'd always slept, even as an infant, a sight simultaneously peaceful-looking and freaky. She sat up on her elbows and squinted at Porter, dazed at first, then annoyed. "What's the hurry?"

"Uh, traffic," Porter suggested. "We've got to get out of here before rush hour."

"What time is it?" Kaylie said.

"Eight-*thirty*!"

"Then it's already rush hour," Kaylie said. "Isn't it?"

"Not if we hurry!" Porter shouted.

In his own room, Ben had risen and was sitting at the edge of his bed.

"C'mon, let's go, you two," Porter said from the hallway. "I mean it. We've got to get going."

He checked to make sure Kaylie and Ben had dragged themselves out of bed, then headed into the kitchen, glad, at least, that they'd gotten everything packed the night before. All that was left were the perishables in the refrigerator and his own toiletries, which he'd simply put off packing, thinking he'd have plenty of time in the morning.

"I'll pack up the stuff in the fridge," Porter yelled at them. "We can have breakfast on the road, okay?"

Porter yanked open the refrigerator door. Orange juice, milk, eggs, margarine, tangerines, yogurt. He put all of it into a box, flipping the items from hand to hand and arranging them lickety-split like an all-star bag boy. He stood up and looked around. What else? Pack the toiletries, check the doors and windows, turn off the AC, and get out.

In the bathroom, he stared into the medicine cabinet and remembered why he'd avoided packing his toiletries last night. His stuff was mixed up with Lucy's: her abandoned toothbrush, makeup, pills. For some reason, this cabinet had been the hardest for him to sort through after she died: all those little vials of hope with her name typed on them, plus her lipstick and cover-up and wig accessories—all the undignified crap she relied on to present herself with dignity.

Well, now wasn't the time. He brought a shoe box up to the edge of the cabinet and emptied the contents of each shelf into the box with a sweep of his hand. He could sort through it later. Maybe on the road it would even be easier?

Kaylie and Ben emerged from their rooms dressed and ready, toting their little backpacks of "personals."

Porter smiled. "Let's go!"

Outside it was already warm; the air was clingy with humidity. As he slid the box of food into the back of the camper, he thought he'd better go ahead and put the milk and other perishables into the refrigerator, and then it dawned on him: He'd forgotten to buy a block of ice! He ran back up to the apartment, forgoing the elevator for the stairs, which he bounded up three at a time. He burst into the apartment, opened the freezer, and dumped the contents of all four ice trays into a large Ziploc bag. Not great, but at least it would keep the food from spoiling until they could stop along the way and pick up a block.

Minutes later, they all piled into the cab, Ben squashed in the middle. Porter looked at his empty wrist. Damn, he'd forgotten his watch. Tough shit. The dashboard clock read 9:03, but who knew how accurate that was? Porter turned the ignition and pumped the gas, but it whined and sputtered and wouldn't start. He tried again. More whining. And what Porter thought then was *This is just like in the movies!* Except in the movies this happened when a ski-masked killer was trying to smash in your windshield, not when a highly skilled mechanic was making a rare house call to inspect your truck for free.

Thinking this way, Porter began to feel small and ridiculous. But he wasn't wrong about Claire's intentions, was he? He hoped not. Then, before he could think it through any farther, the engine caught, and Porter fed it gas until it roared, the cab vibrating with the surging motor. He backed out cautiously, now hyperaware of this vehicle's larger girth, then he lurched forward and rolled out into the street.

Relax, he told himself, but his hands remained clenched to the steering wheel in a white-knuckled grip.

He raced down 10th Avenue, then steered onto Main, making a beeline for the Route 28 on-ramp. But the two-way stream of cars on Main Street crept along in bumper-to-bumper traffic. Finally, when they got within a few blocks of the highway entrance, traffic eased and began to flow. Porter was accelerating to make it through his third yellow light in a row when the driver in front of him slowed with indecision and then stopped, bringing Porter to a rocking halt. The light clicked from yellow to red. Porter struck the steering wheel and gazed across the intersection, fuming. And that was when he saw Jim Nathan's familiar white tow truck stopped on the other side, in the facing lane, no more than forty feet away. Porter was too stunned to do anything but stare at him, but Jim seemed otherwise absorbed, first gazing up at the red light, then yawning, then checking absently in the rearview.

Unbeknownst to Porter, the light turned green, causing someone to honk behind him. That's when Jim, who'd just begun to cruise forward, looked over at Porter, and as they came within ten feet of each other, a wash of recognition passed over Jim's face.

Heading away, Porter watched in the sideview as Jim's brake lights blinked on and he slowed to the curb. The line of cars behind him all came to a brief stop, then began to jockey around in a herky-jerky fashion, trapping him there. Jim stuck his head out the window and looked back, a helpless, bewildered smile plastered across his beefy face, then shrugged and angled his truck into the stream of traffic.

Porter glanced back one last time to see Jim's truck—distinguished at that distance only by the bar lights on the roof—disappear around a street corner, and he was gone. Three blocks and one more red light and they were ascending the on-ramp to Route 28. Porter pushed the pedal to the floor and relished once again that unfamiliar power as they accelerated to the speed of the highway traffic and then began to pull away. Wind rushed loudly in through the windows, whipping at his hair. The line of sweat that had broken out along Porter's forehead cooled and dried, and the thrashing of his heart began to subside.

Ben gazed up at his father with heavy-lidded eyes. "Can I go in the back now?"

"Sure," Porter said. "Go ahead. You want to try to sleep?"

"Yeah."

"That's what this thing is built for. That's the whole point." He looked to Kaylie. "You can go back too if you want. I'm sorry for rousting you guys up this morning."

"I don't want to," Kaylie said. "I'm up now. I might as well stay up. I'll keep you company."

The sky was soft and bright—a low, unbroken blanket of thin clouds. They drove along the Allegheny River toward downtown, the same route Porter had driven to work for the past ten years. It was also the way to Allegheny General Hospital, where Lucy had been. But today he was going to neither of those places. The camper bumped along, rocking gently from side to side with the subtle rolls and pitches of the road surface. Then the front wheels slammed into a gaping pothole, and the whole rig shuddered and shivered, like a boxer trying to shake off a blow.

They'd just cruised past the H. J. Heinz plant, that relic of another era with its brick smokestacks soaring above the river, when Porter heard a muffled beeping in the back of the camper.

"Dad," he heard Ben say. "Something's beeping back here."

Kaylie looked at Porter and grinned. "I wonder who it could be?"

Porter smiled grimly.

"It's gonna be Gramma," Kaylie shouted back to Ben. "She gave me her cell phone."

The phone beeped again, louder this time. Porter looked in the rearview to see Ben rummaging in a box. Then, presto, out came the phone. Ben flipped it open like a pro. "Hello?" Then, "Dad, it's Gramma. She wants to talk to you." He handed the phone through the boot. Before Porter had even taken it, he'd already been able to hear Claire's tinny voice: "Porter? Porter? Are you there?"

He brought the phone to his ear. "Hi, Claire," he said cheerfully. "You found us!"

She started right in—"Where *are* you? Jim Nathan said he just passed you on Main Street. He said you went right by him. Porter, I thought you were going to have him look that thing over. I thought we'd agreed to that!"

"I'm sorry, Claire," Porter said. He was talking loudly, over the sound of the engine and the rushing wind. "Tell Jim I'm sorry, would you? I tried to call him at the shop, but he'd already left, I guess. He didn't get the message?"

"Message? I don't know. He was calling me from his truck. He was on his way back to his garage. What happened, Porter?"

"We were anxious," he said. "And you know what? I remembered last night that the guy at the dealership told me he'd already given the truck a thorough going-over. So I just thought we wouldn't waste Jim's time."

"This is so upsetting to me," Claire said. "We're both very upset, William and I. We think it's so disruptive for Kaylie and . . ." Her voice trailed off into static. ". . . supposed to keep a regular routine, keep their normal day-to-day life as much as possible. That's what *all* of the books recommend. None of the books say to go take a vacation—"

"Claire . . ." Porter interrupted, "I know all that. But this isn't the right time to talk about it. I can't hear you very well, for one. But let me just say this: Why isn't taking a summer vacation considered normal day-to-day life too? Shouldn't that be considered part of their regular routine?" This argument had just come to Porter on the spot, and he was quite proud of it.

But there was no response from Claire. He could hear her whispering to William in the background. Her voice was muffled, as if she had the phone cupped against her hand. Had she even heard him? Then she came back on. "William would like to talk to you, all right?"

"Claire, this isn't the best time . . ." he tried, but once again she'd already begun talking to William, coaching him. He heard Claire say, "Just *tell* him," and William respond with, "I know, I know . . ."

There was the brief clatter of the phone handoff, and then William's voice: "Porter?"

"I'm here, William."

"It's difficult to hear you on this blasted thing," William said. "Your voice isn't coming in clearly."

"That's probably because we're on a bridge," Porter said. "The Fort Pitt Bridge. There's interference. In fact, you'd better hurry, because we're heading toward the tunnel."

"Pardon? Heading toward the what?"

"The tunnel, you know. The Fort Pitt Tunnel."

"Oh, whatever," William said. "Listen, Porter, I'm having trouble hearing you clearly. But I did want to make the point that . . ." and with a *whoosh* they entered the tunnel and the line went dead.

"Hello?" Porter tried. "William?"

"They don't work in tunnels, Einstein," Kaylie said, taking the phone from his hand. "You should turn it off to save the battery."

Porter glanced at her with irritation. "I don't want to save the battery. I don't want them calling me again. I don't even know why you took this from her."

"I *wanted* to take it. Plus, she's right. If we break down somewhere, we'll need it. Or if we get lost."

"We're not going to get lost," Porter said. "We hardly even have to make a turn until Colorado."

Ben stuck his head through the boot and perched himself there as they sped through the dark of the tunnel. "What did Gramma say?"

Porter sighed. "Oh, Benny," he said. "Your gramma misses us, that's all."

Kaylie said, "She wanted to know why we blew off the car guy, right?"

"She wanted to know that too, yes."

Kaylie looked at him with a hang-jaw expression. "Well . . . ?"

"Well, what?"

"Why did we?"

They were hurtling through the darkness, rounding the short bend toward the tunnel's end, when suddenly the light of the exit blinked into view. Porter began to squint with anticipation, and then they shot out of the tunnel. The low cloud cover was so uniformly bright it somehow felt more blinding than the sun. Porter flailed for the visor and pulled it down, causing a nest of napkins and papers to cascade into his lap. "God*damn it*!" He glanced at Kaylie for help, but despite the mess of trash now strewn across his side of the cab, she just looked at him with the same expectant expression. She wanted an answer to her question.

"*What?*" he said.

"Why did we?"

He gathered a fistful of napkins from his lap and handed them over his shoulder to Ben. "Could you put these in the garbage bag, please?" One napkin still dangled from the visor, stuck there from what? a smashed particle of food? a wad of gum? LSD residue? Whatever. He tore it down and dropped it to the floor. More debris from the visor spill was already down there, fluttering and dancing in the wind: brochures, more napkins, and what looked to Porter like ticket stubs. *At least there's no rolling paper*, he thought. Then he turned to Kaylie. "Because he was going to find something wrong, that's why. That's what mechanics do. They find something wrong, and then they fix it. And if they don't find anything wrong, then they act like they find something wrong, and then they act like they fix it."

Kaylie regarded him. "That's a pretty cyclical attitude."

Porter laughed. "You mean cynical?"

Kaylie looked away. "No."

"Then what do you mean?"

She didn't answer.

"Actually, I'm impressed that you know that word," Porter tried. "Or almost know it. Did Gramma teach you that?"

But she just stared out her window.

They cruised due west on the interstate, Ben no doubt already settling in for his nap, Kaylie moping on her side of the cab. Porter finally drew her out by saying, "Look at the tornado." When she looked, he pointed at the loose funnel of paper swirling improbably under his legs. She grinned despite herself, then reached down and began collecting it, stuffing most of it into a trash bag and singling out some items to keep.

"You want to see our route?" Porter asked her. "I marked it on the map."

She nodded and picked up the road atlas from the seat between them. Opening it to Pennsylvania, she traced her finger along the yellow-highlighted route. "We should get to West Virginia pretty soon," she said, "but only for, like, half an inch. Then it's Ohio." And hers were the only words that were spoken until they had entered and left West Virginia in a span of less than ten minutes—soaring over the Ohio River and into the depressing little town of Steubenville—and Porter said, "That was it? That was West Virginia?"

"I told you it was only half an inch." Kaylie looked out the window. "So where is our final destination today? Are we sleeping in this thing tonight?"

"What do you mean, *Are we sleeping in this thing?* Sleeping in this thing is the whole point."

Kaylie scrunched her face up snottily. "I was just asking. You don't have to have a hemorrhoid over it."

"I'm not 'having a hemorrhoid,' " he said. "I don't know. We'll go as far as we can. The far side of Indiana, maybe."

Kaylie began flipping through the stuff she'd retrieved from the floor, scanning ticket stubs, opening brochures. "Whoever owned this camper sure liked the Grateful Dead," she said. "That's what all these tickets were for. *All* of them."

Porter nodded. That hardly surprised him. "I wonder if they caught the last shows," he said. "Before Jerry Garcia died."

"These are all from last summer," Kaylie said.

"Hmm. Then they probably did. I think he died . . . when was it . . . last August? September?"

"Don't ask me," Kaylie said. "Wasn't that band like a hundred years old anyway?" She opened a brochure and started scanning it. "Hey, here's a place we could stay. It's a health resort. It has swimming." She paused, reading. "Listen to this: 'Natural limestone swimming haven. Volleyball courts. Electricity hookups. Weekly rates. Licensed *mass*er on location.' "

Porter laughed. "It's ma*soo*er, not *mass*er."

"Whatever. What is that?"

"Someone who gives you a massage. You want a massage?"

"No."

"You'd probably like it."

"I'd hate it. I hate stuff like that."

"What do you mean, 'stuff like that'? What else is like that?"

"You know. Acupuncture and stuff. Herb compresses. All that stuff Mom did. It's all sort of a rip-off, isn't it? Anyway, that's what Mom thought."

"She didn't really think that. She was just frustrated. She was tired of getting her hopes up and then being let down." Porter glanced at his daughter. She was gazing out the window into the rolling countryside. "Besides, a massage isn't the same kind of thing. A massage is just to relax your muscles, make you sleep better."

"That's not what that ma*soo*er guy told Mom. He told her it would squeeze the toxins out. What a jerk."

"Well, maybe he believed that," Porter said. "He wasn't trying to be a jerk. He gave a great massage, that's for sure. Mom would second that. She loved it. She told me so."

Kaylie turned away. She slumped down in her seat so that her eyes just cleared the base of the window. "She still died."

'Yes, she did," Porter said softly, and left it at that. He knew better than to touch that one. With Ben he would have said, "Yeah, well, but at least . . ." and then come up with some qualifier, some fatherly spin to take the edge off. But with Kaylie he'd learned it was better to let such remarks go without any upbeat rejoinder. For a few miles they rode in silence. Then Kaylie straightened up again, and glanced at him, and this was the sign, Porter knew, that they had passed out of that moment and now could resume their conversation in another place.

"Can you give me the cell phone?" he said to her.

"What for?" she said, fishing for it on the floor.

He smiled. "I'm going to call that place. Set up an appointment for a massage tonight."

"No you're not," she said. "Not unless you want Gramma to find us. She'll track us by the call. They can do that. Find out where their cell phone is being used. I've seen it on TV."

"I was only kidding," he said. "So what's this place called? And where is it?"

Kaylie put down the phone and opened the brochure again. "Umm . . . Uh-oh, get ready. This place might be totally retarded after all. It's called 'Cherokee Charlie's RV Resort and Spa.' That's the name of it. It says it's 'Open to the World,' whatever that's supposed to mean."

Porter laughed. "They call it a spa?"

"That's what it says. What's an RV?"

"All you have to do to call yourself a spa is provide a swimming hole and a licensed masseur?"

"Beats me," Kaylie said. She continued to study the brochure. "So who owned this camper anyway?"

"I don't know. The salesman said they were nice kids. Hippies. Why?"

"Because there's little notes and drawings all over this brochure. People's names and phone numbers. I can't believe they left this stuff in the camper for just anyone to have."

"They probably didn't mean to," Porter said. "My guess is they ran out of money and panicked, thought they could dump off this camper at the used-car lot like you sell a ring at a pawnshop, thinking you can go back in a week or two and buy it back. That's probably why they didn't clean it out so well. They planned on reclaiming it."

Kaylie turned to him. "So we got it instead."

"That's right."

She started riffling through some of the other pamphlets on her lap. "Hey, look at this." She lifted a pressed joint from the pages of a glossy booklet of Grateful Dead paraphernalia and held it aloft, pinched in the tips of her fingers like a bug.

Uh-oh. Porter sucked in his lips. "You know what that is?"

Kaylie squinted at him. "Do *I* know? Dad, how old do you think I am? Three?"

"No," Porter said. "But I think I was sixteen before I knew what pot was. Twelve seems a little young to me." He thought for a moment. "So do kids . . . kids your age . . . do they do that stuff?"

"Sure," Kaylie said without batting an eye. Then she looked at him. "But I haven't, okay?"

Should he believe her? He decided he would.

"In fact," she went on, "when these burnouts at school found out Mom had cancer, this one jerk actually asked me if I could get pot for them. He said Mom would be allowed to smoke it to help with the pain."

Porter felt as if he'd been punched in the stomach. "You're kidding."

"I spit at him, I was so mad," Kaylie said proudly. "I'd never done anything like that before. Except it was really stupid, because I thought I could spit on him by just blowing spit out of my mouth and having it splat on his face or something? But I guess spitting really takes practice to be able to do it like that—did you know that?—and when I spit, it came out in this spray and then, like, dribbled down my chin, which was totally disgusting. So he just laughed and walked away. Which was probably good, because that kid can hurt people."

Porter wished Kaylie had not told him that story.

She put the joint back into the booklet and continued flipping through the pages. "So what if the hippies *do* want the camper back? Wasn't it kind of harsh to buy it if they were planning to get it back?"

"I don't know for sure if that's what they were going to do. It's not a good enough reason not to buy it."

"Well, I'm glad we got it," Kaylie said. "I'm glad we're doing this. It's fun. We should come up with a name for it, for the camper."

Porter smiled. Kaylie hadn't said anything that unguarded in months. "Like what?"

"Like Betsy, or something like that."

Porter laughed. "Betsy?"

"I like the name Betsy."

"You think Ben would like it?"

"He'd hate it. He'd want to name it Destroyer or Supercharger Transformer or something."

"So why don't we compromise and call it Betsy Transformer?"

Kaylie laughed. But then, as if catching herself having too good a time, stopped smiling and looked down at her hands. "No, that's dumb."

The road stretched out before them in a long ribbon of shimmering cement. Budding fields spread out on both sides in a rolling lime carpet. They went through Cambridge, joined up with I-70, crossed through Columbus, and coming out the far side, began to feel achingly hungry.

"Hey, we forgot to stop for breakfast!" Kaylie yelled. And then she started to moan with how much she needed to eat and go to the bathroom, and Porter too suddenly had to piss so badly he didn't think he'd make it to the next exit. Within two miles they were able to pull off the highway and into a suburban strip mall of fast-food restaurants and warehouse-size appliance stores, where Porter steered immediately into the first parking lot—a McDonald's.

After lunch Porter got the truck fueled up and bought a block of ice for the fridge, tossing what had by then become a bagful of cold water. When they were on the highway again, Kaylie went in back for a nap and Ben sat up with Porter, reading the map. Porter solicited his navigational help even though he planned to be on I-70 until Denver. To keep Ben engaged, Porter asked him to compute mileage amounts. "How far between Denver and Kansas City?" And Ben would get out his pencil and add up the numbers—"Six hundred and three miles." And then from Indianapolis to Kansas City? "Four hundred and eighty-five miles." And which way was shorter through Indianapolis, the bypass or the downtown route? "The downtown route is less miles."

For a while they debated the pros and cons of getting caught in rush-hour traffic in Indianapolis until Porter realized that if they stopped for dinner before Indianapolis they'd miss the rush entirely. The only problem, Porter cautioned, was that they would then have to go through Indianapolis after dark. He was worried that doing so would increase their chances of making a wrong turn amid all the merging highways and wind up heading south or north. But Ben misinterpreted, saying that maybe they should go around Indianapolis after all, because he didn't want them to "get robbed in the slums by crooks."

"Well," Porter said, and he found himself struggling through some half-baked statement about how people who live in ghettos and don't have jobs are "probably nice people too" and "not any more likely to rob you than anyone else."

Ben nodded solemnly, accepting this wisdom. But Porter felt ridiculous about what he'd said and was glad that Ben was his only audience. If it had been Kaylie, she wouldn't have let him off the hook so easily.

Ten miles east of Indianapolis they stopped for dinner at the Pizza Barn in a town called Mount Comfort. The place was jammed with what Porter assumed to be the entire population of Mount Comfort— shrieking babies, hormonally pumped teenagers, and pasty-faced moms and dads of every shape and size seemingly having the time of their lives amid a deafening roar of raucous laughter and clanking dishware.

By six-thirty a line had begun to snake its way out the door into the parking lot, and remarkably, the line too was brimming with pink-faced merriment. As far as Porter could tell, the rest of this bump of a town was shuttered and desolate at this time of night, but this red-roofed oasis was pulsing with life.

It was nearly an hour before their lukewarm pizza arrived, and Porter was already two beers into a raging headache. Ben's cheese bread was stale, and Kaylie's Diet Pepsi was, according to her, "*definitely not* Diet Pepsi." After Porter made several futile attempts to flag down their pigtailed waitress, they inhaled the food anyway, and then it was another twenty minutes of trying to get the check. When their waitress finally dropped it off with a quick "Thank you! Ga' night!" before bolting from the table like a relay runner, the bill amounted to one hundred and forty-seven dollars and listed as their order seven pepperoni pizzas and nine pitchers of Bud Light.

Immediately someone bellowed from the booth behind, "Hey, what a bargain!" leading to a round of table-pounding laughter that subsided only when the group's barrel-chested spokesman stood up and approached Porter with a check in his meaty hand. "You get ours?"

Porter smiled and nodded, holding out the check.

"Hey, you can go ahead and pay it if you want!" he roared. "Don't let me stop you!" And this renewed the riotous frenzy in his booth until the man, catching his breath, said, "Nah, I'm only kidding, buddy. Here you go."

By now Porter should have known better, but he held out his

credit card with the bill for a while anyway, hoping for a miracle. Finally he dug into his pocket, retrieved in bills and change the exact amount of the check (no tip), and dumped it in a heap on the table. Feeling bloated and besieged, and already guilty for having stiffed the waitress (it probably wasn't *her* fault!), Porter fought his way through the crush of people in the doorway, Kaylie and Ben trailing along in a safety chain of held hands. As they burst free of the mob and made their way across the parking lot to the camper, Porter looked back upon the flushed, expectant faces of those waiting in line with utter astonishment. He scooted in behind the steering wheel and immediately felt a wave of affection for the camper. Already it was home. Sanctuary.

They passed through Indianapolis—right through the city's center—at nine o'clock, sailing along, though it surprised Porter how many people were on the highway at that time of night. All fast cars full of teenagers in search of sex, no doubt. A rusted-out boat of a car—an old Cadillac, it looked like—cruised by jammed with six or eight longhaired kids. As they passed, the boy behind the wheel honked, gave Porter a big-toothed smile, and flashed him the peace sign (he hadn't seen anyone do that in fifteen years!). "DEAD!" the kid yelled. "*Wooooo!* Jerry!"

Porter grinned and nodded in response. If they only knew the truth of it. Then he gazed over at Kaylie for her reaction and was surprised to find that she'd fallen asleep against the door, her hair tossing in the warm wind.

They reached the west side of Indianapolis and soon reentered the rolling farmland of western Indiana, fields of black carpet stretching out into the night. As Porter drove, everything slipped away from him. He felt nothing but the thrumming of the truck's wheels on the pavement. He thought about trying to find something on the radio, then decided against it. He liked this better, this peace. For a moment he considered driving all night just to get them out of this boring state and even make some headway into the next boring state. That's what his own father used to do. Drive late into the night, with only coffee and the radio to keep him going, before pulling over at a rest stop. Or if they happened to be someplace interesting—on the shores of some beautiful lake or in the midst of a pine forest—they'd stop with a few hours of daylight left so that Porter and Alex could play and their mother could fix a nice dinner. Then their dad would wake up in the wee hours of the morning and creep into the cab and quietly pull away. How many times had Porter and Alex awoken to this same thrumming only to learn they'd already been on the road for hours?

Well, they weren't in the vicinity of anything interesting that Porter knew of, and there was no light left in the day anyway. But he could do the first option, just pull off somewhere convenient, grab some necessary sleep, and then start up again as soon as he woke. Then he remembered his pledge to William—"Only certified campgrounds"—and sighed. But probably better not to push it anyway. After all, what was the hurry? He *was* tired. And besides, he realized, he never liked it when his father was always forging ahead like that! It was one thing to be impressed by his father's ability to drive twelve or fourteen hours a day. But that didn't mean anyone enjoyed it. As he now recalled, he and Alex used to hate waking up on the road when the night before they'd gone to sleep next to a lake. He wouldn't do the same thing to Kaylie and Ben.

Suddenly he remembered the place Kaylie had found, that brochure she'd been reading. The "Resort and Spa." It had been west of Indianapolis, hadn't it? He clicked on the dome light, rummaged with one hand through the pile on the seat, and found the flyer. On the front was a collage of amateurish pictures: people playing volleyball while smiling at the camera, jumping happily from a dock, sipping drinks in front of their ridiculous-looking tepees. Cherokee Charlie's? Kaylie was right: This place probably was "totally retarded."

But maybe it would be fun? On the back was a little map that showed how to get there from the interstate. Ten miles south, only a couple of turns. It looked pretty simple, but it was hard to read with so much ink scrawled all over it. Kaylie was right about that too: Every inch of empty space on the brochure had been filled in with names, dates, phone numbers, directions. He opened it up. More notes and scrawls amid washed-out photos with misspelled captions: "Swim in our gorgous lake!" "Eat our sumptous food!" "Enjoy a relaxing massage!"

Tacky, definitely. But the kids would have a blast. And maybe, before heading off in the morning, he could get a "relaxing" massage. Why not?

He got off on 231 and followed signs to Bloomington and Indiana University as the brochure instructed. He crossed State Highway 46, and then looked for it on his left—supposedly it was .7 miles from the intersection. He went that distance and beyond, but his headlights found nothing, only dark woods and moonlit fields stretching away from the narrow road on both sides. He made a U-turn and headed back. Maybe he'd missed it? God knows he was so tired he was on the verge of seeing things. And then, just as he was about to give up and head back to the interstate, he saw it, or saw *something*—a sign and a driveway leading off into the trees. He pulled to the side of the road, slowed, then came to a stop. The sign was unlit, but he thought he could see the word "Charlie's." He clicked on his high beams and flooded the sign with light. It read:

Welcome to

CHARLIE'S

Open   World!

Squinting at it, Porter realized that some of the words had been painted over, creating this disjointed, off-kilter message. He looked back at the brochure. "Cherokee Charlie's RV Resort and Spa. Open to the World." Well, this was it. But who would have done that to the sign? Maybe some local rednecks had defaced it recently for laughs, and the owners hadn't gotten their act together yet to fix it.

Whatever. He was sleeping here tonight, even if this road led to a locked gate, even if it meant stopping the camper in the middle of the driveway. He knew that Claire and William would certainly "have a hemorrhoid" if they ever found out. True, they were in the middle of nowhere, and there was a chance—a chance—that something bad might happen. But at this point, it would be far more dangerous for him to drive any farther.

The driveway was paved but heavily potholed and dropped away into a shallow, dark valley. Porter peered into the darkness, trying to follow its path, then raised his eyes and saw, in the distance, through swaying tree branches, a little community of twinkling lights.

What do you know? he thought. *This might just work out after all.* He put the truck in gear and lurched forward, down the sloping road. It snaked into total darkness, low branches slicing at the camper; then there was a brief opening, and his headlights played over a small bridge with solid, shiny guard rails, a reassuring sign. He crossed, then crept up the other side. Three switchbacks brought him up the rise and toward the clearing of lights he'd seen from the entrance.

First he came upon a hodgepodge of five or six log cabins, some lit, others dark, all with cars or campers or motorcycles parked in the driveways. The cabins formed a crescent, facing a wide trampled field. On the far side of the field Porter could see the silhouettes of the Indian tepees he'd seen in the brochure.

Porter followed the headlights as they probed the dark, casting black shadows in the rutted dirt roads and off into the woods. A scattering of campsites seemed to ring the field, connecting the cabins at one end to the tepees on the other. A few of the campers looked semipermanent, up on blocks or with fixed wooden steps. A string of blinking Christmas lights dangled in the trees at one site, splashing a rainbow of colors onto a VW bus.

Porter chugged noisily around the half circle of this strange, hushed community, feeling as if he were piloting a tank through a church. Finally his headlights illuminated a small grassy turnoff, an unoccupied campsite with a parking space, a grill, a picnic table. He pulled the truck in and cut the engine, relieved for the silence. He opened the door and stepped stiffly out. It was warm; the songs of crickets filled the air. Across the field, beyond the silhouettes of the tepees, he could see the lake: a flat, shimmering void leading up to a black-rock cliff.

He went around to the passenger side, his boots cracking twigs and leaves, and slowly opened Kaylie's door. He held out his arms, and Kaylie fell into them, her head lolling, her blond hair scattered across his shoulder. Her mouth sagged open. Then she smacked her lips and closed them. He hitched her over his shoulder in a fireman's carry and brought her around to the back of the camper, where he heaved her up and rolled her onto the top bunk.

Ben was asleep above the cab, in Porter's bed, laid out on his back. He'd taken his shoes off, but he still wore jeans and a T-shirt. A purple blanket covered him haphazardly from his knees to his chest. The scene gave the impression that the bed was luxurious, but Porter knew better. His own feet would most likely hang over the edge.

He flipped the latch under the kitchen table, lowered it on its post, replaced the cushions on top, and fixed up Ben's bunk down there with a sheet and pillow. Then he stood up and pulled Ben by the feet until his boy's butt was at the edge, at which point Porter gathered him in his arms and slung him down gently onto the lower bunk. He unbuttoned Ben's jeans and slid them off.

After he'd covered both of his kids with light blankets, he removed his own boots and pants, dropped them onto the floor, and, wearing just his boxer shorts and a T-shirt, climbed up onto his bed over the cab. The clearance was low, less than a couple of feet between him and the ceiling, but he didn't care.

He rolled over onto his side, then rolled to the other side, experimenting. The mattress was great—consistently firm. The sheets felt clean and snug. He reached up and touched the wood-paneled roof.

The paneling looked a little chintzy, but so what? He rolled back onto his stomach and gazed out the window into the field and across to the village of tepees. Each had a little yellow bug light at the doorway, and a couple of tepees were aglow from the inside with what seemed like fluorescent light. Where was the office? In the morning he would find it and pay whatever he owed. This place seemed pretty casual. Maybe he could sign up for a massage then too, and the kids could take a swim.

He drew closed the purple velvet minicurtains, then decided he wanted to look out some more and yanked them open again. Staring out at this strange place, he realized that it hadn't really occurred to him, in the three weeks since Lucy had died, that their lives might become a completely different thing without her. He'd only thought of their lives without her as being the same as their lives with her, except she wouldn't be around anymore. But now look at them.

Suddenly Porter felt rather proud of himself. He was dealing okay. Taking action. To quote Lucy, he was "acting instead of reacting." That was one of the many ways she had intended to battle her cancer, by "acting instead of reacting." Porter had never quite understood how such a philosophy was to be put into practice, and he never had the guts to question her on it. Her only explanation had been "You have to take control of it, not let it control you."

Lucy was stubborn, all right. Absolutely determined to carry on a normal life. As much as she physically could, she still took care of her kids, helped them with schoolwork, went to parent-teacher conferences, made meals, planned little vacations. Porter admired her for this, but it also troubled him—he thought she ought to allow herself to be taken care of. She'd even made a point, with Porter, of trying to keep their sex life active and normal, which Porter had found the most distressing. First of all, they hadn't had an active and normal sex life before she got sick, so he didn't see why they should institute one now.

After Lucy's two deliveries, the second requiring a large episiotomy since she'd ripped with Kaylie (Porter still couldn't hear the word "rip" without cringing and covering his ears), they'd almost never had what they called "real sex" anymore—intercourse. Several months after Ben was born and she was supposedly completely healed, they'd begun to try it every so often, Porter hunched over her, Lucy wincing with each jab, until finally Porter would pause, suspended. "You okay?"

"Yeah, keep going," she'd say, her eyes clamped shut.

So he'd try again, as gently as possible, but then he'd have to stop.

"What's wrong?" she'd say with apparent irritation.

"It looks like it's painful for you."

"It is. But that's just because we're not used to it. We have to get used to doing it this way if we want to have sex like normal people again."

"Well, it's hard for me to concentrate when you look like you're in pain."

"Then close your eyes," she'd say in all seriousness. "Imagine I'm into it."

He'd laugh. "That won't work."

Eventually their lovemaking turned to utilitarian hand jobs and belabored oral sex, which would go on until one of them (usually him) got off. Afterward he'd say, "You want me to do you now?" Occasionally she'd nod, but more often she'd say, "No, that's all right. You can do me next time." And this was the totality of their sex life.

As it turned out, it was Carole Levine who was partly to blame for having encouraged this activity to extend well into Lucy's illness. "Carole says that as long as we have the desire, we should do it," Lucy had said. "And the doctor confirms that there's no physical reason cancer should stop anyone from having sex."

"But what about *your* desire?"

"I have desire. To be involved anyway. I mean, I don't really have any sexual feelings myself, but it's important that we try to carry on a healthy sexual relationship."

As Lucy's condition declined, she would only be able to jerk on Porter's penis for a minute or two before stopping to rest. "I'm sorry," she'd say, breathless. At this, of course, Porter would lose all concentration and start to go soft. "Lucy," he'd say, "Maybe it would be better if we just didn't . . ."

"No, we *should*," she'd say, starting up again. "Just like normal couples." And Porter was always amazed that his penis would respond, oblivious, and sometimes he would even be able to block out everything to the point that he could reach orgasm. Then he'd open his eyes to see Lucy lying across his belly, her bald head resting on her outstretched arm, a sheen of perspiration glistening between her shoulder blades, and he'd think, *That's the last time we ever do that.* But then a week or two later they'd do it again, exactly the same way.

Porter drew closed the purple curtains and rolled over onto his back. Lucy would approve of this trip, that's for sure. She wouldn't want to go on it, but she would approve of it. More than anything, though, he wished he could tell her about it. That's what he felt most robbed of right now. God, she would have loved the Pizza Barn story. As much as he'd hated the experience, it would have been a perfect story for Lucy. She'd be doubled over, laughing so hard that her face would lose color. Laughing like that, Lucy was a sight to behold, well worth whatever effort it took to get her to that point. Over the years Porter had learned just how to play it—how much to exaggerate, which scenes to act out, who to impersonate.

And it was more than just his ability to make Lucy laugh. It was everything, a way of being, a complicated dance that he'd practiced and perfected. Lucy used to joke with her girlfriends about Trainable Men, and how she'd found one in Porter and how, over the years, she'd "trained" him. This was all in the context of encouraging her girlfriends in their hopes of finding Trainable Men.

So he'd been trained. He was the best student ever! Now what? What was he supposed to do with it now?

CHAPTER FOUR

"**HEY,** open up!" *BAM! BAM! BAM!* at the little metal door.

The pounding sounded like a gavel on Porter's brain. But he just lay there—it didn't register. Then he felt the tugging at his feet and heard Kaylie's hushed, desperate voice—"*Dad!* Wake *up*!"

"Open up in there!" A *woman's* voice. "Open the door, you assholes!"

And then Kaylie again—"*Dad!*"

Porter jerked up, slamming his head into the panel ceiling, which cracked and splintered with the impact. He reeled back against the mattress—"Agh! Shit!" He felt his forehead. Splinters. A flap of skin. Warm blood.

"Hey! You came back! Open the fucking door! I can't believe you assholes finally came back." *BAM! BAM! BAM!*

Porter was trying to remember where he was. Then it came to him—Indiana, tepees.

"Dad!" Kaylie said. "What's happening? Where *are* we?"

"It's okay," Porter said, arranging himself, trying to shimmy down from his bed. "We're camping. I'll see about this."

As Porter's feet touched the floor, he saw Benny in the lower bunk, wide-eyed and shivering, his little white shoulders exposed. Huddled like that, peering up from the dark, Ben looked like some nocturnal animal—all eyes and bones peeking out from the cocoon of covers.

"Don't worry, Benny," Porter said. Blood trickled into his eyebrows. He wiped at it, then saw it in his hands.

Ben's eyes widened farther. "Daddy! You're bleeding!"

"I just hit my head on the ceiling, that's all." Porter's forehead throbbed and pulsed, as if his brain had shifted. He grabbed the washcloth from the sink and rubbed the blood off his hands, then used it to dab at his forehead.

Benny started to cry, his mouth a square, blubbering hole.

"Benny," Porter said. "I'm right here."

"I peed," Benny sobbed. "I'm all wet!"

"I hear you in there!" came the voice from outside. Porter could see the shadow of the woman through the curtain, bearing down on them.

"Who *are* you?" Porter shouted. His question was met by silence. He was trying to dress himself and keep the blood out of his eyebrows, wiping at it and then reaching down to pull up his jeans.

"Who's out there, Daddy?" said Kaylie from her bunk. "Where are we?"

Porter watched the shadow of the woman move away from the door. He gathered himself, pushed aside the door's little curtain, and looked out. The woman had retreated to the edge of their campsite where the turnoff joined the dirt road. She was staring back at the camper, touching her hand to her chin uncertainly. And she was tiny! Not much more than five feet tall, and skinny—little stick arms and a flower stem of a neck. She turned and took a few quick steps away, then stopped once more and looked back at the camper with an expression of utter perplexity.

She seemed young—maybe twenty-five—with dirty-blond hair chopped off in a bowl cut. She wore billowy tie-dyed pants, leather sandals, and a faded black T-shirt. The arms of the T-shirt had been cut off to reveal the edges of her bony shoulders.

Porter almost laughed. She was a wisp, a fairy, twinkle-toes in a muscle shirt. She was a fawn he'd startled in the woods. She didn't even seem capable of pounding on the door as loudly as she had. Porter's heart was still jangling in his chest from the commotion, but his fear slid away.

He fiddled with the lock, then swung the door open. "Who *are* you?"

"Who are *you*? You friends of Don and Stacey's?" Now that she wasn't shouting, the soft lilt of a Southern accent emerged.

Porter let out his breath. "I think you must have us mixed up with someone else."

"I don't have that camper mixed up," the woman said, pointing. "I *lived* in that camper. I came all the way from Oregon in that camper." She eyed him suspiciously. "They aren't in there?"

"Just me and my kids," Porter said. He allowed himself a smile. "You scared the hell out of us."

"But that's *their* camper," she said. "It *is*!"

"Well, it's our camper now. I just bought it on Saturday. In Pittsburgh."

She squinted at him. "In Pittsburgh? From Don and Stacey? What were they doing in Pittsburgh?"

"No, from a dealer," Porter said, exasperated. "I don't know Don and Stacey."

She looked as though this remark were especially hurtful. "From a *dealer*?"

Porter felt something wet in his eyebrow and remembered the blood. He reached up with the washcloth and dabbed at it.

"You're bleeding, you know that?" she said. "You really are. You've got it all over your shirt too, in the front."

He looked down at himself, at the maroon smears, then back at her. "I hit my head on the ceiling when you were shouting. I'm not used to sleeping up there. It was our first night."

She brought her hand to her mouth, and the suspicion slipped out of her face all at once, as if it had just occurred to her that *she* had done this, that *she* was to blame for this early-morning scene. "Oh, I'm so sorry. I just never thought . . ." and she began to walk over to him. "It just never occurred to me that it wasn't . . . and then I hear your voice in there and I'm like, *Who the hell is that?* Then I hear some kid start to cry and I'm like, *Who the hell is* that?"

Porter smiled. "That was my boy, Benny. He was just scared."

"So you've got little kids in there? God, what did I say anyway?" She looked away, trying to remember. "I can't believe I was yelling at ya'll like that." She put her hands on her hips and shook her head. "Man, I need to get a grip. I need to get a serious grip."

Porter stepped down from the camper, keeping the washcloth pressed against his forehead to stem the bleeding. "I'm Porter," he said.

"Delilah."

"Delilah? Really? We almost named our daughter that."

"She can have it," Delilah said wearily. "I'm sick of it. It's not even my real name—just what Don wanted to call me. It's what I'm known by *here*, anyway, so I guess I'm stuck with it for a while. But it's better than my real name, which I really hate."

Porter waited a moment. "Which is?"

"Sherry. Can you believe it? Like I'm supposed to be some 7-Eleven clerk for life." She smiled. "So what'd you end up naming her, your daughter?"

"Kaylie," Porter said, and, as if on cue, Kaylie appeared in the doorway wearing her yellow nightshirt and jeans she'd just pulled on.

"Oh, hi," Delilah said.

Kaylie gave her a savage look. "You scared us, lady."

"I know. I'm really sorry about that. I thought you were someone else. I thought ya'll were my friends. I mean, people like ya'll don't just drive in here in the middle of the night. And I really thought it was those guys! And they left me here!"

Kaylie looked at Porter. "Should I clean Benny up? Everything's all wet."

"Would you? That'd be great."

"Let me take a look at your wound," Delilah said, stepping closer. She touched his forehead at the hairline and brushed his bangs up, holding them aside. "Ow. You've got some splinters in there. Nasty ones." Up close, she smelled vaguely of pot and lavender. As she leaned toward Porter with her arm raised, he noticed a tuft of blond hair in her armpit, and he could tell by the way her breasts hung against her T-shirt that she wasn't wearing a bra. *Well. We seem to have landed smack in the middle of Granolaville.*

Porter felt at the top of his forehead. He knew that the splinters were tiny, no bigger than broken-off toothpicks, but at the touch of his fingers they felt like chopsticks. He winced.

"I should get you something for that," Delilah said.

"No, no." Porter waved her off.

"No, really. I've got a whole first-aid kit. Band-Aids and stuff. Disinfectant. Over at my place. Right over there." She pointed across the field toward the village of tepees.

Porter grinned. "You're staying in one of the tepees?"

"I know, isn't it outrageous? This place is so appalling."

"What are they made of?" Porter asked. "Fiberglass?"

Delilah's face became all teeth and dimples. "You got it. I'll bet you didn't even know that Indians invented fiberglass."

"Oh, yeah?"

"You should see the inside," Delilah went on. "Little baseboard heaters. A built-in closet. Beanbag chairs. All the luxuries you never read about in the history books. It's always the suffering and the buffalo hunts and everything."

Porter laughed. "So how long are you here for?"

"Me? Indefinitely, I guess. Pretty much everybody is here indefinitely."

"Everybody?"

Delilah squinted at him. "Just how did you find out about this place anyway?"

"From the brochure. There was a brochure in the truck."

"Ohhh," Delilah singsonged. She grinned at him mischievously. "So you don't know what this place is, do you? You have no idea?"

"The brochure said something about an RV Resort and Spa . . . ?"

She shook her head, smiling. "That was then. Once upon a time. Now this place is . . . ummm, what should I call it? Now it's more like a big holding pattern. All these people are in a holding pattern."

Porter couldn't imagine what that was supposed to mean. "It's not open anymore?"

"Oh, it's open, all right. Didn't you see the sign on your way in? It's 'Open to the World!' " She laughed, her slitty eyes almost disappearing above the expanse of her smile. "All right, I'll stop being so coy. I hate it when other people are coy, so I don't know why I have to act that way myself. No, this place was someone's stupid idea—a guy named Rick . . . Rick . . . I want to say Rick James, but that's not it. God, I can't even remember his last name. Anyway, he's the moron who built this place. Don't ask me the logic of having tepees and a health spa in the middle of Indiana. So the place goes belly up and shuts down about ten minutes after it opens. Well, more like ten months."

"So it *is* closed?"

"Wait, let me finish. So this guy Rick wants to unload the place, but *surprise*, nobody wants to buy it! Meanwhile he can't afford to maintain it either—all these buildings and everything. The expenses are really killing him. So he asks his niece, this girl named Andrea, and her stoner boyfriend, Seri—he's Fijian—if they'll stay here and be caretakers until he can find a buyer. I guess Andrea and Seri are the only people he knows who have essentially no plans in life. They're total Deadheads, and, you know, when Jerry died last August, they were sort of adrift. So they agreed to do it. But what Rick the moron didn't think of with his little pea brain was that all their friends and all their friends' friends were also Deadheads, and none of them had any particular place to go either. All they'd done for years and years was follow the tour, and now there was no tour." She smiled, clearly reveling in the story. "So here they all are. In a holding pattern."

Porter was incredulous. "Since last summer?"

"Most of them. Some came trickling in this spring. I've just been here since March."

"So you're a Deadhead too?"

"Not really. I was just trying this out for a while. Don totally is. I was with him. We came here together. He met Stacey here."

Porter raised his eyebrows. "So you . . . ?" he began, but then he couldn't think of what to ask.

She sighed. "Oh, I can't explain it all now. Don knows Andrea, and he wanted to stop here and see her. But while we were here, the transmission gave out on our truck." She smiled. "On *your* truck. So we got sort of stranded. Then, to make a long story short: Boy meets new girl. Old girl—that would be me—moves into tepee to try to get a grip on her life. Boy gets transmission fixed and blows out of here in the middle of the night."

Porter turned to see that Benny had come into the doorway, naked except for a towel wrapped around his waist. Despite the warmth of the morning, he looked slightly blue-skinned, and he was shivering.

"Benny," Porter said. "We've got to get you cleaned up. What's Kaylie doing in there?"

"Guess," shouted Kaylie.

Benny looked down sheepishly. "She's putting my sheets in a plastic bag."

Porter turned to Delilah. "You know, I'd better get him cleaned up and dressed." Then, realizing he'd forgotten his introductions, he said, "Oh, Benny, this is Delilah. Delilah, Ben."

"So I get to say I'm sorry to you too," Delilah said. Then, to Porter, she said, "While you're doing that, I'll go get the stuff for your head. Then I'll be right back. Okay?"

"It's really not necessary," Porter said. "I think we've got some Band-Aids in the camper."

"Let me, please?" she said. "I'm good at this kind of thing." And without explaining any further, she turned and walked away, ducking under a branch, weaving and bobbing through the little stretch of woods, then high-stepping into the field, her billowy pants flaring out like wind socks in the breeze.

"How retarded is that lady?" This from Kaylie, who'd replaced Ben in the doorway of the camper.

"Oh, Kaylie," Porter said. "She's fine. She didn't mean to wake us up. Look at it from her side. She sees her friends' camper—*her* camper, really—looking exactly the same as when they drove out of here. . . . I would have made the same assumption."

Kaylie stepped to the ground in her bare feet, yawned hugely, and sat down at the picnic table. "How's your head? It doesn't look so great."

"It hurts like hell." He touched it lightly with his hand. Already the blood was becoming lumpy, coagulated. "But I guess she's going to clean it up and treat it. That'll be good. Keep it from getting infected."

Kaylie said, "You're gonna have to be the one to clean up Benny. He doesn't want me to see him naked."

"All right." Porter looked around this place and sighed. So this was the first day of their new life? This was it? What a disaster. He could hardly see straight from the pain pulsing through his forehead, his face and clothes and hands were bloodied, and his boy was a shivering, urine-soaked mess. Only Kaylie, as always, seemed unscathed, sitting at the table with her head on her arms. Her only reason for lifting her head was that her yawns were so large, her upper body couldn't accommodate them from a bent-over position.

Porter stepped up into the camper and found Benny huddled on the floor under an orange beach towel, knees drawn to his chest. "Okay," he said, rubbing his hands together. "We're gonna have to get you dressed and find out about getting everything washed. But first we'll have to give you a sponge bath."

"Won't that be too cold?"

"You know what?" Porter said. "We can boil water on this handy-dandy stove."

Benny gripped the towel around himself. "Won't that be too hot?"

"We'll mix it up." Porter stuck his head out the door. "Can you help me with this, Kaylie?"

She dragged herself up from the picnic table.

Porter got the stove going and began heating a pan of water while Kaylie found some washcloths in one of the boxes Porter had packed. As the water heated, Porter took one of the washcloths, dribbled some warm water onto it, and began to lightly swab his forehead. When he pulled it away, there were smears of bright red blood along with more solid maroon slabs. He folded it over and dabbed some more, being careful not to snag the splinters. He didn't want to break any of them off and leave them embedded. Delilah would no doubt return with tweezers and antiseptic and bandages, and he didn't want to mess anything up before she could tend to him properly. He'd considered just trying to yank them out himself, but they were too obscured by his hairline to be able to see clearly. Kaylie had also offered to pull at the splinters with her fingers even though it would gross her out, but Porter declined.

When the water was mixed and ready, Porter asked Benny to stand up, but Benny didn't want to take off his towel in front of Kaylie, so Kaylie—after rolling her eyes—climbed up onto Porter's bed and promised not to peek.

"Dad," she said once up there, "you really torpedoed this thing. Your head made it all the way to the metal." She started poking at the roof of the camper, which bent in and out with the push of her finger, making a little *ping* each time. "It's like a Coke can. We're living inside a big Coke can. That's reassuring."

Porter soaked the washcloth in the warm water, wrung it out, and began to sponge off Benny's legs, his knobby knees, all that goose-bumped flesh. Benny stood there shivering, covering his crotch with his hands, until Porter had finished. Then Benny took the washcloth and swabbed at his own butt and around his crotch with quick nervous wipes. "When's that lady coming back?" he asked.

"Don't worry," Porter said. "I'm keeping a lookout."

Porter did expect her to rap on the door at any moment, but when he stuck his head through the boot and looked out the front window, there was no sign of her. Benny pulled on his underwear and stepped into his shorts, then announced to Kaylie that she could look now.

"Lucky me," she said, not looking.

They hung around inside the camper a while longer, pulling clothes out of boxes, arranging the kitchen utensils, getting dressed. Finally they all climbed outside and looked off across the field toward Delilah's tepee, but there still didn't seem to be any action over there.

"Where do you suppose she went?" Porter said, but neither of his children responded.

After a moment Kaylie said, "Can we have some breakfast?"

Porter nodded. "Sure. We've got milk and cereal. Even some Pop-Tarts, I think." The morning's blizzard of events already seemed like a dream, and the fact that Delilah hadn't returned and there was no sign of her after nearly an hour only added to his sense of disbelief. But he still had his bloodied, throbbing forehead as evidence. And he had Kaylie and Ben as witnesses.

"I'll get it," Kaylie said. "Where'd you put the cereal?"

"It should be in the cabinets. Under the sink." Porter looked at his son, who sat at the picnic table in his blue sweat suit and white sneakers looking shell-shocked. "You want to set the table, Benny?"

Ben nodded, extricated his skinny legs from under the picnic table, and stepped up into the camper. Once Benny disappeared from view, Porter could hear Kaylie bossing him around inside. "Over there. No, the bowls are in there. No, in *there!*"

Porter looked around. In the blaze of daylight this place was kind of a dump—not at all the impression he'd gotten the night before. Some of it was still beautiful: the towering trees—were they sycamore?—and the broad oval field of high grass. But the village of fiberglass tepees, which had looked so intriguing when silhouetted against the night, now glinted in the sun like a battery of Minuteman missiles. The lake too was no longer the beckoning black oasis he'd seen shimmering in the moonlight. Now the water looked green and stagnant, the only point of access a muddy beach with a plastic swimming dock and a white lifeguard stand that was tipped over on its side.

He had yet to see anyone besides Delilah, but they definitely had neighbors ringing the oval field. Two VW buses, both covered with bumper stickers, occupied two spots near the lake. A full-size Partridge Family–style school bus sat up on blocks halfway around the oval. And closest to them—less than a hundred feet away—was a mustard-colored castle of a tent with a separate, tarpaulin-covered porch.

Porter couldn't believe that his own camper had already spent time here. What did Delilah say, that she'd come in March? So his camper had been here for two or three months. And now it had returned like a goddamn homing pigeon.

"Breakfast is served," Kaylie announced.

Porter swung around to see his two children step down from the camper, Kaylie with the milk, cereal, and a plate of sliced oranges on a tray, Benny galumphing along behind her with a tray of bowls, plates, and paper towels.

"Hey, great job," Porter said. He was always pleased when he judged Kaylie right, playing on her bossiness by giving her a task and a helper. It was his best medicine for her, and had always been, though the credit for the strategy belonged to Lucy.

Kaylie and Ben put their trays down on the table, and Kaylie looked around. "She's still not back?"

"Nope," Porter said. "No sign of her."

"I'll bet she's not coming back," Kaylie said. "She's too embarrassed."

"She didn't seem to me like the type to get embarrassed," Porter said. He poured some Cheerios into his bowl and reached for the milk. "But she was nice at least, don't you think?"

"Well, it was obvious *you* liked her," Kaylie said, sucking on an orange slice. "Forget that she woke us up and made you cut your head and made Benny pee his pants."

Benny said, "I didn't do it because of *her*! I did it because I was *scared*!"

"Same difference."

Porter tried to chew his cereal, but his jaw ached at the joints, all sore from the blow and misaligned somehow.

He wondered if they were being watched. Delilah must have woken the entire camp with her pounding and screaming. But if she had, there was no sign of it. The only sounds were birds chirping and an occasional car in the distance, rushing by on the state highway.

He gazed across the field at the tepees, but still nothing.

Then he heard a crunch of gravel from behind, footfalls, and he looked around to see Delilah approaching from the road. She was accompanied by a longhaired, bearded Jesus figure wearing overalls and leather sandals. Delilah was carrying the first-aid kit like a lunch box at her side. The Jesus figure, who was easily a foot taller than Delilah but somehow thinner, and sunken-chested, looked over at them and gave an embarrassed hand-flip of a wave, as if to say, *You don't know me*. He took one step for every two of Delilah's.

"Sorry!" Delilah shouted from fifty feet away. She held up the first-aid kit. "Took me a while to track this down. These guys stole it from me!"

These guys? But it was only the Jesus figure with her.

The Jesus figure shrugged his shoulders, his ragged beard parting in an affable smile. Porter could see now that he was not a man but a kid, a teenager, sixteen or seventeen. No more, at any rate, than twenty. The beard looked soft, pubescent, as if he'd simply never shaved since his first awkward facial hair poked through. The bottom of it hung from his chin in a brown tuft. Where the beard thinned out on his cheeks, his skin was broken out in a rubble of acne.

At the picnic table, Benny sat gawking, his spoon suspended motionless above his cereal, while Kaylie continued to eat as if nothing were happening.

"This is Jasper," Delilah said. "And you're . . . Porter, right? And I'm sorry. I've forgotten your kids' names already."

"Kaylie and Ben," Porter said. "Nice to meet you."

Jasper blinked shyly.

Porter extracted his legs from underneath the picnic table and stood up. But when he went to shake Jasper's hand, Jasper held both hands up in meek surrender. They were the hands of a mechanic: black with oil, all knobby knuckles and broken fingernails.

"Better not," Jasper said. "Sorry."

Delilah pointed to Porter's forehead. "So that's the wound."

Feeling that he should oblige, Porter lifted his bangs to expose the damage.

"Far out," Jasper said. "You really put your head through the roof?"

Porter would have felt as if he were being made fun of if it hadn't been for Jasper's earnest expression. The kid seemed genuinely concerned, and not the type for sarcasm.

As they stood there, a warm breeze kicked up in the woods behind Delilah and Jasper, stirring the trees, and as the breeze reached Porter, it brought with it a waft of acrid armpit odor from Jasper.

"I told him the story," Delilah said. "He just wanted to see for himself."

"Pretty intense, all right," Jasper said. "You know, that's such a rage that you guys found this place."

Delilah went on, "Jasper also fixes things around here, so I wanted him to check out the hole in your roof. He might be able to patch it up for you."

"Oh, it's nothing," Porter said automatically. Then he realized he hadn't even really seen the damage he'd done. "I just need to get this head wound cleaned up."

Delilah put the first-aid kit down on the picnic table and opened it up. "You'd better sit," she said to Porter, and he did.

Jasper said, "So this was all from her pounding on your door?"

Porter nodded. "I forgot about the low clearance."

Jasper shook his head. "I heard Lilah yelling and pounding this morning. Woke me up too. And I thought, *What the hell is she doing?* When I looked out the window and saw the Brokedown Palace parked here, I thought it was Don and Stacey too. I thought they'd come back. Then I saw you come out, and your kids and everything, and that freaked me out." He laughed. "You know, I heard you guys pull in last night, and I remember thinking, *I wonder if that's the cops coming?* But I was too tired, man, you know? I was *crashed out.* I was too tired last night to even care who it was."

Porter said, "The Brokedown Palace?"

"Tip your head back, okay?" Delilah said, bringing a peroxide-soaked gauze pad to his forehead. "This is going to sting."

Ow! Porter felt as if his entire hairline were engulfed in flames. He gasped a mouthful of air and let it slip out through his gritted teeth in a slow hiss. She dabbed a few times, avoiding the splinters; then, as she pulled away, a piece of the gauze snagged one. It felt as though his forehead were being ripped open.

"Oops, sorry!" Delilah said. "Sorry."

"You okay, Daddy?" This from Benny.

Porter tried to say "Yep," but with his head tilted back and his mouth open it came out more like "Yulk." Finally Delilah backed away and Porter rolled his head forward, his wound sizzling with disinfectant.

Jasper said, "So how's the transmission on the Palace holding out?"

"The transmission?" Porter said, still grimacing. "Fine."

He opened his eyes just long enough to see that Delilah had soaked a fresh gauze pad and was zeroing in for round two. He closed his eyes and braced himself.

But this time he barely felt it. The nerve endings must have still been in shock from the first round. Delilah dabbed away gently, leaning over him. Porter opened his eyes in a pained squint, and there, right before him, were Delilah's little breasts hanging freely within her T-shirt. Lucy's breasts had been completely different—large-nippled and udderlike. Delilah's were more like a boy's chest that had been pulled and stretched to supple points.

"You haven't had any problems with it?" Jasper continued. "It's not leaking any?"

"Nope," Porter said, thinking, *Leaking from where?* "I haven't had problems with anything. We came all the way from Pittsburgh just yesterday. Almost nonstop. And it drove just great."

Jasper smiled, folding his arms over his chest. "That's because *I* fixed it."

"Really?" Porter said. "You did?"

Delilah said, "He's the one who's responsible for Don and Stacey leaving me here. It was the night after he fixed the transmission that they took off without me."

"She likes to blame me. She thinks Don would still be in love with her if I hadn't fixed it."

"Hey," Delilah said, delivering him an icy glare. "Shut your blow-hole, okay?"

Jasper glanced at Porter sheepishly. "I'm sorry, Lilah. But I didn't make them leave. They still would have left, right?"

Delilah picked up the scissors and cut a fresh piece of gauze. "How?"

Jasper shrugged his shoulders. "Hitch?"

"To where?" Delilah said. "Where were they so desperate to go? Look into your crystal-meth ball and answer that one."

Jasper's laugh was almost soundless, a series of short intakes of breath with a wide smile—*huh, huh, huh.* "Crystal-meth ball," he said. "That doesn't even mean anything." Still smiling, he said, "No, but really, Lilah, it looks like they were desperate to go to Pittsburgh, doesn't it?" He turned to Porter. "Isn't that where you guys bought the Brokedown Palace?"

Porter nodded. Kaylie and Ben chomped away on their cereal, apparently too tired to participate in any of this.

"As if," Delilah said. "Desperate to go to Pittsburgh." She approached Porter's forehead with a pair of silver tweezers. "Who do they even know there?"

"Beats me. You were the one who knew them. Or him at least. Nobody really knew her. She was pretty much just looking for a ticket out the second she got here."

"Ha. I can't imagine why."

Porter felt a little tug at his scalp and winced.

"You okay?" Delilah said. After his "Uh-huh," she tugged again. He could feel the length of the sliver sliding out of his skin. She dabbed at the spot with gauze, then moved on to splinters two, three, four, and on it went—Porter counted twelve in total, all done in breathless silence as everyone looked on.

Delilah prepared a final gauze pad and wiped away the fresh blood from the wound, then quickly applied a bandage and affixed it to his forehead with two pieces of white tape.

Porter sat forward and felt at it. It was fairly compact, but he could already feel his head swelling underneath it. He looked at Delilah. "So why didn't you follow those guys to Pittsburgh?"

"Because I didn't know they went there! Plus, I kept thinking Don would feel guilty enough to come back eventually." She laughed. "So then when I saw ya'll parked here this morning . . . I just can't believe ya'll found that brochure and came here. That is just too weird."

"Really?" Jasper said. "That's what happened? How hilarious. That brochure makes this place look like some kind of fancy resort. When Andrea sent that to me, I was like, *I get to live there for free?* And then when I got here I was like, *Oh, I get it.*" He turned to Porter. "So you must've been pretty surprised to find out what this place really is, huh?"

Porter nodded. "I still am."

"So where's the mom, anyway?" Delilah said cheerfully. "Or is this just a dad-and-kids kind of thing?"

"She's dead," Kaylie said, just like that. Didn't even look up from her cereal bowl. Didn't even stop chewing.

"You're kidding," Delilah said with a big squinty smile. "You mean it?"

"That's why we're taking this trip," Kaylie said, looking up. "To get over being depressed about it."

Delilah looked incredulous. "Really?"

Porter felt he should step in and say something. "She did die, yes," he finally said. "But we're not taking this trip to get over being depressed. We just need a break, you know. It's been hard."

Delilah swallowed. "That's tough. I'm really sorry to hear that."

"Thanks," Porter said.

Jasper said. "How long has it been?"

"Just three weeks."

"Wow. So recently."

Jasper's response seemed more out of surprise than judgment, but Porter felt a twinge of unease nevertheless, wondering if maybe Claire was right—maybe this trip was a bad idea after all. "She'd been sick for a long time," he said. "Almost two years."

There was silence among them. A warm breeze stirred the trees. In the distance there was a wash of glinty ripples across the sullen lake.

Delilah looked at Porter brightly. "So then this is kind of a journey, this trip."

"A journey?"

"You know. How you've just sort of set off? Looking for something?"

"Maybe," Porter said. "But I don't think I'd couch it quite that way."

"I know, I know," Delilah said. "You ruin it when you talk about it. I shouldn't have said anything. Awareness isn't everything."

"It's not that you ruin it by talking about it," Porter said. "It's just that there's no 'it' to talk about."

Delilah gave him an amused, patronizing look. "There's always an 'it.' "

Porter was trying to find a way to shift out of this conversation, looking into the woods for a different topic, when Jasper, of all people, bailed him out.

"You know, the Palace looks great," he said. "You guys must have cleaned her up."

Porter nodded. "We sure did," he said gamely. "Spent all day Sunday, practically."

"Looks it." Jasper grinned. "So I'll go check out that hole. See what I can do." And before Porter could respond, he set off for the camper.

"No, don't worry about it," Porter called after him, and then he watched helplessly as Jasper lowered his head and bounded into the camper in one graceful, long-legged leap.

A moment later Jasper shouted out to them, "Man, it's split all the way down. Lilah, you should check this out."

"That's all I need," Delilah muttered. "More guilt."

"I can fix this up for you, no problem," Jasper shouted. Porter could hear him grunting and groaning. "Just rip out this whole piece and put in a new one. You wouldn't want to do a patch job on something like this."

Porter went over to the camper door and leaned in. Sure enough, Jasper was straddled exactly as Porter feared he'd be—one foot on the edge of Benny's bed, the other on the kitchen counter, armpits splayed fully against the edge of Porter's mattress. He had both hands in the hole Porter's head had made and he was *ping*ing the metal roof in and out the same way Kaylie had been doing earlier.

"Could you watch the feet, please?" Porter said. When Jasper looked around, Porter added, "That's our couch and our kitchen." He pointed to where Jasper's feet were planted.

Jasper grinned with embarrassment, then hopped down. "Sorry, man." He knelt down and tried to brush the dirt from the cushion but succeeded only in smearing the footprint into a dull brown smudge. He looked at Porter with an anguished expression. "I live in a pigsty, man, so I don't even think before doing something like this. Not that that's any excuse. You know what, I'll wash this cover for you. I've got the washers here hooked up so it doesn't cost anything. Even for the heavy-duty European one. The Miele."

"Forget it," Porter said. He'd have to wash the cushion covers anyway from Benny's accident. Plus, he didn't want this sweaty Ichabod Crane involved anymore.

"Least I could do," Jasper said. And before Porter could protest any further, Jasper was already unzipping the cover. As he began to pull the foam pad out, he suddenly stopped and looked up. "Hey, this is *wet*," he said. "You guys spill something on it?"

Porter smiled uncertainly. "I guess," he said. Then he added, "You know, I hardly remember most of what happened this morning."

Jasper laughed and continued to remove the cover. "I *bet!*" He stood up but remained slightly hunched in the camper. Porter was exactly six feet tall, and his head came close to the ceiling. He guessed Jasper was around six three. But the kid was really an emaciated stick, all bones and tendons. As Jasper held the cushion cover against his chest, his long, spindly fingers looked almost translucent. "Want me to wash anything else for you?" he said merrily. "I might as well, if I'm going to do a load anyway."

"No, that's okay," Porter said. He just wanted to get the cushion cover back, clean, and hit the road. He thought briefly about his own sheets, now fully smeared with Jasper's armpit oil. But then he said, "Everything else is pretty clean. Like I said, we just started this trip yesterday."

Jasper nodded enthusiastically. "And what a long, strange trip it's been!"

Porter smiled. This guy wasn't so bad. Thinking about Benny's pee soaking into the front of Jasper's overalls, he even felt a little sorry for him.

"So where are you guys headed?" Jasper said.

"Out to Colorado. I want to show the kids Rocky Mountain National Park. Do a little camping."

"Killer choice. Know it well. I lived in Estes Park for a few years. That whole area is killer."

"Lived there with your family?"

Jasper paused. "I guess you could say that, yeah."

There was an awkward silence, during which Porter could hear Delilah talking to his kids at the picnic table. He heard Kaylie utter some clipped response. What were they saying? He wanted desperately to know.

"Well, I'd better stick this wash in," Jasper said. "These days you have to get to the washers early, especially the Miele. I just rigged them up a couple of weeks ago, and now that they're free, everyone's using them all day."

Porter smirked. "I guess that's what happens when you make something free."

"The people *use* it!" Jasper said with gusto.

Porter backed away and stepped outside, and Jasper hopped out like a boy, landing on both feet in a little cloud of dust. When Delilah looked over at him, he said, "I'm washing this for these guys. I got it dirty."

"Isn't that from Benny's bed?" Kaylie asked.

Porter nodded uncomfortably. He wanted to make a face that would indicate to Kaylie that she shouldn't say anything about Benny's pee, but what kind of face would convey such a thing? He tried jerking his head to the side and sort of sticking out his jaw.

She looked at him, perplexed. "He's *washing* it for us?"

"That's right," Porter said.

"Why?"

But luckily Jasper was already ambling away, rounding the front of the truck and heading off into the trees. He looked back at them as he walked, smiling, then turned his gaze warmly on the truck, as if reconnecting with a long-lost friend. Suddenly something caught his eye, and he stopped, then crept back to the front of the truck, where he put the cushion cover on the grass, crouched down, and peered under the engine. Dropping to his stomach, he reached underneath with his long white arm and then brought it back out, the tip of his index finger glistening with black fluid. "Uh-oh."

Porter started to walk over. "What is it?"

"Transmission fluid," Jasper said. "A lot of it. Probably all of it."

"*What?*" Porter said. "It drove fine. You're sure it's not just over-flow or something?"

Jasper rolled onto his side and reached up, feeling around. "Looks like you blew out all the work I did." He seemed mildly annoyed by the prospect. He scooted himself out from underneath the engine, stood up, and walked over toward the dirt road, peering at the ground as he went. Then he stopped and crouched down. "Here's some more," he said. "Some drips." A few yards into the road he found more. "It's possible it happened just toward the end," he said. "Then it all dripped out overnight."

"Are you kidding?" Porter said. "So what does that mean? We've got to call a tow truck?"

Jasper's face darkened. "Oh, I don't think Andrea would want that."

"She wouldn't? Why not?"

Jasper started walking back to the picnic table, where Delilah and Kaylie and Ben all sat watching them. "It's shot again, the transmission," he called out to Delilah. "Andrea's not going to want a tow truck coming in here, is she?"

Porter looked to Delilah with a plaintive expression.

Delilah stood and came walking over to meet them. "You could talk to her," she said as she approached. "But I seriously doubt it. She's not going to be too thrilled about someone like that coming in here."

"What do you mean?" Porter said.

"It's her butt on the line," Delilah said. "She's the one who invited all these people. If her uncle finds out what she's done here, this free ride will be over for everyone."

What is this, Porter thought, *"The Twilight Zone"?* He couldn't even call a fucking tow truck if he needed one? "Well, she can't stop me," he said, but as soon as the words left his lips, he cringed at how juvenile he sounded, as if he were going to take his ball and stomp on home.

Delilah sighed. "No, she can't *stop* you. She's not going to *physically restrain* you. It just seems like you could let Jasper take a shot at it first. I'm sure he could at least fix it well enough to get you into town. It'll just be a real bummer if you call in some mechanic from town, and he sees what's happening here and goes back and blabs it to everyone, and the next thing you know the cops pull in."

Porter thought about it. "Yeah, I guess."

"I mean, I, personally, wouldn't care that much," Delilah said. "I need someone to boot me out of here anyway. But I don't think it would be too cool for everyone else."

Porter looked at Jasper. "So you think you can fix it again?"

Jasper sucked in his lips, considering. "You know, it's just really too bad that you rode her so hard yesterday. All day long on the highway. In this heat? No wonder it blew out. I told Don and Stacey to go easy on her. I told them if they wanted to go all the way to Pittsburgh to take two days, and really nurse it—"

"Wait a minute," Delilah interrupted, "wait . . . You *knew* they were going to Pittsburgh?"

Jasper froze, his mouth stuck in a scared smile. "No, I didn't . . . I mean, I know they *went* there, now, 'cause that's where these guys came from, right?"

"You just said you told them to take two days if they were going *all the way to Pittsburgh*! You just said that!"

Jasper stood there for a moment, biting at his upper lip.

Porter found himself watching and waiting with a sort of sadistic pleasure. It wasn't often that you saw someone in Jasper's situation—exposed, caught in a bald-faced lie, but still trying to figure out if there was some escape.

"But that's not how I meant it," Jasper tried.

"Oh, come on. Yes it was." She looked Porter. "Right? You heard him."

"All right," Jasper said, totally caving. "I knew they were going there. But they made me promise not to tell you!" He held his hands out, pleading, and suddenly he *was* Jesus—that stricken face, those sinewy outstretched arms, the straight greasy hair.

Delilah glared at him. "How *could* you? How could you watch me twist in the wind for the last two weeks knowing all along where they went?"

"Because I promised," Jasper said, looking away. "And that's all I'm going to say about it. I promised, and promises are important to me."

Delilah dug her hands into her sides and pursed her lips. She glanced at Porter with her slitty, angry eyes, then turned them on Jasper. In a fierce whisper she said, "I don't want to make another scene in front of those kids today, lucky for you. But we're going to talk about this later. I am *so* royally pissed at you. I don't care shit about your goddamn Boy Scout promises."

Jasper held up his hands in meek surrender. "All right, okay." And with that he turned and ambled off, walking sort of disjointedly, as if he'd been stung on the foot by a bee.

"Look," Delilah said to Porter, "go ahead and call that tow truck if you want. I don't care. I'm so sick of this place I could burn it to the ground right now."

"DAAAD!" It was Kaylie, calling from the picnic table.

Porter and Delilah spun around.

"Can we *do* something?" she yelled.

Porter started to walk back to her, and Delilah fell in step behind him. "What do you want to do?"

"I don't know. *Something.*"

"How about swimming?" Benny offered.

Porter turned to Delilah. "Is that allowed?"

"Allowed? Of course. Everything's allowed."

"But do you think the water will be warm enough?" Benny asked.

"It's a little cold at first," Delilah said. "But you get used to it pretty fast."

Porter stepped forward. "You guys should go ahead and get your suits on," he said. "It's probably going to be a little while before we get the truck fixed, so we might as well enjoy ourselves while we're here."

"Yay!" Benny said, jumping up. Then to Delilah he said, "Lady, do they have any rafts or anything over there?"

Delilah's eyes glinted with amusement. "This lady doesn't," she said. "But I might be able to find a lady who does."

Kaylie and Ben picked up their bowls and cereal and climbed into the camper, closing the door behind them.

Delilah turned to Porter. "You want me to tell you where ya'll should swim?"

"Not at the beach over there?" Porter asked, pointing to the area with the plastic dock and tipped-over lifeguard stand.

"Well, here's the thing," Delilah said. "In another hour or so, if not sooner, there's going to be a whole lot of naked people on that beach. And it's not a pretty sight, believe me. I mean, think of about two dozen Jaspers, both the male and female versions."

"You're kidding. Really?"

"I don't think you want your kids to see much of that, am I right?" Porter nodded.

"So there's a little cove about a hundred yards to the right," Delilah said. "If you go all the way over, beyond the tepees, there's a little path. But it's not the first path, it's . . ." She paused. "You know what, I'll just take you there, because it's too hard to explain. I'll walk ya'll over. In fact, I wouldn't mind taking a dip myself. I try to take a swim pretty much every day anyway."

Porter smiled. "But you'll keep your bathing suit on?"

"I have to admit I don't have one," she said. "But I'll get something, don't worry. Unlike most people around here, I'm sensitive to the real world. They should appoint me ambassador or something." She looked at him. "Are you going to swim? You know, you probably shouldn't get your forehead wet."

"I think I'll just lie in the sun and let my head swell up to full capacity."

Delilah laughed. "All right. I'll go change. When ya'll are ready, stop by my place and get me. It's the one over there." She pointed to the right edge of the tepee village. "It says 'Silver Squaw II' on the door. Isn't that perfect? Like I'm a Native American cruise ship or

something. I swear, the moron who owns this place is such a moron."
And with that she picked up her first-aid kit and walked off.

Porter started for the camper, but just as he reached for the handle, the door swung open, and there was Kaylie, her white limbs sticking out of a bright orange one-piece bathing suit that Porter had never seen before. Claire must have bought it for her on their Saturday trip to the mall. "Did you pack our flip-flops?" she asked.

Porter shrugged. "Not that I remember."

Kaylie huffed and rolled her eyes. "So what are we supposed to wear?"

"Wear your sneakers. We have to hike a little ways through the woods anyway."

"Dad, the beach is *right there,*" she said, pointing.

"We're going to a better beach," he said. "Delilah says there's a nicer one farther down the shore."

One more impatient huff, and then Kaylie turned back into the darkness, closing the door on him. Porter could hear her saying to Benny, "Wear your sneakers, okay?" Then louder, "We didn't pack them, okay? Just *chill out.*"

Porter wandered over to the picnic bench and sat down, leaning back with his elbows on the table. He gazed at the camper, waiting for Kaylie and Ben. Through the kitchen window he could see their heads bobbing around, getting ready, gathering their stuff. They seemed like such normal kids all of a sudden, excited about going swimming. There were plenty of times over the past month when Porter feared he'd never see them act this way again. But on this afternoon anyway, a raft and a lake were going to make them happy, however briefly. And tomorrow or the next day they'd do or see something else that might be fun, or at least distracting. So maybe this was an okay thing for him to be doing, acting on a whim and then hauling them across the country? Maybe this wasn't going to be such a disaster after all? Or was Claire right in believing they all ought to stay in Pittsburgh and have some stability? Would that have been better?

Porter watched Kaylie and Ben a moment longer, then he drew back and stared at the abstract landscape on the side of the camper. He gazed admiringly at those green-enamel swirls of trees and grass and tepees atop the glossy purple background. And all at once it came to him. He looked over at the field and the tepee village, then back at the side of the camper, and gasped. It was identical. It was this exact view. And he smiled and thought, *Okay, I give up. Just tell me what to do next.*

CHAPTER FIVE

"IT'S called tai chi," Delilah said. "It's like meditating." She was trying to pull Benny out of his goggle-eyed trance by explaining what the naked man in front of them was doing, but Benny wasn't responding. Meanwhile, the man was trying his best to ignore their gawking presence. Perched on one leg like a big fleshy flamingo, he continued to knife his hands through the air in a series of slow-motion karate chops—his pale rope of a penis dangling groundward like a plumb bob. Then he crouched down, lifted the other leg, and angled his body into a slow-motion horizontal kick.

Porter just shook his head. For fifteen minutes everything had been fine. They'd made their way past the beach before anyone arrived and had slipped unnoticed into the woods, the kids yakking away about going swimming in a "real lake." Much to Benny's delight, Delilah had managed to round up an inflatable yellow raft (which Porter now had trundled over his back) *and* a big tractor inner tube (which

Benny was rolling along at his side). Delilah had been leading the way, and when they'd turned the corner into this grassy clearing, she'd stopped so abruptly that Kaylie had run into her, then Benny into Kaylie and Porter into Ben—the four of them stacked up like Keystone Kops. Porter had staggered at first to maintain control of the raft, then looked up from underneath the bow until his eyes had fallen upon the hairy, contorted man. *Oh, great,* he'd thought.

Now, as they all stood there agog, even Kaylie was speechless.

Delilah said, "Well, let's keep going. We'll let Uncle Charlie go about his business in private." She grabbed the tractor tube from Benny and set off, and they all fell into step behind her, rubbernecking their way past Uncle Charlie. As they made their way out of earshot, Kaylie said, "So is this some kind of nudie farm?"

"Nudie farm?" Delilah laughed. "Not exactly."

"Then what was that?"

"Oh, Charlie? He's just trying to get his yin and yang aligned."

Porter plodded along underneath the raft, trying to think through the possible long-term impact of exposing his kids to this place. As he thought about it, his initial shock and repulsion over the "Uncle Charlie" episode meandered into a philosophical debate about the human need to clothe oneself. Sure, he thought, people had to dress to keep warm or to protect themselves, if need be, from the dangers and discomforts of the natural world, but this whole Puritan tradition of everyone's keeping their private parts covered in public—regardless of the weather or situation—was just an invention, wasn't it? It was less about practicality than about sin and shame and keeping a lid on people's desires, right? So maybe it wasn't such a bad thing for the kids to be exposed to it. In fact, maybe it was even potentially healthy to have their view of the world challenged in this way. And even if it wasn't healthy, it could hardly be any more destructive than allowing them to watch *Beverly Hills 90201,* right?

They trudged on for another fifty yards, first away from the water, then up and over a little hill, and finally down to the shore, where they emerged into the peaceful and secluded cove that Delilah had described.

It was beautiful, far more picturesque than the muddy lakeshore of the camp, but the drawback was that there was no beach, just rocks and brush and a sharp drop-off into what looked like pretty deep water.

"This is it," Delilah said. "Ya'll should probably keep your sneakers on because there might be some sharp stuff underwater. Sticks and rocks and stuff." She knelt down and put her hand in. "Not too bad," she said. "All this hot weather has really warmed up the lake fast. Last month it was too cold to go in above your knees."

Porter shifted the raft off his shoulders and, holding on to the rope, dumped it into the water with a splash. "You want to take this?" he said, handing the rope to Benny.

Ben secured the rope under a rock, and then he and Kaylie started to peel off their sweatshirts. When was the last time his kids had gone swimming in a lake? Actually, Porter couldn't remember their ever having swum in a lake. It was always the Winters' pool or Club Med. Could that be possible?

When Porter was growing up in Minnesota, a lake was the *only* place he and Alex swam. There was no pool in their neighborhood, public or private, and as far as taking a trip to Club Med . . . well . . . even if Porter's father could have afforded it, he wasn't exactly the type to want to dance around in a circle of sunburned corporate execs singing "YMCA."

Kaylie and Ben's privileged swimming history revealed itself right off the bat as they ventured cautiously along the rocky shoreline looking for a clean entry point—that apron of white sand perhaps, or a dock with a metal ladder.

"Where are you supposed to go in?" Ben finally asked.

Delilah looked at him. "Anywhere."

"But it's all slippery," he said.

"And there's weeds," Kaylie added.

"Oh, c'mon you two," Porter said, suddenly embarrassed that they were acting so prissy in front of Delilah. "Just go in. It's a beautiful lake. Not every beach is going to be like Grand Cayman."

Kaylie glared at him, but then she turned and began walking gingerly into the water. When she was in up to her waist, she closed her mouth and dropped straight down, popping up a second later as a slick, smiling pinhead. "God!" she squealed. "It's *freezing!*"

Benny hesitated and looked back at his father, but when Porter nodded for him to continue, the boy did, stopping every few feet of his descent to grip his arms to his chest in a little shiver fit. Then he stepped off whatever rock he'd been on and sank in up to his neck, treading water, his mouth drawn back in a playful panic. "Huh-huh-huh," he breathed, smiling. And then the two of them were swimming, their tiny, smiling heads motoring away from the shore.

"Is it cold, Benny?" Porter shouted, pleased.

Benny shook his head. "S'okay." He ducked his head under and popped back up, his Brillo hair glistening. "Could you push the raft out, Dad?"

Porter untethered the raft and kicked it away from shore toward them.

"Ya'll want this too?" Delilah yelled, tossing in the tractor tube.

Benny kicked toward the raft and clambered aboard, and Kaylie disappeared underwater and then popped up inside the tractor tube. She pulled her legs through, plopped her butt down in the middle, and lay back in the sun. And suddenly it was one of those rare moments in parenthood—especially single-parenthood, Porter had been realizing lately—when you could stop wondering about what your kids were going to *do* for more than five minutes.

Porter turned to Delilah. "You going in?"

"Not yet," she said. "Just before we're ready to go, I'll take a quick dip. I don't want to sit around in wet clothes."

In lieu of a bathing suit, Delilah was wearing the same armless black T-shirt she'd had on earlier, but she had replaced her billowy clown pants with a pair of baggy green sweats cut off at midthigh.

Porter looked around for a place to sit and saw a nice flat rock the size of a mattress a few paces down the shore. "You want to sit over there?" he asked. Delilah nodded, and the two of them started off toward it. The lower end of the rock was already baking in the sun, and Porter relished the thought of soaking up that dry warmth, maybe even catching a quick nap when Delilah joined his kids in the water.

The problem with nice flat rocks, however, was that they always looked like such appealing places to sit or lie out, but once you were actually on them, trying to arrange yourself into a comfortable position, every jutting bone in your hips and spine and ankles suddenly made its presence known. Porter shifted and grunted, turning himself this way and that, to no avail. Finally he scooted his butt to the edge and let his feet hang over. Tolerable, he supposed. But what was he supposed to lean against?

Delilah, meanwhile, didn't seem uncomfortable in the least. She tucked her legs underneath herself Indian style, and there she sat, happy as a clam.

How can you sit like that? Porter longed to ask her. *Don't your ankles* kill? But he didn't want to be the one sounding prissy now. Instead he asked her, "So what's the deal with that Uncle Charlie?"

"Oh, he's a trip, isn't he?" Delilah reached into her Bolivian fanny pack and donned a pair of John Lennon–style sunglasses.

Porter instantly coveted those sunglasses. Not only did he love the way they looked, he also wanted them for the more pedestrian reason of shading his eyes from the sun. He was trying to keep watch on his kids, but the reflection off the water was as bright as a halogen lamp. Porter was pretty sure he'd left his own sunglasses on the dashboard of the truck, but he opened his backpack anyway and conducted a quick, futile search, then zipped it closed in frustration. He could already see the elements of the day lining up perfectly to give him an absolutely skull-splitting headache.

"Charlie does his tai chi like that all over the camp," Delilah said. "Although I've never seen him doing it there before."

"He looks a little like David Crosby, don't you think?"

"He does! Except not that big. Have you seen David Crosby lately? God, he's a whale. Was that from prison, or what? But anyway, you know, Charlie's the one who did that paint job on the entrance sign. Did you see that on your way in?"

Porter nodded. "You mean where some of the words had been painted over?"

"Yep. When he saw the possibilities, I guess he couldn't resist. Personally I thought it was pretty funny, but, man, did Andrea ever throw a shit fit. You could hear her screaming all the way across the camp. She thought the local yokels driving by would notice and stop in and then call the cops or something. I told her if anything the new sign would make it less likely that anyone would come in, because they wouldn't know what the fuck it meant—'Welcome to Charlie's Open World.' But she didn't want to hear it. She nearly booted him out."

"So why didn't she?"

"You know why? Because he was teaching her tai chi, and she really wanted to learn it."

Porter leaned back on his elbows for a moment, until they started to hurt, then sat back up. "Actually, I thought about turning around after I saw that sign. But I was too tired to drive any farther."

Delilah brushed her fingers through her blond bangs and looked at him, slightly tousled. The effect, with the John Lennon glasses, was adorable. "Well, I for one am glad ya'll came on in," she said. "This place needs some fresh faces. And your kids are really sweet. That Kaylie is really about twenty-five, isn't she?"

Porter nodded and smiled, then turned and squinted at the lake.

To his surprise, Kaylie and Ben at some point had swapped flotation devices, and now Kaylie was sunning herself in the yellow raft while Benny propelled himself around the cove in the tractor tube.

"So are they okay about their mom?" Delilah asked.

Porter thought a moment. "That's really hard to answer," he said. "No, I don't think they're okay about it. But I'm really proud of how they've handled it. Every once in a while, you know, they snap into this happy mode, like right now, out there, which I envy. I try to do that, but it's like work. It's a project I have to undertake. With them, it seems like something they can turn on or off."

"Maybe they just aren't aware of it all the time, like adults. I think kids sort of forget stuff sometimes."

"That's right. They do," Porter said. "Benny especially. But with him that makes it worse somehow. He's always waking up having forgotten. He expects that she's going to be there making him pancakes or something, and then he really melts down when he remembers."

"What'd she die of, your wife?"

"Breast cancer."

"Huh." Delilah untucked her legs and drew them up to her chest, hugging them. "My sister, Samantha, she died of leukemia when I was little, and there've been times when I've totally forgotten I ever had a sister."

Oh, no, Porter thought. *Here it comes.* He'd heard so many death stories in the past three weeks from friends and strangers alike that he didn't think he could bear hearing yet another. Sure, it had helped at first, maybe the first eight or ten, but after that it had felt like piling on. Death from breast cancer, ovarian cancer, skin cancer . . . cancer of the lung, pancreas, brain, liver, pituitary, colon, cervix . . . And that didn't even count the accidents! Cars, falls, skiing, bicycling, crossing the street, eating a steak. It was all so diminishing somehow, the endless descriptions of emergency procedures and rotten body parts and ceremonies of grieving. "And she was so young!" "And he was so young!" "And they were all *so young!*"

Now another. A little girl struck down decades ago by leukemia? He understood the impulse, and he knew the intentions were good and all that. But c'mon. Enough already.

Still, he said, "I'm sorry to hear that."

"I was only three at the time; she was five. It's not something I remember very well. My aunt's the one who told me all the details like fifteen years later. My parents never wanted to talk about it. But it's a really weird story. It was a lot worse than it had to be."

A five-year-old dying of leukemia? How could you make that worse than it had to be? "What do you mean?"

"It's just one of those bizarre things," she began. "A freak coincidence. I mean, my sister had been really sick for like a year. This was in 1963. And then I guess all of a sudden her body started to give up, and the doctors thought she was going to die soon. So my parents went into this death-vigil stage, and all the relatives came, and everyone was waiting around for her to die. But then she hangs on for like another month, and the relatives come and go. And then the day she finally dies turns out to be the same day Kennedy is assassinated. Can you believe that? I mean, she died less than an hour after he did."

"And that made it worse?"

"You could probably figure it out if you thought about it," Delilah said. "But what it came down to is, *JFK stole her show!* I mean, here were these nurses and doctors who'd been caring for her for months and months. And they were already freaking out about the president when Samantha died. So everyone was like, 'Her too?' But since they all knew Samantha was going to die anyway, it was the president they were really upset about, not her. And I guess it was hard for them to fake it. My aunt said that a lot of people even thought it was a relief when Samantha died, you know, to end her suffering and all that, and because people had been waiting so long for it to happen. So not only was everyone more upset about Kennedy, some even considered my sister's death to be the blessing of the day!

"But the calls to the relatives were the worst. My poor dad. When he called his mother, she picked up the phone, already crying, and said, 'Oh, my God, did you hear? The president!' So my father didn't even tell her. Not until days later. Both of my parents were so bitter about all that for years and years. Which really explains a lot."

Porter felt a little flattened by the story. "A lot about what?"

"Well, how they treated me, for one. I mean, not to sound like Pity-Me Polly, but my childhood was not exactly hugs and kisses."

Porter didn't want to open that particular can of worms right now, so he grinned and said, "Pity-Me Polly? Sounds like some new talking doll."

Delilah laughed. "Oh, if only it were! Wouldn't that be great? A doll for the nineties." She made a pouty face and whined, "I'm unloved! Nobody cares about me! Stop hurting me! I have feelings too!"

"She could be a self-mutilator," Porter said, "and instead of bottles and a teddy bear she could come with little fake razor blades and an X-acto knife."

"Ugh, that's not even funny," Delilah said. "I knew someone who did that. She always had these nicks and gouges on her forearms, and they'd get all infected." She looked off. "I haven't seen her in years. I wonder how she's doing."

Suddenly there was a shriek, and Porter and Delilah swung around to see Kaylie sit bolt upright in the raft, water dripping down her face. Ben was behind her in the tube, giggling. "Oh, you are so DEAD!" Kaylie yelled. "You are TOAST!" And she jumped from the raft onto the side of his tube, sending the raft scooting away. Benny tried to bob and weave, but he was trapped, and within seconds Kaylie got her hand on top of his head and pushed it under. He started thrashing with his hands, trying to surface. After a second Kaylie let him up. He gasped for breath. Immediately she pushed him under again.

"Kaylie!" Porter shouted. "Let him up! Now!"

She looked at Porter but continued to hold Benny under for a few seconds. Then she let go of both him and the tube and pushed herself away.

Benny popped up in the center of the tube sputtering for breath and wiping desperately at his face. He coughed a few times—deep, hoarse coughs—and then began to cry. "Daddy!" he wailed. "Daddy!"

"Swim on in, Benny," Porter yelled to him.

"I can't!"

"Of course you can. Hold on and kick." Porter looked at Kaylie, who was swimming in a breaststroke toward the center of the lake. "Kaylie!" he shouted.

Without stopping or looking back, she yelled, "He started it."

Benny started to kick his way back in. A couple yards from shore he found some rocks under his feet and tried to stand. But then he slipped and went under again, coming up gasping and sputtering once more.

Porter stood up and went over to him. "Come closer," he said, motioning him in with his hand.

Benny finally found some steady footing and emerged all the way to his waist, then his knees. Gingerly, he stepped out of the tube onto dry land, where he rushed to embrace Porter with his wet, shaking body. "Daddy!" he sobbed. "I couldn't breathe!"

"I know, I know," Porter said. "But she was just getting you back. she wasn't going to hurt you."

"I *hate* her! I do!"

"All right," Porter said. "Okay."

From atop the rock, Delilah said, "Is he okay?"

Porter nodded, cupping his hand over Ben's wet hair. Benny's sobs were lessening, and then he let go of Porter and glanced up at Delilah. "I wasn't *that* scared," he said to her. "I just couldn't breathe."

Delilah smiled encouragingly. "I know. I hate that. I'd react the same way."

Porter looked again for Kaylie and saw that she was now within thirty feet of the opposite shore, coasting along in an easy breaststroke. The lake was narrow at this point, no more than forty yards across, so he wasn't worried. Thanks to nearly a decade of summers in her grandparents' pool, she was a strong swimmer. By the end of last summer she was doing nearly forty laps of front crawl without stopping. Porter watched as Kaylie closed to within a few feet of the far shore and then rose to a shaky stand. Hands out to the side for balance, she stepped out of the water and scrambled up onto the flat top of a sun-drenched boulder, where she stood and waved at them.

Porter and Delilah waved back, but Benny, wrapping himself in a towel, just stared at her. Then Benny pointed off to the right and said with alarm, "Hey, the raft."

Porter looked to see the yellow raft, pushed by a light breeze, drifting down the lakeshore. He turned to Benny.

"*I'm* not getting it," he said.

"But, Benny," Porter said, "you're already wet."

"*She* can get it," he said, pointing across the lake. "She's the one who let it go."

On the other side of the lake, Kaylie was now lying on the rock, soaking up the sun with her arm over her face.

"Kaylie!" Porter tried, but she didn't respond. It was possible she couldn't hear him. The breeze had kicked up a notch, rustling the trees, and Porter saw that the raft's pace down the lake had quickened.

"I'll get it," Delilah announced, standing up. "I'm getting hot anyway." She unbuckled her fanny pack and removed her sunglasses, then climbed down from the rock.

"Thanks a lot," Porter said.

"I just hope these clothes don't drag me to the bottom," she said, gesturing at her cutoff sweats. "I feel like I'm in one of those bathing suits from the thirties." Then she crept into the water, dropped in to her neck, and pushed off.

She swam in a rushed, overexerted breaststroke all the way to the raft—a good twenty yards—then hauled herself aboard. For a while she attempted to lean over the side and paddle with her hands, but it was futile; she made slow, circular progress before finally giving up. "I'm gonna have to swim it back!" she yelled. She sat back and started to untie the drawstring on her sweats. "Sorry! But these are just too heavy. Especially when I'm already wearing shoes." She slipped out of the sweats to reveal peach-colored bikini underwear, then crawled over the side and dropped herself back in the water.

As she approached them—laboring now, huffing and puffing—Porter couldn't help wanting to see Delilah emerge from the lake in that peach underwear. *C'mon, get a grip,* he told himself. But as Delilah reached the rocks and rose to a stand, it was all he could do to keep his eyes on her face. The second she turned away to grab a towel, he glanced down, catching an eyeful of wet peach lace.

Luckily, Delilah was quick to wrap a big towel around her waist. "Phew, that was exhausting," she said, drawing another towel over her shoulders. "I thought I was in better shape than that."

"You looked like an Olympian from where I was sitting," Porter boomed, his hormones in full throb. But then, as he watched Delilah pat herself dry and shake out her hair, he felt suddenly alone and lost.

Delilah retrieved her cutoff sweats from the raft and spread them out on a branch to dry, then returned to the rock they'd occupied earlier and lay down on her stomach, arranging the towel modestly over her butt.

On the other side of the lake, Kaylie was still on her back, arm over her face, apparently oblivious to the rescue mission she had caused. Benny, meanwhile, was dragging the raft all the way onto the shore to prevent another such incident. After securing it, he looked at Porter. "Do we have anything to eat?" he asked.

"Some cheese and Wheat Thins," Porter said. "In my backpack." As he went over to retrieve them, he saw Delilah's sunglasses lying temptingly on the rock next to her. She looked as if she was in the process of dozing off—her eyes were closed and her breathing regular—so he went ahead and put them on.

The frames felt too narrow for his face and the arms rode high on his ears, but, *wow*, the lenses instantly turned the world into a soft, cotton-candy playland. Maybe this is what people meant when they talked about seeing the world through rose-colored glasses. Porter handed the Wheat Thins and cheese to Benny, then climbed onto the rock and settled down on the same spot where he'd been before. Surveying the scene before him with his enhanced vision, he noticed that the lake and the trees, the sky, everything—it all looked more vibrant and interesting this way, as if he'd dropped out of the sky into the Land of Oz.

Considering the disaster of the morning, Porter felt pretty good. The headache he'd been expecting had yet to materialize, and the only pain he felt was the same dull throb of the wound as it swelled to accommodate all the blood and pus and whatever other healing juices were cruising through there by now.

After a while, Porter began to wonder about the story of Delilah's sister. How would he have felt in that situation if he'd been the father? Would he have been so bitter about such a thing? After all, how were people supposed to react? It seemed perfectly reasonable to him that the shock of the assassination would overwhelm the little girl's death in the minds of the hospital staff. And when it came to the phone calls to the relatives, what had he expected? Did he have any right to expect that his mother would not be upset about Kennedy when she picked up the phone?

But, he thought, it was easy for him to judge now.

Then, out of the blue, it occurred to him that if Delilah was three years old in 1963, she would be thirty-six today—at least ten years older than he'd guessed she was. It seemed absurd; she was even older than he was. Plus, he couldn't help thinking, *What has she been doing with her life all these years?* It was one thing for her to be casting about on the Deadhead circuit for a few years after college, but thirty-six? That left fifteen years to be accounted for. He wanted to ask her about it, but she seemed to be asleep now, her back rising and falling in an even rhythm.

He looked over at Benny, whose cheeks were so stuffed with cheese and crackers he resembled a foraging squirrel. "Hey, save some of those for me, okay?" he said quietly, then clambered down from the rock.

BACK AT THE campground, Porter was disappointed to find the cushion cover exactly where he'd left it, dried in position, encrusted with Benny's pee. Ignoring it, he walked up to the truck, knelt down beside the engine, and peered under. Yep, there it was, that perfect circle of transmission fluid, untouched. During the walk back from the lake, Porter had allowed himself to fantasize that while they were off swimming, Jasper had taken it upon himself to fix the transmission. Well, so much for that.

Porter stood up and realized that he hadn't the foggiest idea what time it was. One o'clock? Four? He cupped his hand against the glass of the passenger window to see the clock. Two-fifteen. Kaylie and Ben were sitting on the picnic benches, exhausted. Delilah was back at her tepee. When they'd dropped her off, she'd said she was going to get changed and then see if she could "corner Jasper and beat some more information out of him about Don and Stacey."

It dawned on Porter that they were destined to spend another night and probably most of tomorrow here, at the least. It was too bad that Jasper and Delilah's fight had ended the morning's encounter with Jasper walking off. If Porter wasn't going to call a tow truck, he at least wanted to get Jasper to agree to a timeline on this job. But now what?

He turned to his kids. "It's two-fifteen," he said. "What do you guys want to do?"

Kaylie yawned. "Nothing."

"What else is there to do here?" Benny asked.

"Beats me. I could go find out. Talk to that Andrea woman. Delilah said I should talk to her anyway, if we're going to be spending another night here."

They stared at him with droopy eyes.

"Anyone want to come?"

Benny shook his head. Kaylie yawned again—a yawn that expanded into another, larger yawn—and for a while it seemed she might never close her mouth.

Porter too was beginning to feel wiped out. He'd forgotten how draining vacations could be, how debilitating it was to always be planning and executing fun times for everybody. "All right," he said, "I'll probably be back in half an hour. You guys can play cards or something if you want. And there's cereal and milk in the kitchen, if you get hungry." More cereal and milk, he thought. His kids sure must miss their mom when it came to mealtime. If she were here, within five minutes there'd be a spread of tuna-fish-sandwich squares with fresh fruit laid out on the table, complete with napkins and plastic dishware. With him, they were lucky to get hunk of bread and a paper towel.

Porter set off down the road for the log cabins where Delilah had said Andrea and Seri lived. She'd told him to look for the biggest cabin and then find the door that was underneath a biblical phrase from the Book of Acts. She'd been unable to remember the phrase but had said it was "some BS about sharing." As Porter approached the cabins nestled in a grove of pine trees, he quickly identified the biggest—easily twice the size of the others, with three plank doors equally spaced across the front. Above the door on the right, painted in white block letters on a brown piece of plywood, was the phrase:

AND ALL WHO BELIEVED WERE TOGETHER AND
HAD ALL THINGS IN COMMON; AND THEY SOLD
THEIR POSSESSIONS AND GOODS AND DISTRIBUTED
THEM TO ALL, AS ANY HAD NEED.

Huh, Porter thought dismissively. He rapped on the screen door.
Within a few seconds the wooden door behind it swung open. As
Porter's eyes adjusted to the dark, he was able to make out a hunched,
brown-skinned tank of a man wearing only yellow nylon basketball
shorts and a necklace of colorful beads. Hanging down his back was
a bushel of dreadlocks gathered together by a pink shoelace. His face
was brimming with nervous energy in a way that struck Porter as
slightly crazed. Maybe he was on speed?

"Are you Seri?" Porter asked him.

"That's me," Seri said quickly. His eyes zeroed in on Porter's
bandaged forehead. "You the dude from Pittsburgh?"

Porter nodded.

Seri pushed the screen door open with his massive arm and gestured Porter inside. "Ontray-voo," he said. "Have a seat anywhere."

Porter surveyed the room but could not determine what was
meant for sitting. The place resembled the encampment of a nomadic
desert tribe—overlapping oriental rugs with piles of kilim pillows scattered about and a line of flickering candles along the mantel. A haze
of incense hung in the air, making Porter's eyes sting. In the center of
the room was a cardboard box that served as a coffee table. Maroon
Turkish veils covered all the windows, filling the room with a reddish,
hellish glow.

Seri opened a minifridge on the far side of the room, pulled out
two bottles of liquid—one red, one clear—and stood up. He had to
be over six and a half feet tall and close to 350 pounds. "Can I offer
you anything to drink?" he said. "I've got seltzer or cranberry juice.
Or I can mix the two. That's what I'm having myself."

"I'll have one of those too, please." Porter lowered himself into a mound of pillows and sat back. As huge a man as Seri was, there was something effeminate about him. Was it how his face was so lit up? Or the delicate way his pudgy fingers handled such little glasses?

"You know," Seri said, turning, "you look a little like that movie star . . . that guy . . . what's his name?"

Porter blushed. He'd been down this embarrassing road before. "Kevin Bacon?"

Seri squinted at him. "Well . . . maybe. Maybe a little bit in the eyes. But I was thinking about that other guy. You know. The one in that classic movie about the . . . you know . . . where he's trying to save that girl . . . and there's that other guy in it too . . . ?"

Porter found himself racking his brain.

"Well, it'll come to me." Seri turned back to the refrigerator. "I swear, my mind is a sieve these days. Everything just leaks out of it. Andrea says it's because I'm too fat. She says my fat cells are crowding out my brain tissue. But you know what I think? I think it's from smoking weed every day for the past fifteen years."

"So where is Andrea?" Porter ventured. "Delilah said I should come by and talk to her."

"She went into town. She'll be back this evening." Seri picked up the drinks, rose to a hulking stand, and started toward Porter, the wooden floor creaking under his tottering gait.

Fe, fi, fo fum, Porter thought. "So you guys do that? Go into town?"

"What . . . you think we stomp our own cranberries into juice?" He handed Porter his drink and then sat down himself, reclining into a mountain of pillows and crossing his legs underneath him like Ali Baba.

Porter took a sip—it was the most refreshing thing he'd tasted in days. The room was quiet for a moment, with only the sound of Seri's labored breathing and several large flies hurling themselves against the screen door. Porter guessed that the covered windows and darkness were meant to keep the place cool, but the heat inside was oppressive nevertheless. And what was the deal with all those candles on a day like this? Sweat beaded and dripped from Seri's brown face onto his nearly hairless chest. Porter gazed at the glowing red windows, imagining that on the other side of them a howling desert sandstorm was under way.

"So anyway," Porter began, "I just came by to ask if it's all right if we stay here another night. We're having some trouble with our transmission, and it looks like we're not going to get out of here by the end of the day."

Seri downed his entire cranberry-seltzer blend in three big gulps, then wiped his face, from brow to chin, with his fat paw of a hand. "Fine with us," he said. "Jasper told me it might take a day or two."

Porter sat up. "He did? He talked to you about it?"

"Yeah. Stopped by less than an hour ago, in fact. He told me that all the work he did before he has to do over again."

"What else did he say?"

Seri slurped an ice cube into his mouth and began to chew, his big jaw crashing up and down. "Only that he needed some parts from town, and he wanted to borrow our van right away. But Andrea had already left with it to do the shopping."

Porter sat back and crossed his arms over his chest. "Well, that's nice of him to want to get right on it. I was starting to worry that it might take him a while."

Seri leaned forward, his face breaking into a mischievous grin. "You want to know the truth? Jasper's not doing it to be nice. He's doing it because he wants to get you out of here."

Porter shifted uncomfortably. "What do you mean?"

Seri looked into his empty glass, then raised his eyes at Porter with an expression of red-cheeked glee. "Jasper just *loves* Delilah. He's had a schoolboy crush on her ever since she and Don rolled in here. And now he considers you to be a big fly in the ointment."

Porter gasped. "A fly in the ointment? *Me?*"

"I'm such a gossip, aren't I? I just can't keep my mouth shut. But what else is there to do around here? Really?"

"But what's there to gossip about?" Porter said. "We just got here last night."

"I guess you made a fast impression. At least according to Jasper."

Porter sat back, stunned. "All we did was go swimming today."

Seri smiled. "That's what he told me."

"So what, exactly, did he say?"

Seri held up his palms. "Look," he said, "I can't remember his exact words. But it was something to the effect of how he thought you two were sort of flirting with each other, and then when you all went off swimming together, I guess he got a little jealous."

Porter sighed. *Flirting?* He tried to remember how he and Delilah had acted in the morning, while she was patching his wound, and then afterward. Suddenly he felt guilty—maybe a lingering guilt from having peeked at her underwear? And even though it hadn't occurred to him that he and Delilah had been flirting, maybe that was just because of how clueless and out of practice he was. "Well," he said to Seri, "you can tell Jasper he has nothing to worry about. We're heading west as soon as we can. And then I'll be out of his ointment." He paused. "Did he tell you about my wife?"

Seri nodded solemnly. "I was sorry to hear."

The two of them sat in silence. The flies continued their assault on the screen. Seri shifted against his mound of pillows, unfolding his legs and extending them across the floor.

Finally Porter said, "Well, I'd better get back to my kids. I appreciate you letting us stay."

"Happy to," Seri said, smiling again.

Porter stood and moved to the door.

From across the room, Seri said, "Hey, could you leave the door open? It's a sauna in here."

Porter looked at Seri's glistening face and nodded.

Outside, he started across the field for his camper, but after a few yards he stopped and then turned in the direction of Delilah's tepee. He should talk to her about this. He should try to clear up this situation before things got out of hand.

But what would he say? Suddenly Porter felt as if he were back in high school, trying once again to navigate the minefield of adolescent love. One wrong step and you could find yourself slow-dancing with that nice but plain girl to whom you'd already professed your intention to remain "just friends." One misplaced hand or misinterpreted word and she could be breathing hotly against your neck.

That was one thing that had been such a relief about Lucy. They'd never been that way. They'd never had to go through that awkwardness and anxiety. From the beginning they'd always been so in sync, so clearly meant for each other. Life mates, Lucy had deemed them.

Although as things turned out, Porter thought bitterly, apparently not.

CHAPTER SIX

OVER the past year Lucy had thought about her looming death in two ways. The first had been to accept it by trying to minimize the importance of her life in the grand scheme of things—she was just a blip on the radar screen, a collection of cells evolved from mud. "Thousands of people die every single day. Every hour!" she'd say, summing up. "So how much can *I* really matter?"

When Lucy would back herself into such statements, conversation between her and Porter would usually grind to a halt. He'd felt it was better not to respond with patronizing sentiments like "You matter a lot to us!" or "You're a helluva lot more than a blip on the radar screen to us!"

Lucy's second way of thinking had not been a rejection of death so much as an inability to imagine it. "What happens to your thoughts and dreams?" she'd wanted to know. "Do they simply stop happening? How can that be?"

Unlike the first, this second mode of Lucy's would lead them into endless conversations that would spiral deep into the night, each of them guessing about what happens to your mind and soul, where your thoughts go, whether they take a new form of energy, and, if so, whether that energy continues as thought, or turns into rain, or plant food, or into someone else's thoughts.

"If only we had a religion!" they'd say. "Then we wouldn't have all these unknowns. We'd believe. We wouldn't question."

"But we *wanted* to question, didn't we? That's why we rejected religion in the first place."

And on and on it would go, for hours, until Lucy would finally lose her battle to maintain her end of the conversation and fall asleep. A few times, though, they'd managed to talk straight through until dawn, which they'd both loved. In fact, after Lucy had died and Porter was doing his thinking about silver linings and feeling so bitter about it, those all-night conversations came back to him as at least one good thing. But did they qualify as a silver lining? Not by a long shot.

Now, sitting in a faded blue folding chair on Delilah's patio, waiting for her to return from wherever she was, Porter found himself thinking about those all-night conversations. In particular, he was remembering one in which he and Lucy had talked about the nature of love and what happens to the love that two people share when one of them dies. "Assuming the love in the surviving person doesn't die," Lucy had wondered, "where does it go?"

"It probably becomes grief," Porter had said. "Or else longing for the person to come back."

"No, that's different. That's something else."

"Okay. So maybe you shower your kids with it. You give them more than before."

She'd shaken her head. "I doubt it. You can't love those kids more with the love you had for me." Then she'd smiled at him. "You know what I think? I think you have to aim it at someone else. A new person."

"Oh, c'mon," Porter had said. "We're not going to talk about that."

But she'd kept her smile. "It's funny. I used to say I wouldn't mind if you had an affair if it was only for sex. Remember? We even used to talk about that, when our sex life started to get a little old. And I told you that I wouldn't really care if you had sex with someone just to get your rocks off, as long as you didn't fall in love with the person. Remember that?"

He'd nodded.

"And I meant it. I didn't want you traipsing back into our bed with AIDS or something, but I wasn't so worried about that. Mostly I just didn't want you to fall in love with someone else. But now it's the opposite. When I'm gone, I feel like I want you to find someone to love. I don't care whether you have sex with the person or not." She'd laughed. "I mean, I've come to think that sex is just so dumb anyway, even if I feel like we should still try to do it to be normal. But I really hope you find someone to love."

Porter gazed across the field, then over toward the lake, but still no sign of Delilah. He was pissed that he'd remembered that conversation with Lucy. It was ridiculous for him to be floating around in some memory that seemed to suggest he take his love for Lucy and "aim it" at Delilah. And suddenly he started to feel angry at Delilah too, for not being here when he arrived, because it was this goddamn waiting that had allowed those thoughts to enter his mind in the first place.

"DAAAD!"

Porter sat forward to see Kaylie coming across the field toward him, carrying something in her hand. It glinted in the sun, and he realized with a flash of horror that it was Claire's cell phone. *Oh, no,* he thought. *She didn't.*

"DAD!" Kaylie yelled again as she approached. "It's Gramma. She wants to talk to you." Then she brought the phone to her head and starting talking into it.

Porter crept off the patio and tiptoed into the field, as if stealth were somehow called for in this situation.

Kaylie approached with the phone still at her ear. "Okay . . ." she was saying. "Okay. Gram? Gramma? Here he is," and she held it out.

Porter grabbed it. "Claire, could you hold on a sec?"

"Porter, I—"

He brought the phone down from his ear, located the hold button on the glowing green keypad, and pressed it. Then he glared at Kaylie. "You *called* her?"

Kaylie raised her chin indignantly. "No, I didn't *call* her. I turned it on to see if it was still working, and it rang in like a millisecond. They must have had their phone on autodial. I bet it's been dialing us nonstop ever since we turned that thing off yesterday."

Yesterday. Porter couldn't believe that had happened only yesterday. "So what did you tell her?"

"Don't worry. I said we were at this really neat place with a lake, and that we went swimming and everything. I told her we're having fun. You should thank me for not putting Benny on. He kept asking to talk to her, and he would have said like twenty stupid things in ten seconds."

"You didn't tell her about the transmission?"

"No," she said sullenly. "I don't even know what's wrong with the truck." Then she squinted at him with annoyance. "So what were you doing over on *her* patio anyway? It took me forever to find you. I thought you were going to talk to that other woman."

"I did. I was just over there. I talked to her boyfriend. He was this big guy." Porter realized he sounded like he was trying to build an alibi. "I just stopped at Delilah's on the way back. I wanted to ask her something, but she's not around."

Kaylie considered this. "Well, you'd better take Gramma off hold. She's mad enough at you already."

Porter nodded grimly, released the hold, and brought the phone up. "Claire? . . . Claire? . . . Hello?"

"Porter?" Claire's voice sounded like a distant squawk—she'd put him on speakerphone, he realized—and then there was the brief clatter of her picking up the handset. "How dare you cut me off like that. I am livid. Just livid. First you have the gall to turn off the cell phone after we lost the connection, so we have no idea where in the world you are, and then when we finally reach you, thanks only to Kaylie, I might add, you put me on hold in midsentence . . ."

From where Porter and Kaylie were standing in the field, there was an opening in the trees that afforded a full view of the muddy beach area fifty yards away. As Claire berated him, Porter found himself staring at the ugly white butts of about half a dozen scraggly Jasper types who stood in a loose semicircle chatting and drinking from big German beer mugs. They wore nothing but sandals and broad, floppy farmer's hats. After a moment, one of them said something that sent the others into a round of foot-stomping laughter that Porter could hear even above Claire's hissing diatribe.

Suddenly he felt a wave of affection for those ugly white butts. He loved this place. He loved everything it stood for. Glancing at Kaylie, he saw that she too had turned to look at the men, no doubt alerted by their laughter. At first her eyes widened and her lips parted, but as she watched, her face collapsed into an expression of "been there, done that," and after a moment she gazed back at their campsite—a good thirty or forty yards in the opposite direction, where, Porter saw, Benny was hunched over the picnic table deeply engaged in a project that involved gluing together pieces of sticks and branches into an elaborate structure.

Porter's spell was broken by a sudden silence at the other end of the phone. Then Claire said, "Aren't you?"

"Aren't I what?"

Claire sighed. "Have you even been *listening* to me?"

"Yes."

"So, then, aren't you the least bit sorry for what you've put us through?"

"I'm very sorry," Porter said. Then he thought of something. "You know what, Claire? I didn't even know that turning the cell phone off made it so it couldn't ring. I thought that's how you were supposed to hang it up." He shrugged helplessly at Kaylie, who scrunched up her face in a way that said, *You are such a liar.*

Claire emitted the sounds *"Uhfff . . ."* and *"Wuh . . ."* before finally gathering herself and blaring into the phone, "How could you not *know* that? *Everyone* knows that."

The trees at the far edge of the field had begun to shimmer gorgeously in the warm, lazy breeze. Above them, a fleet of billowy, flat-topped clouds pushed their way across the blue sky. "So Kaylie told you how nice it is here?" Porter said brightly. "The kids had a blast swimming today."

Claire was silent for a moment. "I'm glad to hear that," she said in a defeated way.

"You should see Benny. He's at the picnic table building some miniature log cabin out of sticks. He's totally engrossed. That kid's going to be the next Frank Lloyd Wright."

"Oh, Porter," Claire said in a rush, "I miss those kids so much. I was just so upset this morning thinking about them. I just wish—Oh, I don't know."

Porter didn't say anything.

"William and I," she forged on, her voice trembling, "we've been bumbling around this house like blind people. I was so angry at him this morning. You know what he did? At the crack of dawn he stepped outside to get the paper, *but he forgot to disable the alarm!* And then, to make matters worse, he got confused and couldn't remember how to turn it off. He was so frustrated that he struck the code box and cut his hand rather badly. So I woke up to find William with a bloody hand, and meanwhile I was sure that we'd woken up the *entire neighborhood . . .*"

The entire neighborhood? Their closest neighbors—the Honorable and Mrs. Walter Pilar—lived more than a hundred yards away in a gargantuan stone fortress that looked as if it had been built to withstand a nuclear attack.

"I'm sorry, Claire," Porter said. "Is William all right?"

"I suppose. I mean, yes, he is. It was just a little cut—no stitches or anything—but we were both quite upset about it." Claire was sniffling into the phone, wiping her nose. "Oh, Porter, I don't know. I don't want to push our problems into your good time. You three are entitled to a nice time."

"It's not that we're entitled to a nice time," Porter said. "It's not a matter of entitlement." And then he almost laughed. A nice time? After everything that had already happened today? The thought skipped across his mind that around the same time William was cutting his hand and Claire was waking up to that chaos, Porter was slicing open his forehead and Benny was peeing in his sheets. At least their days had begun similarly. Not that Claire would find any comfort in such knowledge.

"That's not how I meant it," Claire said, her voice regaining its strength. "I'm just trying to . . . well . . . Porter, I simply would like you to call us every couple of days, that's all. Is that too much to ask? I don't want to be placed in the position of having to hound you across the country."

"I'm sorry about that, Claire. I'll try to do a better job of keeping you posted. But, you know, it's only been one day since we left."

Claire laughed, a brief exhalation of breath in the midst of her sniffling. "Can you believe it? One day! It's so ridiculous. But when we couldn't reach you, I truly panicked."

"I'll call again in a couple of days. Maybe we'll be in Kansas by then."

"*Kansas?*"

"We're just passing through on our way to Colorado," he said. "If we make good time, we should be there by Thursday." Then he remembered that tomorrow was already Wednesday. They might not even get on the road until Thursday morning, at the earliest. "But we may not get that far until the end of the week," he added.

"Oh, my. Please be *so* careful, will you? Tell Benny I love him. I didn't get a chance to say hi to him. Is he really okay? Is he doing better?"

Porter glanced back at their campground. It looked as if Benny's glued-together structure of sticks had collapsed on the table. His boy was nowhere in sight. "I think so."

"Okay, then. So Porter? Don't turn the phone off this time, please? I promise I'll wait for you to call us if you'll leave the phone on. I want to feel like I'm able to reach you if I must."

Porter thought a moment. "Sure. That's fine."

"Love to everyone."

"You too."

And they hung up.

Porter and Kaylie exchanged glances. She said, "That didn't seem too bad."

Porter slipped the cell phone into his pants pocket and started back toward their campsite. "She really yelled at me at first. But I just let her, and after a while she calmed down. I learned that strategy from your grampa."

"Dad, I didn't know where you were!" Kaylie said, following him. "I told Gramma you'd call her back, but she kept saying, 'Absolutely *not*, my darling. You must find him *now*.' The whole time I was look-ing for you, she was getting all panicked and saying, 'Kaylie, where could he *be*? How could you not know where he *is*?' I went to those log cabins where I thought you said you were going, but I didn't know where to knock, plus it started to feel a little weird over there, like people were watching me or something. And that's when I looked through the trees and saw you sitting next to that lady's tepee."

"I'm sorry you had to deal with that," Porter said. He put his hand on her little neck and gave it a squeeze. "I just wanted to ask

Delilah when Jasper's going to fix our truck. We need to get on the road."

They stepped into the clearing of their campsite and approached the table. The bottle of Elmer's glue Benny had been using lay in the gravel about twenty feet away, as if thrown there. Benny's structure on the table did not look collapsed so much as ripped apart—dozens of footlong sticks, shining with white patches of hardening glue, littered the area around the table, some reaching as far as the camper.

Porter stepped over to the camper and opened the back door. "Benny?" He peered into the darkness.

Kaylie came up behind him. "Is he in there?"

Porter climbed inside and felt Benny's bunk. "I don't think so." He stood up and ran his hand across his own bed. "Benny? You in here?" He looked around at Kaylie, who had stepped up into the doorway. "You didn't see him go anywhere?"

She shook her head. "Maybe he went off looking for us. When I left, I told him I'd be right back, and then I was gone for like fifteen minutes."

"But couldn't he see us right there in the field? When I was on the phone, I was able to see him building that thing on the picnic table."

Kaylie shrugged. "He probably didn't think to look that way. I didn't when I came looking for you. You went off down the road, so I did too. Maybe he only thought we'd come back from that way."

Porter put his hands on his hips and let out his breath. "Well, I have to go look for him. He's got to be around this place somewhere."

They climbed down from the camper and stepped out into the brightness. From where they stood, they did a brief scan of the entire area: down the dirt road, across the field, among the tepees, over toward the beach, and in the woods immediately surrounding their campsite. Porter was surprised to see that suddenly there were many more people out and about than there had been earlier. The beach was populated by a crowd of longhaired women and men dressed in a rainbow of colors, talking in small groups or wading up to their knees in the lake—a scene straight out of Woodstock. Porter was encouraged to see that about half of them wore clothes—loose, flowing dresses or jeans shorts and tie-dyed T-shirts. Porter could hear the tinny rasp of Grateful Dead music, and scattered groups of Deadheads were twirling or swaying to the rhythm, their arms snaking through the air.

Closer—maybe halfway across the field—a gray-haired man Porter recognized as Uncle Charlie was beating a hurried path to the beach wearing work boots and a white robe that looked like the flag of Japan. Then a couple of women emerged from the woods just where Charlie had, adorned like Gypsies—feathers in their hair, bright scarves trailing from their necks. Another trio followed a few paces behind: two men in overalls, a third in knee-length orange shorts, bare-chested, a black cowboy hat perched crookedly atop his head.

"I don't see Benny anywhere," Porter said anxiously.

Kaylie shook her head. "Me either."

"He'd steer clear of that beach crowd anyway."

Kaylie went over to the picnic table, swept a spot on the bench clean of Benny's sticks, and sat down. "Should we just wait here for him?"

"Tell you what. Why don't you stay here, and I'll do one loop all the way around. If he comes back while I'm gone, just stay here, okay? It's going to be time for dinner in another hour. You could start getting things together if you want."

She yawned.

Porter set off down the dirt road. "Benny!" he called out. "Ben?" As he walked, he began to wonder about the way Benny's log cabin structure had been destroyed and scattered around the campsite. Why would he have done that? He was a stressed-out kid, sure, but he didn't have any history of destroying things, especially something he'd made himself. The sticks Benny had been working with had been notched and tapered at each end, no doubt done with his own pocket knife—all careful, thoughtful work. No, his boy wouldn't have created such a thing only to rip it apart and throw it around their camp. But if he hadn't done it, who had? And why?

Jasper? Maybe he was trying to scare them out of there? But all he had to do was fix their transmission. What good was scaring them away when they had no way to leave? Besides, this whole place seemed so gentle and peace-loving. Or was that only a facade hiding a menace that lurked just beneath the surface?

Would you chill out? Porter told himself. He came into the pine forest and the cluster of log cabins where he'd been earlier and decided to check first with Seri. As he approached, he heard voices inside and stopped to listen. The screen door was closed, but the wooden door behind it was angled open.

"You like that?" a woman was saying. "Seri thinks he invented that drink." She laughed.

"Well, *I'd* never had it before." It was Seri. "And I never saw anyone else make it that way. So I did sort of invent it, no matter what Andrea says. I didn't *steal* the recipe from anybody."

"Cranberry and seltzer? A recipe?" The woman exploded in a deep, guttural laugh. "Wait, let me write that down. Ingredients: one bottle cranberry juice, one bottle seltzer. Mix cranberry and seltzer. Pour in glass. Drink." *HA, HA, HA!* "Seri, you are too much. God, I love this big fat guy. He's from Fiji, you know that? You know where Fiji is?"

"In the ocean?"

Was that Benny's voice? Porter stepped closer.

"Bingo," Andrea said. "In the middle of the Pacific Ocean. Ten thousand miles from here. But you know what else . . . ?"

Porter rapped on the screen door. "Hello?"

"Dad?" Benny said.

Seri's huge form moved over and filled the doorway, then his hand pushed the screen door open and he lowered his big head into the daylight. "Hey, Porter," he said, smiling. "Come on in. Your kid's in here."

Porter stepped inside, and there was Benny, sitting cross-legged on the floor with a glass of juice in his hand. "Hi, Ben," he said. "I've been looking for you."

Benny looked up at him sheepishly. "*I* was looking for *you*. Kaylie left a long time ago to find you. Gramma called."

Seri took Porter by the elbow and turned him. "This is Andrea. Andrea, Porter." He jerked his thumb at Andrea. "She's the one who runs this place."

"Runs it?" Andrea said. "Hardly. I just try to keep a lid on it." She stood with her hands on her hips, wearing a brown tank top and a green, ankle-length skirt. She was a bear of a woman herself—nearly as tall as Porter, with an electric blaze of red hair, breasts like melons, and a butt so big it looked strapped on. She came right up to Porter, smiling warmly, and as he reached out to shake her hand, she opened her arms and engulfed him in a smothering hug, trapping his arm between them in the folds of her soft belly. As she squeezed him, Porter inhaled the pot-laced aroma of her hair and, for just a moment, felt the embarrassing, childlike sensation of having his feet leave the ground. "Happy to have you here," Andrea said, releasing him and stepping back. "Your boy is a sweetheart. He kept saying he should go and find you, but we wouldn't let him!"

"I'm glad I found him," Porter said. "I was worried."

"Worried?" Andrea boomed. "Worried about what?"

"I don't know. That he'd get lost?"

Andrea waved her hand. "Nonsense. First of all, everyone here is lost, right, Seri?" She gave him a broad grin. "That's the whole point." Then she turned back to Porter. "No, but really. Don't worry. He's fine." Glancing in Benny's direction, she said, "We were just talking about music and dancing, weren't we?"

Benny nodded obediently.

"Because there's gonna be a whole lot of music and dancing over at the beach this evening. In fact," she said to Seri, "we should be getting over there, shouldn't we? We're late."

Seri nodded, then tipped his head back, causing his layers of dreadlocks to fall away from his face and behind his shoulders.

"Your son said he doesn't like to dance," Andrea prattled on. "Is that true with you too?"

"I didn't say I don't *like* to dance," Benny corrected her. "I said I've *never* danced."

Andrea directed a bewildered look at Porter. "Is that so?"

"Benny, you used to dance all the time when you were little," Porter said. "You marched all over the house, carrying that stick. Remember? You loved to march."

Benny squinted at him.

"That's different," Andrea said, looking miffed. "Marching."

Porter said, "I didn't mean *military* marching."

Andrea dismissed him with a wave of her hand. "Whatever. Listen, if you guys want to, you should come over to the beach. Every Tuesday night we do a concert." She looked at Seri and grinned. "It's our only organized event, right?" She cast her eyes back at Porter. "It even has a name, our little concert series. We call it 'Music Never Stops.' "

"You're part of a band?" Porter asked.

"No!" Andrea said, exasperated. "The *Dead*. We pick a Dead concert to play. From tape. The whole thing. From start to finish. We rig up speakers outside and everything."

Seri brushed past Porter and pushed the door closed. On the back of the door, tacked in the middle, was a calendar. "Let's see," Seri said, stooping over to read it. "Tonight is . . . oh, yeah, that's right. We've got the Capitol Theatre, Passaic, New Jersey, June nineteenth, 1976. A classic, man. We kick off with 'Might As Well,' then straight into 'Sampson,' and then into a killer 'High Time.' Man. I remember every second of this one."

Porter smiled. There was something so harmless and likable about Seri. "So you guys went to this concert?" he asked.

Seri drew back his head in surprise. "In 1976? I was *twelve*, man! I was still in Fiji!"

Andrea giggled. "He was a skinny island boy running around in a loincloth. That was three hundred pounds ago."

Seri looked hurt. "Not three hundred."

Porter wondered why Seri didn't retaliate with a cutting remark about the tonnage of Andrea's breasts or butt. Maybe he was scared of her. Or maybe he just had the decency to keep his language clean in front of Benny.

"So you think you'll go?" Andrea asked Porter. "Delilah will be there." She smirked, pointing at his forehead. "I understand she's the one responsible for that bandage."

Porter reached up for it and was surprised to feel the taped gauze under his fingers. He'd forgotten it was there. "It already seems like days ago."

"You know, you shouldn't worry about Jasper," Andrea said out of the blue. "He just needs to grow up. He's like a little boy." She glanced down at Benny. "Not that's there's anything wrong with being a little boy . . . if you *are* a little boy. "

"I shouldn't worry about him doing what?" Porter said.

Andrea said, "Just about him in general, as a presence."

"I only want him to fix our transmission. I mean, I'm grateful for your hospitality and everything. This place is great, really. But we only have about ten days. And we hoped to make it all the way out to Rocky Mountain National Park to do some camping."

"Oh, I know," Andrea said with an air of disappointment. "No, Jasper's good at that sort of thing. He'll be able to do it."

"Speaking of which," Seri said, "you think Jasper can borrow the van tomorrow morning? You know how I told you he needs to go into town to get parts."

"I don't see why not," Andrea said. "As long as he goes to the service station and *only* to the service station. I don't want him cruising up and down Main Street with the music blaring like last time."

"That was only to impress Lilah," Seri said, casting a sidelong glance at Porter. "He won't do that when he's just by himself."

Andrea regarded him. "If you say so." She walked over to the mantel and began blowing out the candles. As each flame was extinguished, the room plunged farther into a maroon darkness. Before the last one was out, Seri pulled open the door, flooding the room once again with fresh, sparkling light. "We gotta go," Andrea said, turning around. She gazed down at Benny, who looked like a man overboard, awash in that sea of pillows. "Thanks for stopping by, sweetheart," she said, bending over to kiss him on the cheek. "You gonna be okay now? You feel better, child?"

Benny nodded shyly, and Andrea moved toward Porter. He braced himself for another crushing hug, but she just put her hand on his shoulder and said, "So come on over to the concert, will you? Bring the kids. They'll love it, I swear. There might be some other kids there." She looked at Seri. "Don't Jack's kids usually come? Aren't they the ones who are so cute? The ones who spin around and around?"

Seri nodded. "Plus there's Mary Anne's daughter, Wilderness. She's ten."

"See," Andrea said to Porter and Benny, her eyes twinkling, "we're not just a bunch of old fuddy-duddies."

Wilderness? Porter thought. "First I think we're going to make some dinner back at the camper. Also, we're all a little wiped out, so I'm not sure how much we're up for. But thanks for the invite. We'll see."

"Oh, there's food there," Andrea said. "People bring stuff. There's tons."

Porter waved her off. "That's okay. We brought all this food that's going to go bad if we don't eat it soon."

Andrea looked at him curiously. "You don't have a refrigerator in that thing?"

"Yeah, we do."

"Well, you can plug it in, you know. Electricity is free. It's on the house."

"I saw that," Porter said, remembering the silver outlet sticking out of the ground like an odd weed next to their camper. "No, that's great." And then he realized that he'd never plugged the camper in! *Damn it.* The ice block would be completely melted by now, after almost two days in the heat. All that food they'd packed—eggs, milk, chicken, salami. Would all of it be spoiled? Come to think of it, the milk had felt slightly warm this morning, when they'd had their breakfast. Why hadn't he thought of it then? Had that blow to his head knocked the sense out of him?

Seri held the door open, ushering everybody past.

Outside, under the towering pine trees, Seri and Andrea didn't look quite as gigantic as they had inside their cramped Saharan mugwump, or whatever you called it. Seri laid his brown arm over Andrea's shoulders, then gave Porter and Benny a quick wrist-flick of a wave, and the two of them set off.

Porter headed down the road with Benny, still dwelling on their food situation. How were they supposed to buy anything to eat now, without transportation?

"They were nice," Benny said, yanking Porter out of his thoughts.

"Yeah," Porter said absently. He looked at Benny, and in the early-evening light he could see that his boy's eyes were all red and puffy, rubbed raw. He stopped. "Benny?" he said. "Were you crying?"

Benny gazed down at his shoes. "Uh-huh."

"When you went to them?"

He nodded.

Porter crouched down and put his arms around his son. Benny leaned into him and began to breathe in sharply. Then Porter felt the familiar warmth of tears on his neck and Benny's humid puffs of breath.

"I . . ." Benny said, his voice wavering. "I didn't know where anyone was! And I was making this thing . . . this thing with sticks . . ."

Porter put his hands on Benny's shoulders, held him away, and looked into his boy's face, which was flushed with anguish.

". . . and it was so neat," Benny said, averting his eyes. "It was like a castle. There were all these doors and windows and everything. Big guns and stuff. And I wanted to show it to someone. I wanted to show it to *Mommy*!" Then he burst into sobs, and Porter gathered him in again.

"So you wrecked it?" Porter said. "You did that yourself?"

Benny nodded against Porter's neck.

"Oh, Benny." He squeezed his boy, and Benny heaved against him for a while, breathing hotly. "I'm so sorry."

When Benny's sobbing finally subsided, he pushed himself free and turned away, wiping at his eyes and nose. "I want to go home," he said, sniffling. "Can we go home now?"

Porter sighed. "We can't go anywhere yet. Not until the truck's fixed. But, Benny, we just started this trip. You've liked it so far. You liked swimming today, didn't you?"

Benny nodded.

"It'll be fun. Don't worry. You're not going to feel any better being back there," Porter said, "in our apartment."

"Okay."

Porter took his son's hand, and they set off that way, their clasped hands swinging between them. It had been a while since they'd done that. It reminded Porter of those toddler years, of Kaylie and Ben stomping along on either side of him as they crossed the street, Porter constantly checking both ways for cars, certain that some out-of-control vehicle was about to come hurtling out of nowhere and barrel them over.

He was so fearful in those days! He saw danger in everything. Every trip in the car was an opportunity for a bone-crushing collision, every hot dog and peanut and grape a potential choke item. Leashless dogs that came bounding up—even friendly, tail-wagging ones—were psychotic carnivores that could snap without warning, removing one of his child's limbs.

Porter couldn't remember when, exactly, he'd gotten over that debilitating phase of parenthood. But he did recall that the feeling of getting over it was one of surrender. *You can't stop it,* he'd told himself. *You can't protect them from everything.*

But still, every so often, he'd feel a surge of that familiar fear, that premonition of imminent harm.

Years ago, Porter had made the mistake of watching some TV docudrama where they re-created real-life emergencies using actors, but the story was narrated by the actual person who'd been hurt by the tragedy. And this one woman, whose son had been struck by lightning while playing in a friend's backyard, said that at the moment her son was struck she'd had a feeling something bad was happening to him. She *knew* he was in trouble. She just didn't know where, or what, and it drove her crazy for about ten minutes until she got the call that her boy had burns all over his body and wasn't breathing.

After seeing that show, Porter started feeling that way several times a week. *Something bad's happening,* he'd think, and panic would surge up his spine. But it would turn out he was wrong. Nothing had happened. Everyone was fine. Ironically, the day he got the call from Lucy saying her gynecologist had felt "something weird" in her breast, Porter couldn't have been feeling more carefree. He was in the midst of a rare slow day at work, winning his third game of computer chess in a row, and thinking, *Man, this is excellent! I get paid for this?* Then the phone rang.

Porter and Benny made the turn into their campsite, still walking hand in hand, and then saw Kaylie standing there waiting for them.

She was scowling, her hands dug into her hips. Next to her, the picnic table was beautifully set with plates, silverware, glasses, and folded blue napkins.

"Guess what?" she called out. "The food's all bad. The whole refrigerator *stinks*." She shook her head with disdain. "So what do you want to do now?"

CHAPTER SEVEN

THE feast was spread out across a dozen picnic tables lined up end to end, and Porter quickly realized that Andrea hadn't been exaggerating—there was *tons* of food. Pots of pork and beans. Ceramic bowls of fruit salad. Fresh loaves of sourdough bread laid out on cutting boards. Corn on the cob simmering in steamy barrels of water. Vats of coleslaw, potato salad, green salad. Plates of hummus, tabouli, Indian rice, white rice, brown rice. Juice and wine in bottles. Cans of Coke, Sprite, root beer, and seltzer submerged in ice-filled metal drums. Beer by the keg. Beer in bottles. There was even a station for kids with peanut butter, grape jelly, and Wonder Bread.

An orderly procession of Deadheads snaked past the tables, filling their plates, moving to the music. The main crowd danced in a dusty frenzy just beyond the tables. But everywhere Porter looked—off into the field or down the road or up on rocks—people were dancing, often alone, in that familiar, loose-limbed reverie Porter remembered from the Dead concert he'd gone to during his freshman year of college, an event so remote it seemed like a hazy childhood memory.

Music blasted out of six coffin-sized speakers that had been rigged up directly behind the food tables, making any conversation within twenty yards impossible:

> *Goin' down the road, feelin' bad*
> *Goin' down the road, feelin' bad, bad, bad, bad*
> *Don't want to be treated this way.*
> *Goin' where the climate suits my clothes . . .*

Porter shouted to Kaylie that she and Benny should just grab a plate and help themselves, but she put her hand to her ear and mouthed, "What?"

"Decide what you want and help yourselves!" He did a brief pantomime of eating with an imaginary utensil.

His kids stared at him.

Fuck it, Porter thought, suddenly ravenous. He handed them paper plates, then turned to the tables and began shoveling food onto his own plate, overloading it with a scoop or two of nearly everything before him. Kaylie and Ben followed suit, moving among the crowd, grabbing at the free bounty like street urchins.

From the metal drums at the end of the serving line, Porter grabbed a bottle of Bud. His kids picked out cans of soda, and he motioned for them to follow him. The sun was a fiery white ball on the horizon, its brightness making their exodus from the food area a squinting, stumbling journey over uneven terrain. They cut a swath through pockets of twirling bodies and emerged at the edge of the tepee village. Porter looked to make sure his kids were still with him, then turned into the sun again to forge ahead, but his path was blocked by a short, silhouetted figure.

"There ya'll are!" Delilah said.

Porter shaded his eyes with his beer bottle. "Hi."

"I came to tell you about this, but you'd already left."

"Andrea told us about it," Porter said, smiling. "It's great. All this food."

Delilah was wearing a green print dress that ended in a stringy fringe at the tops of her thighs. On her head was a floppy blue hat. Her feet were bare. Porter was surprised how glad he was to see her. She somehow seemed like a long-lost friend. He glanced at his kids. They stood expectantly, their paper plates sagging under the weight of their dinners. "We should find a place to sit down, I guess."

Kaylie said, "Can't we go back to our *own* picnic table?"

"No—well—you want to go all the way back there?" Porter said. "You sure?" Then he thought about how nicely Kaylie had laid everything out—those blue napkins especially, folded like little tricornered hats atop the plates. The image filled him with sadness. "Yeah, okay," he said. "I'll catch up to you, okay? I need to talk to Delilah for a minute."

They nodded and started to move off, but a few steps away Benny's plate buckled, and his rice and half of his mashed potatoes plopped onto the dirt. He looked back at them helplessly.

"Aww," Delilah cooed. "Here, let me get ya'll real plates." She stepped up onto her cement patio, disappeared into her tepee, and came back out a second later with white plastic plates for both of them. She helped Benny slide the remains of his dinner onto the new plate, then, despite Kaylie's objections, did the same with hers.

As they walked away, Porter shouted after them, "Okay, I'll be over."

Delilah started toward her patio. "C'mon," she said, looking back. "You wanna sit?"

Porter followed her. She ducked inside her tepee and came right back out dragging a beanbag chair through the doorway. The chair was made of blue jeans that had been sown together, zippers and all. She sat down, grinding her butt to mold the chair around it, then crossed her legs at the ankles and lay back. Porter sat down in the same blue folding chair he'd occupied a couple of hours earlier, balanced his plate on his knees, and started to eat.

"So you met Andrea," Delilah said. "That's good."

"Yeah," Porter said, chewing. "I met both Seri and Andrea. They were nice. And I have to tell you, they had some interesting things to say about Jasper."

"Oh, God," she said. "Jasper. He and I really had it out this afternoon. I'm still so pissed at him for not telling me where Don and Stacey went. And he just *refuses* to acknowledge that he did anything wrong. I mean, what do you think about that?"

"What *I* think," Porter said, stabbing at his scalloped potatoes, "is that he didn't tell you because he wanted you to stay here. At least that's what I gather from what Andrea and Seri told me."

Delilah rolled her eyes. "What. Because he *loves* me, right? Is that what they told you? Because he has a *crush* on me?"

Porter stopped in mid-chew. He nodded.

She shook her head. "I swear, this place drives me nuts! It's like junior high school."

"I think Seri was just trying to clue me in," Porter said. "I was asking what Jasper's deal was, and when he might be able to fix the truck, so Seri started telling me about him and you. He wasn't trying to be catty." An image of Seri's huge face, lit up with gossipy delight, flashed across Porter's mind.

"Oh, I know." She sat back and let out her breath. "Seri's nice. Andrea's nice. It's just that the hypocrisy around here gets to me after a while. You know, it's supposed to be this place where everyone is so open-minded, and everybody accepts everybody else for who they are, and blah, blah, blah. But they only really accept you if you're open-minded in the exact same way they're open-minded. If someone asks you if you want to have an orgy or do mushrooms or get stoned or something, and you say no, they accuse you of being closed-minded. How warped is that? I mean, you'd think it would be considered *more* open-minded *not* to want to do stuff like that when everyone is doing it, wouldn't you?"

All Porter could think was, *Orgy?*

"I guess I'm just bummed out that the same interpersonal shit that goes on everywhere goes on here too. I wanted to think it was at least possible to get beyond that."

Music filled the air, skipping across the treetops. Porter gulped his beer until his neck tingled and he felt that brief, soaring feeling in his chest.

Delilah sat forward, wrapping her arms around her legs. "So, what are you going to do now anyway?" she said. "With your life, I mean?"

Porter laughed. "With my life? Well, I'm . . ." he began, gazing at her with a goofy smile. He took another swig from his beer and lowered his gaze into his plate of food, as if trying to jog his memory. Finally he looked up. "I'm just going to live it, I guess," he said idiotically.

"I know *that*," she said. She let go of her knees and flopped back into her beanbag. "But live it for what? What do you *want*?"

"What do I want?" This line of interrogation reminded Porter of his painting workshops in college, all those gloomy girls crouched in their chairs like gargoyles poised for attack. "What are you trying to communicate?" they'd demand of him, or "How am I supposed to experience this?" Their questions seemed like riddles, crafted from a language he didn't know, and he never knew quite how he was supposed to respond. Clearly there was a specific answer they were searching for, something deep and profound that he ought to be able to articulate—the very essence of his art, or of his being, which were possibly the same thing. *Look,* he always felt like asking them. *Do you like the fucking painting or not?*

He looked at Delilah and sighed. "I want to be a good father, mostly." At first this answer pleased him, but as it settled into the void between them, he began to have doubts about its sincerity. He wanted a lot more than that. But what did she really expect him to say?

"Well, yeah, of course," Delilah said. "But I'm more talking about what *you're* looking for. For *you*."

Porter shifted uncomfortably. "I don't know," he said. "What do *you* want?" As he watched her mull over her response, he took the opportunity to shove another forkful of beans into his mouth.

"That's easy," she said, launching right in. "First of all, I'd like to figure out why I can't forgive my parents enough to call them up and tell them where I am in the world. That's one goal. Then I'd like to understand why I can't stay in one place for more than three months and actually make a life. I'd like to know why I'm so fucking afraid of just being a normal person, whatever that is, instead of this weird, flaky person I seem to be."

Porter smiled. "You're not so weird."

"Oh, thanks." She laughed. "So does that mean I'm flaky?"

"I think the term is 'colorful.' "

"No, the term is 'flaky.' " Her face took on a wounded look. "That's what Don called me. His parting shot."

They were silent for a moment. Porter took another swig of his beer and let his head roll back. He stared into the purpling sky, the music washing over him—acoustic guitar and hissing drums followed by a bright tinkling of keyboards. He sat forward once again and looked down at the remains of his dinner—some rice, a little chicken—searching for some last morsel to end his meal. "So what have you been doing for all these years anyway?" he said, poking his way around his plate. "After you told me that story about your sister, it occurred to me that you aren't as young as I thought you were. I mean, since that happened in 1963, I started to think—" and he looked up at Delilah and saw that she was about to cry. Her eyes were glassy and brimming with tears. She made a chokey sound in her throat, then reached up with both hands and wiped at her face. "Hey, I didn't mean . . ." Porter said. "It's just that you look so young. I wasn't saying . . ."

"What?" she said.

"I wasn't saying you were old."

"Oh," she said, waving him off, "it's not that." She took the sleeve of her dress and dabbed at her eyes. She wiped some more, then opened her eyes wide and tried to smile.

"Then what is it?"

She gathered herself, crouching forward in the beanbag chair and crossing her arms over her chest. "I really need to find Don," she said finally. "I have to find him."

Porter was surprised to feel his heart sink. "You do?"

She nodded, gripping herself. "In fact—and you have to stop me if I'm overstepping my bounds here—but I was wondering if maybe there was a way you could help me out somehow. I know it's not fair. I mean, here you are stranded, and you want to start your vacation and all that. The last thing you need are my problems heaped on top . . ."

Porter watched her mouth move and thought, *This is fine. This is a good thing that she wants to find Don.*

". . . so I was thinking," Delilah went on, "that the place you bought the camper might have some information about Don and Stacey. Maybe an address or a phone number? Do you know if you have to give any of that information when you sell a used car?"

It took a moment for Porter to realize she'd stopped talking. "What?"

"The place you bought the camper," she said. "Do you think they'd have an address or phone number for Don and Stacey?"

"Um . . . that's a good question. I don't know."

"Think we could call the dealer and find out?"

Porter tried to think of the name of the dealership, but all he could remember was the sign that said USED CARS. "Actually I can't think of the name of the business, but I remember the name of the guy who sold it to me. I could probably get his home number through information."

She brightened. "You'd do that?"

"Why not?"

"Like, now? Tonight?"

Porter looked at his empty wrist for the umpteenth time since he'd forgotten to put on his watch yesterday morning. "Do you know what time it is?"

"Maybe around eight-fifteen? Eight-thirty? I think that's when the sun goes down around here. Think it's early enough?"

Porter imagined Joe Hinchcliff plopped in front of the TV in his cramped row house, beer on the armrest, feet up on the coffee table, blue boxers, white socks. Wife? Yeah. Probably an Edith Bunker type. She'd be the one to answer the phone. "I guess it's early enough. I'll give it a shot if you want."

"That would be *so* great." She lowered her chin demurely. "Now, here's the other thing. And tell me the truth, okay? But would you be willing to use that cellular phone you have? Andrea banned me from using her phone for long distance."

"How'd you know I have one?"

"Wasn't Kaylie carrying it around earlier? That's what I heard anyway. Everyone was talking about it."

Porter raised his eyebrows. "Everyone?"

"Well, not *everyone*."

A feeling of humiliation rose in him. "It's not mine, actually," he said. "It's my mother-in-law's."

"So does that mean you'd rather not use it for something like this?"

"No, it's okay." He put his plate down on the patio and stood up. "I'll go get it. I should go check on Kaylie and Ben anyway."

"You sure? You don't mind?"

"It's fine," he said. "Really." And he set off into the field in a stiff-legged walk. Across the field he could see Kaylie and Ben at their campsite, both sitting on the same side of the table, their backs to him. As he drew closer, he saw the lone place setting on the other side meant for him.

"Hi," he said, coming up behind them.

Kaylie turned around. "Where's your food?"

"I left it back there. I'm sorry. Delilah needs to borrow our phone."

"For what?"

"She wants to find her old boyfriend, the one who left with the camper."

"And we're supposed to help her?"

Porter opened the cab and grabbed the phone off the seat. "This might take a little while," he said, facing them. "I'm going to help her try to track him down. You can go back and get some more food if you want."

Benny gazed at him groggily. "What about sleeping?"

"You ready for bed?"

He nodded.

"You need my help with it?"

Kaylie said, "We never washed anything, remember? From Benny's accident?"

"Oh, right. Okay, let me see." And Porter went into the camper, stripped Benny's bunk, and covered the cushions with fresh sheets. Then he remembered the splinters and dried blood—not to mention Jasper's armpit oil!—on his own sheets and decided to change those too. By the time he came out, it was dark, and Kaylie and Ben were heading toward the camper with their plates.

"Is that music going to be shut off soon?" Kaylie said, delivering him an icy glare as she stepped past him into the camper.

"I don't know," Porter said. "Are you going to sleep now too?"

She looked back through the doorway and said breezily, "No, I think I'm going to stay up awhile and write about today in my diary."

Porter hadn't known she'd planned to keep a diary of their trip. The thought cheered him. "Really?"

"No," Kaylie said. "Not really." And she disappeared inside.

Porter stood there a minute, trying to think of what to say to her, then stepped up into the camper. Benny was sitting on his bunk, untying his shoes. Kaylie was at the sink rinsing off their plates under the warm dribble of the kitchen faucet. "I'm sorry about having to leave," he said. "I just need to make a couple of calls for her. I need to call the guy I bought the camper from."

Kaylie kept rinsing, not looking at him.

"And then I'll come straight back, okay?"

She didn't say anything.

"Okay, Benny?"

Benny yawned and blinked hard. "All right."

"And then tomorrow we leave for Colorado, right?"

Kaylie turned to face him. "So that guy's really gonna fix the truck?"

"He better. We can't stay here forever."

"Aw, why not?" Kaylie said snottily. "It's so peaceful."

Porter grinned. "Okay, I know. So tonight's a little loud, with this concert and everything. But these people actually *are* about the most peaceful people you'll ever meet. They're completely nice."

"Well, Benny's a little scared of them. He thinks they're doing voodoo."

Porter laughed. "Voodoo?"

Benny gazed up sheepishly. "I'm not really scared. I was just wondering if they were putting hexes and stuff. You know, like when they're twirling their arms and everything?"

"They're just dancing, Benny. It's just how they dance. You know, like when you do square dancing in gym?"

Benny frowned.

"Do you want me to stay here, Benny?" Porter said, crouching next to him. "Are you really scared?"

"Not really," Benny said.

"Believe me, they're just having fun. They're happy people, not mean."

Kaylie turned off the kitchen faucet and looked around. "Don't worry, Benny," she said, wiping her hands on the dish towel. "I'll protect you." And then she pursed her lips and nodded encouragingly at him in the exact way Porter had seen Lucy do a thousand times before.

THE GRATEFUL DEAD had been meandering through an incongruous jam of banging drums and cymbals, and now someone (Jerry Garcia?) launched into an eerie guitar solo that made Porter think of the mating songs of whales. As he waited for the operator to find listings for Joe Hinchcliff, Delilah—rocking back and forth to the rhythmless noise— flashed him a smile and said, "This tape is great, isn't it?"

Porter nodded agreeably, then sat up at attention, pen to paper, as the operator came back with numbers for three J. Hinchcliffs. He jotted them down, pressed the keypad for a fresh connection, and dialed the first. Instantly a voice barked, "Hinchcliff here."

Startled, Porter said, "Joe? Joe Hinchcliff?"

"Yeah, who's this?"

"Joe Hinchcliff the used-car dealer?"

"Who's askin'?"

Now Porter recognized the voice. "Joe, sorry to bother you at home. I'm, uh . . . I'm the guy who bought a camper from you a few days ago. Porter Ellis. It was that purple camper. The one from the hippies?"

There was a silence at the other end of the line. Finally Joe said, "That vehicle was sold *as is,* you know."

"Oh, I know, I know," Porter said, raising his voice as a surge of thrumming bass guitar and crashing drums filled the air. "I just have a question about the previous owners," he shouted. "Those hippies!"

"Those what? Hey, turn down the music, why doncha? I can't hardly hear you."

"Hang on." Porter cupped his palm over the receiver and yelled to Delilah, "Can we go inside? He can't hear me."

Delilah pulled open the door of her tepee, and Porter strode in.

The inside was surprisingly neat and spartan, not at all what he'd imagined. There was a small metal cot done up smartly with white sheets and a gray wool blanket and a card table that was bare except for a pair of toy-soldier salt and pepper shakers. Laid across the middle of the floor as a rug was an orange beach towel. The four corners of the towel, Porter noticed, had been affixed to the cement floor with silver duct tape. A white fiberboard dresser stood awkwardly against the curved wall, on top of which was scattered jewelry and a couple of pictures: one of a smiling, bearded guy (Don?) and the other of an older, gray-haired woman (her mother?).

Delilah motioned him to the bed, then reached back through the doorway and started to drag in her beanbag chair.

"Joe?" he said, sitting down. "Is this better?"

"Yeah. What're you . . . at a bar or somethin'?"

"Sort of a concert, actually. But listen, Joe. I just have a question about the previous owners. You remember? Those hippies? Believe it or not, I ran into an old friend of theirs at this campground where we're staying. She recognized the camper. And she was wondering if you might have an address or anything for them. Maybe a phone number? She wants to get in touch."

Joe laughed. "Funny you should ask. They were just here yesterday."

"They were? They came back for it?" He nodded at Delilah, and she smiled expectantly, eyes wide.

"They couldn't believe it was gone," Joe went on. " 'Who would have bought it?' they kept asking me. And I kept tellin' them, 'This guy did. He's takin' his kids camping. And you know what? Now that I think of it, they actually wanted *your* phone number. Wanted to make you an offer, I guess."

"You're kidding." Porter cupped his hand over the mouthpiece and turned to Delilah. "Don and Stacey asked him for *my* phone number. They wanted to buy it back."

"So how's she driving anyway?" Joe roared.

"Not so good, I'm afraid. It was fine until we got here. Then the transmission gave out. It's shot. All the fluid's gone."

Joe was silent. "Aw . . ." he said. "Aw, man." Porter pictured him wiping at his broad forehead, maybe scratching at his crotch. "Porter, I'm real sorry about that. *Real* sorry. Hey, you must think I'm some sort of cheat."

"No," Porter protested. "Not at all."

"Well, I'm not," Joe said. His breathing was suddenly labored, as if he'd gotten up and was pacing the floor. There was the sound of cabinets opening and closing, water running, and then a tremendous sneeze *(WhAAAA-chOOO!)*, followed by three nose blows *(honk, honk, honk)*. "Uch," he said. " 'scuse me." Porter heard the clink of a glass and then the *glug, glug, glug* of swallowing. "Hey," Joe exclaimed suddenly. "You aren't the guy with the dead wife too, are you?"

"That's me."

"Aw, *phooey*!" Joe breathed in and out. "Oh, jeez . . . I feel like a real *turd*! You guys stuck out there with a broken-down vehicle I sold you?" More labored breathing. "Hey, tell me, Porter, where are you anyway? How far'd you get?"

"Central Indiana. Not too far from Bloomington. We're at a campground here."

"About a day's drive?"

"Yeah."

"Tell you what," Joe said. "You find a way to get that truck back here, and I'll replace that transmission for free. Just stick a new one right in there. Or whatever it takes. Okay?"

Porter thought a moment. "How am I supposed to get it back?"

"It just lost the fluid, right? It's not all seized up, is it?"

"How would I know?"

"Did you lose your speedometer when you were driving? Did it stop working?"

"Uh, no . . ." Porter said, trying to remember.

"Was it hard to shift? Feel like molasses?"

"No. Not at all."

Joe sniffed, then cleared his throat with several loud hacks. "Good. Good. I think you just lost your fluid. Okay . . . so, see if you can find someone around there. Any service station. I want you to tell them you need to make it to Pittsburgh and that the leak is okay as long as it's slow. Then I want you to buy, let's see, three or four pints of transmission fluid. Now, listen." He cleared his throat again. "When you're driving back, as soon as the shifting starts to get sluggish, you pull over, okay? You wait for the engine to cool down, then I want you to pour in a whole pint of fluid. Okay? You should be fine. When you get back to town, come straight here with it, all right? I'll have you on your way the next day."

"Really?" Porter said. "That's great."

"Least I could do. Hey, I feel *terrible*. I'd come fix it myself if you weren't so far away."

Porter glanced at Delilah, then remembered about Don and Stacey. "So I'll try to take you up on that," he said. "But also, do you happen to have anything on those kids who sold it? For this woman I met? She just wants to call them."

"Probably." He paused. "No, you know what? I just got an address for 'em. A place they're staying with their friends. Their friends don't have any phone, can you believe it? Welcome to the twenty-first century, you know? 'Cause I offered to call them if you happened to come back with the camper, and they said all they could give me was their friends' address. Oh, and now I remember, because I laughed and said, 'What, am I supposed to make a house call if he comes back with it?' And that cute girl smiles and says, all sincere, 'You could send us a postcard!' And I was like, 'Right. A friggin' postcard!' "

Porter laughed. "So do you have it? The address?"

Joe coughed, then cleared his throat. "Nah. Not at home. Got it in the office. But I'm not gonna be there till Thursday. I'm still fighting off this bug." He sniffed. "People don't like to buy a car from a sick man. That's rule numero uno."

"Okay, then," Porter said. "I'll get back to you on all this."

"Bring it on in," Joe said. "I'm telling you."

"Thanks. I'll try."

And they hung up.

Delilah sat forward. "So does he really have it? Their address?"

"At his office he does," Porter said. "But he's not going to be in until Thursday. He's sick."

"Well, that's okay," Delilah said, smiling. "Think you'll still be here then? Or should I call him back?"

Porter sighed. "Here's the thing. He felt really bad about the truck giving out on us. So he offered to replace our transmission if I can nurse it back there. And I might just take him up on it. I mean, chances are Jasper's not going to fix it any better than he did last time. And it would cost a fortune to have it replaced out here somewhere. Plus it would probably take just as long as it would to drive it back to Pittsburgh and have him do it right away. He said we'd be back on the road the next day."

Delilah pushed her fingers through her blond bangs and cupped her hands behind her head. She held herself that way for a moment, staring down, then released her hands, sat forward, and grinned up at him, pressing her palms together like a beggar. "I know you're going to say no to this," she began, "and you have every right to, but I'm going to ask you anyway, okay?"

Porter nodded.

"Take me with you to Pittsburgh. *Please?*"

Porter let out his breath and shook his head. "Seriously?"

"Then I can find Don and talk to him face to face. It's the only way. I was going to write a letter, but that wouldn't do any good. Besides, Stacey would probably intercept it."

Porter thought a moment. "So what are you . . . I mean, why do you think . . . ." He looked off, struggling to find a diplomatic way of putting it. "What makes you think he'll take you back?"

Delilah shrugged. "I doubt he will. And I'm not sure I want him to anyway."

"Then why do you want to go to all this trouble to see him?"

"Because I need to tell him something. There's something he needs to know. And if I don't see him there, I doubt I'm ever going to see him again in my life."

"What do you need to tell him?"

Delilah looked at him wearily. "It's the old story. The *oldest* story." She put her hand against her stomach and rubbed. "Guess what's in here."

Porter felt a stupid grin break across his face. "Really? You're pregnant?"

"Yep." She buried her face in her hands. "Six weeks, give or take."

They were silent. Despite Delilah's apparent gloom, Porter felt oddly happy. A baby. A cute, tiny Grateful Dead baby rocking away in her belly, grooving to Jerry's strumming in what he imagined to be Delilah's tie-dyed amniotic sac. Then a chill crept up his neck. "Are you going to keep it?"

She groaned. "Beats me. I guess. I'm thirty-six."

"So the time is right?"

"I wouldn't say that." Delilah twisted her hair in her fingers. "But I'm at an age where I could probably deal with it. I certainly wouldn't have much of an excuse to get rid of it. I mean, I'm not some clueless fifteen-year-old. And you know what else?" She looked at him, suddenly angry. "I'm getting so sick of all this *me, me, me* around here. Everyone's always so wrapped up in doing whatever they want at all times. And after a while it's just so *selfish,* don't you think? I don't want to be the focus of all my energy anymore. It wears me out."

"I know what you mean," Porter said, thinking of his brother and Chloe. Was that their problem? That they were too much the focus of their own energy? Nah, that wasn't really it. Their problem, it still seemed to Porter, was that they didn't have any problems. They led fake lives. "Well," he said happily, "a kid will wear you out too. Believe me."

"But that's different, isn't it? You're talking physically. I don't mind being worn out physically."

It's more than that, Porter thought, but he didn't want to preach. "So how are you feeling so far? Okay?"

"Fine." She smoothed the fringes of her skirt over her thighs. "I hardly feel anything. Not sick at all. Except I do feel a *presence* in there, you know? A soul. I feel like there's another soul in me."

"Lucy, my wife, she always felt so sick the first few months." He smiled, remembering. "She hated it. She never threw up, but she'd walk around spitting into sinks and toilets, wherever she could. In fact, she was six months pregnant with Kaylie when we got married. It was scandalous. Her parents were so embarrassed."

Delilah made a face of mock astonishment. "You think *ya'll* were scandalous. My parents are way beyond embarrassment when it comes to me." She pushed herself up out of the beanbag chair, grabbed the picture of the gray-haired woman from her dresser, and handed it to Porter. "That's my mother," Delilah said, sitting down next to him on the small bed. "She's pretty much disowned me. When I was twenty-one, I had an abortion—didn't even think twice about it, you know. I wasn't with the guy anymore, and I wanted to have *fun*! I wanted to *do* things. But my mother hated me for it. It was like I ripped her heart out."

Porter looked at the woman in the picture. She appeared pleasant enough—slitty eyes like Delilah's over a small, worried smile. "She's antiabortion?"

"That's the *thing*," Delilah exclaimed. "She's *not*. They live in Austin, and she's this big liberal. Both my parents are. So I actually *told* her about it, thinking she'd support me. But instead she just hated me for it. She cried and cried. I don't know; it must have had to do with my sister or something. I think even *she* was surprised by how she reacted. Like it was fine in the abstract, abortion, but when she started picturing her little grandkid thrown out with the trash . . . I don't know . . . she just flipped."

Porter handed her back the picture. "So you're not in touch with them anymore?"

"For a long time I still talked to them a couple of times a year. I at least made an effort, and so did my mom. But we've hardly spoken at all since I met Don and started traveling." Suddenly her face filled with longing. "I mean, I loved Don! And I loved traveling around! But my parents thought I was wasting my life. They think you have to suffer for your life to be meaningful. You can't just have fun. Life is *serious*! They used to say that all the time. I swear, my whole childhood was like that. And you know what the scariest thing is? Now *I'm* starting to think that way! I'm turning into my mother! Sometimes I look at everybody here, all these people just vegging out, not harming anyone, and I start feeling all pissy and want to say, *Get a job! Get a life!*"

Porter smiled and shook his head. "I always think people like that are going to pay for it somehow. Like you can't just blow off everything and not pay for it. I'm one of those justice types. Or that other principle—what's it called? Where every action causes an equal but opposite reaction? Something like that? The older I get, the more I hear myself saying all those things my father used to say, like, 'If it sounds too good to be true, it probably is.' I mean, I look at people who've won the lottery, and right away I think, *Oh, well. Their lives are fucked.* Because I believe, deep down, that the equivalent amount of luck it took them to win the lottery is going to now have to come back to them as bad luck. And you know what? It usually works out that way. Their friends and relatives all come to hate them, and they go crazy trying to manage all that money, and then they end up blowing their brains out."

Delilah laughed, tipping her shoulder into his.

"But as much as I say stuff like that," he went on, "I really would like to see those rules just blown to hell sometime. I'd like to see someone win the lottery and never have anything bad happen to them from that point on."

"Well," Delilah said, "then it would just mean that they'd had a shitty life up to that point, right? And that nothing bad happening after winning the lottery was to equal out that long shitty part?"

"But say there wasn't a shitty part before either. It was just normal, everyday life—not out of balance one way or the other. Then, after the lottery, everything was fantastic."

She looked at him. "I think the lottery is a bad example. People who play the lottery are such morons in the first place. It's hard for me to think of a moron's life as being fantastic no matter how much money or good luck he has."

Porter grinned. "I guess." He gazed up into the tip of the tepee, which was sealed off about twenty feet up by a ceiling panel the size of a bicycle tire. He briefly wondered what was in the cone above the panel. A secret storage area? A little water tank? "I just wish," he said, still staring up, "that Lucy had gotten something good in exchange for what she had to go through." He turned to Delilah. "I mean, she went through total hell and got nothing for it. Zippo."

"Well, that's because she probably passed it on to ya'll, that good thing she was owed." Delilah smiled, her eyes almost disappearing in the crinkles of her cheeks. "Ya'll are going to get it, you and your kids. You'll see."

Porter felt a warm, melting feeling at the base of his throat. "You think?"

Delilah nodded and then leaned against him, slipping her arms around his waist. She gave him a gentle squeeze.

Porter didn't move. He felt his breathing go shallow.

Finally Delilah said, "You're so tense."

"Really?" Porter said. "I don't feel tense." And, as if to prove it, he draped his arm stiffly around her shoulders. And this is how they were holding each other when the cell phone rang, bleating against the surface of the card table.

"Oh, God," Delilah exclaimed, laughing, then withdrew herself and flopped back on the bed.

Porter reached for the phone and flipped it open. "Hello?"

"Hey! I got you finally!"

"Alex?"

"I've been trying this number for two days," Alex said. "I was thinking I'd gotten it wrong."

"I had it turned off for a while. To keep Claire from calling."

"Good. I'm proud of you." Alex crunched down on something. A carrot? "So where are you anyway? Kansas? Missouri?"

"Indiana."

Crunch, crunch, crunch. "No, really? That's all?"

"That's all."

"Well, tell me about it. At least the basics. Plus, I've got a story about Mom and Dad that you're gonna love. They called me Sunday night. I've been trying to reach you ever since."

Porter looked over at Delilah, trying to affect an apologetic smirk. *My brother,* he mouthed. She waved him off and turned herself onto her side so that her stomach was against his back, her knees drawn up around him. "Our trip?" he said to Alex. "We're grounded. The transmission blew out on that truck after our first day."

Alex gasped. "Bummer! So where are you staying?"

"We're camping. It's fine."

Crunch, crunch. "So how're you going to get it fixed?"

"This guy's working on it. A local guy. We should be on our way again soon. By tomorrow, probably."

"Well, that's good. So you want to hear this story about Mom and Dad?"

"Yeah, I guess."

"Porter, you're not gonna believe it. But anyway. They called Sunday night, right? And I told them about you buying that camper, you know, and how you were taking off for Colorado with Kaylie and Ben. And Dad got all excited, thinking back to when we were kids, I guess, and how he used to drive us all over the country? So he says to Mom— she was on the other phone—and he says to her, 'Well, we ought to go on up there and meet them. Get out of this bullshit place and away from all these bullshit people for a while.' And Mom sort of hems and haws but then comes around like she always does. So anyway, the short of it is that they already took off this morning. They'll probably get to Rocky Mountain National Park before you do."

Porter was almost too stunned to speak. "But how are they going to find us?"

Alex laughed. "They told me to arrange it. I said I could call you. I'm like the—what's it called?—the dispatcher. I'm supposed to track down both parties and arrange a meeting place and time."

Porter pushed his fingers through his hair. "You know what, Alex? This isn't such a good idea. I don't know when we're going to make it out there. I don't know when this transmission is going to be fixed."

"I wouldn't sweat it." *Crunch, crunch*. "If they get there earlier, they'll just hang out. They'll be so happy to be out of Thatcher they won't care how long it takes you."

Porter sighed. "Alex. The fact of the matter is, we're heading back to Pittsburgh first. And then I don't know where we're going after that."

There was a small, hesitant *crunch*. "What do you mean, you're going back to Pittsburgh?"

"The guy I bought the truck from. He said he'll replace the transmission for free. And it's just that after we go all the way back there, I'm not sure we're going to have enough time to drive across the country again."

"Oh, *c'mon*," Alex said. "You've got enough time to do whatever you want. Don't be a martyr about this. Enough with being a martyr. Take the kids out there. Do it for them. Fuck work."

Porter almost laughed. His job was the farthest thing from his mind. In fact, at that moment, it seemed inconceivable to him that he'd spent most of his life for the past decade perched in front of a computer screen in that stuffy, windowless box of an office. "It's not about work," he said. He looked at Delilah, who lay behind him with her hands under her head, eyes open, listening. "It's about something else."

"What, then? What else?"

"It's a favor I'm going to do for someone."

Delilah's eyes flicked up and met his. She smiled.

"Favor for who?"

"Someone."

"*Who?*" Alex huffed.

Porter didn't say anything.

"Hey, why are you being so coy, huh? What's the deal? You know, Mom and Dad have already left. All I'm supposed to do is leave a message for them at the ranger station, telling them where to meet you. There's no turning them back now.''

"Well, I can't turn back either," Porter said. "I already left too."

"But I thought you *were* turning back. That's what you just said."

Porter took a long breath and let it out. "You know what, Alex? I'm too tired to talk about this anymore tonight. I'll call you later."

"Wait," Alex said. "What message should I leave them? At the ranger station?"

"I don't know," Porter said. "Make something up. You're the one who invited them."

"*I* didn't invite them. They invited themselves."

"Right," Porter said. "You're just the dispatcher."

Alex exhaled into the phone.

"I'm sorry, Alex," Porter continued. "But I don't feel responsible for this situation. I don't."

Another long silence. Finally Alex said, "What is that noise anyway? Where are you?"

"You mean the music?"

"Is that what it is?"

Porter grinned. "It's the Grateful Dead, circa 1976. There's sort of a concert going on here. I happen to be listening from inside of a fiberglass tepee, so the sound is a little muffled."

No response. The line hummed and crackled, transmitting Alex's stewing displeasure all the way out into space and back. Finally he said, "Are you okay, Porter? Is everyone there all right?"

"We're fine."

"Kaylie and Ben are with you?"

"No, they're sleeping. Back in the camper."

"And you're in an Indian tepee? By yourself?"

Porter sighed. "No."

"Wait, let me guess," Alex said caustically. "You're with *someone*, right? This *someone* you're going to do a mysterious favor for?"

Porter didn't have the energy to explain himself. Besides, why did Alex even deserve an explanation? All he'd done was gleefully arrange with their parents to ruin Porter's trip and then call him up to rub his nose in it. "Alex," Porter said, "I have a question for you. Is there a character in your novel who's just like me?"

"Uh," Alex stammered, "not really."

"There's not a character whose wife gets breast cancer and dies?"

Alex paused. "Well, actually there is, yeah. But he's not you. This guy lives in Cincinnati and his name is Phil. Plus, he smokes a pipe. He's nothing like you."

"Whatever," Porter said. "So what does this guy Phil do after his wife dies? What is he looking for? What does he *want*?"

"What does that have to do with anything?"

"I'm interested," Porter said casually. "Believe it or not, I happen to be in the same situation myself."

Alex cleared his throat. "Well, you know . . . it's just that . . . it's really too hard to talk about my writing that way. Anything I'd say would be an oversimplification."

Porter smiled. "*Exactly*. That's what I say too." And with that he lowered the phone and turned it off.

CHAPTER EIGHT

DELILAH sat up on her elbows. "Your brother wrote a book about you?"

So Porter launched into the whole story of Alex and Chloe, starting with his suspicions about *Lifetime Moon* and what crap it was that his brother had stolen his life like that. Then he ranted on about their "carefree" existence in New York, where they only had to worry about themselves and couldn't care less about "society at large." He felt small and catty to be trashing Alex and Chloe this way, to a relative stranger, but he couldn't stop himself. "The main problem is they've never really grown up," he said with a huff. "It's like they're avoiding real life or something."

Delilah squinted. "Avoiding real life? What's real life?"

"You know. Taking responsibility. Rolling with the punches. That sort of thing."

"I don't get it. How have they not taken responsibility?"

Porter shook his head. "How? Well . . . uh . . . lots of ways. I mean . . ." but his mind was blank. He almost started to say something about how they had no plans to marry or have kids, but what did that prove, and how ridiculous would he look saying such a thing? He could feel a dim anger begin to pulse in the back of his head. "Well, for one, they don't even have health insurance." He was looking away, speaking into the middle of the tepee. "I mean, what if they were to get pneumonia or fall in front of a subway or something? Could you imagine the medical bills? And who would pick up the tab? Not them. And not our parents, that's for sure—they're on a fixed income. So would it fall on me? Would it take food out of the mouths of *my* children to pay for *their* lack of responsibility?" He turned to Delilah, his face flushed. "Or would society have to pay for it? Just dribble away everyone's tax dollars?"

Delilah drew her knees up to her chest and wrapped her arms around them. "Sounds like I touched a raw nerve."

"It's not a raw nerve," Porter bellowed on. "It's about how society operates and how it depends upon personal responsibility. I mean, who wouldn't want to have someone else pay for their health-care costs? Who wouldn't? But a successful society just can't function that way. Look at places like Russia. Look at how everything fell apart there."

"But that was about more than health care, I think."

Porter let out his breath, exasperated. "I'm not talking *only* about health care. I'm talking about the *big picture*! I'm talking about *personal responsibility*!"

A grin spread across Delilah's face. "I swear, you are so afraid of everything!" She put a hand on his knee and gave it a little push. "You've got to stop being so afraid!"

He regarded her. "Afraid?"

"Tell me. When was the last time you took a real risk? Really jumped off a cliff?"

He shrugged defensively. "What do you mean?"

"Just went for something. Threw caution to the wind."

Porter looked at the palms of his hands. "How about going on this trip? Does that count?"

"I don't know," she said. "Does it?"

"I don't know."

She rolled her eyes. "Well, is it a risk?"

"You mean like physically risky? Like dangerous?"

"Whatever. You have to define it. But a real risk has got to have potential gains and losses. You have to be fully exposed. Has this trip fully exposed you?"

"To what?"

"*Grrr* . . ." Delilah said, baring her teeth. "You're like a stone wall. Hello! What did I just say. Exposed you to the possibility of *gains and losses?*"

Suddenly Porter felt as if he were back in that office with Carole Levine, being pressed to reveal his "fantasies." So is this what he was in for all the way to Pittsburgh? One long therapy session about his feelings and vulnerabilities? And what was it about him anyway that always seemed to attract this level of unsolicited analysis? Why couldn't he take his kids on a camping trip to fucking Rocky Mountain National Park and have it be just that? A fun time? A fucking vacation? Why did he have to be stalked by his in-laws every step of the way, tethered to their goddamn cell phone? And why must he constantly be subjected to the condescending snipes and machinations of his happy little brother from a thousand miles away? And what about his parents, breaking camp in Thatcher on a moment's notice, hauling ass up to Colorado and awaiting Porter's arrival like some nightmarish welcome wagon? Did the whole country have to mobilize itself to thwart his simple camping trip?

And now this. Okay, so he liked Delilah. She'd been really nice to them. He liked talking to her. But did that give her carte blanche to go snorting across his emotional landscape like some truffle hog?

Dancing around the edges of his anger, however, was the feeling that Delilah was right. He *was* afraid of taking risks. Of course he was. After all, who was going to jump off a cliff when you had two kids clinging on to you for dear life?

Then an image of Alan Weiner popped into his mind. Alan Weiner was the adjunct professor who had led Porter's senior painting workshop at Carnegie Mellon. Porter thought the guy basically knew his stuff, but the students didn't respect him. Part of the problem had been his buglike stature—he skittered around the room like a bipedal roach in his shell of a black coat, worn shiny from overuse. And if you turned too quickly in his direction, he'd shrink back—some primitive insect survival instinct. But the larger issue was his admission that he had essentially stopped painting, years before, because his life had simply grown "too hectic."

Porter was the only student in the workshop who wasn't openly hostile to Weiner. He actually liked the guy, though he hadn't held him up as an idol or even as much of a mentor. Porter's real idol, he was embarrassed to admit (even to himself), had been Bruce Springsteen. Privately he'd fancied himself as the emerging Springsteen of the art world. God knows the painting world needed a Bruce Springsteen to cut through all the elitist crap and reveal what a pure struggle life was for most working people out there—the meat-and-potatoes stuff artists used to care about but didn't seem to bother with anymore. No wonder the average person didn't give two shits about going to art galleries or museums. Nothing inside spoke to them. It all had to be explained, and even then the explanations wouldn't make any sense unless you'd studied cubism and feminism and postmodernism and had read Kant and Freud and Kierkegaard and had memorized the complete history of all the world's religions.

Porter didn't want to come across as an anti-intellectual, but he had to admit that he hadn't the faintest idea what most of his fellow students were trying to do. Much of their work just seemed like laziness to him: multimedia kindergarten gunk with yarn and glue, or else monochromatic shapes that were supposed to . . . *what? break your heart?*

Porter's paintings were mostly of dingy buildings and urban streets, factories and blue-collar workers—the whole sagging postindustrial age and its related human suffering. In workshop, his paintings were generally received with glazed eyes and stifled yawns. But Alan Weiner always praised Porter's work and on several occasions— much to the spitting horror of the rest of the class—had even singled him out for prizes.

Just before graduation, Weiner had invited Porter into his office and droned on for twenty minutes about Porter's strengths and weaknesses, ruminating about his "career" and "potential." Then Weiner leaned across the desk and pointed a finger at him. "But, Porter," he said, "don't let yourself get sucked out into the sea of mediocrity. You've got talent, but talent isn't going to get you anywhere unless you have real persistence, real staying power."

As far as Porter could tell, if anyone had been sucked out into the sea of mediocrity, it was Alan Weiner, who'd been treading water for ten years already teaching three classes as an adjunct and supplementing those slave wages with part-time secretarial work. By his own admission, the man hadn't painted so much as a spin-art in more than four years. He had a wife and three young boys to support, and Porter imagined the entirety of Alan Weiner's life to be that of a mother bird flying back to the nest, dropping worms into the open mouths, and then desperately flying off to find more.

If your advice is so good, Porter felt like asking him, *how come you didn't follow it?*

But most of his professors had been like that, a bunch of disillusioned dreamers all eager to lecture you about how to steer clear of the dead end they'd wound up in.

It was eight years before Porter saw Weiner again. He'd taken Kaylie and Ben, who were just seven and three at the time, to the

Allegheny County Fair. They'd spent the morning strolling among oversize vegetables and clean-scrubbed pigs and had finally settled in at the main stage, where a gymnastics troupe of chunky girls was demonstrating tumbling routines.

The girls looked perfectly happy, all smiles and ponytails and little nervous waves to the audience. Yet Porter couldn't help but feel sorry for them, crammed into those smudged leotards, their graceless bodies hurtling through the air in a series of low dives and handless flips. Nearly every third flip wouldn't end well, and the girl would plummet to the mat with a loud *smack*, eliciting grins and giggles from the audience.

All that practice, only to be laughed at, Porter was thinking. Then he felt a tap on his shoulder, and there stood Alan Weiner. Porter smiled dumbly. "Professor . . . ?"

Weiner nodded. "Porter Ellis, right?"

Porter reached out his hand, and they shook.

Weiner stared at him, mouth agape. "You know, most students, you can't even remember their faces a week after class ends. But you. I always wondered what became of you."

Porter laughed. "Not a whole lot." Then he put his hands on his kids' shoulders and turned them around. "Actually, these two happened to me. This is Kaylie, and this is Ben." He lowered himself between them. "Guys," he said, looking up, "this is Professor Weiner. He used to teach me about painting."

"Oh, *you* used to teach *me*," Weiner said. "I loved your work." He glanced behind himself, where his three sons stood. "You remember my little boys?" he said, jerking his thumb back. "They're not so little anymore."

The apocalyptic trio glowered at Porter. They were all huge— nearly a foot taller than their father—and beefy, flushed. Their hair had been hacked at, shaved into angled designs. The tallest had a silver chain and cross dangling from his right nostril.

"So," Weiner said, "how's your work going? Are you working?"

"Working?" Porter stood up. "Yeah. Oh, it's going fine. I'm a graphic designer. It's a firm over by the . . . the—"

"No," Weiner interrupted. "I mean painting. Are you doing any painting?"

Porter felt a surprising shame rise in his face. "Nah, not really. It's hard to find the time, you know? With the kids and everything."

"I know," Weiner said. "Believe me, no one knows that more than I do."

"Yeah, well. That's what happens, I guess. Your priorities change."

Weiner beamed. "But they can always change back." He held out his hands, and Porter saw that they were flecked with orange and blue, the fingernails coated with chipped enamels. "I've been at it full-time for about five months now. God, it's all crap. But I'm having a ball. I don't even sleep at night."

Porter looked Weiner up and down. The man appeared physically ravaged. His pants hung on him. But his eyes were alive, burning. "So you quit your job?"

"Quit everything. All my classes. My temp jobs."

"What about money?"

Weiner shrugged. "I managed to save a little. We'll see how long it lasts. My wife picked up some hours at the library, so at least we've got that coming in. And who knows? Maybe I'll sell something!"

Sell something? Porter grinned derisively, shaking his head. All he could think was what a selfish fool Alan Weiner was, tossing his family's security down the toilet so that he could jerk off with his "art" all day and night. How long did he think he was going to get away with that? Sooner or later, those three boys would make him pay for it. They weren't going to stand for a father who wouldn't provide for them. Why should they?

That night, however, after Kaylie and Ben had gone to bed, Porter got out his old stuff—his easel and brushes and a blank canvas. He even managed to find some paint that hadn't dried up. "I just want to see what I've got here," he finally said to Lucy, who'd been watching him curiously from the kitchen table.

Porter set himself up in the living room, just out of Lucy's view, and picked up a brush. And there he sat, for nearly an hour, feeling more worthless and hollow than he'd felt in his entire life. Finally he packed it all up and went to bed, grimly comforted by the thought that he would spend the rest of his days cranking out brochures for the Three Rivers Youth Chorus and the Montvale Marching Band and get paid the same no matter what.

So how had Weiner done it? How had he decided that he was going to take the road less traveled and do whatever the hell he wanted, regardless of who he hurt or neglected or left behind in the process?

Porter looked at Delilah with a grin. "You know what? I don't think I want to be fully exposed just yet. In fact, how about if I let your friend Uncle Charlie be fully exposed on my behalf?"

Delilah laughed. "I already saw him down by the beach tonight. He asked me who you were, and he couldn't believe the story about ya'll buying Don's camper and coming here with it." She rolled her head sideways in the pillow and gazed at the tepee wall. "Uncle Charlie really liked Don. Those two were like Frick and Frack, cracking up over the same stupid jokes. I think he was as hurt by Don taking off as I was. Charlie thinks that if Don had known I was pregnant, he wouldn't have left. Or maybe he was just saying that to make me feel good. But who gives a shit? I wouldn't want him staying with me just because I'm pregnant anyway. I mean, what good does that do me?"

There was a tentative knock at the door, and then Kaylie's whispering voice: "Dad? Are you in there?"

Porter froze.

Delilah said, "Yeah, Kaylie. Come on in."

The door came open a crack, and Kaylie stuck her head in.

Porter felt a mortified smile spread across his face. "Hi, sweetie," he said. "You're not asleep?"

Kaylie stepped into the tepee, closing the door gently behind her. The cuffs of her pajama bottoms were wet with dew, and her bare feet glistened. Her tiny toenails still bore remnants of the red polish Lucy had applied during one of their last family visits to the hospital more than a month before. Kaylie did a quick survey of the tepee's interior, and Porter could almost see her little brain processing the scene, evaluating, trying to piece together the plot of what had happened before her arrival. Finally she settled an accusing gaze on Porter. "What are you still doing here?"

Porter rose to his feet. "Oh . . . uh . . . we're just trying to figure out about the trip back, that's all. Just how to go about it, you know . . ."

"The trip back where?"

"To Pittsburgh."

Kaylie stared at him.

"Oh . . . I guess you don't know about that yet, do you? Um . . . well . . ." Porter suddenly wanted to hold the floor to keep Delilah from blurting out that she was coming too. "It's the transmission, you know. To get it fixed, it turns out we've got to take it back to the dealer."

"So we're going all the way back?"

Porter nodded. "I . . . yeah . . . the guy . . ."

"And I'm coming too," Delilah said, all smiles.

Kaylie's mouth dropped open. "She *is*?"

"Ya'll are going to give me a ride so I can find my friends," Delilah said. "It's just because we're headed to the same place. But, you know, I could always take the—"

But Kaylie had spun around and was already outside, the screen door slamming behind her with a *whap*.

Porter cast a helpless glance in Delilah's direction.

"I'm sorry," she said, smiling weakly. "I really should've kept my mouth shut. I'm so bad at that sometimes."

Porter started for the door. "Don't worry about it."

"Hey, you forgot this," Delilah said, holding out the cell phone. "You want it?"

Porter grabbed the phone and pushed it into his back pocket, then stepped out into the darkness. The Dead music was still blaring away, echoing across the valley, and there was the low buzz of voices all around, but the floodlights that had illuminated the food tables and the beach area had been extinguished. As Porter's eyes adjusted, he began to make out shapes of people silhouetted against the moonlit lake—a mellow, swaying mass. The air smelled of cigarettes and pot and spilled beer.

He saw Kaylie beating a path across the field, her arms swinging stiffly at her sides. "Kaylie!" he called out, but she didn't even look back.

Porter entered the field and started through the tall grass. When Kaylie entered the clearing of their campsite, Porter called out her name again, and this time she spun around to face him, her hands clamped against her hips.

"Wait up, will you?" He jogged a few yards, then bobbed and weaved his way through the trees and brush that divided their campsite from the field. "Kaylie, let me explain." He was breathing heavily from the fast walk and had to pause to catch his breath.

"Are you already in love with her, Dad?" Kaylie said without missing a beat. *"Already?"*

Porter stood up straight. "No! . . . I . . . what do you mean? How can you ask me something like that?"

"Then why is she coming with us?"

"Because, you want to know why? Because she needs a ride to Pittsburgh, that's why. And we're already going there, okay?"

Kaylie looked down at the ground. She was standing among the sticks of Benny's ripped-apart castle. "But I don't *want* her to come."

Porter felt a flash of irritation. "Well, that's not a very nice thing to say. After how good she was to you and Benny today, finding that stuff for you to swim with and everything?"

No response.

Porter drew in a deep breath and let it out. "Kaylie, look at me, will you?"

She turned a half step farther away, hunching her shoulders against him.

Porter moved forward and reached for her arm, but she spun out of his grasp, dashed for the camper door, and disappeared inside.

"Kaylie!" he called out, but the door slapped shut and then he heard the click of the lock.

Damn it! He went over to the door and tried to turn the knob. Then he stepped away and circled around to the cab just in time to see Kaylie's feet slipping back through the boot. He pulled on the door handle. Yep, she'd just locked the cab doors too. "Kaylie! Hey!"

He stood on his tiptoes at the kitchen window and tried to peer in, but it was pure darkness inside. He couldn't even tell if the glass slats were tilted open or not. "Benny!" he whispered loudly. "Hello? Benny? You up?" He could pound on the door, but he didn't want to have his boy wake up petrified. *Again.*

"Kaylie. Where am I supposed to sleep?"

"With *her*!" Kaylie yelled. Then, softly, she added, "Just go away, Daddy. Just . . ." and her breath caught, and she sniffed, emitting a squeaky whimper.

Okay, Porter thought. *Okay. Don't push it.* He went over to the picnic table, sat down with a huff, and promptly felt the crack of plastic under his left butt cheek. *Oh, that's fucking great.* He stood up, pulled the cell phone from his pocket, and examined the split down the side that ran the entire length of the piece of shit. He pressed "ON," and the keypad sprang reassuringly to life. Then he tried "OFF," and nothing happened. He pressed it again. Nada. He pressed it so hard the tip of his finger turned white. Zippo.

Porter reared back and hurled the thing into the trees, where it did a few harmless tumbles before coming to rest in a bed of pine needles. And there it sat, the green pad glowing back at him like a dare.

He turned away and once again faced the camper. So now what? How was he ever going to get the hell in there? He put his hands on his hips and took a deep breath. *Okay,* he thought. *Just think. What could I use to open it? A hairpin?* And before he could think this through any further, he heard the lock click again, and the door opened a crack. In the sliver of moonlight he saw half of Kaylie's face peering out at him.

Porter didn't say anything. He felt as if he were dealing with a wary rabbit—just the slightest twitch might send her scurrying back into her hole. Finally he said, "So are you going to let me in?"

The door opened a little more, revealing Kaylie's whole face, her blond hair looking steely in the moonlight. "I guess."

Porter started over to her. "I'm sorry about the whole thing with Delilah," he said as he approached. "But she's really just getting a ride with us so she can meet up with her old boyfriend. That's all it is."

Kaylie retreated, disappearing in the shadows.

"In fact, she's even pregnant." Porter gave a quiet laugh. "Can you believe that?"

"She is?" Kaylie said, her face emerging once again.

"Yep. Just a few weeks."

"And that's why she wants to go there?"

Porter nodded. "That's why."

Kaylie considered this. "So we're really going back home tomorrow?"

"I hope so. I hope Jasper can get us on the road first thing in the morning. I talked to the guy who sold us the camper, and he said all we need to do is keep fluid in the transmission the whole way back. He didn't even seem to think we needed to get it completely fixed just to get back there."

"Really?" Kaylie said. She was trying her best to stay at least semi-pissed-off at him, but her eyes were suddenly droopy. "Well, whatever."

"C'mon," Porter said with a smile. "Let's go to bed. It's going to be another long trip tomorrow."

Inside, Porter got Kaylie arranged in her bunk and even managed to wrangle a reluctant hug and a kiss out of her. Within five minutes she was snoozing away.

Porter sat down and started to take off his boots, but then he thought of something—Jasper was still planning to go to town in the morning to buy parts for the transmission. *Great.* That's all this situation needed: Jasper blowing a few hundred dollars on unnecessary car parts and then spending the next two days clanking around under the truck's chassis.

Porter stood up and looked out the kitchen window. There was a faint glow in Jasper's yellow tent. Maybe he'd ended his night early and was already over there?

Porter laced his boots back up and stepped out into the night, closing the camper door behind him. He set off for Jasper's tent, the gravel crunching under his feet. He turned off the road and lightened his step as he approached the yellow tent. A twig cracked loudly underneath his foot, and inside the tent a shadow moved—somebody sitting up. Porter froze. The shadow got its legs underneath itself, moved to the entrance flap, and out popped Jasper's greasy-haired head. Porter sighed with relief.

"Who's out there?" Jasper called.

"It's me. Porter."

"Who?"

"Porter. The guy with the kids."

"Oh, man." Jasper stepped out onto the porch. He was wearing the same overalls he'd had on earlier. He slept in them? And something was dangling from his hand. A headband? "You scared the fuck out of me, man. Where are you?"

"Over here." Porter stepped toward the tent and into the light of the porch.

"What the fuck are you prowling around out here for? I thought it was the cops."

"Sorry."

"I could've shot you, man."

Porter swallowed. "You've got a gun?"

"Wrist rocket," Jasper said, holding it out. "Just as fucking deadly, man."

"You'd really shoot a cop with that?"

"No! Are you kidding me? I'd be in prison for life!"

So who would you shoot? Porter wanted to ask. But instead he said, "Hey, I'm sorry for startling you. Really. I didn't know you were sleeping. It's just . . . I wanted to tell you about the transmission."

"What about it?" Jasper said.

Porter briefly recounted his conversation with Joe Hinchcliff. "And so," he said, wrapping it up, "I think maybe all we need is some pints of transmission fluid and we could be on our way."

"And he's gonna fix it for you? The used car dealer?"

Porter nodded.

"I could do a good job on it, man. I don't know if you want to be out on the highway with it leaking like that."

"But the dealer said if it's just a small leak we'll be fine. As long as we keep checking it."

Jasper shook his head dismissively. "All right, man. It's your life." He paused. "So you just want me to get you some fluid in the morning? That's all?"

Porter smiled. "Yeah, that'd be great."

They looked at each other through the screen in awkward silence.

"So thanks again," Porter said.

"No problem."

"So, then, we'll talk tomorrow?"

"Yeah, whatever."

"Okay, great," Porter said, and then he just stood there, smiling dumbly, feeling like he should say something to alleviate Jasper's evident disappointment in him. But what?

Finally Jasper said, "So you want to come in? Take a little toke on my peace pipe?"

"Oh, I better not. I've gotta get to bed."

"No, really," Jasper said. "I mean it." He reached for the screen door and started to unzip it. "But I gotta warn you, man, this place is a little stanky."

Porter was about to protest more, but he didn't want come off as some yuppie candy-ass who was too afraid to set foot in Jasper's tent. He shrugged his shoulders and stepped inside.

"As you can see," Jasper said, "we've got enough pot in this place to sink a ship."

Porter gazed to his right and left in dropped-jaw silence. There were bales—*bales!*—of marijuana leaves stacked against the sides of the tent. "This is all pot?" he said. "You guys smoke all of this?"

"That's the official party line," Jasper said, grinning. "It's all for personal, recreational use. No, actually it's for medicinal use only," he added with a wink. "Most people here are pretty sick puppies. They need this shit to ease their pain."

Porter smiled.

"So what do you say? A little smoke?"

"Oh, I'd like to," Porter said. "But my kids are asleep back at the camper and I—"

"Man, c'mon," Jasper said. "You're the one who fucking woke me up. Now I've gotta nurse myself back to sleep, okay? The least you could do is partake of one joint with me."

Porter grinned gamely. "All right. Maybe just one. And then I've really got to go."

"There's the spirit," Jasper said.

"You know," Porter said with a laugh, "I haven't smoked a joint in years. But back in college I used to smoke all the time. I was like this artist type, a painter, and smoking pot was like drinking coffee for my crowd."

Jasper was rummaging in his pockets. "No shit?" He pulled out a lighter and then a joint the size of a Magic Marker. "You're an artist?"

"Not so much anymore. Gotta pay the bills, right?"

"Nah, fuck that," Jasper said. He gestured at the floor, which was not the floor of the tent as Porter had expected but just hard-worn dirt. "Here, have a seat." Mounds of trash and clothes were scattered here and there: milk cartons, bottles, cereal boxes, underwear.

The two of them squatted on the ground. Jasper put the joint between his lips, flicked the lighter at it, then sucked a few times until the end flared up. "Nah," he said as slips of smoke drifted from his lips, "you don't need that. There's families here. Kids all over the place doing just fine. People just doing whatever the hell they want to do. Whatever *they* want. And there's no harm being done. People sharing the wealth. Living off the bounty. Living in peace. Nope, you don't have to buy into that whole crock of shit if you don't want to. *Bills.* What're they? There's no bills here. Everything's free, practically. And we work, you know, to keep the place up. We have skills. I could make some serious fucking money as a mechanic if I wanted to. If I wanted to spend my life taking money from people. But that's a disease, man. That's a sickness."

Jasper took another hit and then passed the joint to Porter. "Watch it, man," he said. "This stuff is *potent.* It's a special blend."

Porter sucked in, felt the burn all the way down to his gut, and almost hacked it right back up. But he held steady, then let it out slowly, controlled. Hey, he hadn't lost his touch with this. And almost immediately his head began to soar. *Whoa.* Un-fucking-believable. He felt a shiver in his brain, and his hair went cold. His eyes turned to glass. He took another long hit and felt his mouth expand into what felt like the goofiest smile he'd worn in years.

Jasper grinned. "Welcome to Howdy Doody Land, am I right?"

Porter breathed in and out, trying to collect the scattered bits of himself, then brought the joint up to his lips again. Sucked hard. *God.* That taste. That scorched taste. He felt a pulse in his groin and saw a vision of Lucy. That leather couch in the Winters' cabana. Her little white tennis outfit and those smooth, smooth legs. He looked at Jasper. "What's in this? There something in this?"

"Special blend, man! I told you."

"Of what?"

Jasper shrugged. "Different shit."

Is it dangerous? Porter wanted to ask. But if Jasper did it all the time, well . . . not that Jasper was the picture of mental health, but at least he wasn't dead, was he? What the hell. Porter brought the joint up for one more hit, but this time Jasper reached out and snatched it from his fingers. "Hey, brother. You better take it easy. You're already looking a little starched."

"Rightee-o," Porter heard himself say.

Jasper took his hit, held it in his lungs for what seemed like minutes, then breathed out a long white column of smoke. He seemed completely unfazed. "So what's your job?"

Porter wiped at his face and blinked. "Graphic designer. I make posters and stuff. Brochures and stuff. For concerts, you know, and stuff."

Jasper drew back with a smile. "No shit? For concerts? That's a higher calling, man. Did you ever do any of that for the Dead?"

"Nope. Mostly classical music. All around Pittsburgh. Classical-music festivals and the like."

"Sounds like a noble enterprise."

"I don't know about that. It's just selling. I'm a two-bit huckster." Suddenly the word "huckster" sounded hilarious to Porter, and he had to press his lips shut to keep himself from laughing.

"But at least you're selling something worthwhile, right? You're bringing music to the people." Jasper held out the joint. "Hey, you want some more now? You look like you can handle it again."

Porter took the joint and this time just sucked in a short, cautious drag. But it still sent him flying. "I used to think like that. I thought, well, it's okay because I'm pushing something of value, you know, to society. I even used to think I was sacrificing my own art to help promote other people's art. Like I was some martyr." He paused and took another puff. "But that's all just one big rationalization. Because the truth is, I'm sick of it. Sitting in that fucking cubicle every day. Staring at that computer. Always thinking that something's going to change somehow. But you know what? Nothing's gonna change. In fact, if anything, with my wife gone, I've just got more heaped on me. I'm more stuck than ever."

Jasper sighed. "You don't *have* to be, man."

But Porter pressed on, ignoring him. "It's really a joke, you know? It's such a joke. But I really thought I was above all that crap. The workaday life. I had this ego that kept telling me that the sort of shit other people had to put up with in their lives, I wasn't going to have to put up with. What a fucking cliché. Tell me, does everybody think that way? Is that really the way every person thinks? That they're the Chosen One? Is that what *you* think?"

"That I'm the Chosen One?"

"Yeah, you know, like protected? Special?"

Jasper looked down at his hands. "Man, I do not know. I'd have to think about that one." He picked for a while at the cuticles of his blackened fingers, then reached up and started gnawing on his cracked nails. "You know," he said, chewing, "I'd have to say no, I don't feel like the Chosen One. I really don't. Now, Jerry. He was the Chosen One. He was the fucking Magic King. And now he's dead. So how do you like that? Everybody else has got to be pretty fucking Chosen if they're still alive while Jerry's dead. That's one way of looking at it, I guess. If God sees fit to keep me living and strike Jerry down—strike down the Magic King of the Planet while my sorry ass gets to keep on truckin'—well, then I must be made of some golden shit myself, right? And you too. And everybody else on this dumb fucking spinning planet. We all must be made of some pretty golden shit if you look at it that way."

"And my wife's dead too, just like Jerry," Porter said, riding the momentum of Jasper's revelation. "She's dead. And here we all are. Here I am, and my kids . . ." but then he couldn't figure out what point he was trying to make. What had Jasper's point been? That we must be Chosen if we're allowed to keep living after others have died? "Or maybe that's our punishment," Porter said. "To have to live on while all the better people get snatched away, one by one. You could look at it that way too. That's the flip side of your coin, wouldn't you say?" He took another hit and held it in.

"Punished for *what*?" said Jasper. "I haven't done anything wrong. All the wrong in my life has been done to *me*." His face darkened, and he raised a finger at Porter. "You know what my mom did to me the last time I saw her, when she was flipped out on acid? She tried to cut all the hair off around my dick, all my fucking pubic hair, she and her friends did. While I was asleep. Can you believe this shit? Pinned me down. She said it was dirty and wanted it all clean. But she slipped and cut me instead, the scissors scraped right across my dick, and I started bleeding. That was the last time I ever saw her, that night. I called for the ambulance, and they took off, and that's the last time I ever saw her. I was fifteen. Nobody believes this shit when I tell 'em. But I got the evidence."

Porter felt vaguely nauseated. "So you . . . ?"

"So I am not on this earth to be punished. Not me. I *better* not be anyway. Maybe you think *you* are for the sins you've committed against humanity, or whatever shit you believe in. But I'm here to have a good fucking time. And I'm *havin'* it."

Had Porter committed any sins against humanity? None that he could think of. Not any major ones anyway. "But here's the thing," he said. "I didn't say you had to deserve the punishment. Just because you're being punished, it doesn't mean you have to deserve the punishment. I didn't *deserve* to have my wife die. She didn't do anything to *deserve* to get cancer. My kids didn't *deserve* all the crap they've been through. That's why all of this is so fucked. You know what? I wish I *had* sinned, big time. I wish I had, and I wish my wife had, and my kids too. Then at least I'd have a reason for everything that's happened."

Jasper shook his head. "Man, you are really a case, you know that? What exactly makes you tick? You've got to be about the most twisted-up dude I've ever met. You're all twisted up in knots, man! You're a fuckin' pretzel!"

Porter's mind was whirring at a million bytes per second. He was crashing. He lay back against a bale of pot and stared up at the tarpaulin roof as his brain raced forward and backward and sloshed from side to side. "I'm no pretzel," he said and then started laughing. "I'm a human being." Suddenly he was laughing so hard his stomach hurt. His eyes were streaming tears. The muscles of his face strained against his jaw and skull.

Jasper leaned over him. "Man, I'm cuttin' you off." He reached down and after a brief struggle was able to extract the mangled joint from Porter's clamped fist.

Porter felt a blanket being pulled over him, up to his chin. He flailed at it, still laughing, then rolled onto his side and vomited the warm flow of his stomach's contents onto the ground at Jasper's feet.

"Hey," Jasper cried out. "Not here, brother!"

But Porter was helpless. He retched again. Yellow bile and chunks of carrots and corn pooled in his sagging cheek and dripped coldly into his shirt.

"Fuckin' stanky!" Jasper cried, leaping about from foot to foot.

Porter closed his eyes. His mind had gone white. Where was he? And where was Lucy? He knew something terrible had happened, but what? And where were his kids? What had he done with Kaylie and Ben?

CHAPTER NINE

IT was the morning after. The whole camp had that look. Nobody was out. A haze hung over the lake. Paper plates and cups littered the field. Over by the beach a couple of the tall speakers had been tipped over, dragged a few feet, and then left that way, forming a little black Stonehenge.

Porter sat at the picnic table, head in his hands. Scattered about him were the various remnants of their visit thus far: the dirty cushion cover, broken sticks from Benny's castle, a white wrapper that had once enclosed the gauze pad on Porter's forehead. He was massaging his temples with his fingertips, trying to keep his brain from exploding. Kaylie and Ben sat across from him in mopey silence. Kaylie had already told him her story of the morning's events, and Porter was still trying to get his mind around the idea that William and Claire Winter were at that very moment soaring through the clear blue sky, bound for Indianapolis and the rental car that in a matter of hours would bring them to this very spot.

Porter stopped massaging for a moment and gazed blankly at his daughter. "And when do you think they're going to get here?"

Kaylie sighed theatrically. "I told you I *don't know*. Gramma just said they'd take the first flight out."

Porter shook his head. "But why would you think somebody kidnapped me? Just because you found the broken cell phone?"

"It wasn't only that," Kaylie said. "We couldn't find you anywhere! We tried. We walked around calling your name. We went to Delilah's. She didn't know where you were. We went over to those fat people's cabin."

Benny nodded solemnly. "Andrea and Seri."

"Nobody'd seen you." Kaylie pushed her hair from her face. "*Nobody*. Not until Jasper got back from town and said you'd slept on his porch. But by then I'd already called Gramma."

Jasper's hovering face had been Porter's first horror of the morning. Those yellow teeth. That moonscape of acne dotted by tufts of adolescent facial hair. That acrid body odor. Porter had slept next to a puddle of his own vomit, but it was the waft of Jasper's armpits that had brought him fully to consciousness, slicing through his nasal passages like smelling salts. "Hey," Jasper had whispered, jostling Porter's shoulder. "Your kids are outside. They've been looking all over for you. You gotta get your shit together, man. It's almost *noon*." With Jasper's help, Porter had managed to get himself into a sitting position, from which he'd been able to gaze out through the screen and see Kaylie and Ben's little moon-pie faces peering in. It had taken him another couple of minutes to rise to a shaky stand and make his way out the door into his children's huddled, uncertain embrace.

Porter picked up the cracked cell phone and examined it. "I'm surprised the batteries still had enough juice. This thing must've been on all night." He tried the "ON" button, but the phone was dead.

"It didn't have much. We could hardly hear each other, it was so staticky. That just made her panic even more."

"You know what, though?" Porter suddenly grinned. "They're never gonna find this place. How'd you tell them how to find us?"

"I read her those directions. From that flyer."

Porter tightened his lips. "Well, that's just great. Really great." He looked around, settling his gaze on the tepee village. "They're sure going to love us around here once your gramma calls in the cavalry. She'll probably have the whole Indiana State Guard at this place within fifteen minutes." Then Porter remembered the bales of pot on Jasper's porch. "You know, I've got to warn them about what's going to happen. We can't just let Gramma and Grampa roll in here un-announced."

Benny sat up and smiled. "Can I show them the place where we went swimming?"

Porter stared incredulously at his son, at the boy's animated and happy face. "Are you kidding?" He laughed. "What makes you think they'll want to go touring around?"

Benny's face fell. "I don't know."

"They're going to be *pissed off*, Benny. At *me*. Don't you get it?"

Ben looked away, off into the field.

"They're not coming here for the fun of it, to see where we went *swimming*, for God's sake. They're coming here to rescue you guys. From *me*." Porter could feel the anger rising in his throat. *Just shut up*, he told himself. *Shut the fuck up*. But then the first tear slipped down Benny's cheek, and somehow this made him even angrier. "Oh, *come on*, Benny. Don't cry again. Enough crying already."

"Okay." Benny sniffed and blinked, his eyes glassy with tears.

"You've got to stop acting like such a *baby* about all this stuff," Porter blared on. "You're not a baby anymore. Come on, Benny. Grow up, will you?"

Kaylie leveled a hostile gaze at Porter. "*You* grow up," she said. Then she scooted over and gathered Benny into her skinny arms.

Okay, he deserved that. If only his brain would stop expanding for five seconds maybe he could get a grip on himself. He could make up with his kids, apologize all over himself, give his fragile, whimpering boy a big hug and tell him not to worry, everything was going to be fine.

But everything *wasn't* going to be fine. In fact, as far as Porter could tell, everything was only going to get worse. This disaster of a vacation was just the tip of the iceberg. It was rapidly dawning on him that he wasn't up to this job, this carrying on cheerily without Lucy. He couldn't put a happy face on this crap anymore. His energy for that was officially gone, drained away overnight like the cell-phone battery. And sooner or later Benny was going to have to figure out how to deal with that, wasn't he? He was going to have to acquire some skills at playing the rotten hand he'd been dealt, and he might as well start now.

The three of them sat in sullen silence. The air was still. A low blanket of gray clouds obscured the sky. Even the trees looked exhausted, their branches sagging. Finally Porter said, "Ugh, I don't feel so good."

"Plus you stink," Kaylie shot back. "You smell like total puke."

"I know. I know I do. Yeah, something in that dinner definitely turned on me. But you guys still feel okay? You sure?"

No response.

Porter pushed himself gingerly to a stand. He felt as if he'd slept on bowling pins. His lungs burned. His stomach was caving in on itself. "Well, I'd better go talk to Andrea. Tell her about what's to come." He waited a moment for his children to look at him, for them at least to take notice of his herculean struggle to gain his feet, but no such luck. "Don't worry," he said to the backs of their heads. "I'll only be gone a few minutes." Then he turned and started to hobble away.

On the way to Andrea's, Porter stopped in the camp bathroom

for a piss and a quick cleanup. The mirror was just a hazy square of scratched sheet metal bolted to the wall, but Porter didn't mind; he didn't want to see himself clearly anyway. Even in the metal he could tell how ravaged he looked: three days of stubble, hollow eyes, the gauze bandage on his forehead with that disgusting yellow circle of hardened whatever smack dab in the middle. He removed the bandage, tugging gently where the gauze had affixed itself to the scab, and began to splash some cold water onto the wound. But the whole area up there felt so damaged and numb that he gave up on cleaning it and decided just to blot it dry with some toilet paper. Which promptly disintegrated into gloppy spit wads all in his bangs and along his hairline. Which he then couldn't pick out because he couldn't see himself well enough in the goddamn metal mirror.

Fuck it. If Claire and William were to arrive in the next thirty minutes, before Porter could clean himself up more fully, they would simply have to deal with the full horror of what had become of their son-in-law. At least they'd be relieved that he hadn't been kidnapped. Or would they?

Porter stepped outside and squinted. His brain felt as if it were floating in a larger sack of liquid, bashing against his skull with each tip and turn. He forged ahead into the little pine-tree enclave that surrounded Andrea's cabin, then approached her door and knocked.

"Who goes there?" Seri called out.

"It's me. Porter."

The door opened. Seri stood there in his yellow shorts, his bare chest and gut thrust forth like a bellowing walrus on parade. "Hey! There he is. Returned by the forces of evil. They let you go, man? No ransom?"

Porter grinned. "Oh, there's a ransom, all right."

Seri ushered him in. "Here, have a seat."

Porter lowered himself into that nirvana of pillows and lay back.

"Andrea and I felt bad for your kids this morning," Seri said.

"They were pretty flipped out when they couldn't find you anywhere. But Jasper tells me he fucked you up good. He said you really tripped out on him."

"You'll have to take his word for it," Porter said. "I can't say that I remember much after my first couple of hits of that stuff."

Seri lowered himself to the floor, his brown thighs flattening against the rug like two sacks of mud. "If it's any consolation, at least he got the stuff for your truck. You guys will be on your merry way before too long."

"That's sort of what I've come to talk to you about," Porter said. And he quickly filled Seri in on Kaylie's phone call and its unfortunate result—that his in-laws were on their way. "They could arrive as early as two or three, I'm guessing. It's not that far from Indianapolis, assuming they don't get lost trying to find this place."

Seri's face broke into a devilish smile. "Andrea's gonna have a shit fit about this. You know that, right?"

Porter nodded. "I just thought you guys might want to prepare everyone. I don't know what they're liable to do. But if my mother-in-law has gotten herself all worked up about this, which is highly likely, she could really cause some trouble."

"Like what trouble?"

"Well, it's just that, you know, I get the feeling there's a lot of drugs around here. And she's not too savvy about that kind of thing, but if she brings anyone in with her—you know, if she's managed to bully the local sheriff or somebody into checking this out—"

There was the sudden sound of footfalls outside the door, then the maroon-dressed, electric-haired mass of Andrea filled the doorway. In her hands she held plastic grocery bags, which banged against the door as she fumbled to pull it open. She got herself in, nodding at Seri and then charging ahead into the darkness. She was halfway across the room before she saw Porter reclined in the pillows.

He sat up on his elbows. "Hi."

"Hey there." She knit her brow in apparent concern. "You okay? You all recovered from your little psychedelic adventure?"

"No, not at all. I feel awful."

Andrea frowned, shaking her head. "That stuff will melt your spine. Jasper should know better." She moved through the room with her bags, disappearing into the dark kitchen. Porter waited for a light to come on, but Andrea proceeded to unload the bags and near-total blackness. He could hear cans being slid onto shelves. Then she stepped back into the relative brightness of the living room.

"Andrea, my dear," Seri began, "we've got something to tell you." His big face was drawn slightly with apprehension, but his eyes danced with what Porter could only identify as a kind of masochistic delight. "So Porter just told me that apparently his in-laws are coming here to pay us a visit today. His daughter called them this morning when they couldn't find him, and I guess the mother-in-law freaked out a little."

Andrea's face dropped. She looked at Porter. "Today? What do you mean 'today'?"

"They caught the first flight out," Porter said. "To Indianapolis. Then they're renting a car to come here."

Seri grinned, casting a sidelong glance at Andrea. "So who's in charge of mixing up the cyanide Kool-Aid? You or me?"

Andrea shot him a toxic look. "This is no *joke*," she snapped. "You want to find us someplace else to live? You want to be the one to explain to Uncle Rick what all these people are doing here?"

Seri brought his hands to his face in mock cowardice.

She directed her anxious gaze at Porter. "So are these people cool, your in-laws? Or are they gonna fuck things up for everybody?"

"I wouldn't say they're 'cool,' no. But I don't know that that means they're going to cause any trouble."

"You think there's a chance they already called the cops?"

Porter sighed. "That's what I was just saying to Seri when you walked in. I've been wondering about that. But don't you have to be missing for twenty-four hours or something like that before you can get the cops involved? Isn't that what they always say on TV? That you need to wait twenty-four hours to file a missing-persons report?"

"I think he's right on that one," Seri said. "I've seen that before too."

Andrea made a big show of rolling her eyes. "Oh, well, that's reassuring. They said that on TV? Is that right, Seri? That's the sort of thing you use your brain cells to remember? Instead of remembering what color my eyes are?"

Seri shook his head. "I can't believe you still give me shit about that. That was like a year ago."

Andrea put her hands on her hips and stared resolutely at Porter. "You've gotta keep them out of here, your in-laws. That's all there is to it."

"Keep them out of here? How am I supposed to do that?"

"Meet them at the entrance," Andrea said, gesturing outside. "Out at the highway. Intercept them out there and keep them out there."

"But my truck . . ." Porter said.

"Jasper will just have to take care of that. He got the stuff he needs this morning, right? Well, now he's got to get you guys on the road ASAP. Unless he wants to risk getting his ass thrown in jail for the rest of his life. Tell him that. Tell him I told you to tell him."

As Porter marched his way over to Jasper's, it occurred to him that Andrea was absolutely right. Jasper was the one sitting on the time bomb around here. One glance into that screened-in porch by some curious cop and it's bye-bye Jasper in handcuffs. Shouldn't be a hard sell to convince him that it would be in his best interest to check out their transmission pronto and get them on the road.

But Jasper said, "Fuck that. How long before they get here?"

"I'm not sure. It could be anytime."

"Well, then fuck that. I gotta hide this shit first." He was gnawing away at his thumbnail; then he brought his hands up on either side of his greasy head and squeezed. "I can't believe you've got the cops coming in here. I just can't believe that."

"Well, I doubt the cops will come. At least not in the first wave."

But Jasper was already scrambling around, pulling bales of pot frantically this way and that and muttering under his breath.

"You don't have to fix it, remember?" Porter said. "You just need to put new fluid in and make sure it's just a small leak. Get us on the road."

Jasper wheeled to face him. "I told you I've gotta *hide this shit*. I'll be *over,* man."

Porter stepped away and walked back to the road, and there he stood in a stupor of disbelief. So what now? Should he go back and tell Andrea what happened? Have her flip out on him? Or just head back to his camper and wait for Jasper? Or for Claire and William? Whoever came first? It could be like a little game. He could drag his lawn chair out of the back of the camper, pop open a beer, lie back, and place little bets with himself about who was going to arrive first to kick his ass.

Porter started back toward his campsite, surveying the area for Kaylie and Ben, but they had evidently left the picnic table for greener pastures. Actually, they were probably inside the camper having a secret bonding session over what a pathetic father Porter was and how shitty this trip had turned out to be and how much they missed their mother and their grandparents and their home and their friends and their *90210* and Pop-Tarts and Hot Wheels and Nintendo and all that crap, *all* of it, the whole comfortable, familiar cocoon he'd yanked them out of. And for what? For *what?* What was he really trying to find out here? Whatever it was, he wasn't finding it. And whatever it was, it wasn't for Kaylie and Ben. That much had become clear.

He opened the camper door, stepped up and in, and there they were at the kitchen table: Kaylie facing him with her stony gaze, Ben tucked in against the side window, and then a smiling face appeared, craning out from the near corner. Delilah.

"Hey," she said. "I just decided to come by. I heard there might be some action, like about you taking off? And I didn't want to be left standing at the station."

Porter put his hands on his hips. "So you already know about my in-laws? That we're supposed to try to meet them at the entrance?"

"Word spreads fast around here."

"So she's right?" Kaylie said. "We're leaving finally?"

"Well, that depends on Jasper. On how soon he can get the truck ready."

Delilah said, "I wouldn't hold your breath. In fact, Andrea already put Plan B into effect. She let it be known that all residents should go on a little hike today . . . you know, like scatter into the hills and not come back until tomorrow?" She pointed out through the window behind Benny and the view it afforded of the field and the tepee village and, beyond it, the beach. "See? They're already heading out."

Porter bent down and squinted. Sure enough, this strange community, or at least what he could see of it, was on the move. A cluster of people with backpacks and fanny packs and bedrolls, trailed by a gaggle of mop-headed little boys and girls, was disappearing into the woods at the water's edge.

"Man, I'm sorry about this," Porter said. "I really am."

Delilah waved her hand dismissively. "You think they care? If anything, they're grateful to have a planned activity for the day." Then she narrowed her eyes at Porter and leaned closer. "What's all that in your hair?"

Porter reached for his hairline and felt the dried spit wads of toilet paper. "Oh . . . uh . . . I was just trying to clean myself up a little."

Delilah smirked. "With Kleenex?"

"That's all I had. And I couldn't see myself."

"Here," Delilah said, standing up. "Let me." She soaked a washcloth under the faucet and wrung it out. "Sit," she said, gesturing at her empty spot. "We've got to make you presentable, right? At least as much as possible." She dabbed gently at his wound and then used her fingernails to pick out the pieces of toilet paper, flicking them one by one into the sink. Instead of replacing the gauze bandage, she decided to cover the wound with two Band-Aids. "So the story is that you just walked into a low tree branch, okay?" she said. "I don't want your in-laws hating me right off the bat."

"All right," Porter said with a smile.

She turned to Kaylie and Ben. "And that goes for ya'll too."

They nodded obediently.

Delilah stood back and looked at him, holding his face in her hands. "You know, you really need a shave too."

"*I* can do that," Kaylie said with an edge of desperation. "Right, Dad?"

Porter grinned. "Yeah, okay. That'd be nice."

How long had it been since Kaylie had shaved him? A year? Two? For a while it had been their regular morning routine, the "quality time" they shared before Benny and Lucy had woken up. He'd sit on the toilet seat with a towel over his lap, and she'd work back and forth from the sink to his face, using her fingers as he'd taught her to pull his skin tight before stroking it clean with the razor. Porter used to love the seriousness her face took on then, her pursed lips and appraising eyes. And she was good at it, although occasionally at the men's room at work he'd see a patch she'd missed, and this would lead him to think fondly of her all over again.

During Lucy's sickness, however, that routine had ended, like so many other things, almost without notice. Porter couldn't remember when it had stopped, or why. It hadn't seemed important. That was one part about handling the whole ordeal that Porter wished he'd done differently. He'd let the fact that Lucy was sick cancel out the importance of everything else. He was often having to tend to Lucy in the morning, since she was no longer sleeping in, or sleeping at all. Sometimes he had to help her into the bathroom to throw up. So how important could it have been for Kaylie and him to spend twenty minutes shaving every morning while Lucy literally was dying on the other side of the wall? How important could such a small thing have been? But of course it was important—more so then than ever before. Why had he been so dense about things like that?

But now, as Porter sat at the kitchen table, head tilted back, the warm water dripping down his neck, it was as though they had never stopped. Kaylie's face immediately took on the exact same expression—exactly!—as all those times before, and her fingers moved knowingly around his face, stretching and pressing.

Delilah had taken Benny outside, and the two of them were cleaning up the campground, picking up the sticks from his ill-fated castle, throwing away the trash from their meals. Delilah had on the same green fringed dress from the night before, and she'd taken off her sandals. Her hair was flared out on one side and mashed down on the other, giving her head an off-kilter look. Benny dashed about happily, fetching crumpled napkins and plastic forks, while Delilah pointed him in this direction and that. They even expanded their cleanup efforts to include the near end of the field, gathering paper plates and litter from the night before, lest that evidence raise any questions.

During the shave, Kaylie took the opportunity to tell Porter again how much he still smelled like "total puke," so after she'd finished, he grabbed his toiletry kit and a towel and headed off to the camp shower, which, as Delilah had pointed out to him, was a white cinderblock building near the lake. Porter disliked public showers. The floors were always cold and slimy and invariably littered with disgusting items you had to tiptoe around: used Band-Aids, globs of pubic hair, unidentifiable pools of liquid. Plus, Porter had a lingering sense of embarrassment (which had lingered since adolescence; those awful days of high-school gym) about showering in front of other men, soaping up his groin and butt crack, drying himself and stepping into his underwear in such close proximity to other nudity.

And then, of course, there were the more mundane concerns of not being able to get the temperature right, of being scalded when someone flushed the toilet and then chilled after you'd flailed at the nozzles to compensate. And what about the pathetic water pressure, especially at a camp shower like this? But, whatever. He had to take a shower, and he would feel much better after he had.

Porter approached the near entrance of the building first. A carved wooden sign that read SQUAWS had been bolted to the door, but beneath it someone had written in black Magic Marker "All People." *Great.* He strolled around to the other side. Yep, there too. The wooden sign read WARRIORS but underneath, again, was "All People." He sighed and went in. Empty, thank God. Maybe they'd all taken off into the hills by now.

Porter disrobed, turned on the shower—testing it with his hand until the temperature had achieved perfection—and then stepped into the powerful spray. Wow, this shower was terrific. It felt like a pulsing massage on his sore back. He let the bullets of water thrum against him, luxuriating in it, but he knew he had to hurry. He was afraid that Claire and William might pull in at any moment, and he wanted to be there to greet them when they did. Plus, he was unnerved by the fact that the showers had no curtains or doors or anything to shield you from the changing area—just a divider from the next stall. So after he'd let his shoulders and back and chest get a sufficient beating, the skin blooming red from the abuse, he started to scrub and shampoo at a manic pace, trying hard to keep the soap out of his wound.

He was on his second round of shampoo when he thought he heard the door open, and he squinted out through the stinging spray to see a twenty-something redhead in an orange terry-cloth robe stroll by. She glanced at him casually before turning to face the lockers.

Porter slunk back into the stall until his butt came up against the sharp nozzles. The hot water streamed down his body, draining like piss from the tip of his penis. His eyes burned with shampoo. *Fuck.* Now what was he supposed to do? He peered longingly at his towel, which hung on the pegboard about ten feet away, only a few pegs down from where the woman had set up shop. His towel might as well have been on the moon. Out of the corner of his eye he could see the woman hang up her own towel and begin to search through a plastic bag.

Okay, he told himself, *just turn off the shower and walk out.* It was ridiculous; he felt like a cop trying to talk someone down from a ledge.

Plus, hadn't this woman already been through this situation two hundred times by now? Hadn't she already been exposed to such a parade of dimpled asses and shriveled penises that she probably wouldn't even care to look at his? Yes. Yes. But he still couldn't make a move. He felt positively stricken.

Porter thought, *Why not just wait until she gets into her stall, then make a dash for it?* But when he glanced out again to check on her progress, she turned to face him, her mouth breaking into a warm smile and her robe falling open to reveal the inner slope of her breasts. Her face was sharp, birdlike, the nose hooked and freckled. Porter's eyes were drawn down, lured by the glinting silver ring in her belly button above that wedge of red crinkly hair. "Hey, you must be that guy, right?" she called to him. "The one with Don's camper?"

She was really going to engage him in a conversation? "Uh-huh," Porter shouted. "Yeah. That's me." He moved about in the water, trying inconspicuously to hold his shampoo bottle in front of his groin.

She sat down on the bench and continued the search of her bag. "So you're the reason we're all supposed to clear out of here today?"

"Oh, yeah, I guess."

"And why are the cops after you? You on the run from something?"

Porter put his head under the spray. "No, it's not that they're after me . . ."

"What's that?"

Porter closed his eyes. *Okay,* he thought. *Okay, here we go.* "Wait a sec," he called out. Then he turned off the water, grabbed his shampoo bottle, and stepped out of the stall. As he walked across the small space that separated them, Porter felt as if his penis were bouncing around before him like a sprung jack-in-the-box. Did it always bounce around that much when he walked?

But the woman didn't even look there. She kept her eyes on Porter's face, waiting for an answer.

Porter grabbed his towel, secured it around his waist, and turned to her. "It's not that they're after me," he started to say. But then she stood up, her robe fell open again, and that belly-button ring and the whole exposed area down there—the triangle of hair, those skinny freckled legs, even her delicate jutting kneecaps—were just too much for him to handle. "Um . . ." he said, and then he had to stop talking for a moment, look away from her, and sit down. Even so, as he hunched forward, he could feel the tip of his erection beginning to press at where the towel was stretched across his lap. He crossed his forearms over it, mashing it down. "It's really just my in-laws coming here," he said, staring at the floor. "My kids' grandparents. They got worried about us. My kids couldn't find me this morning." He looked up at her, sensing that she wasn't following his tortured explanation. "It's a long story," he added, smiling gamely.

The woman nodded uncertainly, then slid out of her robe, draping it on a peg next to her towel. "So it's not the cops? Is that what you're saying?"

Porter stared at her, his mouth agape. "Uh, I doubt it."

"Well, good," she said happily, putting her hands on her hips. "Then I'm glad I didn't postpone my shower." She picked up her shampoo and a little plastic travel box of bar soap and held them against her stomach with one hand. "I, like, *really* wanted to take a shower after last night." She gazed off dreamily. "Oh, God. Last night. *Wow.*"

Porter found himself trying to fill in the blanks, wondering just how much sex she'd had to make her this in need of taking a shower.

She looked back at him. "So anyway, then when I heard Andrea wanted everyone to clear out . . . I was like, 'Shit.' So I was, like, trying to sneak in and out of here before the cops came. I didn't want Andrea pissed at me. I've already been through that once, and I barely lived to tell about it." She laughed and leaned forward, her hair falling around her face, her breasts bobbing slightly.

Porter's hard-on was so powerful it ached. He wanted to ask this woman if he could have sex with her right now. On the bench. Or in the shower. Anywhere. She'd probably do it. What was one more orgasm added to her night of plenty? He could reach out and touch her if he wanted. There she was, smiling before him, only two feet away. He could stand up and let his towel fall and just embrace her, press his hard-on up against her belly, against that silver ring, and start grinding away. Or how about if he said something like, *You're beautiful, you know that? You're really sexy,* and see what happened? All it would take was opening his mouth and having words fall out and then waiting for the consequences, good or bad. It would be exactly what Delilah was talking about, wouldn't it? He would become fully exposed to the possibility of gains and losses.

And so what if he lost? So what? Nobody gave a shit. People did stuff like this all the time. Around the world people were groping each other in closets and in stuck elevators and in the backseats of cars. Total strangers were stumbling out of bars and humping in dark alleys. This sort of thing was happening every minute of every day in every town, village, and city on the planet. It *was*!

But Porter didn't open his mouth, no words fell out. He didn't stand up and embrace her. He didn't reach out and touch her. Instead, shame filled his face and a kernel of regret lodged itself high in his throat, making it impossible for him to speak.

"So good luck dealing with your in-laws," the woman said with a small smile, and then she moved off to the shower.

CHAPTER TEN

PORTER jogged through the little pine forest to the camp bathroom and locked himself into a stall. He dropped his pants and boxers, leaned against the cinder-block wall with his head on his forearm, reached down for his hardening penis, closed his eyes, and quietly began to jerk off.

He could still see her in the spray of the shower, soaping her thighs and shoulders and the pale undersides of her breasts, her red hair becoming a thick, dark slab down the middle of her back. Those delicate shoulder blades working like tiny wings beneath her freckled skin. And that butt. *God.* That small, muscular butt.

And suddenly he came, the little mound of sperm pooling warmly on his fingers. Porter let out his breath and opened his eyes, sagging against the wall. He stood there for a moment, just holding himself, breathing deeply. Then, with his free hand, he reached for the toilet paper and began to clean himself up. He wiped at his fingers, then knelt down and cleaned up what little had dripped to the floor.

He was surprised by the minor output—not that he cared one way or another. But he'd been expecting some sort of explosion, because didn't it just keep accumulating? Or was that only a myth? The last time had been in his own bed, a couple of nights before Lucy died. The kids were off at Claire and William's, and Porter was completely exhausted, but he'd been unable to sleep. It was two in the morning, then two-thirty, then three. Finally he'd begun absently to grope at himself, not really expecting to get anything started. Lucy was dying. Pretty soon she wouldn't be a person anymore. She was going to vanish and leave him with nothing but her body, that rotten and failed thing.

Earlier in the night, feeling anxious and depressed, Porter had watched Letterman, then an hour of Headline News. He'd found it oddly comforting to be reminded that around the globe people were dying by the thousands. Shot and stabbed and burned and strangled. Crushed in train wrecks. Buried under mudslides. Porter imagined all those souls drifting up and away in a silent skyward chorus, leaving behind their dumb bodies to be raked into the topsoil and composted by the great hand of God.

But later, in bed, Porter had found himself thinking about a previous version of Lucy's body. He was remembering her suspended above him, her crotch spread over his face and her mouth at his groin, an image from so long before, from college, in that swanky apartment her parents were paying for in Squirrel Hill. He could almost feel her warm breath and her small, darting tongue on the shaft of his penis, her nipples grazing his belly. And this image had been enough. It had been just enough to do the trick. Afterward he had fallen asleep that way, his wet hand on his shrunken penis, the sheets cast aside.

Porter tossed the wad of toilet paper into the bowl and flushed. He pulled up his boxers and pants. Tucked in his shirt. Did his belt. And then, before he could make another move, he felt a powerful gloom beginning to descend. He lowered the toilet seat and sat back against the cold fixture, and then it was upon him. First the weight pressed down on his entire body like a lead blanket, flattening him, and when that finally eased, the feeling recomposed itself into a lightness in his chest, swarming up his throat, nearly bringing tears to his eyes.

God, what was *this*? He'd felt plenty awful before—nearly incapacitated by sadness—but nothing quite so swift and ravaging as this. Porter knew grief and the various forms it could take, both the hand-wringing anxiousness and the bone-melting lethargy. He knew loss, was well acquainted with that hole in himself, that missing lung. He knew what it was like to have your kids so twisted up with hurt that they flinched when you tried to touch them. But this was something else, this blackness. He wasn't sure what this was.

Porter wished, of all things, that he could talk to Carole Levine right now. Maybe his therapy would have been different, and certainly more productive, if he'd told her the truth about himself. ("No *duh*," Kaylie would say to that.) Maybe if he hadn't been so concerned with presenting himself to her as a good person, he would have gotten more out of those expensive, torturous sessions.

"Do you ever wish you'd never married Lucy?"

"No! What do you mean? How can you ask that?"

Fuck, yes, he should have said. *You think this isn't God's way of saying I made the wrong decision?*

"Do you find yourself blaming her for dying, for leaving you?"

"Not really . . . I mean, how can I blame her for getting cancer? That's ridiculous."

Of course I do. I hate her. I fucking hate her for this.

But what would Carole Levine have thought of him if he'd admitted such things?

At the end of *Ordinary People,* the Timothy Hutton character discovers—through Judd Hirsch's skillful prodding, of course—that he is actually *good* inside, that *he* was the stronger one, that his brother let go of the little sailboat but *he* managed to hold on. He survived not because he was weaker than his brother but because he was *stronger.* And, damn it, he finally comes to understand, that strength is nothing to feel guilty about.

But what was inside of Porter except for lust and selfishness and a barren soul that could produce only a charade of caring? Is this really what he was composed of—this weak, empty stuff—or was there something else underneath, deeper down, that was pure and good and strong too? And how was he supposed to know? Had he opened himself up more fully to her, would Carole Levine have been able to lead him to that promised land, to the discovery of that better part of himself?

Porter felt his eyes grow glassy and warm. He took several gulps of air, trying to fight it off, but then he lowered his face into his hands and began to cry. It was mostly a muffled, whimpering affair, although at one point his mouth opened into a moaning yowl that he could not control, his stomach pumping in and out with little sobs. He wiped his face, rubbed at his eye sockets with balled fists, then put his hands on his knees and made a conscious effort to regulate his breathing. *In and out,* he told himself. *In and out. Come on, man. C'mon.*

And in this way the moment passed. The pressure lifted. Porter rose to his feet, grabbed his towel and toiletry kit from the coat hook, and headed for the door.

Outside, the day was the same. This place still existed. Nobody had pulled the plug on the lake, or collapsed the pine forest like a bunch of umbrellas, or rolled up the field, or lifted the tepee village into the stage rigging. Everything was exactly as it had been. Claire and William were still on their way, if they hadn't arrived already. Lucy was dead, gone without a trace, yet Porter's life marched forward inexorably.

AT THE CAMPER, Porter put on a short-sleeved, denim button-down and his best pair of khakis, then crouched in front of the half-length mirror. *Perfect.* He looked as if he'd just walked out of a fucking J. Crew catalog. If nothing else, this outfit would be a great preemptive strike against whatever opinion of him Claire and William had already armed themselves with.

It was three in the afternoon by the time Jasper arrived with his toolbox and four pints of transmission fluid, dragging a shovel. First he shoveled out the fluid-soaked area, heaving the goopy soil into the bushes, and then set to work under the truck's chassis, his bare feet sticking out like those of someone trapped.

Delilah had brought over some lunch—leftovers from the night before—and as Jasper lay under the truck, they all sat at the table eating.

Presently Jasper scooted himself out and rose to his feet, his hands black and slick with grease. "I think I found it," he said. "The leak. Just this small crack in the casing. I think that's where it's coming from."

Porter stood up and stepped over to him. "So what does that mean? You think we can make it back?"

Jasper shrugged. "Probably. I'd do what the dude told you. If the stick shift starts to feel all gluey, you know, while you're driving, then you're gonna want to pull over and get some fluid in her. I filled her up, and you've got three extra pints. Maybe stop every hundred miles and check the level. Make sure it's not draining out too fast."

"Thanks, Jasper. Thanks a lot. What do I owe you?"

"I already told you I'm not into that shit—owing. I hardly did anything anyway. Just the fluid. You're still gonna have to get major work done on that thing."

"Well, I really appreciate it." Porter pushed his fingers through his hair. He wanted to get them all in the camper and out of there, *now, this minute.* But how was he going to get Delilah into the camper without creating some big scene with Jasper? The love-struck fool still didn't know Delilah was coming along with them, did he? Porter hadn't told him. And he didn't think Delilah had. *C'mon, Jasper,* he thought. *Leave, man. Leave.*

Instead, Jasper turned to Delilah with a shy smile and said, "So, Lilah, I hope you find Don. Say hi from me if you do."

"I will," Delilah said, moving toward him.

Jasper held up his blackened hands. "Not *too* close. I got that Pigpen cloud around me today."

But Delilah went right up to him, grabbed him by the ears, and planted a big kiss on his scruffy, pockmarked cheek. "I'll see you again," she said, stepping away. "I know I will."

"Hey, I hope so," Jasper said, looking down.

Humbled by this display, Porter felt that he should at least go shake Jasper's hand. But he didn't want to get his own hand all black and greasy. That stuff's not so easy to get off. Plus, he'd muck up the whole kitchen sink with that shit, not to mention ruining the soap and the hand towel.

But something pushed him toward Jasper anyway and made him reach out his hand. "Good meeting you," he said.

"Hey, man, you too," Jasper said, ignoring Porter's hand. "Sorry about the"—he glanced sheepishly at Kaylie and Ben—"well, you know," he continued in a whisper, "the special blend. I swear, Andrea almost took my head off when I got back from town. 'What'd you do to him?' she yelled at me. 'What were you thinking?'"

Porter laughed. "That's all right. I think I needed my system cleaned out anyway."

"Good luck with the trip back," Jasper said, backing away. And then he turned and walked off.

Porter faced Delilah and the kids. "Well, should we get going? Try to cut them off at the pass?"

They all smiled and nodded, rising to their feet in unison. And with this small gesture Porter's mood—against all odds—turned cheery. He knew he'd still have a mighty pissed-off Claire to contend with, but he couldn't quite focus on that yet. In every other respect, life was looking up. With some food in him, Porter was finally feeling better. His head had cleared. He felt well scrubbed and groomed for the first time since they'd left Pittsburgh. And just in the last fifteen minutes the day had broken open into a breezy, blue-skied celebration. The trees were stirring noisily, and the lake was awash with ripples.

The entire scene was so stunning that when Claire and William's bright red sedan cleared the crest of the entry road and began to drift into the campground, its wheels grinding and popping over the gravel, it almost struck Porter as just one more festive element of this suddenly dazzling day. Sunlight blazed from the windshield. The chrome grille sparkled. Then the sedan slipped into the shadows, and Porter caught a glimpse of his in-laws' drawn faces, their severe gray hair and squinting eyes, and it was like the part of the movie when the orchestra music crashes in, heralding the impending doom.

The car circled toward them, creeping along at an agonizing pace. William was crouched behind the wheel, peering straight ahead. Then he gazed over and saw them, drew his head back, and turned to say something to Claire. The car leapt forward with a jerky motion, moved past Jasper's tent, turned into their space, and pulled to a stop behind the camper.

Claire and William were perched sternly behind the dashboard, their faces pinched. Then Benny took off for the car in a blind dash. "Hi!" he yelled, slapping his hands against Claire's window. "Hi, Gramma!"

Claire managed a weak smile through the glass, nodding at him, but both she and William couldn't seem to figure out how to free themselves from their seat belts. They were looking around their laps, fiddling, until Benny yanked open Claire's door and her seat belt retracted automatically.

Claire climbed out straight into the full assault of Benny's excitement—"This is where we've been camping! Our truck broke! We went swimming in that lake over there! A real lake!" He was leaping about, pointing this way and that, and all Porter could think was *Thank God for Benny.*

Despite its being at least eighty degrees out, Claire had on one of her yellow cardigan sweaters over a collared white shirt. She'd put it on for the plane, no doubt.

William had parked the car too close to the bushes on the driver's side, and he was in the process of trying to mash them back with repeated blows from the door. Finally he extricated himself, hugging the car as he worked his way past the bushes to the rear. Already flustered by that struggle, he put his key in the trunk, popped it open, and lifted out a black garment bag.

Claire looked at him with irritation. "May I ask what you're doing, dear?"

"Well, I . . ." he began.

"It seems that Porter has been located," Claire said. "Unless you'd like to stay the night anyway."

William stuffed the garment bag back into the trunk and slammed it shut, scowling.

Poor William. Who but Claire would insert the knife *and* twist it in such a situation? The guy already must have had an earful from her. She probably hadn't let up for five minutes since Kaylie's phone call.

Porter felt that he should go to them and begin the process of apologizing and groveling and kissing butt—just get it over with—but he couldn't bring himself to take a step. Instead, he raised his hand in a mild wave and called out, with more of a sarcastic edge than he'd intended, "Welcome!"

Claire glowered at him. Then she and William gathered themselves and strode forward. Benny was leading Claire by the hand, bouncing along beside her.

"Hi, Gramma," Kaylie called out.

"Oh, dear ones," Claire said with a prim smile.

Kaylie rushed toward her, and they embraced, Claire kissing her on the top of her ponytailed head.

"Dad was over at this other guy's tent this morning," Kaylie said, looking up. "He told me about it, and I just forgot. And then the phone didn't work anymore, and—"

"Shhh . . ." Claire said, cupping Kaylie's head against her chest. "Shhh, now. Don't worry. I'm just so glad to see you again. I'm so glad everyone's all right. I doubted anything was seriously the matter, really," she said, glancing at Porter. "But I thought we should come anyway."

"I'm actually glad you did," Porter said, feeling generous. "We ran into a little trouble here."

Claire regarded him, squinting. "What did you do to your forehead?"

Porter felt for the bandage. "I, uh . . . I walked into a branch when we were hiking. It's nothing. No, the trouble had to do with the truck. There was a leak in the transmission, and we kind of got stranded here."

"What happened?" William said gruffly, as if car talk were his area.

"Just this small leak, I guess. But all the fluid drained out."

"Poor things," Delilah said, stepping forward. "They really got stuck."

William looked appraisingly at her.

"I'm Delilah," she said.

"Oh, I'm sorry," Porter said. "These are my in-laws, William and Claire. This is Delilah. She's also camping here."

"Hello," Claire said, nodding at her. "And where is your campsite?"

"Over there," Delilah said, pointing vaguely.

"She's been great," Porter gushed. "She showed us a great swimming place. Right, Benny?"

"Yeah," Benny said. "But Kaylie dunked me. I couldn't breathe, Gramma. I got water up my nose!"

"Porter," William said, "what say we have a look at that leak?"

"That's not really necessary," Porter said. "I've put some fluid in, and—"

"Let's have a look," William said, grasping Porter by the elbow and turning him toward the truck. As the two of them walked off, William said, "Transmissions are tricky things, you know. I once had a problem with the Mercedes where the blasted thing wouldn't shift, and even Jim Nathan couldn't, ah, couldn't . . ." and he lost his train of thought.

Porter popped open the hood and gestured for William to look in, but William just gave it a cursory glance and said, "Yes, very well. So you've got some new fluid in her? That's good." He looked distractedly into the woods. "That ought to do the trick. These transmissions . . . they most certainly can be a headache, from what I gather."

And that's when Porter realized that William wasn't interested in the transmission at all; he was on assignment. Claire had assigned him this duty.

"Porter," William said, still gazing away, "I hate to bring up something like this. I really do. But Claire and I feel . . . We've come to believe, ah, that where it concerns the children . . ." Finally he looked directly at Porter. "Oh, blast it all." His eyes searched Porter's face. "I *know* you wanted to have a good time with the children on this trip. I know you love them terribly, and you thought this camping would be a fun thing for everyone. But we feel, Claire and I . . ."

"That you want to take them back home with you?" Porter said.

William sighed. "Oh, Porter, it's not that so much as . . . I don't know. Claire is so distressed over this trip, and I simply wish . . ."

"I think you should take them, William. I really do."

"You do?"

"I'm not giving them what I expected to out here. I thought we'd be hiking and fishing, cooking over a fire, talking, you know, sorting things out. And it's just not working out that way. I mean, we've had some fun. It's been a little adventure for them. But I think I over-estimated my ability to take on something like this so soon after losing Lucy." Porter peered into the engine. "Plus, I'd rather not have them traveling around in this truck until I can get it fixed."

William gazed warmly at Porter, his hands on his hips. "You're an able fellow, Porter. But this frankly has been too much for all of us. Too much for me, certainly. At the start I didn't think this camping plan was such a bad idea. I wasn't against it, not like Claire was. But it does seem to have gone a bit awry, wouldn't you say?"

Porter smiled.

"So is your injury bad?" William said, peering at Porter's fore-head. "That's an awfully big bandage."

"It's just a scrape. Actually I was lucky I didn't poke my eye out."

"You don't look so good, if you don't mind me saying so," William said. "Rather pale. Tired."

"I'm exhausted."

"I am too," William said. "And I'm injured as well. Have you heard?" He grinned and held up his left hand, which was bandaged with gauze and white tape across the heel and up the meat of his thumb. "Cut myself up on that damn security box. I simply detest that thing. I mistakenly activated it the other morning, and damn it all, I *still* can't figure out how to turn the thing off under those circum-stances. And I must admit I lost my temper. I have never been quite so angry in all my life, Porter. I scared myself." He gave a little laugh. "And I believe Claire actually was afraid of me too. I'd never seen her afraid of me before. When I spun around to look at her, she retreated a few steps from me, and there was fear in her eyes. *Fear.* And I can imagine why, with the blood all over my hand, and elsewhere too, of course. And my face must have been crazy, my hair all mussed up. In fact, it was seeing Claire so afraid that startled me out of it, really. I don't know if I would have stopped pounding on the blasted thing otherwise."

In all the years Porter had known him, he'd never heard William speak so openly. Not once during Lucy's illness had William spoken about being scared or angry or out of control. And now, with this, Porter didn't know quite how to respond. "So how is the hand today?" he said.

"Oh, it's getting better. Sure enough."

They were silent. Porter looked over at the picnic table where Claire and Delilah and the kids were all chatting in a loose circle. Benny was holding Claire's hand while kicking at the dirt with his shoe. Delilah nodded at Claire, then pointed at something in the direction of the lake. Her tepee?

Porter couldn't imagine what Claire must think of this place. Well, that wasn't true. He could imagine. Although on occasion she could surprise him. Sometimes she could be struck by a lightning bolt of open-mindedness, like the time, not longer after Kaylie was born, that Porter got his ear pierced with a little diamond stud. It had been an admittedly pathetic act, a meek demonstration of . . . *what* exactly? The fact that he was still an artist, even though he hadn't picked up a brush in over a year? Or did he intend the earring to shout out to friends and strangers alike that, despite all evidence to the contrary, he was actually some kind of rebel?

In any event, Claire's response upon seeing it had been one of honest admiration—"You know, I've always liked that sort of jewelry on men," she'd said, casting a sidelong glance at William. And later, Porter and Lucy had had a good laugh imagining William perched grumpily on a stool the next day at the Piercing Pagoda, a gleaming diamond punched through his droopy lobe.

Despite Claire's approval (and Lucy's too—she'd thought it conveyed an air of "urban sophistication"), Porter's earring had lasted only four months. He'd decided to remove it and allow the hole to close up after three other graphic artists in his office (plus his *boss!*) all got doofy-looking studs of their own.

"So will you go on to Colorado?" William said. "By yourself?"

"Actually, no, I'm heading back to Pittsburgh too. The dealer said he'd replace the transmission for free, so I'm going to take him up on it." Porter surveyed William, trying to judge his mood. Then he just plunged ahead: "And I'm also giving that woman a ride," he said, nodding in Delilah's direction. "She needs to meet up with her boyfriend. It turns out they're pregnant."

"Really? You're taking her along?" William looked over at Delilah, then back at Porter. "She has no transportation of her own?"

"He took it," Porter said. "The boyfriend. It's a long story."

"And you feel you've come to know her that well in a couple of days? You trust this woman?"

Porter nodded. "Yeah, definitely. She's helped me with the kids too."

"She doesn't look pregnant."

"Well, she is. Just a few weeks."

"But how do you know for sure? This might very well be some kind of ruse. I've read about these Gypsies, you know. They can be real con artists. Real pros. They marry wealthy widowers and then poison them. They give them digitalis to bring on a heart attack, and then they make off with the inheritance."

Porter grinned. He was about to say it was a good thing that he wasn't a wealthy widower until he realized he *was* a widower—he just wasn't wealthy. A *widower*. He was a fucking *widower*.

"She looks like she could be a Gypsy," William said, glancing over at her. "I'd be careful if I were you."

"But I don't have much money. Plus, I'm a little young for a heart attack."

William waved him off. "I'm sure they have other schemes."

"Don't worry," Porter said. "She's not a Gypsy. She's really not. She just wants to hook up with her boyfriend in Pittsburgh. He doesn't even know she's pregnant."

William frowned. "Well, but how did . . ." he began, but then stopped himself. "Oh, I suppose it's not my concern. Not my concern at all. But I do advise caution, Porter, please? This place gives me an ill feeling, I must tell you. I don't know how you managed to land yourself in such a spot." William gazed for a while in the direction of the beach with its knocked-down speakers; then he seemed to conduct a quick survey of the entire camp, his eyes sweeping over the tepee village, the VW bus with the blinking Christmas lights, and finally, Jasper's yellow castle of a tent.

Porter was glad that Jasper had taken off before their arrival. He was glad, in fact, that everyone had taken off. No explanation of this place, however well articulated, would ever penetrate William and Claire's glossy veneer, and Porter didn't want to be put in the position of having to explain it. Let Kaylie give it a shot during the car ride to Indianapolis. Let Benny have a go at it, for God's sake. Once they all piled into that rental car and headed off into the sunset, Porter didn't care what was said or done or admitted to. The next time he'd have to face Claire and William again somehow seemed like years away.

"It was late," Porter said. "I was tired. So I was just looking for someplace to camp . . ." and then he remembered the brochure, and he didn't want to get into all that. "But we've had a great time here. It's a great place."

William cocked his head and grinned in a way that suggested he didn't believe a word Porter was saying. "Yes, well, whatever," he said. "I trust you can find your way back safely. When do you expect to arrive?"

"By tomorrow, I hope. Or maybe the next day, depending on how it goes with the transmission."

"Okay, fine, then," William said with a small smile. He leaned against the truck and ran his hand across his hair. "Oh, you know, your brother phoned from New York this morning, concerned with your whereabouts."

"He did? Alex?"

"Yes, he did. Only a moment after Kaylie had called, in fact. Porter, he told Claire some rather troubling things. She was quite upset after getting off the phone with him."

Porter looked over to see Claire shed her yellow sweater, place it neatly on the picnic table, and then follow Benny into the edge of the field, where Benny crouched down to show her something in the grass. Kaylie and Delilah hung back, talking. "Like what things?" he said, turning again to William.

"He was worried, Porter, as we all have been. He expressed concern about your state of mind. Apparently you told him you were away from the children, that they were sleeping elsewhere, and then not long after that you hung up on him? Is that right?"

Porter bristled at the idea that Alex, of all people, was calling his mother-in-law to blindside him in this way. He felt his face flush with anger. "*He's* worried about *my* state of mind? That's a fair comment coming from a selfish asshole like him."

William's face darkened. He was not one to participate in a conversation where a word like "asshole" was tossed so freely about. "I don't believe he was intending to malign you," William said. "After you hung up on him, he couldn't reach you all night or this morning, so he called us. When Claire told him about Kaylie's phone call, I guess the two of them began to compare notes."

"Compare *notes*?" Porter felt a renewed throbbing in his temples. "Christ. That's fucking beautiful. I can hear it now. I can just hear the two of them going at it."

William straightened his back and clasped his hands together. "Well," he said, "nobody likes to be talked about in such a manner, that's true. But I think you underestimate their concern for you."

"Do I?" Porter shot back, his voice rising.

William didn't respond. Instead, he put his hand on the hood of the engine and peered into the array of black tubes and belts. After a while he said, "Engines. You know, I wish at some point I'd taken a course about this sort of mechanical hoo-ha. Because it is just beyond me how a simple engine like this works." He gazed up at Porter with a hopeful expression. "It's a miracle that someone dreamed this up, isn't it?"

Porter shrugged.

"A miracle," William said again, removing his hand from the hood. "So, Porter, what say we join the others? And then, before too long, I'm afraid we should get going. I'd like to try to catch a flight back to Pittsburgh tonight. I have absolutely no interest in spending the night in Indianapolis." He smiled and reached out for Porter's shoulder, clamping down with an iron grip. "Okay?" He squeezed Porter's shoulder twice. "Shall we join the others?"

Under the weight of William's steady grip, Porter felt himself relax, and finally he sighed with an odd relief. "Yeah, okay."

IT TOOK A surprisingly short time to pack all of Kaylie's and Ben's belongings into duffel bags and load them in the trunk of the red sedan. Both readily agreed that it was better to fly back home with their grandparents, especially since, as Porter explained, he probably would see them the next night or the day after that anyway. They would simply be spared the drive and the danger that the transmission would fail somewhere along the way, leaving them stranded yet again. This potential danger also allowed Porter to make the point that Delilah would be a valuable traveling companion should they break down, so that one of them could go get help while the other waited with the truck.

Unfortunately, Claire then seized upon that possibility as a reason to insist that Porter take yet another cell phone to replace the one he'd broken. He was about to protest when it occurred to him that, since he would no longer have the kids, Claire would have no reason to call him every five minutes. In fact, she would have no reason to call him at all.

Much to Porter's surprise, Claire had been completely charmed by Delilah. Or at least she was acting that way—laughing uproariously at the same jokes Delilah used on Porter ("I'll bet you didn't even know that Indians invented fiberglass." "No, I didn't. *Ha, ha, ha.*") and touching her affectionately on the shoulder. Maybe Claire had been expecting a pitched battle over the children, and when it turned out to be so easy to snatch them away, she had all this excess energy to spend. In any event, the result was that she could barely contain herself. She hugged Porter several times, telling him to "Take care, love. Take care. Be safe. And take extra time if you need it. Please, don't rush. The children will be fine with us, so don't worry about them. Do what you have to do . . ." and on and on. Porter wondered if, upon his return, he would actually be welcome at all.

Everything was fine until the final bell, when the last door was shut and the waving began and the car started to back away. That's when Benny melted down. "Daddy!" he wailed. *"DAAAD!"* Porter could see him in there, struggling against his seat belt, as hands reached back to comfort him. Then the door popped open and out he rushed, arms flailing as he barreled toward Porter. He collided with Porter's waist, and they hugged strenuously for a moment. Then Porter picked him up, Benny's legs dangling, as the boy sobbed against him.

"I don't wanna go!" he cried. "I don't. I don't."

Claire had gotten out of the car too and was approaching cautiously, her face drawn. "Don't worry, Benny," she said. "We'll have fun. You'll see your daddy soon."

"But I . . . I . . ." he sobbed.

"You know what, partner?" Porter said, lowering Benny to the ground. He crouched slightly, grabbing his boy by the shoulders. "I'll bet you'll get a movie on that plane. How about that? And earphones and everything?"

"Really?" Benny said, looking up through tear-filled eyes. "Gramma said no."

Claire rolled her eyes. "The flight's too short, Porter. You should know that. It's only half an hour. A puddle jumper."

Of course. "But you still get the earphones, right? With all those channels?"

"And a meal?" Benny said hopefully.

Porter looked to Claire for guidance. He didn't want to fuck up again, although it did give him a certain satisfaction to see Claire struggling this way.

"I'm sure they'll have those peanuts you like," Claire offered. "And any drink you want."

Benny wiped his nose on his arm and sniffed. "Okay," he said, then let go of Porter and turned to Claire.

She took him firmly by the hand and started to lead him away, but Benny stopped for a moment, looked once more at Porter, and said, "I love you, Daddy." Then his eyes flicked to Delilah. "I love you, Delilah."

Porter was momentarily speechless, but Delilah stepped forth into the void. "I love you, sweetheart," she said, blowing him a kiss.

Porter lifted his hand and gave a childlike wave. "Me too!"

Claire delivered them a pained smile. "Come on now," she said, tugging on Benny's arm, hauling him off to the car even as he continued to gaze wistfully over his shoulder at Porter and Delilah. "We've got a plane to catch."

FORTY-FIVE MINUTES LATER, Delilah returned from her tepee with all her worldly possessions packed into a large, stitched Mayan bag. Or Incan bag. Or whatever advanced society it was that liked to paint black stick figures of warriors and goats on everything.

Porter was relieved not to have to think about his kids' needs for a while, but without them he felt oddly exposed, as if their presence had sheltered him somehow. Since the moment William had driven away in that red sedan, dropping out of view into the valley, Porter had felt a mounting tension between himself and Delilah that he hoped wasn't sexual. But it had started instantly, this vague discomfort. "Well," he'd said when the car was gone, turning to her with a smile.

"Well," she'd said. "I guess I'd better go pack, right?"

"Right."

"Okay." But she'd just stood there, smiling.

"Okay."

It had been agonizing. He'd hoped it would pass. But now, with her return, everything was immediately charged again. He couldn't think of anything to say. For the past two days they'd done nothing but talk, a nonstop stream of family history and personal philosophy and exchanged witticisms. So why had it suddenly turned into such a struggle?

"Where should I put this?" she said, holding up her bag.

"Oh, anywhere."

"Okay. Like just up front?"

He dropped the hood with a slam, an act that made him feel self-consciously masculine. "Sure, if you want."

"Okay. That's great." She opened the door and climbed in.

He came around to the driver's side and scooted in beside her. It was hot but comfortably dry. Delilah's knees had little blond hairs that glistened in the sun. "Boy, I'm wiped out," he said. "I didn't really feel it until just now."

"You want me to drive?" she said. "I feel fine."

"Oh, no," Porter said. "No, that's all right. I'll be fine. Besides, this truck is a little hard to handle. It doesn't have power steering."

She grinned, rolling her eyes. "Did Jasper's pot wipe out your memory or something? This was *my truck*, remember? I've driven this thing about twenty thousand miles. Even without power steering."

Porter shook his head. "I'm a true idiot, aren't I? Not to mention a sexist pig. I'm sorry."

"I know my arms are toothpicks, but they're strong. I'm a massage therapist, so my hands and arms, especially all up in here"—she ran a finger along her forearm—"are pure muscle."

"You're kidding." Porter laughed. "You're a masseuse?"

She looked hurt. "Yeah. So?"

"No, I didn't mean it that way. I just mean, that's the whole reason we stopped at this place." Porter hung his hands in the steering wheel, smiling at her. "In that brochure, you know, it says something about a licensed masseur on location, and I was joking with Kaylie, saying how, after a day of driving, I really needed a massage."

"Really?"

"Sure. No, that's cool that you're a masseuse. That's totally cool."

She turned to him, folding a knee up underneath herself. "Well, I could give you that massage tonight if you still want it. I don't usually toot my own horn, but I am really, really good at it. You'll feel like you have a brand-new body."

"Oh, no, that's okay. No. I just need some rest."

"Don't worry," she said with a devilish grin. "It's not a sexual massage. I won't make you get naked or anything."

His face flushed. "I wasn't thinking that. It's just that I don't really need one anymore."

"Hey, I saw you walking today, after your fun night at Jasper's. You looked like my grandfather. Don't tell me you couldn't use a massage."

"Well, we'll see," he said. "But I will let you drive. How about that? I actually would love to take a nap while you take the first shift."

"Yeah, sure. It'll be fun to be back behind the wheel of this thing again." She started to shimmy over to his side.

Porter opened his door and stepped down. As she got herself situated behind the wheel, Porter closed the door and leaned in the window. "Just head up to I-Seventy. Then we're on that almost all the way to Pittsburgh."

"Okay." She was doing a little mock driving to get comfortable, moving her hands over the wheel and reaching for the stick shift.

"And remember what Jasper said. Keep testing the stick to make sure it's loose. If it starts to get tight, pull over and we'll put some fluid in."

"Got it." She reached down, turned the ignition, and the engine sprang to life. She fed it gas, and it revved with power, the metal shuddering against his hands. She turned to him. "You'd better get in, chief," she said with a smile. "We're on our way."

Porter jogged around to the back door and closed himself in. As Delilah drifted out of the campsite and then pulled slowly away, he crawled up to the bed and nestled under the damaged paneling to watch their exit from the long window. They dropped into the valley, branches scraping at the roof of the camper, crossed the little bridge, and then climbed the other side to the state highway. One last look at that defaced sign—the handiwork, he now knew, of Uncle Charlie, that oddest of the odd.

Good-bye, Charlie's Open World, Porter thought. *Good-bye, Andrea and Seri. Good-bye, Jasper. Good-bye, Shower Girl. Bye-bye, tepees and lake. Good-bye.*

The phrase "good riddance" then skittered across his mind, but the truth was, Porter already felt a little nostalgic for the place. He thought about Delilah down below, driving him home, driving him into the night as his father had so many times.

It still surprised Porter that he was now the father. He was the person in charge, the decision-maker, the caretaker. But now, as he lay in this bed watching the Indiana farmland roll by, *he* was being taken care of. For the first time in years, it seemed, he was being taken care of.

The thrumming of the highway soon brought Porter around to the absolute state of exhaustion he knew he had to yield to sooner or later. He kicked off his shoes, let them fall to the floor below, curled up on his side under the blanket, and closed his eyes. And immediately his mind sagged and darkened. Twisted memories began to course through the folds of his brain. He felt a dull flash of panic, remembering William's stern warnings about Gypsies, which briefly caused Porter's limbs to stiffen and twitch like those of a nightmare-stricken child.

Finally he succumbed. His head lolled back and forth, and his mouth fell open. His hands loosened from clenched fists to splayed, nimble fingers that lay unmoving upon the sheets. But his mind, as always, raced over the familiar terrain of his fears—casting him off boats into a molasseslike ocean, pummeling him with fists and bottles and sticks, slowing him time and again into the grasping hands of his mysterious, relentless pursuers.

No! he kept trying to scream as they grabbed at him. *Help!*

But of course he was asleep and, despite his frustration, could not speak.

CHAPTER ELEVEN

DELILAH had no idea where this rest stop was. Western Ohio? Eastern Ohio? West Virginia? "I wasn't really paying attention," she said. "You said just stay on Seventy, right? Well, we're still on Seventy."

She and Porter sat on opposite sides of the camper's little table with the road atlas spread open between them. It was nearly midnight. Porter was still trying to orient himself after being jarred awake by the slam of the hood; Delilah had been checking on the level of the transmission fluid. ("You didn't wake up the other two times I did it," she'd said by way of apology, "so I didn't think you would this time.") Outside, the fluorescent glow of the streetlights made the surrounding landscape—the grass and trees and picnic tables—seem cast in pewter.

"Well," Porter said. "Did we go through Columbus? You would

have remembered that. It's a pretty big city. You know, like tall buildings?"

Delilah shrugged. "Beats me. At night it all looks pretty much the same to me. But what does it matter? We're about five hours closer to Pittsburgh than we were five hours ago."

Porter supposed she was right. It didn't really matter. But as a lover of maps—a *connoisseur* of maps—it gnawed at him not to know where the hell they were spending the night.

"You could go out and ask one of them," Delilah said, nodding out the window at the handful of tractor-trailers lined up down the asphalt. "If you really have to know."

"Oh, yeah, right," Porter said haughtily. "If I want to get my head busted open. No, that's okay." But what was that supposed to mean? That your average long-haul trucker liked nothing better than to commit felony assault when asked for directions? He looked at Delilah with a befuddled squint. "It's not that I really have to know. I just can't believe you don't pay any attention to where you are. It's so completely foreign to me not to know exactly where I am when I'm driving somewhere."

"Porter, look," Delilah said. "I appreciate you letting me come with you to Pittsburgh. I really do. But you've got to find something else to do with this anger. Because I don't really want it."

Porter scoffed a single laugh of disbelief. "Anger?" he said. "I'm not angry."

She smirked, raising her eyebrows.

"I'm *not*."

"Oh, c'mon. Look at yourself. You're totally angry. You're about to pop a vein."

"Well, yeah, I'm angry now," he said. "Because you keep saying I am when I'm not."

She cocked her head playfully, grinning. "You're not serious."

He looked down at his hands, then out the window.

"Really," she said. "You're not going to stick with that statement, are you?"

Had he been angry at her before? Maybe a little irritated, but not angry. But why should he even be irritated with her after she'd done all the driving while he snoozed away? Just because she hadn't paid attention to where they were when, true enough, it didn't really matter anyway? "All right," he said. "Whatever."

"So is that supposed to be an apology?"

He let out his breath and gazed at her. "I guess, yeah. I'm sorry. I don't know why I'm so irritable."

"You don't? You really don't?"

"Well," he said. "I always seem to get a little worked up after a run-in with my in-laws."

She smiled. "Now we're getting somewhere."

"And I do feel kind of bad about sending Kaylie and Ben off with them. But it *was* the best thing to do. You have to admit that. I didn't want them out on the road with us when this truck is so unreliable."

Delilah just sat there expectantly.

"Also, I mean, this trip *has* pretty much been a disaster. It hasn't exactly been the wholesome, healing process I thought it would be."

"Maybe not wholesome," Delilah said. "But I thought you were doing a great job with them. They're really smart, both your kids. I don't think you have to protect them as much as you think you do. And, God, that Claire. They don't stand a chance with her. If it was up to her, she'd stick those kids in a sealed jar until they were about thirty."

Porter grinned. "You just wait," he said. "You wait until you have your own kid. Then you'll see how protective you feel."

"I know, I know," she said. "I'll probably change my tune, right? But I hope I don't. I hope I don't shield my kid too much. I hope I'm able to let it experience the world without me standing guard all the time."

"And you think that's what I do? Stand guard too much?"

"Not really, no. But, well, sometimes maybe it seems like you do a little."

Porter could feel himself getting pissed off all over again. Nothing lit his fuse faster than receiving a condescending lecture on child-rearing from the childless. "Like when?"

Delilah sat back. "I'm not judging you. I'm just trying to figure out how I might, like, do some things differently, you know? Because I'm starting to think about all this stuff now that I'm pregnant, and I'm trying to decide how I'm going to handle it when I'm in your position."

Porter took a deep breath. "So what would you have done differently?"

"Oh, it's not anything specific. I mean, it's obvious you love them so much. But sometimes, with Benny especially—like at the lake?—you sort of protect him, when, I don't know, he might be better off in the long run if he learned to fend for himself."

"Fend for himself? He's *eight*!" And Porter was about to really unload on her. An entire platoon of his best sarcastic slings was poised at the front of his brain for immediate deployment. But instead, he gave a short, breathy laugh and shook his head. "You just wait," he said. "Wait until that kid of yours is as old as Benny. And one morning your boy doesn't want to go to school. He just refuses. So you say, 'Are you sick?' and he says, 'No.' So you say, 'Do you have a hard test or something?' 'No.' So why don't you want to go to school?' And he says because some kids on his bus have started calling him 'Cue-ball boy.' So you say, 'Cue-ball boy?' And he looks up at you and says, 'You know, because of Mom's head?' "

Delilah sighed.

"So first do that," Porter said. "Go through that. And then come back and tell me that you don't you need to protect your kids as much as you think you do."

"Yeah, I guess," she said. "I mean, that's really tough. But isn't that just life, kids being mean to each other? Isn't that something they've got to learn to deal with on their own sooner or later?"

And this, it seemed to Porter, was perhaps the greatest parenting dilemma of all time, one that he'd spent a good part of the past decade trying to figure out. How much are you supposed to do when it comes to shielding your kids from unpleasantness? How much coddling is too much? How much is too little? Get out the Spock, see what he says. Now get out the Brazelton, see what *he* says. And how long does Ferber say you're supposed to let the baby bawl at night before going in to comfort him? Thirty minutes? Forty-five? Don't let him wail away for too long or it will damage his sense of trust and security. Don't rush in too quickly or he'll become too dependent on love and affection and develop separation problems later on. Too dependent on love and affection. A *baby*. Now there was a concept.

"But don't listen to me," Delilah went on. "I mean, my kid's not even going to *have* a father. At *all*. Then, to top it off, it's gonna have *me* for a mom." She grinned. "I dread the day it gets old enough to figure out what a curse that is."

"Oh, you'll be fine," Porter said. "You'll do just fine. But also, don't you think Don might stick it out with you, once he finds out?"

"He already made his decision," she said sourly.

"But he didn't. Not a well-informed one."

"Oh, come on. I don't want him to come back to me just because of this. I told you that. That's not why I want to tell him. I just thought he should know."

"But he may decide to come back anyway, regardless of why you want to tell him."

"I hope not." She curled her fingers up against the heel of her hand and started to scrutinize them.

Porter found himself gazing at Delilah's tiny hands, at those narrow fingers with their clean, clipped nails. The hands of a masseuse? They seemed too thin and fragile.

The only real massage Porter had ever gotten was a year or so before at the Allegheny Racquet Club, a pricey outfit near work where some of his DINK co-workers (Double Income, No Kids) were members. And one day after he'd been up all night tending to Lucy and really felt like crap (and must have looked it too), those swell DINKs pitched in to buy him a massage from the best therapist there, a guy named Anton.

Anton tipped the scales at about two seventy-five, his mouth hung open as he worked, and his hands felt like warm, boneless sirloin. Those slabs worked their way lovingly around Porter's back for the better part of an hour. Afterward, Porter couldn't even stand up. It was as if he'd become boneless himself.

But a massage with Delilah's miniature digits? It wasn't that Porter didn't believe her; he just couldn't imagine it.

Finally he cleared his throat and said, "So did he ever tell you why he left you for what's-her-name? That other woman? Stacey?"

"No."

"You guys didn't talk about it?"

"No."

"So you have no idea?"

Delilah shook her head. "Not besides him calling me flaky." She lowered her face wearily into her hands.

Porter watched her. After a moment he asked, "Are you crying?"

"No. I'm thinking."

"About what?"

"About why he left me." She looked up, her face suddenly flushed and anxious. "Because, you know, he didn't even *like* her that much. Sure, I mean, she was cute and young. But she was *so* spaced out. A flower child extraordinaire. Don even made fun of her when she first arrived. 'Oh, *wow*,' he'd go, imitating her. 'Oh, like, *wow*, like, I think we must have been lovers in a previous life. Do you want me to toss your I-Ching? I'd love to toss your I-Ching.' "

Porter laughed. "What's an I-Ching?"

"Oh, God, who the fuck knows? It's like some mystical, Eastern fortune-telling bullshit. She tossed my I-Ching, looked at it for two seconds, and then gave me this look of total pity. 'Oh, no!' she goes. 'What?' I go like a total sucker. 'Tell me!' And she goes, with all this fake sympathy, 'It's not positive, Delilah. The energy is all bad. It says that you're going to lose something. Not everything. But something, like, really, really important to you.' So two days later she lures Don into her little butterfly net, and that was it for us."

Porter was trying to think what Don might look like. What sort of guy would Delilah go for? Some good-times surfer-dude pothead? Or more of a troubled, intellectual, poet pothead? Then he remembered that picture he'd seen on her dresser, the one of the bearded guy. Nah, that guy had to be a friend. She wouldn't have kept a picture of Don on her dresser after he'd dumped her that brutally. "So," Porter said. "You don't think Don really loves her?"

"I can't imagine he does. But I guess you can never imagine your ex falling in love with someone else, right? It's always going to seem like someone who's totally wrong for them, and who's probably the complete opposite of you."

Porter sat back, closed his eyes, and started to rub at his temples. He could hear the sound of cars rushing by on I-70. It was now well after midnight, but he wasn't going to bed anytime soon. He'd just slept for five hours. The smart thing to do, he supposed, would be to get right back on the highway and let Delilah get her rest while he drove. But what was the hurry? Besides, he liked the way this conversation was turning; he liked talking to Delilah about love and relationships. He just wished he had something to drink. "Hey," he said, looking at her. "You didn't happen to pack any alcohol in that bag of yours, did you?"

"No. I'm not much of a drinker. I'm too little. I get drunk too fast." Then she smiled. "I've got a few joints, though, if you want."

Porter held up a flat hand. "I better not. That stuff of Jasper's nearly killed me."

"Don't worry. This isn't that. This is just regular stuff. It's pretty mild."

Porter glanced out the window, trying to assess their chances of getting caught by the state police. It made sense that the police would patrol a rest stop like this for drugs, prostitution, and whatnot associated with the trucking trade. But where would the hookers and dealers come from? This place seemed to be in the middle of nowhere, although, for all Porter knew, it very well could be on the outskirts of *somewhere*. In any event, he could already envision the whole thing like a scene straight out of *Cops*: the flashlight shining in the window, the barking of orders, then the handcuffs and the humiliating trip in the patrol car, followed by the standard offer to make his one phone call.

And who would he call? Not Claire and William. And certainly not his own ridiculous parents, who were out of touch anyway, unless Porter felt like leaving a message for them at the goddamn ranger station. Not Alex, who, beneath his veil of concern, would be brimming with superiority and probably taking notes for his next book. How about somebody from work? Nah, too risky. He could already see the gossipy e-mail circulating, popping up on everybody's screen. So who? He couldn't think of anyone. Not a single person. Then suddenly a name leapt to mind—Joe Hinchcliff. Maybe he'd call Joe Hinchcliff. "Joe," he'd say, "you gotta bail me out. Take the truck as collateral." And Joe would say, "Aw, jeez, Porter. Honest to Pete. Oh, all right. I'll be there. Just tell me where you are, and I'll come take care of it for ya."

"So you want some?" Delilah said. "It's totally mellow, good-feeling stuff."

Porter sighed. "Yeah, I guess so. Why not?"

Delilah leaned over and rummaged in her Mayan bag, producing a silver cigar tin. Inside were three joints, some loose grains of pot, a few scraps of rolling paper, and a turquoise-studded lighter. She plucked out a joint, grabbed the lighter, and snapped the tin closed.

"Believe it or not, pot actually gets me all revved up," she said. "I won't be able to go to sleep after this, but what the hell. Looks like you're not going to sleep anytime soon either."

Delilah fired it up and started toking away like a pro. It was a sexy thing to see her doing that, so fluid and comfortable with that turquoise lighter, and the squinty way her eyes got when she held in her hit. Finally she breathed it out and handed the joint to Porter.

He sucked a few times, tentatively at first. But Delilah was right—this pot was good-feeling stuff, nothing at all like Jasper's. Already he felt fine. Happy, even. This was more like the feeling he remembered from college. That chemically induced urge to create, to love, to laugh, to forget about the drudgery of your life for an evening. Done right, drugs could be pretty fucking great. Too bad they had to cause so many problems and destroy communities and kill people, earning the scorn of proper society. Because the simple fact of the matter was that drugs had the power to make you feel good when you weren't feeling good, and that was such a blessing. It really was. Porter had forgotten.

Why hadn't he and Lucy gotten stoned when she was sick—especially toward the end, during that last month before the final, hospitalized decline? What would there have been to lose? Maybe it would have seemed frivolous, to have shared a false happiness at such a truly miserable time. Maybe there would have been no benefit to that. But what had been the benefit of the alternative?

Porter sucked in deeply one last time, then closed his eyes and allowed the juices of pleasure to roam freely around his brain, triggering warm spasms of happiness in the joy centers of his frontal lobe. *I'll be forever thankful for this,* he thought. And then he grinned, picturing Thanksgiving at the Winters', and how Claire always insists that everyone go around the table and say what they've been most thankful for over the previous year. "Besides my loving family, of course," he would say this year, "I'm most thankful for the joint I smoked on the way back to Pittsburgh, somewhere between Indiana and Pennsylvania."

Finally he tipped his head forward and looked at Delilah. "You know," he said, "I wonder if you should be smoking this stuff when you're pregnant."

She made a face. "It's probably not great. But I've cut back so much. This is, like, rare. You know how they say it's all right, even healthy, for pregnant women to have a glass of wine every so often? I figure it's probably the same thing with this. A few hits of mellow weed once a month can't really hurt, can it?"

Porter had taken another hit while she was talking, and now, holding it in, he couldn't answer. Truly gifted potheads seemed to be able to talk while holding their breath, or at least manage to talk and keep the smoke down somehow. But not Porter. He'd surely scorch his throat and go into an embarrassing hacking fit. So instead he held up his hand as a placeholder in the conversation. Eventually he let out his breath and then said, "I hope not. I mean, you hear about crack babies. I guess I never heard anything about pot babies, though."

"I'm only going to have one more hit anyway," she said, taking it from him. She looked down and rubbed her tummy. "So don't worry, Sam."

"Sam?" Porter said.

"That's what I've decided to name it. Just this morning I decided."

"But what if it's a girl?"

"It'll still be Sam. Samantha was my sister's name. So it'll be in honor of her either way."

Porter cocked his head quizzically. "Your sister?" And as soon as the words left his lips, he remembered, and his face flushed with shame. Christ, what had the little girl died of? A brain tumor? Spinal meningitis? No, it was leukemia, wasn't it? Yeah, on the day JFK was assassinated. "Yeah, well," he said, trying to recover. "Then that's a great idea. Just great."

"It did make me feel great this morning, thinking about it. I mean, it's not like I knew my sister that well, or at all, really, because I was so little. But I always feel like she's been with me somehow. And now, with this baby, I feel like she going to reveal herself in a new way, you know? Like her energy is going to come back in this baby?"

"Yeah, uh-huh," Porter said, but he wasn't really listening. He was trying to figure out what his fucking problem was. Why hadn't he been able to keep track of one of the most important stories of Delilah's life? Was he was really that self-obsessed, or just forgetful, or simply too weak to carry the burden of other people's sorrows along with his own?

"But I have to say that you get a lot of the credit," Delilah said. "Just being with you and your kids these past couple of days."

"Credit for what?"

"For helping me decide to keep it."

Porter blinked with astonishment. "You mean, instead of having an abortion?"

She nodded.

"But I thought you'd already decided."

"Not completely, I hadn't. I mean, this is pretty scary, going into this all alone, with hardly any money or anything. No place to live. No insurance. I have no idea how I'm going to pay for any of this, or what I'm going to do for money after it's born." She looked off, out the window, as if searching the rest stop for career ideas. Then she turned to him again, her face suddenly alight. "But seeing you with those kids! I swear, ya'll are like this little self-contained unit, you know? A little island in the middle of some big storm. And I just said to myself, 'I can do that too. I can make my own little island.' "

Porter felt a thump in his heart and a warmth emanating through his chest.

"That's why it made me so sad to see Kaylie and Ben carted off like that, by your in-laws. Even though I can see now how it's more practical and everything, with the problems with the truck. But I really wanted to say to Claire, I wanted to yell at her, 'Hey, what are you doing? You can't take those kids! They're part of the island!' "

Porter grinned. "She would have written you off as a total lunatic if you'd tried to explain something like that. She's so closed-minded. She never thinks about how other people live their lives or what problems they have. She never even thinks about her *own* life. Talk about denial. I'll tell you something. The main reason she wants those kids back—the whole fucking point about getting the kids back into that walled castle of hers—is so she doesn't have to think about the fact that her daughter is dead. She's as much as admitted that to me."

"Really?"

Porter nodded aggressively. "Just doesn't want to think about it. And you know what's even worse? She tries to brainwash my kids into acting that way too. She's been telling Kaylie and Ben that the most important thing for them to do right now is to 'stay busy,' which of course they interpret as meaning they should try to forget about their mother." He paused a moment, fuming. "She's just such a condescending bitch sometimes. Always judging everybody else, when meanwhile *she's* the one in total denial." Porter folded his arms over his chest, shook his head, and then emitted a *hrumph* of disgust—the precise trio of actions, he realized, that his father so often relied upon to close out his huffy tirades about the various things that drove him "nuts."

"She didn't seem that bitchy to me," Delilah said. "Just a little controlling."

"Well, yeah, of course," Porter said. "She's a control freak. But you don't even really know her. She was pouring on the charm for you. That's her public face. That's her country-club face. You should see her when she's really scheming. She gets all . . . you know . . . like . . ." But when Porter tried to draw an image of this into his mind, what he saw instead was Claire as William had described her to him earlier—desperately afraid, and shrinking away, as William pounded his bleeding fist against the security box.

Over the past couple of years Porter often had seen in Claire the manifestations of fear suppressed: the chewed hangnails, the sharp tongue, and of course the compulsive busyness—the endless errands and "must-do's" and manic supervising of the hired help. But he'd never seen her openly afraid. Not when Lucy was first diagnosed ("Nonsense!" had been her response), not when it was announced that the cancer had spread throughout Lucy's midsection ("You'll just have to stop it," she'd snapped at the doctors), not even after Lucy had died ("Porter, you're going to have to get ahold of yourself," she'd told him, gripping his shoulders. "We've all known this was coming. Now you're going to have to get ahold of yourself for those kids").

But now, thinking about Claire trembling in that hallway, Porter felt a dark hole open up inside him, and suddenly he didn't know what to say.

"Porter?" Delilah said.

"Oh," he said with a sigh. "It's just, you know, Claire. She's such a head case."

"Yeah, sounds like it."

And they were silent. Porter stared out into the colorless night, at the concrete picnic tables and the gray, trash-strewn lawn. An information kiosk stood guard at the entrance to the bathrooms, its bulletin board empty. Braced against the far side of the bathrooms was a dense thicket of trees and brush that had clearly drawn the short stick in nature's placement lottery. They were probably no different from their brethren trees and brush that had wound up in more glorious locales. But this was their place, this rest stop, and here they would stay.

"So," Delilah said, rubbing her hands together, "you want that massage now? This would be a perfect time for it. I'm completely wired."

"Really? You mean it?"

Delilah's face broke into a crooked smile. "I've gotta work this out of my system somehow."

"Okay. Yeah, sure. Like right here?"

"I've done it right here before."

A few minutes later, Porter was on his stomach, shirt off, and

Delilah's bony little fingers were prodding their way forcefully up the valley of his spine. It was a painful but not altogether unpleasant experience. A few times Porter cringed—"*Ow!*"—and she'd say, "That's where you carry your tension." Then she'd work through that area, pulverizing it, until the muscle felt flattened and slightly bruised.

At first Delilah was standing next to him, resting one knee on the bunk as she worked. But then she said, "This angle is just too awkward," and she hitched up her dress and climbed aboard, straddling Porter's butt. He could feel her bare knees against the sides of his stomach; the warmth of her thighs radiated through his khakis. From this vantage point, Delilah was able to go at him with a renewed vigor. Her fingers probed his neck, working their way around his brain stem and behind his ears before settling in for one last assault on his shoulders.

Eventually the pressure of her strokes eased into a gentle pushing-around of his skin, and after that the massage became nothing more than light finger caresses up his sides and down his spine to the top of his pants, giving him goose bumps. She traced the ridges of his ears, of his jawline, then reached for his arms and out to his hands, where she ran her fingers back and forth across the hair of his knuckles.

"Is this still part of the massage?" Porter mumbled, his face buried in the cushions.

"Yep," she said, drawing her fingertips along the rims of his armpits. "It's the best part. The cool-down."

"More like 'the heat-up,' " Porter said.

Delilah scooted back off of Porter's butt onto his thighs and resettled herself. Then her fingers continued their merry journey from his armpits down his sides and along his ribs, slipping briefly into the cavity of his stomach before finally reaching land's end at the top of his pants, where, after a moment (of indecision?) they began to worm their way under the elastic band of his boxers. "You know," she said, "we could fool around if you want. Unless you think that'd be too weird."

Porter stopped breathing, her words hanging in the air above him. "Fool around?"

She put her hands on her thighs. "Would that be too weird for you? I'd totally understand if you thought it was."

"It'd be sort of weird, yeah."

"So does that mean you want to do it?"

"Do you?"

"Yeah, I do. But I'm all horny from that joint. That's all it takes, can you believe it? I had like three hits."

Porter made an effort to roll to his side, and Delilah rose up on her knees to let him turn beneath her. "I guess we could," he said, glancing warily up out of the corner of his eye.

She laughed. "There's some enthusiasm."

"Well, it's a little awkward," Porter said. "I mean, I feel guilty."

"I know you do. I know. But you shouldn't. I mean, just try to think of it as a free, good thing, okay? Not all twisted up with everything else? Sex doesn't have to be so loaded, you know. It's just your fucked-up childhood that makes you feel that way."

Was it? Was it from his childhood? Or was this kind of guilt a part of your genetic makeup, passed on through the generations? "But also you're pregnant," Porter said. "That makes it doubly weird, doesn't it?"

"No. That makes it *safe*. I can't get pregnant again, right? Besides, I think that must be the other reason I'm so horny. All those hormones. Isn't that kind of screwed up, now that I think about it? That women should get horny *after* they're pregnant? What's that supposed to accomplish?"

Porter didn't know what to say to that. It was the first time he'd ever heard of such a phenomenon. Lucy certainly hadn't become horny after getting pregnant. Only nauseated, depressed, claustrophobic, and short-tempered. In fact, Porter had spent most nights of Lucy's first trimesters on the living-room couch.

"I just don't want to make it all awkward between us," Porter said. "And awkward when we get together with Don."

Delilah sat back. "Why do you think it has to be awkward? It doesn't have to be. It's not foreordained."

"Just a prediction," Porter said.

She looked away, shaking her head. "Then don't even think of it as sex. Let's try that. Think of it as a continuation of the massage. And if you feel like massaging me at some point, jump right in."

Porter cracked a wry smile. "A continuation of the massage?"

Delilah crawled back on top of him, leaned down, and kissed him on the earlobe. "You tell me if you want to stop," she said quietly. "How about that? Or just push me off when you've had enough. I'm used to that." She kissed his earlobe again, and then her dry lips brushed against his jaw and moved toward the edge of his mouth, where, after a small peck, she pulled back and gazed at him. "Okay so far?"

"Maybe we could just turn out the light?"

Delilah reached blindly above herself, and the camper went dark.

CHAPTER TWELVE

W A S this how his father felt all those years ago, rocketing down an empty highway in the wee hours of the morning, carrying his slumbering cargo above? Was this what made him such a happy man in those days? Because he *was* happy then, wasn't he? And Porter's mother was also happy, or so it seemed. They had been a little island too, their family, packing themselves into that old camper and hauling ass to Colorado and Montana and Texas and going fishing and hiking and swimming.

Back then, Porter had pitied his father for having to wake up before everyone else and start driving. "Gotta beat the heat," his father used to say. "Get most of the driving out of the way before the sun's too high." It had sounded so self-sacrificing. But now Porter understood the pleasure his father must have felt. Actually, no, it wasn't that he understood it. He just happened to feel the same mysterious pleasure.

Or maybe what Porter felt was simply relief. Relief about being back in the saddle again, about being back on task and focused after his and Delilah's guilty indulgence. Because, despite Delilah's optimistic preamble ("just try to think of it as a free, good thing!"), what they'd done weighed on him. And the funny thing was he *had* been able to think of it as a free, good thing, both as it was happening and for a short while afterward. But eventually that idea in itself became part of the problem. Why should he have a free, good thing? Why should anyone? What had he done to deserve it, and now what would he have to do to pay for it?

Part of the problem too was the fact that Porter had never in his life had such an experience, and it had him turned completely upside down. What *was* that anyway? What had *happened*? He could scarcely believe that people experienced physical pleasure like that on a regular basis simply by taking off their clothes and doing things to one another. Sure, sex with Lucy had been great at the beginning. They'd had some adventures. They'd even fucked once in the woods behind the Winters' tennis court. But even at its best, he now realized, theirs had been just typical collegiate sex, routine suburban maneuvers acted out within the parameters of what was expected.

But, *God*, last night. All Porter could think about, with a sort of stupefied amazement, was how Delilah had played his body as if she were tuning a musical instrument, how she'd put her fingers in places and done things with her mouth and tongue and had taken him into her in ways that had rendered him absolutely dumb with pleasure, unable to move or speak or close his eyes. And most of what had happened Porter couldn't even remember. He'd been trying to reconstruct it as he drove, but those memories were already long gone, blasted out of his brain before they'd had a chance to take hold.

Afterward they'd dozed in a sticky embrace. When Porter had awoken a couple of hours later, he'd had to peel his stomach from hers, a process that had tugged at his gut hairs as if he were removing a large Band-Aid. Delilah had remained limp, dead to the world, her body like baggage. He'd covered her with the sheet, dressed himself, then stepped quietly out into the warm night.

Crickets were chirping at an irritatingly high pitch, and a small breeze pushed through the trees, but otherwise it was silent. Porter strode into the grass, out beyond the apron of fluorescent light, and looked up. The sky arched over him in a glorious purple swath, its zillions of stars twinkling with apparent significance. Smack in the middle hung a dramatic full moon, its craters visible to the naked eye. The entire universe seemed cocked and loaded, anxious to nudge Porter in the direction of a life-altering revelation, or maybe just a glimmer of understanding, or at least *some* kind of epiphany . . . *some*thing.

But what? What did he feel? And what was he doing out here, having sex with this woman he barely knew, not even a month after Lucy had died? And why hadn't he taken better care of his kids? Delilah was right—he shouldn't have banished them to Claire and William's just because that might make things easier somehow. Their lives together should be about more than simply taking the path of least resistance. Ideally they ought to be able to embrace the difficulties, right? Because aren't the difficulties the more substantial and complex side of life, the real meat of it? And isn't that what life—a *real* life, a fully lived life—is supposed to be all about? *Life is what happens while you're busy making other plans.* And that pretty much said it all, didn't it? *Life is what happens while . . .* Where had that quote come from anyway? Porter had first seen it only a couple of months before, but where? Had Lucy read it to him from one of her New Age, coping-with-cancer books?

Then he remembered. He'd seen it on his daily planner at work. It had been the "Quote of the Day" presented in tandem with the day's Dilbert cartoon. Well, that's just fucking great. Porter put his hands on his hips and sighed. He retreated into the gray glow of the streetlights and headed for the bathrooms to take a piss.

And—*ow!*—that had hurt. His whole deal down there felt engorged and kind of strangled, tender to the touch. Plus, his piss stream

was partially blocked and not coming out smoothly, and Porter had
to angle himself creatively in the stall to keep the wayward spray within
the confines of the urinal.

Back at the truck, he'd quietly gotten the engine going and crept
out of there, slinking down the on-ramp to the highway, where he
floored it and kept it floored until his little rig was hurtling through
the night at eighty miles per hour, then ninety—the wind buffeting
him with loud gusts. He shot past an exit sign for Zanesville and
instantly knew where they were: maybe an hour from West Virginia,
less than three hours from home. And this was just the medicine he
needed, this news. Delilah had really covered some ground during her
shift. Porter sailed along, exhilarated, his eyes watering from the rushing air, until he remembered about the fragile transmission and decided he'd better slow the hell down before he blew the whole engine
to pieces.

BEST USED CARS. That's right. That was the name of this place. *Best.*
How perfect. Porter steered into the entrance, drifted toward the office, then came to a stop and cut the engine. He looked around. Everything about this place gave Porter a soft spot for Joe Hinchcliff: those
grimy plastic flags—in Steelers' black and gold—strung across the lot
in mild celebration, and the gargantuan retaining wall, the size of ten
stacked tractor-trailers, that preserved this slice of hillside for all these
crappy cars, or at least that was the hope. At the base of the wall sat
Joe's tiny mobile-home of an office, propped up on cinder blocks and
fronted by a rickety set of steps and an intact row of bleacher seats
from the old Forbes Field ("Demolition contractor's a buddy a mine,"
Joe had said with a wink).

It was only eight in the morning; the office was dark. Porter
walked over and climbed the steps, but he couldn't find any office
hours listed on the door or in the window or anywhere else. The place
would probably be open by nine, ten at the latest. What to do until
then?

He sat down on the top step and gazed out across the lot. It didn't take him long to locate Lucy's Mazda, boxed in against the retaining wall by four decrepit K-Cars. Porter couldn't help but feel a little sorry for the Mazda; he'd so readily cast it aside after all those years of loyal service. And now here it sat, huddled beneath that looming wall, hemmed in by a gaggle of the nerdiest cars ever to hit the market. Evidently, by its placement, Joe Hinchcliff had deemed the Mazda to be among the least salable cars on the lot, which was really saying something. Porter figured its future was pretty bleak. Maybe it would appeal to a poor college student in desperate need of a set of wheels? Because that's really all it was, a set of wheels.

Delilah was still zonked out in the bed, and Porter was glad for that. He'd enjoyed the solitude of the drive, and now he liked being alone in this lot, back in Pittsburgh, under the familiar gray sky. He was looking forward to seeing Joe Hinchcliff, although he was a little embarrassed by the unwarranted level of fondness he harbored for the man. Was it some misplaced father-figure thing he had going on, or what? Because, after all, he barely knew him. Although, the more Porter thought about it, Joe *did* remind him a little of his father—the Pittsburgh version. Goofy and provincial but somehow trustworthy and lovable nevertheless.

Porter and his father's only real bonding had taken place before he was a teenager, back when he was the eager Boy Scout listening breathlessly as his father preached about how to build campfires and dig rain trenches. It wasn't until later, during Porter's sophomore year of high school, that he slipped out of his parents' clutches into the lost and subversive world of art. First it was photography class, where he brewed up black-and-white "studies" of St. Cloud's disaffected youth (mostly backlit shots of his friends slumped in chairs or leaning against walls, trying to look drugged out and hopeless). The photography teacher, Mr. Ziffaleski (the "Ziff Man"), loved Porter's stuff, fell for it completely, and Porter might have gone on to become a photographer if the class hadn't been such a joke. Nobody took it seriously. Porter could never perfect his technique because the other kids were always busting into the darkroom to French-kiss and stick their hands down each other's pants. So it was on to painting, which he could do at home, in the privacy of the basement. Every so often Alex would tromp down the stairs to ridicule him, or his father would pass through and survey the scene with a nervous grin, but otherwise it was pure bliss. This was what he wanted to do for the rest of his life.

Porter's father had never quite gotten the "art thing," had never understood Porter's desire to be a painter. But he also, much to his credit, never made any attempt to stop him, or even to dissuade him from following such an ill-advised path. Toward the end of Porter's college career, his father even made several attempts to "get it" and to be proud of it by asking Porter, during their infrequent phone conversations, what he was trying to do when he painted and whether the creative process made him feel at peace, "like fishing."

When Porter's parents traveled to Pittsburgh for the graduation festivities, his father patiently examined rack after rack of Porter's stored canvases, saying he liked this or that, and he even singled one out for special admiration. Of course, it had to be the one painting Porter was most embarrassed about—a realistic Schenley Heights streetscape of typical working-class row houses fronted by a curbside garden of crisp orange tulips. It was an early painting from the fall of Porter's junior year, and the gloomy girls in his workshop had really blasted him for it, calling the effort, among other things, "surfacy" and "saccharine sweet."

At the session's merciful close, one of the girls approached him and asked in a friendly way, as if to make amends, "So what's the title anyway?" But Porter just looked away and mumbled that it was un-titled. He didn't have the guts to tell her that the painting was actually called *Garden of Hope.* He just wanted to shove the fucking thing in the closet and never look at it again.

But his father stood back and gaped at *Garden of Hope* with a wide smile. "Now *that* looks real," he said. "I'll be goddamned. I can hardly tell it's even a painting. Looks exactly like a picture. How'd you do that?"

Porter tried to explain that how "real" the painting looked wasn't necessarily the point. "I mean, Dad, if you look at one of these over here you'll see—"

"But those are all a little dark and out of focus, don't you think?" his father said, gripping Porter's shoulder. "This one, though, is really stupendous. In this one you really nailed it. And I like the bright colors too. That gives it a happy look. I mean, art should make you feel good, am I right? It should lift your spirits. What's that famous saying? 'Art is the food for the soul of the downtrodden'? Something along those lines?"

Food for the soul of the downtrodden? Porter shrugged.

"Well, whatever. That's the gist of it. That art should fill your soul with light . . . you know, brightness and light? But these other ones over here, if you'll pardon my saying so, seem a little—I don't know—fuzzy. I don't mean to say they aren't good. They're terrific. But they don't really knock my socks off like this one that's so bright and in focus. That's all I'm saying."

At the time, this pratfall of a lecture had really pissed Porter off. But now, remembering his father talking so earnestly about how art should "fill your soul with brightness and light," Porter felt more embarrassed about the kind of person *he'd* been back then. And suddenly he felt ashamed of those dark, blurry paintings he'd tried to pass off as being the product of real emotion, when in fact he'd just been trying to pander to the gloomy aesthetic of the black-clad girls in his workshop.

So his father had been absolutely right—*Garden of Hope* really *had* been the best of the lot, or at least the most honest. Because Porter was just a kid then, after all, and he'd had a fun childhood and was basically happy and healthy. He had love. Nobody to take care of but himself. He was a little in debt, sure. But he had a big shining ego that was strong enough to make him believe he was on the verge of becoming the Bruce Springsteen of the art world. For all he knew, success and happiness stretched out before him like a bright, colorful, in-focus promise.

And what else had his father been right about—his dumb, working-class father who never went to movies or read books because "they just make all that stuff up anyway"? Maybe he'd been right about the trip to Colorado too, about trying to meet up with Porter and the kids there for the week. For as much as Porter had scoffed at the idea, maybe it would have been a great time. Kaylie and Ben hardly spent any time with his parents anymore, and Rocky Mountain National Park probably would have been an ideal place to have them catch up. His father could have taught Benny how to build things and chop wood and carve; they could have whiled away hours in that kind of huddled concentration. And Kaylie might have been able to discover that her grandmother was actually an interesting, talented person beyond the quavering phone voice that asked her several times a year, "So how tall are you now? So how much do you weigh now?"

Porter pictured his parents bumbling around Rocky Mountain National Park, checking with the ranger every fifteen minutes to see if he'd called, and then bickering endlessly about what might have happened to him and the kids and what the proper course of action should be. He thought about his father, bored out of his skull in Thatcher, pouncing on this opportunity for an impromptu family camping trip and then rallying to pull it off, only to arrive and find that he was still stuck with the same person he'd been stuck with all along (Porter's mother), only in a different place.

And she too—sublimated as she was—would also be terribly disappointed that Porter and the kids weren't going to show, although, in the face of her husband's disappointment, she'd have to assume the plucky, optimistic role. And while he'd get to vent unrestrained, muttering his fucks and goddammits for all the world to enjoy, she'd be resigned to saying things like "Oh, I'm sure they'll try to make it if they possibly can" and "These mountains are just so beautiful, aren't they?"

Porter leaned back against the office door and sighed. He should try to reach them to let them know what had happened. He really should. He didn't want them to worry. And who knew what kind of message Alex had left for them, if he'd left any message at all? But it would be too early to call two time zones west, and he didn't have the number anyway. He would have to call his brother.

Would Alex still be asleep? Or already at his desk typing away? Or would he and Chloe be lounging in bed, sipping from mugs of Lemon Zinger and chomping away on bagels topped with cream cheese and boysenberry jam, trying to decide if their life was as fabulous as it possibly could be or whether, with a minimum amount of effort, they could even boost it up a notch?

Porter went over to the truck, retrieved the cell phone from the seat of the cab, and strode back to the steps. What he dreaded most of all was the screening process that had become standard procedure with Alex and Chloe. Apparently, even when they were both home and doing absolutely nothing, they'd still wait for the answering machine to pick up to see who it was. Then, once the offending party was identified, a swift evaluation would ensue, which Porter imagined involved an exchange of raised eyebrows around the following, unspoken question—"Worth our time, or not?"

Porter usually passed this test, as far as he knew. But it irked him to have his plaintive spiel broadcast into their personal space before they'd deign to pick up, as if he were auditioning before some unseen casting director. "Porter, I'm glad it's you," they'd always say upon answering, which Porter took as a not so subtle reminder that *he* should feel lucky, *he* was on the approved list, while the other assorted rabble seeking an audience with The Great Alex and Chloe had to leave a message and perhaps get called back, perhaps not.

Porter dialed, and amazingly, Alex picked up after the first ring. "Bro! Hey. Where've you been?"

"I'm back in Pittsburgh. Just got back this minute."

"So the truck got you back okay?"

"Yeah. But anyway, listen—"

"Porter, I was *worried* about you. Yesterday I had to call *Claire*, of all people, to track you down, only to find out that you'd pulled a disappearing act on Kaylie and Ben? What the fuck's happening, brother? What's going on?"

Porter didn't even know where to begin. "Have you talked to Claire since then?"

"Yeah, of course. We've agreed to keep each other informed. That's how I found out you were on your way back last night. And you're still with that girl? Some pregnant girl?"

"She's not a girl," Porter said. "She's older than I am."

"But Claire said she's, like, some Gypsy? What's that all about?"

"She just wanted a ride to Pittsburgh. Her boyfriend's here. I'm going to drop her off at his place as soon as I get his address."

"Oh," Alex said, apparently mollified. "You're going to drop her off, then?"

"Yeah, at her boyfriend's. That's what I just said."

"And where is he?"

"Alex, I *don't know* yet. I've got to get his address."

"She doesn't have it? The girl?"

Porter felt like hurling the phone against the retaining wall. "No, she doesn't *have* it. That's why I have to *get* it."

Alex paused. "You know, you sound really stressed out. Are you really stressed out?"

"I'm fine," Porter said. "Really, I am. But the reason I'm calling is to find out what happened with Mom and Dad out in Colorado. Have you spoken to them at all?"

No response to that. Which meant what? Was Alex disappointed to discover that Porter was okay after all? And not only okay, but even of sound enough mind to be inquiring into the status of others? After a moment Alex said, "No, we haven't talked. But I left them a message at the ranger station that you wouldn't be coming after all."

"You didn't give them any reason?"

Alex huffed. "The ranger was taking *dictation*, Porter. And not very willingly, I might add. I didn't feel like it was fair to explain your whole situation to him."

His whole situation? What was his whole situation anyway? Porter wouldn't mind hearing Alex's take on that. "Could you do me one favor, then? If Mom and Dad call you, could you tell them to give me a call at this number?" Porter briefly held away the cell phone and read the number off the keypad. "Did you get that?"

"Yeah."

"I just want to tell them I'm sorry for not making it."

"Okay, sure."

Silence.

"So how is everything?" Porter said.

"How is everything? Oh, just dandy."

"That's good. Chloe's fine?"

"Couldn't be better."

"Tell her I say hi, will you?"

There was a crackle of static mixed with unintelligible speech.

"Did you say something?" Porter said.

"No."

Porter took a deep breath. "Alex, are you pissed at me?"

"Oh, c'mon, Porter. Get off it."

Porter paused a moment. "So does that mean you are?"

"Well, *yeah*, kind of. I mean, you hung up on me, Porter. You know, here I am, trying to do you favors and make your life a little easier at a time when my plate is pretty fucking full as it is. I'm working like a dog on this novel thing, trying to stay on top of all that, plus doing my night job at the restaurant, and then twisting myself into knots keeping in touch with you and arranging for you and the kids to get together with Mom and Dad. And you hang up on me?"

"You caught me at a bad moment," Porter said.

"I must have," Alex said. "I must have indeed."

Dead air.

Finally Porter said, "Do you want to know the truth, Alex?"

"The truth about what?" Alex said hesitantly.

"About me. The truth about me."

"Uh, yeah. I guess."

"Well, the truth," Porter began, but then he wasn't quite sure where he wanted to go with this. "The truth, Alex," he said, stumbling ahead, "is that I'm trying my best to figure out which way is up these days. I really am. And I know I may not be acting like a model citizen in the process. I know that. I know I've been a little loose in my responsibilities, and, yeah, with Kaylie and Ben especially. I feel bad about that." An image of Ben struggling to get out of that rental car flooded Porter's mind, and suddenly he felt choked up. "But," he continued, fighting it off, "but, Alex, I *am* figuring some things out, okay? I really am. I feel like this is all going to mean something someday." And then he did feel a tear slip down his face, and he sniffed and wiped at his nose.

Alex said quietly, "You want to tell me about it?"

Porter sniffed some more, embarrassed now. He cleared his throat in an attempt to strengthen his voice. "Someday, maybe," he said. "But not right now."

"Well, I'm always here for you," Alex said with obvious relief. "Whenever you want to talk. I mean, I'll be in and out a lot during the next few days, and, you know, evenings are always a bad time. But otherwise . . ."

"Thanks, Alex."

"So are you going to be okay, then, from here on out?"

For some reason this question made Porter feel as if he were utterly on his own. *From here on out.* Where the hell would he be when he was out? Or would he ever be out? "Yeah," he said. "I'll be okay."

"That doesn't sound very convincing," Alex said.

Oh, fuck you, Porter thought. But he said, "Don't worry, Alex. I'll be fine."

There was an excruciatingly long silence, during which they each took turns breathing into the phone. Finally Alex said, "Well, I guess I should let you go."

"I guess so. Talk to you later."

And with one press of a button their conversation was put out of its misery.

Porter put the phone in his lap and rubbed at his face for a while. Then he heard a familiar voice call out, "Hey, who sold you that piece of crap?" When he looked up, there was Joe Hinchcliff walking toward him across the lot. He wore a tan leisure suit with lapels the size of pizza slices and carried a cute little lunch box at his side, which he swung merrily as he walked. The top of his head glistened with perspiration; dark ovals stained his underarms. He came right up to Porter and gave him a powerful, sweaty handshake, smiling all the while.

"You *walk* here?" Porter said.

"Gotta. Only exercise I get. About nine months ago my doc said it's either walk a lot every day or get a triple bypass a few years down the road."

"How far away do you live?"

"Down there in Bloomfield. About three-point-six miles each way, give or take, depending on the route."

Porter was speechless. The guy looked like a poster child for Couch Potatoes of America. *Then how can you have absolutely no butt?* he wanted to ask. But maybe that hike was the reason. His butt had worn away.

Joe gestured at the camper. "So it got you back here, I see. You have to stop and fill it with fluid much along the way?"

"I didn't," Porter said. "But my traveling companion did most of the driving last evening. I think she filled it up a couple times."

Joe eyed him. "She the one who's friends with those hippie kids?"

"That's right. She's still asleep in there."

"Well, they ain't been back, so I don't know if they're still around. But I do have the address they left me in the office."

The door to the camper opened, and they both turned to see Delilah emerge in her green fringed dress. She stepped down to the asphalt like someone leaving a movie theater, dazed and squinting, using her hand to shield her eyes from the dim sky.

"Hey, missy, you'd better put some shoes on," Joe called out. "There's broken glass all over."

Delilah waved dismissively. "I've got calluses."

"Joe, this is Delilah," Porter said as she approached. "Delilah, Joe." He jerked a thumb in Joe's direction. "He's the one who sold me the camper."

"But I didn't know about that bum transmission, ma'am. We just turn the inventory around here. We turn it around."

Delilah's hair was gorgeously mussed, and you could see the shape of her nipples pushing against the fabric of the dress. Porter felt his groin flare and throb. He smiled at her to convey that he was cool about last night even if he wasn't, but she wasn't looking at him anyway.

"That used to be *my* truck," she said to Joe. "Did he tell you that?"

Joe's face rattled with confusion. "But you're not the . . . that girl who . . . the one who kissed me?" He smiled, his face reddening.

"No. Somebody kissed you?"

Joe looked down at his feet. "Well, it was just a silly thing. It was the girl who was with the guy. The one who sold it to me. She was just thanking me for the money. But that wasn't you, ma'am, I can see that now."

"That was Stacey," Delilah said. "She's about fifteen years younger than I am."

"Oh, that can't be," Joe said, turning on his sales charm. "That would have to make her, let's see, about five years old, right? 'Cause you don't look a day over twenty, ma'am, if you don't mind me saying so. Not a day over twenty." He glanced at Porter. "Does she?"

"Nope."

Delilah grinned. "Such chivalry in these parts."

"You're not from around here?" Joe said.

"Austin, Texas."

"Oh, yeah?" Joe said. "Now that you say it, I can hear the accent a little. Austin, Texas. *Austin City Limits,* right? You ever go to that?"

Delilah shook her head. "I haven't lived there in a long time."

"Did you know they film that thing *inside*? Somebody told me that, and I just can't get over it. You know all that background of the skyline and everything? All fake. An optical illusion."

"That's what they do, I guess," Delilah said.

"But what great music, huh?" Joe said. "Just great, great music. I love that music." And for a moment his eyes glazed over as he stood there holding his lunch box, lost in a little reverie. He actually had to shake his head to bring himself out of it. He looked at both of them with a squinty smile. "You know, it's amazing to me that some people are able to do that with their lives, make great music like that, and here I am, doing *this*, pushing this crap on decent people like you that only ends up getting you stranded."

Porter had an urge to say, *Hey, Joe, it's all relative*, or some such pithy statement. But how was that supposed to make anyone feel better? Because, after all, it *was* all relative, and what some people were doing was relatively a hell of a lot better than what other people were doing.

"Anyway," Joe said, looking at Delilah, "so I got your friends' address, the place they're staying." He turned to Porter. "It's over in Homewood, over there by Westinghouse Park? You know that area?"

Porter nodded. "In college we used to go there to buy kegs. It was the only place you could go without getting carded."

"Sounds about right," Joe said. "One of those drive-through places?"

"Yeah. Where you pull in and they close the garage door behind you? Do your business in cash only? Used to freak me out."

Joe crossed his arms over his chest, the bulk of the lunch box making his elbow jut out. "So these people who your friends are staying with," he said to Delilah. "You happen to know if they're black or African American or whatnot?"

Delilah gave a little laugh. "That's a good question. I don't know."

" 'Cause if they're not," Joe said, "they've got to be about the only ones."

"You know," Delilah said, "now that you say it, I remember Don telling me he was in an R&B band for a while, and most of the band was black. Maybe he's staying with one of them."

Joe's face gathered itself in concern. "I don't mean to sound racist or anything. I like black people. Most of my customers are black people. This isn't saying anything about black people, okay? But this place, Homewood, this is not a place where, as a white person, you want to hang out for too long, if you catch my drift. You planning on staying there with your friends for a while?"

"Just long enough to talk to him," Delilah said.

Joe sniffed. "That's good. I mean, I don't mean to put a scare in you or anything. I'm sure your friends are okay and all. But I'm just saying . . ."

Delilah turned to Porter with a smile. "Well, what do you say? Should we go get this over with?"

"You sure you still want to go see him?"

She made a face. "What, because of the neighborhood?"

"No, I mean, you don't have any cold feet about seeing Don with Stacey? Surprising them together?" But Porter *had* meant the neighborhood. The thought of coasting around those Third World streets with his big white face blaring out from behind the windshield already had him nervous. "But I also worry a little about the truck in an area like that," Porter said, "you know, where there aren't a lot of services."

Joe said, "No, what are you talking about? Leave the truck. I'm going to get somebody started on it right away. Take your Mazda. It hasn't exactly jumped off the lot in the last couple of days."

"Oh, okay," Porter said. "Thanks."

"So let me go get that address for you," Joe said. He headed up the steps, put his key in the door, and disappeared inside.

Delilah turned to Porter. "You know, I can just go by myself. I don't need to drag you into this any further."

"No, are you kidding? I'm the one who knows my way around this city."

"I'm sure I can find it," she said.

Porter laughed. "You didn't even know what state we were in last night. You expect me to let you wander off into the crime capital of Pittsburgh by yourself? Sorry."

"But you shouldn't have to do this. You should get back and see your kids."

"I *want* to do it," Porter said. "I do." And then he realized that he *did* want to do it, his fear of getting mugged or carjacked aside. He wanted to meet this guy, Don, and maybe have a positive impact somehow. He wanted to help make something good happen, because something good needed to happen here. He could not stand to see one more thing end badly.

"Okay," Delilah said. "Thanks."

"Well, thanks for last night," Porter said.

She gazed up at him with a mischievous smile. "No, thank *you*. For being my willing subject."

They looked at each other, and there was a moment when something seemed to be urging Porter to say, "I love you." But then that moment passed, and Porter was relieved it had. Because he didn't want to say such a thing, didn't know if he believed it or felt it or even what it meant anymore. But he did know what trouble it could get you into and how swift and devastating the damage could be. Already he could sense the depth of the ravine he'd nearly stepped into and hear the rush of the black, bottomless void.

"Maybe we could do it again sometime," Delilah said.

Porter's mouth was dry. "Yeah, maybe."

"But not up there," Delilah said, gesturing at the camper. "God, I forgot about how low that ceiling is. I've actually got scrapes." She lifted the hem of her dress, and, sure enough, there was a slight abrasion on the edge of her right knee. When had that happened? She must have been on her back at some point, though Porter couldn't remember it.

"Yeah," Porter said. "Definitely not up there." But whether in the camper or not, or on the face of the moon or in the rings of Saturn, for that matter, Porter could not imagine himself and Delilah ever doing anything like that again. He couldn't fathom the circumstances that might cause the doors of his life to swing open a second time to usher in such a thing. In fact, he could hardly believe circumstances had allowed them to swing open a first time.

Joe reappeared at the top of the steps, jingling a set of keys in his fingers. "Here," he said, tossing them to Porter.

Porter snatched the silvery glint out of the air. "Thanks." And when he opened his hand, there they were, his old keys—Lucy's, really—strung on a rubber band along with a hole-punched piece of cardboard: Don's address.

So he was getting the Mazda back after all. It had waited faithfully for his return, and now, as a reward, it was going to be reclaimed, however briefly. Or maybe he should just keep the thing. Just give in and keep it. And while he was at it, he ought to give in with the camper too, let Don buy it back from him. Then Don and Delilah could go off and start their new life with baby Sam as if none of this had ever happened. Plus, the camper deserved to be rewarded as well for its persistence—for methodically pursuing its original owners from state to state like some lovesick bloodhound.

Porter just didn't get it. He didn't understand why inanimate crap like this had to keep worming its way back into your life while the things you really longed for—your most sacred dreams, the stuff you clutched against your heart, that vision you had of yourself cloaked in light, protected, looked out for, and loved—remained stubbornly beyond your grasp or else abandoned you entirely.

"So give me a call tomorrow afternoon," Joe called out. "I should have it all ready to go by then."

"Okay," Porter said with a wave. He turned to Delilah. "I'll bring the car around, if you want to get your stuff together."

"Thanks," Delilah said. "I really appreciate you taking me." She grinned, then did sort of a ballet move of a spin on the ball of her foot and padded off toward the camper.

Porter watched her walk for a moment, appreciating the movement of her butt in that pretty green dress. Then he started across the lot for the Mazda, gazing down at the keys in his hand with a sort of detached amusement, when suddenly he was struck by the sick, empty feeling that this was it, this was the beginning of the rest of his life. First he would deliver Delilah to Don, which would put an official end to all of that, whatever it had been. Then would be the trip to Claire and William's to retrieve the children. And where else would there be to go after that except back to the apartment? And then, come Monday, back to his job? Was this really the whole of his future, this narrowing tunnel? Was this his life? Or was something else still possible?

These dark thoughts had brought Porter to a stop. And as he stood there in the middle of the lot trying to figure it out, trying to come up with some sort of plan or idea that might make him feel better, he heard Joe yell out, "Hey, you're trapped. You can't get out."

Porter wheeled around, startled.

Joe came up to him in a hobbled jog and put a hand on Porter's shoulder. "I've got to move some cars around. It'll just take me a minute."

Porter almost laughed. *Okay,* he thought. *Okay.*

CHAPTER THIRTEEN

HOMEWOOD. So it wasn't quite what Porter had expected. No gangs roaming the streets. No turf wars for him to get caught in the middle of. No swaggering thugs calling him "honky." In fact, the place seemed to be populated almost solely by young mothers and their babies, most of them nicely dressed and well fed, strolling down the sidewalk while conducting loud, laughing conversations. None of them paid any attention whatsoever to Porter, who was parked curb-side, his bucket seat in half recline to make himself less conspicuous. The only person who'd noticed him at all, it seemed, was a big bruiser of an infant who'd drifted by, riding high in his stroller, a pacifier plugged into his shining brown face. The kid's eyes had widened and locked on to Porter's, his head rotating like a melon on a stick, and then he was around the corner and gone.

In Porter's little river town, Aspinwall, there were almost no blacks. And up in Fox Chapel, where Claire and William lived, there were even fewer, possibly none. For a few minutes Porter allowed himself to muse sadly about our segregated society and how destructive slavery had been for our nation. *How incredible,* he thought, *that people once owned other people.* He wanted to delve more deeply into this subject and perhaps even bring it to a satisfying conclusion, but then he felt a pang of hunger and started rooting around under the seats for the bag of pretzels he used to store down there, or how about that jar of peanuts? Nope. He'd cleaned out all that stuff when he traded in the car.

Porter adjusted his seat back a little higher and gazed out the window. Across the street, maybe twenty feet away, two boys were playing chess on the hood of a car, their skinny bodies bent over the fenders in silent concentration. Porter had noticed them before, when he and Delilah were creeping along looking for house numbers, and the sight had been among the first to ease his fear about the neighborhood. (The second had been a FedEx van that had zoomed by and jerked to a stop halfway down the block, where the smartly dressed driver had hopped out, climbed the stairs of the dilapidated building before him, and delivered his bright, urgent envelope.)

Unlike the camper, the Mazda had no dashboard clock, so Porter was starting to lose track of how long he'd been waiting. Half an hour? Forty-five minutes? Or did it just seem that long because of how anxious he was? Porter could now see that one of the chess-playing boys wore a watch. But it wasn't worth disturbing them, was it? After all, the fact that they liked chess didn't necessarily mean anything—they might still whip out switchblades and tell him to go fuck himself. He decided to hold out a while longer. But if Delilah's little session with Don wore on too long, he was going to have to go in and see what was happening. He couldn't just wait out here forever.

Porter was dying to know what was going on inside. He'd insisted on walking Delilah to the door, had waited with her until an ancient, stooped black man had answered her knock, and, upon hearing Don's name—she'd had to repeat it as he'd cupped his hand to his ear— had ushered her in.

The house was a two-story, clapboard-and-tar-paper death trap with bars on the windows and a pile of bricks around the side where the chimney had been. The front porch, where he and Delilah had stood waiting, evidently had been designated as some kind of feline feeding and shitting zone. In one corner was a bucket that Porter had guessed contained water, although it was hard to tell what, exactly, lay beneath that velvety layer of dead flies. Scattered from one end of the porch to the other were dozens of half-eaten cans of Friskies Buffet. And to the immediate left of the door, as a sort of welcome basket, was a litter box that featured perhaps seventy dried cat turds. Porter assumed that this level of activity had to be the work of more than just the two scruffy calicoes who lay sprawled, either asleep or dead, on the cement steps.

Porter had never much liked cats, had never quite understood the appeal of their snobby independence. But Benny was nuts about cats and had frequently pushed for them to get a kitten ("I'll take care of it all by myself! I *will*!"). Luckily, however—or at least that's how Porter saw it—their landlord strictly had forbidden pets of any kind.

When Lucy got sick, though, and Benny was having such a hard time with it, Porter and Lucy decided that maybe they ought to take the risk and get him a kitten for Christmas. After all, what was their landlord going to do? Throw them out on the street? But when Lucy mentioned this plan to her doctor in an offhand way, the doctor said, "Maybe you should wait until you're all done with the chemo. You know, chemo makes you weaker, and sometimes you can react to things you wouldn't have a reaction to under normal circumstances. So you really need to limit your exposure. And cats can be really problematic in that way."

So they'd decided to put it off. "I promise that once Mom is a little stronger, we'll get one," Porter had explained to his pouting son.

"The doctor just recommended that we wait until Mom's out of the woods with all this, and then we can get one. Okay?"

But, of course, Lucy never got out of the woods. She had her ups and downs, and on several occasions, during the ups, Benny would again plead his case. "Just be patient," Porter had told him. "We have to wait a little while longer, just to be sure."

Now, remembering it, Porter wondered if Benny had thought about this subject since Lucy died. No doubt he had. No doubt he wanted a kitten more than ever. But how was he supposed to ask for one under these circumstances? "So *now* can we, Dad? Since Mom's dead? *Please?*"

Well, that's one thing he could do today. On the way to Claire and William's he could swing by the Animal Rescue League and get Benny a little kitten. But then, he realized, he'd also have to buy all the other mandatory kitty accessories: food, a litter box, litter, a scratching post, maybe even some catnip? Did you need that? And what would be Kaylie's equivalent gift? She didn't want a pet, so what could he get her? Some nerdy sweater or blouse for her to hate and feel guilty about?

A screen door slapped shut. Porter sat up, peered through the windshield, and there, on the porch, was Delilah with a guy Porter assumed must be Don. Yep, that was the guy, all right, the one he'd seen in the picture on her dresser. He had that same beard, though it was fuller, bushier, spreading down his neck. She and Don exchanged a few words, then they hugged—a long, tight embrace—followed by a brief, lips-to-lips kiss. As Delilah turned away and started down the steps, Don remained on the porch for a moment, hands on his hips, watching her. Finally he dropped his head and went back inside.

Porter opened his door and stood up. "What happened?" he called out across the roof of the car. "How'd it go?"

She didn't look at him as she approached. "Fine," she said, tight-lipped.

Porter started to come around in front of the car, but Delilah went straight to the passenger side, opened her door, and got in, leaving him with nothing to do but return to his side and get in too. He pulled the door closed, then angled himself in the seat to face her. "So tell me about it."

She looked over at him with a weak smile, and now he could see that she'd been crying. "Well, he's not with Stacey anymore. That's the good news, I guess. I knew he never really liked her. So at least it was nice to have that confirmed."

"Where'd she go?"

"East. To Boston, maybe? I think that's what he said. Who cares?"

"But what about the baby? What did he say about that?"

"He already knew about it. He already fucking knew. In fact, that's the whole reason he dumped me. Can you believe that?"

"But I thought you didn't tell him?"

"I didn't. I didn't tell him because I wasn't sure what I wanted to do yet, whether I was going to keep it or not. But I told a couple of other people, and he found out somehow, big surprise. He wouldn't tell me from who. What does it matter anyway?" She gazed stonily into her lap. "I just can't believe I came all this way to tell him something he already knew. That is so fucked. I felt like such a loser in there."

"What an asshole," Porter said.

"No, he's not. He's really not. He feels terrible about this. He almost seemed more upset about it than I was, saying how much he missed me and everything, and how much he still loves me. I mean, you should've seen his face when I first walked into that basement. He was sitting there with his bass, you know, just plucking away, and that old guy who took me in, he says, 'Don, you have a visitor,' and I thought Don was going to fall through the couch. He, like, went into total shock."

"So what gives him the right to be so upset?" Porter said, irritated. "He didn't have to leave you over this."

"And you know what else?" Delilah said. "If we hadn't come

today, we would've missed him completely. They're off to West Virginia tomorrow, to do a gig, play at a wedding. And after that they're heading south. I never would have seen him again. Never."

Porter slumped in his seat, facing the front. "So you didn't try to talk him into staying with you?"

"I didn't want to talk him into staying with me."

"But you still love him?"

Delilah looked away. "Yeah."

"Then why didn't you tell him that?"

"Because I didn't want to tell him that."

But what about the baby? Porter wanted to say. Poor little guy. Growing up with no father whatsoever. Or, actually, worse—a father who didn't care enough to know him. What was the right age, Porter wondered, to explain that to him? How would Spock handle that one? You could break the news when he's four or five and really unhinge him at a tender age, or wait until he's older and more mature. But with each year you put it off, of course, the lies and evasions would be compounded. The kid might be better equipped to handle it, sure, but there also would be more damage to undo.

Finally Porter said, "Then what did you say to him about why you came here?"

"I told him I wanted to let him know, that's all. I told him I'd decided to keep it and that he was going to have a kid in the world. He kept asking me how I found him here, like that was the most important goddamn thing, but I was like, 'Who cares?' "

Porter sighed and looked away.

"What?" Delilah said.

He faced her again. "I don't know. It just seems to me you should tell him how you feel. I mean, how are you supposed to get what you want otherwise? That's what you'd say to me, right?"

"Porter, look," she said. "There's only so much I'm gonna rub my own face in shit over this. I mean, first he dumps me, in front of everybody, for Miss I-Ching girl, okay? Then he takes off in our truck with her in the middle of the night. Which pissed me off more, even though it was really *his* truck. I still felt as if it were part mine. So I swallow my fucking pride and hunt him down anyway. Okay, I'm thinking. So he didn't know I was pregnant. Maybe that would change things somehow. I didn't want that to be the reason anything changed, like I've been saying, but still, I don't know. I thought he should at least know, and that maybe it might mean something to him. But it didn't, Porter, okay? It didn't mean anything. And today I had the pleasure of finding out why. Because it was the whole fucking reason he left me in the first place."

Porter took a deep breath. Then he sat up and turned to her. "Would you mind if I went in and talked to him?"

She gave a caustic laugh. "Don't you dare."

"But I just want to meet him."

"No you don't," she said with a grin. "You want to try to shame him into living up to his responsibilities, right?"

"I won't say anything you don't want me to say."

"I don't want you to say anything."

Porter opened his door.

"Hey, I'm serious. I'll be so pissed if you go in there."

"I want to meet him," he said. "Don't I deserve that much for driving you here?"

"No."

Porter pushed his door shut and crouched in the window. "I also have something else to tell him. About the camper. I've decided to give it back to him, if he wants."

Delilah squinted, leaning toward him. "What are you talking about?"

"I feel like he should have it." Porter smiled. "That's what my I-Ching is telling me."

Delilah grinned despite herself. "Your I-Ching doesn't tell you something like that," she said. "Your I-Ching—"

But Porter was already walking around the car to the sidewalk.

"Hey," she yelled at him, craning her head out the window. He looked back.

"Oh, fuck it," she said. "Do whatever you want."

Porter climbed the steps two at a time, his adrenaline surging. He did want to give the camper back to Don, yes, but that was secondary. What he was most curious about, he had to admit, was finding out what Don was like. Who was this guy? And what was so great about him? Or maybe he wasn't great, and that would be revealing in its own way. Porter strode forth to the screen door and gave it three powerful raps—*whap, whap, whap*—a man who meant business. Ten seconds passed. He opened the screen door and knocked on the main door, a hollow piece of crap that you could splinter to bits with a good karate chop. Again, no response. And it wasn't until he'd been waiting for half a minute or so, standing there amid the stench of the litter box, that he began to have second thoughts about this little stunt of his. And once he gave life to that anxiety, the little voices in his head started to blast away at him: *You can still turn around. Just walk away. Go. Go!*

Porter gazed back at the Mazda for some sign from Delilah, but she wasn't looking at him. The two chess boys were, though. They were standing on either side of the board, arms crossed over their chests, their squinty, grinning faces aimed at him. Porter nodded and smiled, gave them a little wave. At this the boys' grins broke open wider, and they exchanged a glance and shook their heads, as if sharing a joke. And suddenly it occurred to Porter that they'd probably heard his and Delilah's conversation. They'd probably heard every stupid, white, middle-class word of it. And instantly shame rose in his face and started to tingle at the tops of his ears. He was a fool, and those kids knew it. They might live in squalor and have only a car hood for a table and crack vials for chess pieces, but they knew a fool when they saw one, and they saw one now.

Then, behind him, the door opened and a voice said, "Who are you?"

Porter wheeled around. It was Don. "I'm uh . . . I'm a friend of Delilah's. I'm the one who drove her here."

Don looked him up and down. "She told me about you."

"She did? Oh. Well, anyway, I just wanted to talk to you for a second, if I could."

"Yeah, okay." He pushed the screen door open and ushered Porter in. And it was just like walking into Andrea and Seri's. The same smell of incense. The exact same stuff. Maroon curtains on all the windows. "I'm staying in the basement," Don said, leading the way.

They tromped down the stairs into a black-walled, subterranean hovel of music. Don's bass was on the couch, and before it, on the floor, sat an amp, its red lights aglow. Pushed back against the wall was a set of drums and keyboards. A trombone rested in its rack in the middle of the rug, rising out of the purple shag like a piece of ornamental plumbing.

"I hear you're a musician," Porter said idiotically.

Don dropped himself into the couch. "Yeah." He slumped back and put his feet on the coffee table—a piece of plywood on two milk crates.

"That's cool."

"Yeah, I don't know."

Porter clasped his hands before him and said, "Well."

"You want to sit?" Don said, patting the couch next to him. "There's room."

Porter looked at the couch, but he couldn't quite picture having this talk, or any talk, sitting next to Don on the couch. It just wasn't right. "Nah," he said. "Thanks. Floor's fine." And down he squatted, crossing his legs underneath himself Indian style. But that felt weird too, as if he were ten years old and at summer camp, gazing up doe-eyed at his counselor. So he stretched one leg out and kept the other under him, which at least got him close to the casual but confident air he was trying to convey.

Don did look a little wiped out, but it was hard to tell if this was from his session with Delilah or just from a lack of sleep. He pushed his fingers back through his hair, leaving it in a greasy, wind-driven clump. Then he cast Porter a sheepish, sidelong glance and said, "So is she really pissed at me?"

Porter grinned, then began to gesture with his hand as if conducting what he was about to say. "No . . . I mean, I guess she's upset, yeah. But not pissed. I wouldn't say that."

Don shook his head. "I *told* her I didn't want kids. I told her that when we first met. No kids."

"Yeah, well, but you never know," Porter said. "Maybe you think you don't want kids, when you don't have any."

"I know what kids are."

Porter smiled. "I'm sure you do. But not your own kid. You don't know what having your own kid is like."

"I don't want to know what having my own kid is like."

"But you're going to have one."

Don leaned forward, resting his arms on his knees. "Not really. She's going to. And that's as it should be. Because she wants the kid. She's the one who wants it, right? That was her decision. And, you know, I knew that's the way it would be with her, if she got pregnant. I just knew it, man, because her abortion was such a big deal for her, you know, like a big, cosmic, life-altering event. And I knew that if she ever got pregnant again she was going to keep it. So that's why I made it really clear to her up front. No kids for me, I told her. I don't want kids. You can have one, but I don't want any part of it."

After a moment, Porter said, "You know what? I was in your position once. I didn't want kids either. I wanted my freedom, you know. But my girlfriend, Lucy, she got pregnant—we were both, like, twenty, just out of college. And I wanted her to get an abortion. I pleaded with her. *Get* it. *Please.* I was on my knees. I kept thinking about this thing growing inside her and how it was going to ruin my life. I kept trying to figure out ways to get rid of it. Stick something up there and break the sac, cause a miscarriage or whatever. Anything.

I was crazy, I swear. Because I didn't feel like I could just walk away from it. I felt like I was trapped."

Don scratched at his beard. "So what happened?"

"We got married. We got married and had the kid."

"How long ago was that?"

"About twelve years."

"And what happened to the kid?"

"What happened to her? She's my daughter. And I have a boy now too, who's eight."

"So do you see them very often? Your kids?"

"Of course." Porter laughed. "We live together."

Don frowned. "You're not divorced or something?"

"No."

"So what's the deal with your wife then?" Don said, hunching forward. "Where's she?"

Porter paused. "My wife died. She's dead."

"Oh," Don said with surprise. "I'm sorry to hear that." He sucked at his lips and sat back, laying his arms across the top of the couch. "But at least that explains it."

"Explains what?"

"You know. How you could be with Delilah when you've got this whole family in the wings."

"I'm not *with* Delilah. I just gave her a ride. She asked me for a ride to Pittsburgh so she could find you."

Don shook his head. "That's not what she told me. She told me that you and her are lovers."

Porter gasped. "She said *what*?"

"I told her I'd send some money when I got some, you know, to help out with the baby. And she said she didn't need me for anything because she had you."

A cold thrill surged through Porter's heart. "You're kidding."

Don raised his eyebrows. "So you two aren't together?"

"No."

"You know," Don said, "I wondered if she was telling the truth about that. Seemed a little soon to me. But she probably just said that because she was hurt. She probably wanted me to think she had her own deal all worked out and she didn't need me anyway. She's like that. She never wants anyone to think she needs them."

Porter didn't much care for that explanation.

"I mean," Don went on, "her parents could help her out with this baby if she'd just let them. Her parents are rich. They're fucking loaded. Her father's some computer guy, owns some high-tech company. They're practically billionaires. But Delilah won't go to them. She's flat broke, has been for years, but she won't turn to them for anything. To her credit, I have to say. I mean, I still love her. She's the best. I never wanted us to break up. But I knew this kid thing was going to come up sooner or later. I just knew it."

"You know, there's a lot worse things than having a kid," Porter said. "Kids can be pretty great."

"Well, not for me," Don prattled on. "I've got other things I want to do, things I want to see and experience. But also I don't think this world is such a great place to raise a kid anyway. This planet is totally fucked, if you ask me. Plus, it's already overpopulated. There's kids all over the place that nobody wants. And all the systems are going to break down one of these days—all the feeding systems and communications and everything. People are going to starve. There's going to be these monster hurricanes and killer droughts because the ecosystem is so screwed up from the greenhouse effect. The polar icecaps are already shrinking. This stuff is documented. So the next thing is the oceans are going to rise and flood the low-lying areas, wipe out all that shit, all the rice paddies and coastal fishing villages and everything. It's going to be total disaster, I'm telling you, and not that far down the road either. And you think I'm going to bring a new life into all that? No way. It's just not fair."

"But you *are* bringing a new life into it," Porter said. "You're just choosing not to take care of that life."

Silence.

"Right? I mean, the life you created is coming anyway."

Don scowled. "So why don't you take care of it, if you're so concerned?"

"Because I already have two kids to take care of. All by myself."

"And you resent it, don't you?"

"No, I don't resent it."

"Then what's your problem?"

"I don't have a problem."

Don tipped his head back against the couch and stared at the ceiling a moment. Then he rolled it forward again, settling his gaze on Porter. "So do you mind telling me what you're all wound up about this for? About *my life*? I don't even *know* you."

Porter brought his legs up underneath him. "I'm *not* all wound up about it," he said. "It's just that, you know . . ." He paused a moment. "Actually, if you want to know the truth, I envy you a little, being able to shut out other people's needs and just do what you want for yourself. I couldn't do that when I was in your shoes. I mean, believe me, I was every bit as afraid as you are. I was terrified. But I didn't feel like I had any choice."

"Afraid?" Don said, rising to his feet. "Afraid of what? You think I'd hang around in a war zone like this for very long if I was afraid?"

"People are afraid of different things."

"Oh, are they? And what are you afraid of, since you're the big expert?"

"These days, just about everything. That's one thing kids will do for you. They'll make you afraid of everything."

"Well, there you go," Don said with a huff. "Who would want that?"

"I want it," Porter said. "I'll take it."

Don walked a few steps toward the trombone, his hands on his hips and his head sagging, looking as if he wanted to rear back and kick the thing across the room. Then he turned to face Porter. "Man,

I *told* her," he said. "I *told* her I didn't want kids. I told her that the first time we met. So, I'm sorry, man, but I *refuse* to feel guilty about this."

"Then don't."

"I won't. I *refuse* to."

Porter pushed himself to his feet and stood opposite Don, his arms crossed over his chest. "You shouldn't feel guilty," he said. "You really shouldn't. I'm sure Delilah wouldn't want that."

"I won't," Don said, not looking at him. He put his hand on the mouthpiece of the trombone and started rocking it gently from side to side.

"But I also came in here to talk to you about something else," Porter said. "I have an offer for you, something you can't refuse."

The trombone stopped moving.

"I want you to have your camper back, if you want it."

Don wheeled around, his face broken open in a broad smile. "Seriously?"

"I mean it," Porter said, "I feel like it's more yours than mine."

"Man, I went back for it only a couple of days ago!"

"I know," Porter said. "I heard that."

"And you know what else?" Don said. "We are in desperate need of cargo space for this road trip. Desperate. We were all going to be packed into, like, two cars."

"It's all yours," Porter said. "And I'm having a new transmission put in it too, as we speak. Just go back to the dealer and remind him who you are. I'll let him know what's up."

"I will," Don said. "I definitely will. Man, I really appreciate this. How much do you want for it? That dealer gave us four hundred."

"I don't want any money," Porter said. "But here's the thing, and I mean it. You've got to come back and see your kid when it's born, okay? That's all I ask. You don't have to stick around. You don't have to do anything. Just come back and introduce yourself."

Don squinted at him. "But how am I supposed to find her?"

"I'll keep track of where she is. You can call me." He looked around the room. "You got a piece of paper?"

Don went over to the keyboards and came back with a piece of sheet music and a pencil. Porter scribbled his name and number and handed it back.

"Okay, that's cool," Don said. "I'd like to come back and see it anyway. You know, see what it looks like and everything. But I probably won't stick around. That's just not what I'm about."

"No pressure," Porter said. "You don't have to." *But you will*, he thought. *You will. Once you see it. Once you hold it in your arms.*

Don let out a big breath. "Man, I am *so happy* about getting the Palace back, I can't tell you. I've been fucking sick about it. I never thought anyone would buy that thing. Something that old. And all painted like that. I just needed the money for a couple of days, to get us oriented here and track down my friends, and I thought I'd be able to get it right back. Fucking Stacey. She's the one who came up with that brilliant idea. I was so pissed at her. I was glad when she took off, that's for sure."

Porter was about to ask Don some perfunctory question about where Stacey had gone, but then he thought, *Fuck it.* This conversation was over. It had run its natural course. And he'd had it with perfunctory questions. He'd had it with perfunctory anything. From now on, if he didn't have something he wanted to say, he wasn't going to spew out a bunch of unfelt nonsense just to fill the void. Instead, he was going to embrace the void.

The only problem with deciding to embrace the void, however, was that it didn't stop other people from going ahead and spewing their unfelt nonsense into it. And sure enough, after about twenty seconds of beautiful, virgin silence, Don blared out, "So, is it another warm one out there today?"

Porter smiled and nodded, then started up the steps. He was not going to talk about the weather. Not with Don or anyone else. No more. Maybe never again in his life. *Nicht wieder.* He just wasn't going to do it.

PORTER SLID IN behind the wheel and looked at Delilah with a big, goofy smile. "Hi, lover!"

Delilah was slumped down in her seat, her bare feet on the dashboard. She glanced at him, unamused. "Sorry about that," she said. "But you can figure out why I told him that, can't you? C'mon, put your thinking cap on."

Porter put his hand on her knee and squeezed it. "Because it's true?" He turned the key and fed the Mazda gas until its tiny engine whirred like a coffee grinder. Already he missed the truck. But no regrets. No regrets.

"So what are you in such a good mood about?" Delilah said. "Did you guys have a little male-bonding session in there?"

"Hardly," Porter said, pulling way from the curb. "There was one point where I thought he was going to hit me."

Delilah laughed. "Never," she said. "Don is a total marshmallow. He'd never hurt anyone."

"At least not physically," Porter said.

"Yeah, well, right."

With only two fingers on the wheel, Porter whipped the Mazda around the corner and then pushed the accelerator all the way to the floor to climb the hill. But they immediately slowed to a crawl anyway, and he had to downshift to second, then to first. Compared with the truck, this car made Porter feel as if he were in the soap-box derby. He glanced over at Delilah. "So I made a deal with Don for the Palace. It was a trade."

"For what?"

"That's a surprise," Porter said. "Maybe you'll find out sometime. If he's true to his word."

She rolled her eyes. "He's not."

"This time I think he will be. I hope."

Porter crossed out of Homewood into Squirrel Hill, and like magic, the black people disappeared and white people filled their places, shopping and eating and conversing with other white people. The whole thing seemed so ridiculous. It was, in fact, unbelievable. He cruised down the avenue like a visitor from another planet, trying to unravel the mysteries of these dumb, plodding creatures.

"We have to stop by the car lot," he said. "Tell Joe that Don's coming for the camper. Plus, I've got to get all my stuff out of it. Then I need to do some shopping before we pick up Kaylie and Ben."

"And what's my destination?"

"I don't know," Porter said. "Where do you want to go?"

"Nowhere."

"Well, that's easy, then."

CHAPTER FOURTEEN

THE Animal Rescue League. Furry little heads and triangle ears. Row upon row of round, glinting eyes. And the mewing! *Pick me* is what it sounded like to Porter. *Pick me!*

This was not turning out to be such a cheery, heartwarming event after all. Porter strode among the stacked cages feeling like a benevolent concentration-camp guard, trying to decide whose life to spare. The kittens were one thing. Some were cute and oblivious, rolling around and playing with torn-up newspapers, while others huddled in the corner, terrified. But at least they all had a fighting chance. At least you got the sense that they'd get snapped up by *someone*. And even if they didn't, they were too young and naive to know what was to come anyway. But what about the older cats, cast aside after all these years? Sure, a few of them were all fluffy and hopeful-looking despite the odds, rubbing up against the wires, blinking affectionately, licking their paws and spiffing themselves up, possibly to tip the scales in their favor. But most seemed resigned to their fate and sat hunched, in full scowl, as if thinking, *Fuck this. Take me if you want, but don't expect me to put on any goddamn show.*

Somehow, though, the old dogs were the worst. Not a prayer for them. *My name is Ted*, read the card on the cage of a panting cocker spaniel. *I am eight years old and I have a bone problem in my hips. I am not good with children, but I like adults and would very much like to find a loving home.*

Porter turned to Delilah. "I don't know if I can do this."

"I know," she said. "This really sucks, doesn't it?"

"Could you pick out a kitten for me?" he said. "For Benny? I know that's asking a lot, but I'm not going to last very long in here. I'm just not up to it right now."

"Sure," she said. "Any kind in particular? Help me narrow it down?"

Porter did a quick survey of the nearby cages. *Maybe one of the black-and white-ones?* he was about to say, but then he made eye contact with a tiger-striper and lost his nerve. "Can I leave it to you? I'm sorry. I'm afraid in my state of mind I might pull a PETA stunt and open up all the cages or something."

She smiled. "Don't worry. I'll get him a good one."

Porter made his way to the front desk, where he smiled at the blue-aproned volunteer who earlier had admonished him for sticking his fingers into the cages ("We're not liable for bites and scratches!"). Then he turned and quickened his pace down the hallway, fleeing past posters of trapped foxes and clubbed baby seals until finally he reached the door and burst out into the fresh air.

He took several deep breaths until his head began to clear, then walked over to the Mazda. The backseat was jammed with his belongings from the camper, and that wasn't even all of it. He'd left some stuff for Don: kitchen utensils, food, a couple of blankets, plus a few other items that hadn't fit. He didn't want to have to make another trip, and they already had too much of that kind of crap at home anyway.

Joe Hinchcliff had said, "Hell, make the kid drive it on over to you. Least he could do for a free camper." Joe hadn't been at all pleased about the car-swapping arrangement. "I still think you should make him pay you," he'd kept saying. "At least something. *Something.*"

After Porter had written a check for four hundred dollars and held it out to him, Joe had waved him off and said, "Aw, I'm not taking that."

"But, Joe," Porter had said. "Why should *you* be out four hundred bucks? You don't even know him. You don't really know any of us."

"I know *you,*" Joe had argued. "I know *you,* Porter." But then he'd grudgingly stuffed the check into his shirt pocket.

Joe had also been upset about the fact that Porter's cell phone had been ringing in the cab, at regular intervals, while Porter and Delilah were gone, and he'd had to agonize over whether he should answer it or not. "I didn't know if it might be an emergency," he'd said. "But then I couldn't figure out how to work the friggin' thing anyway, so I figured I'd wait until you got back."

My parents, Porter had thought. And although he didn't really feel the need to speak with them anymore, he was happy they'd tried to reach him. He was glad too that Alex had followed through, however resentfully, in contacting them on his behalf. "They'll call again if it's important," he had told Joe. "So don't worry."

But they hadn't called again. At least not during the unpacking of the camper and the subsequent trip to the Animal Rescue League.

Porter opened the Mazda's passenger door and grabbed the cell phone, then locked the car and wandered off to the edge of the parking lot, where a patch of lush green lawn, complete with park bench, recently had been installed. On the far side of this postage-stamp park the natural world resumed—a dense tangle of trees, vines, and assorted weeds, all held at bay by a brand new chain-link fence. On the bench's upper-right corner an engraved silver plaque identified Brenda Hahn (1931–1994) as the former Animal Rescue League volunteer whose bequeathal had led to the creation of this so-called Park of Tranquillity. The plaque then went on to claim: WHEN IT CAME TO ANIMALS LARGE OR SMALL, SICK OR WELL, BRENDA'S HEART KNEW NO BOUNDARIES. Beneath the plaque, a white sticker of equal size boasted that the bench was composed of 90 percent postconsumer content.

Porter sat down, spread his arms across the top of the bench, and sighed. Both messages clearly were meant to make you feel better about the world, but they failed to have this impact on Porter. To him, they served only as a reminder of death and waste and misdirected goodwill. If Brenda Hahn had really wanted to make an impact, he thought, she should have spent her money building an animal shelter where they didn't have to slaughter every dog and cat whose only crime had been to grow old. That might have served a higher purpose than installing this scenic viewing area of the local Auschwitz for unwanted house pets.

Just then a minivan pulled up to the entrance, and out hopped a girl about Kaylie's age and a woman who presumably was her mother—a sensible-looking, Fox Chapel type in jeans and white sneakers. The mother lifted open the rear door, the two of them leaned into the back for a moment, and then they emerged holding a large cage. As they backed away, Porter could see that the cage was full of kittens; there must have been eight or nine at least, all climbing the sides and falling back down, mewing as loudly as their tiny lungs would permit. And off the two of them went with their delivery, straight inside, quickly vanishing down the long hallway.

Porter thought it would take a while and was surprised that they'd left the van running, doors open, in front of the entrance. Didn't they have to register each one or something? Check for fleas and kitty leukemia? But within a few minutes the door swung open again, and the mother and daughter stepped back out into the sunshine with their empty cage, mission accomplished. Porter continued to watch in a haze of disbelief as they climbed into their minivan and pulled away, chatting and smiling as if nothing had happened. And he was on the verge of becoming really upset about this when the cell phone emitted its shrill ring.

It was with a sense of relief that he reached for it. "Hello?"

"Porter?" his father said. "Porter? Is that you?"

"Yeah. Dad?"

"Are you on a portable telephone? Is that what this is?"

"A cellular phone. Uh-huh. It's Claire and William's."

His father cleared his throat. "I *hate* those things. Jeez, I really do. You know, your brother saw fit to get himself one of those things, and now you never know where the hell he is! You hear everything— sirens, honking, people talking all around him. Once he told me to hold on for a second, and I could hear him giving his *food order* to a *waitress*!"

"That's life in New York, I guess," Porter said.

Silence. "What's that?"

"Nothing," Porter said. "Look, Dad . . ."

"What's that?"

"Dad," Porter said, raising his voice, "I just wanted to say I'm sorry we didn't make it out there. We broke down in Indiana."

"Yeah, Alex told us. We spoke to him this morning."

"It was something having to do with the—"

"Hey, we're having a *great* time," his father blurted out, as if Porter had asked.

"I'm glad to hear that, Dad."

"I was saying to your mother that we haven't been here since you boys were just kids. You remember that? The trip we took here?"

"Not really," Porter said. "I mean, all those camping trips are sort of blurred together in my mind."

"But this is where you boys nearly drowned," he said. "You re- member that? That happened here."

Porter vaguely remembered being told about such an incident, but it was one of those family myths where you were never quite sure if it had actually happened.

"You couldn't have been more than five, Porter. And Alex was three, if that. You'd walked out on some log—this big fallen tree going off into the lake. You had your fishing sticks, you know, these sticks I'd carved for you and tied some string onto the ends of, and you were out on that log pretending. I don't know what your mother and I were doing, but we weren't looking. We took our eyes off you for a second. And I remember hearing the splashes, one right after the other, small sounds, really—*bloop, bloop*, like that, and you were gone. There was just the waves. By the time I scrambled out there, you boys were floating in your clothes like sacks of grain. You'd held your breath, Porter, and you were still moving around. But Alex . . . he was full of water. He was nearly dead. You don't remember any of this?"

"I can't say that I do."

"Well, it's not something I've thought about for a long time. But it just so happens we found that very spot, your mother and I. Stumbled right onto it when we were hiking yesterday. This little clearing by the water. There's a big boulder where we laid Alex down and hit him on the back until he coughed the water out. It was your mother who recognized the place. She said she *felt* it. She sat down on that very boulder and said, 'This is it. This is where the boys almost drowned.' And then she got all broken up, of course. You know your mother."

Porter didn't say anything.

"You know, Porter," his father said, his voice wavering, "I'm just so sorry about Lucy. I'm really sorry about that. It's so damn unfair, isn't it? And for Kaylie and Benjamin? I can't stop thinking about it. I can't."

Porter sniffed and pressed his eyes shut.

"The thing is, Porter, I just don't know what that's like, what you've had to go through. All the people I've ever been close to, you know, are still alive. Mom and Dad probably won't be around much longer, but, jeez, they're *ninety*. And I just can't believe that you have to know what that's like, at your age. And for Kaylie and Benjamin . . ." And his father's voice caught, and he whimpered slightly. "Anyway," he continued in a high voice, trying to gather himself. "So that's . . . I just wanted to say that. Because at the reception, you know, at Claire and William's house, it just hadn't hit me yet, or something. I just didn't feel it yet."

"No, I didn't either," Porter said, wiping at his eyes. "Not then."

"But remembering you boys here . . ." his father said, and again his voice broke, and he had to clear his throat several times before he was able to continue. "You know, you and Alex," he said with a laugh, "you two were such little men. Marching around in the woods with those wooden rifles I'd carved for you. And those army helmets we got you? Those plastic helmets? That's what you boys had on, you know, when you . . ." He took in a sharp breath and then let it out—a long, sighing exhale. "Your mother and I even used to call you that sometimes—the little men. 'There go the little men,' we'd say as you marched by."

There was a long silence, during which Porter lowered the phone and used his shirtsleeve to wipe his entire face. Finally he said, "Dad, I wish we could have met up with you out there. We'll have to really do it sometime. The kids would love it."

"Oh, we will," his father said. "Your mother and I have decided that we're going to travel a lot more. Get out of that godawful place. So we'll be up for anything. You give us a call, and we'll be on the road in a heartbeat."

"Well, you know, it turns out that camper I bought isn't really reliable enough for long trips, but I'll have to find something else that is. Then we'll plan something, okay?"

"Okay."

Porter paused. "Dad?"

"Yeah?"

"You and Mom shouldn't feel bad for me, all right? I mean, yeah, for Kaylie and Ben, sure. They've had a tough time of it. But I think I'm pretty lucky person, all things considered. I really am. I feel pretty blessed. I'm happy about my life."

"Okay," his father said. "All right, then. If you say so."

After they hung up, Porter leaned back on the bench and closed his eyes.

So was that true? Was he a lucky person? Was he blessed? He'd really only said it to make his father feel better, but was there some truth to it? By all rights he was not a lucky person. Perhaps he should not consider himself to be blessed. Yet he often felt that he was anyway. And the feeling was a true one, not the kind of rationalized, goody-goody bullshit that people acquired from elsewhere during times of crisis and brushed onto themselves like varnish. This wasn't something that came from inspirational books or sappy TV shows or life-affirming quotations. This was more like a tide of brightness that inexplicably would rise within him every so often, releasing a hallucinogen of contentment and hope to course through the folds of his brain. And after a while, just as mysteriously, the brightness would subside.

So what *was* that feeling anyway? Porter could call it being blessed if he wanted to. He could call it happiness. Who was going to say it wasn't?

Porter tipped his head forward again and opened his eyes. And what he saw made him smile. There, standing next to the Mazda, was Delilah, and in each hand was a cardboard kitty carrier. She held them up in the air and did a little curtsy. "I did it!" she shouted.

Porter stood up and started over to her. "You got *two*?"

"They practically *made* me. They said it was much better for them if they each had a friend. Plus, they're brother and sister."

He shook his head. "We can't keep two." As he approached, he could see the little striped paws reaching out of the holes, batting at the air. On the side of each carrier it read: A PACKAGE OF LOVE FROM THE ANIMAL RESCUE LEAGUE.

Delilah made a face. "Then *you* pick one to send back."

He grimaced. "Okay, you win. But they're really going to destroy my apartment. I can already see it."

"Do you have nice stuff? Nice furniture and rugs?"

Porter grinned. "No."

"Expensive drapes?"

"No."

She smirked. "Then who cares?"

"Yeah, I guess."

There was no room in the backseat, so Delilah held the carriers on her lap. As Porter drove, she peeked in at the kittens and offered soothing words—"Ya'll are going to *such* a good home," she said. "Benny's going to love you *so much*. And I bet Kaylie will too. They've got so much love to spend, and ya'll are going to get it, you lucky ones." She glanced at Porter with a grin. "And even this curmudgeon over here might pet you every now and then if you push him. He's got it in him. I know he does."

AS PORTER EMERGED from the overgrown tunnel of the Winters' driveway and started up to their house, he noticed a pair of red-and-white SafHom vans parked in front of the garages. Porter drifted up to the house and shut off the engine, a mild panic rising in the back of his brain. What was going on? Had something happened? Two SafHom employees in red-and-white jumpsuits were working on their knees at the Winters' front door, while another was perched on a ladder leading up to the second-story windows. Then Porter saw a fourth dangling from the chimney on ropes.

"Nice place," Delilah said. "What's with the paratroopers?"

"I don't know," Porter said, opening his door. "Just wait here a minute, okay?"

He walked around the side until the backyard came into view, and then he put his hands on his hips and breathed with relief. There they all were at the pool, laid out in deck chairs. Everyone was fine. "Hey!" he called out.

Kaylie sat up in her orange swimsuit, squinting, her hand cupped over her eyes. "Hi, Daddy!"

Claire looked over her shoulder, and William lowered his newspaper. Only Benny didn't move. He had a Walkman on. Then Kaylie punched his arm and pointed.

And then everyone rose to their feet and started up the grass. "Daddy!" Benny yelled, breaking into a run. Porter braced himself for the collision, but this time Benny stopped short, looked up at him with a huge smile, and then stepped forward and hugged him tightly. Porter could feel Benny's wet suit soaking into his pants, but he didn't let go. "I'm so happy to see you," he said.

Kaylie was next, wrapping her arms around him and tucking her little blond head into the nook of his underarm. He put his hand on it and squeezed. As Claire and William approached, Porter called out, "What's with the security people?"

Claire frowned and shook her head. "We're having the damn thing deinstalled. We got in late last night, after *such* a long day, and I did everything right to disable the alarm. Everything. Exactly right. And it went off anyway!"

Porter smiled. "You're kidding."

"I was so angry I decided not to call and tell them it was a false alarm. Right, William?"

William nodded agreeably.

"Bring them on, I thought. Now I'll finally get that Armed Response Team I paid for."

"And did you?"

"I certainly did. Within ten minutes, as promised. They came roaring up the driveway in their silly little jeep with the red light flashing."

She laughed. "And you know what it was, Porter? They said the code box was all out of whack from this lummox beating on it the other morning. They said they'd have to send a new team in the morning to have it replaced. At *our* expense. And I said, 'Like *hell* you will. Get rid of the whole damn system Get rid of it *now*. This *minute*.' "

"Dad, she was awesome," Kaylie said.

Claire smiled. "They were just kids, you know. Scared kids with badges and guns. And they said to me, very politely, 'But ma'am, we're not Installation. We're Response.' And I yelled, 'I don't want *Installation*! I want *Deinstallation*!' They said, 'Ma'am, that's still Installation. Installation does that.' And I was about to yell at them some more, but luckily William stepped in then and handled it from that point on."

"So are you going to get someone else? A new service?"

"Never," Claire said. "I'd rather be robbed blind. I almost think it would be a favor at this point."

"Oh, Claire," William said. "You don't mean that."

"I do! I do mean it."

There was a silence among them. The SafHom Team member who'd been dangling from the chimney lowered himself to the ground, unhooked his harness, and flashed a thumbs-up in their direction. "Almost done!" he shouted. Then he set off in a bowlegged, hulking walk around to the front.

"It's good to see you guys," Porter said. "It's good to be back."

William said, "So that truck made it? You didn't have any trouble along the way?"

"Not at all."

"Is it parked out front?"

"Actually no," Porter said. "I decided to trade it back for the Mazda. I just didn't trust it anymore."

"Oh, really?" Claire said, unable to hide her glee.

"But I might look around for something else," Porter said. "Something not as old. I still want to do this, take a few camping trips. Maybe even meet up with my parents out West. But now probably isn't the best time anyway. Maybe the end of the summer would be better."

Claire took this in without comment.

Porter saw William's eyes move and narrow, focusing on something in the distance, and then his face registered alarm. Porter turned around to see Delilah standing at the corner of the house, paused there uncertainly, a small smile on her face.

"Hey, ya'll," she called out with a wave, then started down toward them.

"Delilah!" Benny said, running toward her.

To Porter's surprise, Kaylie smiled too and set off after Benny.

The three of them converged about twenty yards up the slope, where they exchanged hugs. "Sorry," Delilah called to Porter. "I waited for a while, but I wanted to know what was happening."

Claire turned to him, her face collapsed in concern. "She's still with you?"

Porter could already feel the battle fatigue coming on, yet the battle had barely begun. He sighed. "Apparently."

"But what about the boyfriend?"

"That didn't work out."

William sucked air in through his teeth. "So what will she do?" he said. "Where will she stay?"

"She'll stay with us, as long as it's okay with Kaylie and Ben. At least until she can figure out what she wants to do."

William rubbed his chin gravely. "Porter, I really caution you about this. I tell you, I've read about this sort of thing."

"You know what, William? She's not after my money, okay? Her parents are billionaires. Her dad owns a computer company in Texas. He *owns* it. You can ask her about it if you want. And she doesn't want *their* money. Not a cent. So I hardly think she's plotting to swindle me out of my nonexistent fortune."

"I wasn't suggesting—"

"She's a wonderful person, if you want to know the truth. And I see no reason to start banishing wonderful people from my life right now."

Claire said, "But it's just so soon, Porter. And quite frankly, that makes William and me worry a little about your decision-making. I mean, take your decision to buy that camper, for example . . ."

"Porter," Delilah called out, gesturing toward the driveway. "Can I show them the you-know-whats?"

"Yeah," he shouted. "Just be careful. Don't let them get out." He watched the three of them troop happily around to the front, Benny holding Delilah's hand while bouncing along beside her.

"What's she getting?" Claire said.

Porter smiled. "Kittens."

And Claire had no comeback for that. She just stared at him for a moment and then looked away, off where Delilah and the children had disappeared. Porter watched the twist of emotions work their way through his mother-in-law's face while she evaluated this new development—*So is this a good thing? A bad thing? Will there be consequences? Heartache? Pee on the rugs? Allergies?*

"Kittens?" William finally said.

But then Claire laughed and said, "*Oh!* Oh, my *goodness.*"

And Porter and William turned to see those two tiger-stripers come prancing around the corner of the house. Kaylie and Ben were shepherding them along, bending over every few steps to give them a nudge or put them back on their feet. Delilah brought up the rear. She'd donned her John Lennon sunglasses. "Don't worry, Porter," she shouted. "They're much too small to get away." And she was right. In fact, they could barely stay on their feet in the stiff grass. Every few steps they'd stumble and roll, then pop up again, eyes and ears on full alert.

"Gramma, look!" Kaylie shouted. She scooped one up and held it tightly under her chin as she approached. "Look at how cute! This one's *mine.*"

Claire leaned down and nuzzled her face into the kitten's belly. "Oh, she's just scrumptious. Oh, I could just *eat you up*! Just *eat you up*!" Then she pulled away and looked at Kaylie. "What are you going to name her?"

"I don't know yet."

Benny was on his back in the grass with his kitten on his chest. "I'm naming mine Tiger," he said.

Porter grinned, shaking his head. "Oh, c'mon, Benny. That's too obvious. You should try to come up with something a little more creative."

"But I *want* to name him Tiger."

Porter was about to press the case further, but then stopped himself. Why shouldn't Benny name him Tiger? Why the hell shouldn't he? Who cared how obvious it was? Benny *was* obvious, after all. Benny was as obvious as they come, and this attribute, Porter had to admit, was one of the best things about him. "All right," he said. "Tiger it is."

William got down gingerly on his hands and knees and petted Tiger on the top of his tiny head. Then he rubbed the kitten under the chin while saying, "Chicky, chicky, chicky-poo."

At that, Tiger squatted, a glazed look came over him, and he discharged a little spray of pee into the lawn.

"Oh, *ish*," William said, jerking his hand back. He looked over his shoulder at Claire. "I hope that doesn't harm the lawn. Make a brown spot. Should I put some water on it, do you think, to dilute it?"

"Oh, William," Claire said. "It can't have been more than a thimbleful."

William said, "But even so . . ."

Benny said, "We could take them down to the sandbox."

"Yeah," Kaylie said. And off they went down the lawn with the kittens secured to their chests, those glinting eyes peeping over their shoulders.

Claire turned to Porter. "Where did you get them?"

"At the Animal Rescue League. We just got them half an hour ago. Actually, Delilah's the one who picked them out."

Claire gazed at Delilah, and Porter could tell she was trying to figure out how she should feel about her. "You picked well," she said flatly.

"Thanks," Delilah said. "It wasn't easy."

Porter looked over at the play area and saw one of the kittens hop unnoticed out of the sandbox and start to dash away, but then Benny glanced back and leapt out to retrieve it. "You think they're all right down there?" he said.

Delilah said, "I'll go look after them." And she started off down the lawn.

William rolled back onto his feet and then rose cautiously to a stand, his arms out to the side for balance. "You know," he said, dusting his hands off, "we had a cat once, when I was a boy. A lovely, lovely Persian. Used to sit in this sunny window on a pillow. She'd sit there for hours on end. Now, *that* was contentment. Still, to this day, that is my vision of contentment. Isabelle was her name. A wonderful animal. But she died, of course."

"Well, at least she had a nice long life, though, right?" Porter said. "The woman at the Rescue League told me that the dogs and cats down there get put to sleep if they aren't adopted after two weeks. Even the puppies and kittens get euthanized if they aren't taken in that time, although she said they usually find homes."

"It's just so awful, isn't it?" Claire said. "It makes you think you should try to do something to prevent it, but what can you do? There will always be more pets than there are nice homes for them. And of course you can't rid the world of all the nasty people who mistreat them or cast them aside simply because they no longer amuse. Oh, those poor animals." She sighed, shaking her head. "But what can you do? You just have to not let it get to you, that's all."

"Or the other option is to let it get to you," Porter said. "To let yourself feel really awful about it."

Claire looked at him as if he'd sprouted horns. "Well, that's a silly thing to say," she said. "Why? To what end? Unless you plan to take some sort of action to rectify the situation, I don't see what good is achieved simply by feeling awful about something."

And maybe Claire was right. Maybe at the end of the day, after all the votes had been counted, she was absolutely right. But the only problem was, Porter couldn't rectify the fact that Lucy had died. He couldn't rectify it. There was no action to be taken. All he could do was feel really awful about it or not. And all Claire could do was feel really awful about it or not. That's all any of them could do.

Porter looked down the yard at Kaylie and Ben and Delilah, all huddled together in the sandbox. Finally he turned to Claire and William. "You know what?" he said. "I loved your daughter so much. Lucy was such a good thing in my life. And these kids she brought into the world . . . these kids . . ." And he had to stop for a moment. "And I just . . ." he continued, his voice breaking, "I just wanted to thank you both for her, because, you know, if it hadn't been for you, none of this would have been possible, and she wouldn't have been the person she was, and all of this we made together, our family, and this life . . ." and then he lost it. The tears came, and Porter's arms were moving helplessly before him, gesturing without the accompaniment of words, and in the end he had nothing to do but reach for Claire and embrace her. He crouched against her, placing his wet cheek into the cave of her neck, and he could sense the bewilderment in her face and the stiffness in her hands as she placed them tentatively upon his back.

"Porter, come now," she said, patting him between the shoulder blades as if he were a frightened child. "It'll be okay. Everything will be fine."

"Will it?" Porter said, his face in her hair.

Claire nodded, but a moment later Porter heard a sharp intake of breath—*"uh!"*—and felt Claire's body seize and then soften in his arms. Then suddenly she was clutching his shoulders and leaning fully against him, her damp face upon his chest, the warm weight of her engulfing him like a wave. And then Porter saw the shadow of William approaching and soon felt his father-in-law's soft hand on his neck.

And Porter knew then that this was it, this was the beginning. Finally they were on their way to a new place. Maybe it would take them a long time to get there, or maybe they would never arrive at all. But at least they were on their way. At least something else was possible. True, the basic elements of Porter's life would remain the same. He would work. He would be a father. He would be a son-in-law, and a son, and a brother. He would continue to haul around this grief like a block of ice in his gut. He would do so forever.

These things would not change, but Porter didn't need them to. As long as a few other things were possible. As long as Delilah's baby still came and arrived healthy in the world. As long as his own children still could stumble into happiness every so often, and he too. And maybe he would be able to find love again, as Lucy had hoped for him? Or even companionship? Companionship would be fine, really. More than enough.

That's all. Just those few possibilities. A relatively modest set. But Porter cherished them. He cherished them.

ACKNOWLEDGMENTS

I am especially grateful to Cathi Hanauer, Kate Christensen, Amanda Urban, and Henry Ferris for helping me with this book. I also wish to thank Vacil Richards, Betsy Jones, Lonnie and Bette Hanauer, my colleagues at New Visions for Public Schools, and the writing community at the University of Arizona.

And many thanks and much love to my parents, Charles and Vera Jones, and to my brother, Joe B. Jones.

Please check out this book at the Circulation Desk, using its scan label. Thank you.